The Princess of Panchala

A TerraMythos Novel

Tom D Wright

Visit the TerraMythos website at www.TerraMythos.com

Author website: www.TomDWright.com

This book is a work of fiction. All of the characters, names, places and incidents described within existed in other parallel universes, so any resemblance to actual people, events or locations is strictly an effect of quantum entanglement.

Cover design: Mark J Ferrari

Editing: Barbara Kenyon

Interior Design: Tom D Wright

ISBN: 1500696234
ISBN-13: 978-1500696238

For Nancy, Amanda and Alexia -

It has been a journey to remember

And for Stephen -

Sorry it has taken so long

PART ONE – THE CHOOSING

CHAPTER ZERO – THREE YEARS BEFORE

Demie knew she wasn't dead, at least she didn't think so. Not that she was any expert at the age of thirteen, but she figured being dead was like being crazy. If you can ask whether you are, then you probably aren't.

Well, ruling death out didn't help much, she still had no idea what was happening. As she floated weightless and confused in stone-cold darkness, a writhing knot of dread grew in her core. And gnawing at the back of her mind like a pet gerbil in a cage, was the sense that her little sister Kori was in trouble.

Then she noticed them, suspended in the dark, staring at her. Glowing, fuzzy and nebulous. Creepy eyes. Cheshire Cat in Wonderland eyes. They didn't move closer, but Demie felt them look over her, within her, like groping hands. They read through her every secret thought and emotion, as if reading her diary.

She wanted to run from this thing, but when she tried to move her arms she felt no sensation of any sort. It was as if she didn't even have limbs. That triggered a wave of panic which nearly overwhelmed her, and then she remembered—whatever the hell these eyes were, it had taken Kori. Anger pushed aside her fear and Demie screamed, "Why do you want my sister?"

She did not hear the response with her ears. Rather, the words formed in her mind, a ragged echoing voice so deep in pitch that she almost couldn't follow it. "She is meant for somewhere that isn't yet, but which will be."

Then the eyes drew back; that or she was falling away. She

couldn't tell which, because she had no sense of up or down, right or left, as the voice followed her. "Whenever you go to, I will find the when you have chosen and come for you. Next time, you will not escape."

Whenever? What the heck did it mean by choosing a 'when'? Then, the eyes faded while Demie floated into a mental fog, along with a growing wave of dizziness as if she was on a playground merry-go-round. A distant, steady chirping sound beckoned to her, and she let herself drift toward it. Demetra Anderson had no inkling that she drifted within a dimension that lay between universes, nor that she had just chosen an alternate timeline.

But she was about to find out.

Tony McClure walked down the hallway toward his new office, restraining an urge to pump his fist. The one-on-one session with the TerraMythos CEO went better than he could've dreamed.

The meeting invite came the previous afternoon, with a subject of simply 'Panchala Project Shutdown' and throughout the rest of that afternoon he kept receiving vague condolences from his co-workers. He was unable to eat that night, and finally around 12:30 he took half a sleeping pill. So in the morning, Tony picked out the sportcoat which best complemented his chocolate brown skin, listened to his favorite playlist on the drive to work and took a deep breath as he walked into the meeting. He knew the ax was falling on his dream project.

But something changed overnight. The executive not only supported Tony's proposal for a new gaming realm based on Hindu mythology, by the time Tony walked out of the office he had new workspace assigned for the project. Notifications were already on the way to the new senior members of his team. Apparently a brother could get a break, every now and then.

The biggest surprise, in more than one way, was the server applications manager assigned to his team. Over the previous year Tony had encountered Karen in the hallway a few times, and she was widely regarded within the company as one of the most talented devs within the organization. Karen had a reputation for being fiercely independent and unpredictable, and the few times they talked she had been openly flirtatious.

For the past few months he had fantasized about asking her out,

CONTENTS

but as a rule Tony didn't believe in getting involved with people in the workplace. Still, Karen was known to blow right past the rules, and that aroused both hope and fear in him. She would be a handful indeed.

There was no time to waste, because the CEO set a firm project deadline of three years to get the new game world online. Tony hummed softly to himself as he walked down the hallway to the office space for the Panchala Project.

The sharp hiss of drawn curtains snapped Demie awake. She was disoriented and woozy, and something covered her mouth and nose. When she reached toward her face, stabbing pain shot through her arm and she found an IV inserted into her hand. As she paused to stare at the tubing taped to her wrist, Demie realized a breathing mask was strapped over her face.

What? She must be in a hospital, which explained why she felt drugged. But where was Kori?

Movement to the right caught her attention and she turned her head, immediately groaning when it felt like someone buried an axe in her skull. A dull one at that. At the end of the bed stood an older, thin man in a white coat and a young woman wearing light blue scrubs. The man was focused on a chart which he thumbed through while the woman looked up, noticed Demie and came over smiling.

"We're awake now, are we?" The nurse glanced at the wall behind Demie's head and pressed some buttons, making adjustments. She must be a parent, Demie thought; they have a universal ability to ask questions without waiting for an answer. She pulled the mask away from her face.

"Whhhaaa..." Her voice emerged as a croak. She tried to speak, but the back of her throat felt as stiff as dried leather, and her tongue like a solid chunk of wood. Overpowering thirst shoved forward for her attention, pushing ahead of the splitting headache, and Demie gestured for the nurse to lean closer.

"Water," Demie managed a husky whisper. "Please!"

The woman nodded and followed the doctor out of the room, returning with a small cup that she held to Demie's lips. "Just take a few sips, sweetie, and swirl it around. If you can keep this down, I'll bring you a cup of ice chips."

Demie couldn't taste the water but as she swished the refreshing liquid, her mouth started to soften and she treasured it as long as she could, until it trickled down her throat.

"Is that better?" the woman asked, and again without waiting for an answer she lightly pressed a digital thermometer to Demie's forehead, then checked the IV tube. Demie managed a pathetic croak and a weak smile. The nurse patted Demie's hand and continued, "I'm sure you'll have a sore throat for a few days. Are you strong enough to write notes?"

When Demie carefully nodded her head, the woman left and came back with a pen and small pad of paper. Immediately, Demie snatched it up and ignored the wincing pain in her upper arms as she wrote down the question that haunted her from the moment she woke up.

"*How is my sister?*"

The nurse glanced at the pad, tilted her head and frowned. "I wouldn't know that, dear. You'll need to ask your mom. She said she'd be here this evening, sometime soon."

"*What happened to me?*" Demie scrawled on the pad, and turned it to the nurse.

"I probably shouldn't say anything, but..." The nurse glanced out into the hallway as if looking for guidance, but finding none continued, "All I know is that your chart says you were attacked by some kind of animal while you were camping." Then she pointed to bandages on both of Demie's upper arms. "It got your arms pretty good, but you're going to be okay now."

Those creepy eyes sure as heck weren't like any animal she could think of.

Chandar Partharajan weaved his way through stacks of moving boxes that filled the small living room, and stepped outside to check out the backyard of the new home his family moved into. Not that he had any choice. His friends were all back in Denver, and if he had been a year older and out of High School, family or not he seriously might've stayed there.

When the opportunity arose for his father to move up from just being a college professor to the head of a department, it didn't matter that the college was in a small town which even Google hadn't heard of. Okay, there were a few references, such as the fact that the Broncos football stadium held more people than the population of the whole county he now called home. Heck, the city they moved away from had more population than this entire freakin' state.

After looking around the large grassy yard and concluding he could add mowing the grass to the list of things he hated about this new home, he went back inside to get something to drink. Maa was in the kitchen, sitting at the table and talking to one of their new neighbors. That was his mother, always being the social butterfly.

"So I'll bring over some dinner tonight for y'all, since I'm sure you'll be unpacking for a good long time." A frosty-haired woman with the puffiest hair Chandar had ever seen, sat across the table from his mom. The woman looked and moved like a life size bobble-head doll.

"Everyone here is so kind," Maa replied. "I did not expect such a warm welcome."

Chandar poured a glass of iced tea from the fridge and turned to make a hasty retreat.

"We take right good care of each other here," the Bobble-head woman said, "Cause we have to. Fer instance, take your next door neighbor, Cassandra. You hain't met her yet cuz she took her daughter camping this week. Anyhow, Cassie's divorced with one daughter, and tough as it is being a single parent, she's also a volunteer paramedic."

He paused in his tracks for a moment and frowned. That's strange, he thought and then continued down the hall to his new room. He was certain the real estate agent told them the afternoon before that a family with two girls lived next door. Chandar almost died of embarrassment when Maa joked about arranging a marriage with one of the girls, and the agent said Maa had better talk to their father first because the girls were nine and thirteen.

Chandar began to unpack the room that would be his for the next three years, until he finished High School and graduated from the two-year college. Then he would move back to Denver.

As he began to set up his computer, Chandar dismissed the contradiction about the neighbors from his mind; the agent must have been thinking of someone else.

Demie rested her head on the pillow and closed her eyes. After demonstrating how the TV remote control also signaled for help, the woman left Demie alone with her fragmented thoughts. She recalled bits and pieces of what happened, of Kori and herself with their parents on a family camping trip for Kori's ninth birthday.

They were asleep inside a tent, when the small, stocky blond girl whimpered and scrambled out of her sleeping bag to worm in with Demie. "I had a nightmare," Kori had whispered. "I saw a big man standing over me, all dark and wearing some kind of shadow. A Shadowman." The younger girl shivered as she snuggled up to her sister. "He said he was sorry, but I had to leave this world."

Then, something happened to Kori, something so terrible she couldn't face it. The memories were locked away, as inaccessible as a bank vault in her mind. That thing with the Cheshire Cat eyes was the Shadowman Kori had seen. Her sister's words, along with the Shadowman's dire promise to come back for Demie, brought a cold shiver that penetrated into her bones.

She didn't want to be alone, so Demie groped around desperately on the bed for the remote, before remembering that the nurse hung it on a bar at the head of the bed. Reaching up, Demie pressed the call button and asked for an extra blanket, which the woman brought in along with a cup of vanilla pudding. The smooth snack wasn't half bad, and felt soothing to her throat as it went down.

Still, the image kept replaying in her mind: Kori, fading into darkness, silently mouthing the same question over and over again. 'Why?'

Demie was just finishing off the pudding when her mom walked in. She wanted to jump out of bed and run to her mother. But the best she could manage was to raise her hand in greeting, and then stare.

This was a different Mom who walked across the room. Instead of the long ponytail that always hung between her shoulder blades, Mom's hair was cropped short. Her eyes had slight bags and lines that weren't there before. She even walked like she was tired. It was as if Mom had aged ten years since Demie last saw her. And when her mother walked up, Demie smelled a trace of cigarette smoke. Since when had Mom smoked?

A shiver coursed through Demie as this stranger-who-was-Mom-but-not-Mom took Demie's hand and gave a weak smile.

"How are you doing, honeybear?" Mom asked. As a preschooler, Winnie-The-Pooh had been Demie's favorite book, so Mom started calling her "honeybear." Demie hated it, but she still gave a thumbs up. At least it was one thing that hadn't changed.

Since Mom was here, Demie could ask the question. Making a hoarse croak and pointing at her throat, Demie grabbed the paper and pen, and wrote, "*How is Kori?*" Her hand shook, so afraid of the answer that she could hardly write.

Mom read the message a couple times, frowned, and then looked at Demie, puzzled.

"Who's Kori?"

Cold trembles pierced Demie's body. She had imagined all kinds of answers over the past few hours, few of them good. But none came close to this. Anger surged within as Demie glared at her mother and scribbled, "*My sister, Kori. How is she?*"

Mom stared at the pad, then slowly shook her head as she replied, "Honey, you don't have a sister. You're an only child."

What the heck was wrong with Mom? This couldn't be happening. A pounding ache erupted in Demie's head as she wrote back, "*Not funny! Where's Dad?*"

Mom snorted, "Where do you think? My ex-husband is too busy with his girlfriend to be here."

Mom's EX-husband? Since when, and why would she even say something like that? For some reason, Mom was playing some real sick joke on her. Her hands shook as Demie snatched the pad back, "*You're NOT divorced. Why are you DOING THIS*?"

Mom read the message as the doctor walked in and then, dropping the pad on the bed, she pulled him aside for a whispered conversation. Over the beeping of the machines and the hiss from the ceiling vents, Demie overheard snatches of the conversation as the doctor calmed Mom down.

"...very traumatized...classic symptoms of PTSD...just an imaginary friend."

Demie scribbled, "*Kori is REAL!*" and threw the pad at her mom. The lies about Kori and being divorced had to be covering something up, and apparently the doctor was in on it.

Whatever they were hiding, she needed to find out what was really going on and why they were doing this to her. Maybe they were punishing her for not saving her sister from the Shadowman. She couldn't remember, didn't want to remember exactly what happened, but Demie knew with a sickening certainty that she had somehow thrown Kori under the bus to save her own self.

Demie thrashed in the bed as she pushed the side rail down, slipped over the edge and dropped to the floor. She tried to crawl away while Mom and the doctor held her down and the nurse scrambled to get a sedative injected into the drip line. Demie kept picturing Kori's eyes, asking the question Demie couldn't answer.

The sedative slammed her into unconsciousness, as she directed her last, fading thought toward her sister.

'I promise, Kori, I'll never forget you. Ever.'

CHAPTER ONE

Demie wailed at the shaft of light entering through her bedroom window. Turning over away from the window made it worse, since the mirror above the dresser reflected the whole freaking ball of fire. In that moment she just wanted to rip the thing right off the wall. Moaning, she covered her face with a pillow. What day was it?

Saturday.

Shit! She shot up into a sitting position to pull the shade down and then buried her head back in her pillow, wishing she could keep it there until the sun went around the world to rise again. This was an anniversary of the encounter with Kori's Shadowman.

Three years later, that creepy voiceless promise still echoed in her mind: "I will find you and come back for you." She couldn't say why, but she was certain of two things--it would indeed come back for her, and it would do so on an anniversary day. Which made the rest of the year bearable, in this world that was similar-but-not-the-same as the world she once knew.

The first few months after she awoke in the hospital, nightmares had haunted her every night. Even now Demie still woke up in the middle of the night at least once a week. It was always the same, an image of Kori dangling above a river within a dark fog and pointing an accusing finger. So anniversaries were a special kind of bad.

The first anniversary, Demie spent the whole day in her closet crying and refusing to come out, half paralyzed with fear and half with shame over acting like she was four instead of fourteen.

Whatever world this was that she got dropped into, it wasn't the one she came from, because the 'old' Mom would not have yelled and threatened Demie with punishment for not coming out. Then again, Old Mom didn't smoke and go to AA meetings every week either. Eventually, New Mom got tired of yelling and later that evening brought supper in to Demie. When they spent the night curled up together in blankets and comforters, it was almost like being with Old Mom again.

Through the pillow over her head, Demie heard a muffled cell phone chirp. She felt around for her phone, pulled it under the pillow and read the text message from her mother. 'Breakfast ready, we leave in 30 minutes.'

Today was also the championship softball game, and had it been any other day of the year Demie would bounce out of bed. After groaning, she sent Mom a quick 'brt' reply and slid out from under the covers. Maybe it wouldn't be too bad. Just stay away from rivers and swirling fog, and she might see tomorrow.

Demie shuffled to the dresser to embrace the framed portrait she had drawn of Kori. When Mom brought her home from the hospital, Demie insisted on signing up for every art and drawing class she could get into. Six months of obsession produced this finely drawn sketch that she treasured, so she wouldn't forget what her sister looked like. Eyes damp with tears, she brushed the picture with her lips and replaced it among the small pentagram of crystals and weird herbs from that lady at the Mystic Pyramid shop. Those things were supposed to help communicate with the dead, but even that special $50 black candle hadn't helped Demie contact Kori.

Probably because Kori wasn't dead. She just wasn't.

"Kori, I know you are out there somewhere," Demie fiercely whispered. "Don't give up, I haven't forgotten you." Nor forgotten that she had done something to her sister.

The words felt strange as she spoke, because for three years Demie refused to talk to anyone. Ever. Since the morning she awoke in the hospital, the only time Demie spoke was to her sister, when she was alone. The shrinks used some fancy words for it, some kind of trauma thing. After a year Mom gave up and stopped taking her to see them.

Snatching her robe off the floor, Demie went downstairs with her cell phone. Her mother, Cassandra Morris, was in the kitchen washing dishes when Demie wandered in and tapped on the table to let Mom know she was there.

"Oh, morning honey." Mom brought over some waffles. "How did you sleep?"

Texting on her cellphone by feel, Demie replied, "*oki*." Why did Mom always ask that? Questions like that always annoyed her. She had been asleep, how the heck would she know?

Mom glanced at her own phone for Demie's response and replied, "So are you ready for the big game?"

"*Yea imma hit a home run*"

"Really? You sound awfully sure." Mom brought over a plate of crispy bacon, just the way Demie liked it. Probably Mom's way of making up for being so mean the night before.

"*Sensei says think it will it do it*" Demie snatched up a piece of bacon like a t-rex, tearing at its prey; the crunch of the bones as satisfying as the salty flavor.

Mom went back to the waffle iron. "Aren't you glad I made you take Karate? Sounds like you're getting more out of it than you thought."

"*Maybe*" Demie reluctantly admitted. It was always dangerous to let Mom think she was right about something. Demie had carefully planted the idea of taking martial arts, as part of preparing to find Kori. If she ever figured out how to find her sister, she might need to know some self-defense.

"*Dad wbt at game?*" Demie fed butter to each of the hungry little mouths in the waffle, and gave each square a solid drink from the syrup hose that hung off the bottle.

"He didn't even come to your sixteenth birthday last month, so why would you think..." Mom paused, then turned back toward the table, "I'm just tired of seeing you get...Stop!" Demie was so focused on making sure each mouth got a good drink, she didn't notice the syrup almost overflowed the plate.

Demie gestured that it was okay, and set the syrup down.

Mom let out a sigh, and sat at the table. "Look, sweetie, I'm sure he'd like to come, but your dad has priorities that come with owning his own business. But even if he doesn't make it to the game, I do know that he loves you very much."

Demie glared at her plate. Yeah, she could tell how much he loved her; enough that she was lucky to see him once a month over the past three years. In that respect, New Dad was worse than New

Mom. But she wasn't going to try setting Mom straight, she never got anything that Demie tried to explain to her. Mom must've come from some foreign country, because she just didn't understand English.

While Mom cleaned up, Demie raced upstairs to get ready for softball. She pulled the jersey over thick shoulder-length black hair and examined herself in the mirror. Tying back the hair that framed her oval face and light green eyes, she tucked away a few loose strands and applied some quick touch-ups to her features. A few tugs to adjust the jersey was the best she could with what she had. At sixteen she was almost as flat as she had been at thirteen, those buds had become little more than big bumps. They were the least of her problems, in more than one way.

Slipping on the rest of her softball outfit made her feel like she was getting ready for battle. Avalanche was an idiot name for a team, but she didn't care what Coach called the team as long as she played each game. In a world where she didn't belong, bouncing between parents that weren't her real parents and shunned by peers who wanted nothing to do with the weird mute girl, the team was the one place where she truly belonged. She trembled with anticipation, yearning to be on the field. If they won today, they would advance to the state championship.

Mom called upstairs, "Come out to the car, we're going to be late! And bring your poncho, it might rain later."

Demie stuffed her shoes and mitt into the sports bag and then hesitated, stopped by that uneasy sense of being watched. It was an itchy feeling she frequently experienced, which spooked her at times. Enough that she once spent an evening tearing her room apart looking for peepholes or hidden cameras. When Mom asked, Demie said she was looking for a lost earring.

Shrugging off the edginess, she pondered which bat to take? The trusty wooden one she used in the last two tournaments, or the new aluminum bat Dad had given her?

She reached for the familiar wooden one that never let her down, when a wave of dizziness swept over her. The moment she touched the wooden bat, a churning bile rose in her throat. Then in her mind she heard the hollow 'thwack' the metal bat would make when she hit her home run. Smiling, Demie snatched it up and ran down stairs to join Mom. She didn't need a stupid poncho.

In the house next to Demie's, Chandar smiled as he opened the browser on his computer. The previous night, while buttering popcorn at the movie theatre and filling sodas, his thoughts were anchored to this moment. The morning he waited months for.

Chandar impatiently tapped the keyboard as the browser homepage opened on the TerraMythos website. Several times he battled with his parents when they couldn't understand why he wasted countless hours playing characters in the worlds of TerraMythos. But he smugly pointed out that he kept his college grades up and managed to reach the final semester of his A.A. degree with a 4.0 average, all while holding down a weekend job. So what difference did it make how he spent his free time?

Once he tried making the case that TerraMythos was educational, teaching about ancient cultures and myths. But when they asked if India was one of those cultures and he said no, his mom threw up her hands as if he had just made their point. Which made him wonder why he even tried with them sometimes.

Until today, that is. TerraMythos was opening the beta version of a new realm, the world of Panchala, based on Hindu mythology and the world of the Vedic texts. Now Chandar quivered with excitement in his chair, because long time customers were the first players to launch a character.

The TerraMythos site came up with the usual roll of thunder, clanging swords and animal cries. Licking his lips and fidgeting, Chandar eagerly clicked through, skipping the opening graphics and music. There, right at the top, was the link to Panchala: a pair of massive wooden doors which had been padlocked for the past month. The locks were gone.

Chandar clicked on the doors, and the screen slowly panned in as the doors swung open. Heavy groans of rusty metal hinges mixed with the sigh of a wind blowing through the dark opening beyond the gate.

Demie frowned as her team headed into the dugout. It was the top of the sixth inning and her father still wasn't in the stands. No big surprise. Not being around was what New Dad did best. With her team losing four to three heading into the last inning, they were running out of time to win. And Dad was running out of time with

Demie, in more than one way. She still remembered what Old Dad had been like, but after three years those memories were fading fast.

Giving up on searching the bleachers, she turned back to the game in time to see the first batter, Molly, get a single. The Bears pitcher was killing them with a wicked pitch that kept hitting the corners, and Molly was the only Avalanche player to get on base since the first inning.

Demie groaned when Kelly and Ursula both struck out, and then it was her turn. The tight pressure of being the team's last hope aroused a fierce focus as she grabbed her bat and glanced once more at the bleachers, knowing Dad still wouldn't be there. Of course not, but then a tall, stately blonde woman in the stands waved, and a wrathful anger burned inside as Demie pretended not to see and quickly turned away.

Dad's stupid girlfriend, Lauren. It figured he wouldn't come and send her instead. The only reason he liked Lauren was because she had big boobs, at least that's what Mom said. And maybe there was something to that, because they were ginormous, which made Demie want to rip her fricking face off that much more.

Shaking with anger, Demie walked to home plate and locked her eyes on the pitcher, a tall stick-thin girl who looked like she belonged in an anorexia clinic rather than on a softball mound. That was, until she wound up and a large white ball shot out from under her arm toward Demie. The ball came closer, and Demie imagined it was Lauren's head. A big, white head that made dumb jokes Dad always laughed at. The head Dad spent all his time with.

Demie swung, her only thought to crush Lauren's head into the next county. She connected with a scream that sent the ball flying up, up and toward left field. The left fielder took a few steps, then just stopped and watched the ball clear the fence by at least twenty feet.

When she crossed home plate with the go-ahead run, Demie didn't care who was in the stands.

The circular room which included Tony's office featured a huge window facing onto a California beach. In some ways it looked more like a dorm room than an office, with a small fridge, TV and gaming consoles in one corner and posters on the walls. The room only lacked beds. He led the small group which directed the teams working on the TerraMythos Panchala project, and they cultivated reputations for personalizing their work space.

Tony was a die-hard Star Wars fan, and much of the paraphernalia on his desk and shelves had once outfitted a movie set. The dark-skinned, six foot tall, square jawed man held a six-inch Wookiee figurine in his hand, pointed at his coworker, Joachim Butler. "Hell yes, if a Wookiee went mano-y-mano with a Klingon, he would kick Klingon ass every time!"

Joachim, just as devoted to Star Trek and surrounded by an equally impressive collection, countered Tony with a comparable Klingon. "No way. Klingons have genetically engineered mitochondria, which give them strength and endurance that a Wookiee couldn't match."

"Man, you're making that crap up. And strength doesn't matter anyway, look at Yoda. Wookiees have an internal source of midi-chlorians that draw on the Force."

Tony glanced at Karen de Havilland, who sat between them and more often than not was caught in the line of fire. She had gotten used to ducking when he and Joachim decided to relieve some stress, but she drew the line the day they pulled out water guns. There was a reason their office space was named The Sandbox.

Turning her chair around, Karen announced, "Come on boys, you'll have to put away your toys. It's showtime."

After a final gesture toward Joachim, Tony set the Wookiee in place and rubbed his hands together in anticipation while he turned to the keyboard. As the creative brain behind the newest virtual world, Tony would issue the computer command that brought the servers online, even though they were a hundred miles away. It was a TerraMythos tradition akin to breaking a bottle of champagne on the bow of a ship.

This had been his dream since he started as a programmer for the first mythical world of Babylonia. Inspired by IBM's Jeopardy-champion Watson project, he developed a question answering logic for how the Panchala servers handled Non-Player Characters and the events that all the live players interacted with. So Panchala was not just another realm; it was a whole new experimental approach that, for the first time ever, used true artificial intelligence. The AI never slept, saw everything, and allowed players to create their own adventures.

They all nodded in turn as Tony asked how their systems looked, and then he turned back to his PC. It was time. He typed '/launch brahma' and hit Enter, then the darkness beyond the heavy wooden doors began to change on thousands of computer screens across the world. The brightening dawn of Panchala revealed green, grassy fields surrounded by jungle.

Demie felt that uncanny itch again which made her skin crawl, as she headed out of the dugout. It was the sense she sometimes got in her room, that some creeper was watching her.

She tried not to look around as she took her position in center field, while the first batter for the Bears took some practice swings and then stood in the batter's box. The girl hit a ground ball out to first and Demie's team cheered, and when the second girl struck out, they cheered even louder. But the cheers cut short as the girl who represented the final out hit a double into center, just short of Demie. The best she could do was to hold the runner at second, and she fumed as she paced back to her position.

The next batter for the Bears was the one who drove in all four runs, once with a single and the others with a three-run home run. If this girl got another hit, they would be lucky to hold the Bears to a tie.

The first pitch looked low, but the girl swung hard and Demie saw the ball fly up. As it headed for the field behind Demie, she turned and raced toward the chain-link fence. Tracking the ball over her shoulder, she raced across the grass like a gazelle, and just before the three-foot chain-link fence she leapt up. The ball smacked into her glove at the same moment her hip crashed against the wall. When she went over the world spun around, but she hung onto that ball with all of her strength, until she felt the earth thud into her back.

Through it all she kept her arm out, and when she stood and pulled the ball from her glove, the Avalanche broke out into wild cheering. Her teammates raced across the field and met Demie after she climbed back over the fence.

As they carried her around the bases on their shoulders, Demie felt like the luckiest girl in the world. At least for one moment, here was a place she really belonged. When they set her down on home plate, Demie looked around for Mom but didn't see her anywhere in the stands. That was when Lauren came walking up, and drove the good feelings away.

"Great game, Demie! Listen, your mom had to respond to an emergency call."

What the heck was wrong with Mom, that she let them put her on call today? For some reason that Demie could never figure out, Mom spent every other weekend on call as a volunteer emergency paramedic, which was something else Old Mom never did. And she didn't even get paid for it. Demie didn't want to grow up, if being an adult meant being that stupid.

"So," Lauren continued, "Your mom asked me to give you a ride home."

Demie simply stared, shocked that Mom could be so clueless. Then again, Mom didn't even know Dad was seeing Lauren before he moved out, something Demie overheard during a monthly visit.

Whipping a small pad and pen out of her bag, Demie angrily jotted a note and thrust it at Lauren. "*No! I need to cool my muscles down. Best way is to walk home.*"

Lauren looked up at some heavy clouds moving in quickly from the west. "But it's going to rain, are you sure you don't want a ride? Really, I don't mind at all."

You mean you don't have a mind at all, Demie thought, or you'd realize I'll never like you. Although her team was still in the midst of celebrating, all Demie wanted was to be alone and at home. Anywhere that Lauren wasn't. Which made returning to her old world somehow all the more urgent, because there was no Lauren where she came from.

"*I'll walk, thanks,*" Demie wrote. While Lauren read the note, Demie grabbed her gear and dashed across the field. She barely heard the woman shout, "But I told your mother..."

Home was only a half-mile. She knew from experience she could be there within ten minutes. Which was a good thing, because Lauren was right. Those were some pretty ugly clouds rolling in.

Dawn broke beyond the doors leading into Panchala, as Chandar clicked his way through them. He ran long, slender fingers through his thick, dark hair while the screen loaded, then took a deep breath as he started the process of character creation. Even though he had a couple of high level characters in Babylonia and one in the ancient Greek world of Mycenae, a character could only move into a new game world through reincarnation. The re-born character would start empty-handed at a high level, without any of the items, weapons or armor it had before. Plus, character migration was a one-way trip; one could never return to a previous world and that was just too painful for Chandar to do.

So he generated a new female character that would be a warrior/thief. This gave the most flexibility, and later he could change her class if he wanted. After selecting some background details such as hair color and build, he adjusted the vital statistics that determined attributes such as strength, agility and intelligence. The strength was rather low, but he could compensate for that with good magical items. Speed and dexterity were at the maximum values for a new character and the other characteristics were decent.

After adjusting his microphone, Chandar reviewed the character voices and selected a sultry female voice with a slight British accent. Although the game would take keyboard responses if one's computer mic failed, most of the interactions were driven by Voice Activated Response. As long as he was in character, whether he spoke to game characters or other players the game interface would modulate his voice according to his character.

Now he had to think of a name. One name had always been at the top of his mind, since his family moved into the neighborhood a few years before. He was outside at the time, cleaning up some debris that Baba asked him to take care of, when he came across her hiding in the bushes by the garage door. The dark haired girl silently gestured for him to crouch down beside her, as if inviting him to join in on some secret.

"What are you doing?" he had whispered. She seemed kind of young, maybe early-teens, but there was something feisty about her that intrigued him. In just a general way, of course, because he was a high school senior at the time and a bit old for her. That would've been too creepy.

"*Playing kick the can,*" she jotted on a pad of paper, showing the words to him. And in that moment her twinkling eyes swallowed his soul, with a smile that was half-playful, half-provocative and totally teasing. She scribbled another note that she tore off and handed to him. "*We can play with each other, but first you have to catch me if you can!*"

Then she darted off, like a rabbit startled into full flight. Chandar merely watched her dash into the night, but he had wanted to catch her ever since. As he watched her blossom over the years into a young woman, his heart raced every time they occasionally spoke. He would get so lost in her emerald eyes that his tongue froze like a browser window, and sometimes a half-sad smile slipped onto her face. Hopefully he kept his feelings well hidden, because the fact that he was four years older was just one reason nothing would ever happen between them.

He kept her note tucked away in his dresser, because his parents would absolutely kill him if they knew he fancied not just a younger girl, but an American one. Their sights were set on some Hindu girl who moved over from India with her family when she was very young. He had not yet met Sanjali, but they were already referring to her as their future daughter-in-law, which he tried not to think about.

Demie was just a harmless attraction that he never acted on. But fantasies were what online games were all about, so there was no reason why he couldn't spend time with Demie in Panchala.

The rain started when Demie was about halfway home, with a few scattered drops that were more like watery marbles.

Coming around a street corner, she startled an orange tabby cat. The moment it saw her a vicious hiss burst out of the feline, its fur standing up as if it had been electrified, followed by a horrible howl that could only come from a dying cat or a bagpipe. The animal crouched, made a half-hearted swipe at her, then turned tail and fled.

It wasn't the cats fault, but Demie made an annoyed token jab toward it with her bat and continued on. Since coming home from the hospital she always got that reaction from cats, as if they saw something only visible to felines. During a biology class field trip last year, a cougar at the zoo hissed at her before retreating into its den. Of course, that spawned an unending stream of snide comments from her classmates the rest of the day about how even animals didn't want anything to do with mute freaks.

Demie stopped musing about cats when she noticed a black funnel cloud form in the clouds above. It didn't appear to be dropping but it rotated slowly, and Demie felt a shiver race up and down her spine like a centipede when she saw what appeared to be an eye in the center. Fine, if the Shadowman came back, just let him try to catch her.

"Catch this," she said as she defiantly flipped her finger at the cloud. She could outrun a slow moving mist.

As if responding to her gesture, scattered raindrops exploded into a full shower and she switched from a trot to a full run. Just as she made the last turn onto her street, the sharp crack of a lightning strike off to her right made her leap sideways. Too close for comfort, but still seven or eight blocks away.

She gripped her bag and bat tighter, and opened her stride up for the final dash home.

The rest of Tony's team had departed for the beta launch party. Since it was a Saturday, he let the team take off after the flawless launch. Now it was time to turn the reins for running Panchala over to the AI. He stood up as he reached to turn off his monitors.

Chandar typed 'DemiGirl' in the name field and clicked on the 'Save' button.

Demie came racing down the street, started to turn into the driveway to her house, and then barely had time to register the flash. She never heard the sound of the lightning strike that reached through her body, along her bat and then up into the sky.

Three things happened at precisely the same instant.

The lights went dead in Chandar's house as the lightning struck, and his computer shut down.

Tony saw the Panchala game world do the one thing it was designed to never do: it froze.

And Demie's body landed on the grass next to her driveway.

CHAPTER TWO

Cassandra Morris felt terrible about leaving during Demie's big game without even saying goodbye to her daughter, but Demie was tough and she'd get over it. Cassie sat in the back of the EMS vehicle, finishing paperwork that seemed to take more time than the emergency response itself. Not that this had been a real emergency. Rachel Darwin took a spill in her front yard and twisted her ankle. Her swearing caused the neighbor's dog to bark madly until the neighbor came outside and called for help, despite her protests that she was perfectly fine aside from a whole lot of stupid, and she just needed to rest. They took the spry seventy-two-year-old to the local clinic for x-rays, and her family was on the way. Which meant that Cassie and her driver, Mark, were off the hook.

One more form, with the same questions as the other three, and Cassie would be finished with her volunteer service. She might even have time for a quick smoke before the AA meeting. They were driving back to the volunteer fire station when the call came in over the radio.

"Unit Two, code red. Girl down at 513 Oak Street. Status unknown but she is not responsive." Mark flipped on the lights and siren, spun the van around and gunned the engine as they headed across the small town. Cassie sat staring at the radio, not wanting to believe what she had heard, even as her blood turned ice cold.

"Cassie!" Mark smacked her arm. "Confirm that we are on the way."

She looked at Mark with a blank stare, then experience and training took over. "Central, this is EMS Two, we are on the way. Do you...do you have any more details?"

Eternal moments passed, and Cassie wanted to beat a response out of the radio when the reply came back. "Negative. All we know is that there was a lightning strike about the same time, but the caller didn't know whether the child was hit. Is that you, Cassie?"

"Yes," she whispered back, afraid to respond, but more afraid not to. "Yes, it's me."

"I'm so sorry, Cassie. It's Demie. Are you sure you can do this?"

"Tell me, who the hell is going to do this, if not me?" Cassie yelled, then choked up and several loud sobs escaped before she got them under control. "I'll do what I have to. You just make sure the ER is ready if we have to evacuate. Okay, we're coming onsite, so stand by."

They raced down the street Cassie lived on, and Cassie gripped the door handle, more to keep herself together than to keep from being tossed. Mark swung into her driveway and there, lying on the grass, was Demie. Kneeling next to her was that foreign boy who lived next door. Chandar.

Cassie grabbed her medical kit and raced over to her daughter. Demie was bare-foot, her shoes blown off by the lightning strike, and Cassie gasped when she saw how badly Demie's right hand was burned. God damn it, I can't lose it now. Check heartbeat and breathing, she reminded herself. Oh God let there be a heartbeat.

When she palpated she found a faint flutter of a heartbeat that was irregular, and then stopped. Cassie screamed at her driver to get the automated external defibrillator, while she started resuscitation. Training took over: clear the airway, two breaths, and chest compressions. Check for breathing and repeat.

Mark was taking forever, how hard could it be? As she desperately applied compressions, Cassie yelled at her daughter, "Damn it, come on Demie, do this. You're not going anywhere!" She checked for breathing and pulse, but still found nothing.

Then Mark hooked up the AED, as Cassie's tears bathed Demie's face and she breathed for her daughter.

The server Tony logged into from his computer was the primary controller for the Panchala cluster. He shook his head, stunned that the primary was still frozen and unresponsive. Opening the TerraMythos site from Karen's computer, he tried to log into Panchala as a regular user. When it also failed to respond he slammed the mouse down on the desk and turned back to his own system. This time the Panchala primary replied and he accessed the operating system; it was active but he gaped, disbelieving, at the huge amount of data it was processing.

The primary was not supposed to process data, but rather distribute the load among the bank of twenty servers that made up the world of Panchala. Even their most pessimistic estimates projected no more than a 10% load on the cluster from this first wave of beta users. But now the primary CPU was running at a full 100%. Tony actually started to sweat as he switched from server zero to server one, and on up to nineteen. Every CPU was running at 100%, all processing some kind of data.

What the hell did they miss, to cause a screw up this bad? There would definitely be a team-wide root cause analysis, but first Tony had to get Panchala back online, even if it meant physically bouncing all the servers. They would lose whatever data they were processing, but it was only a game. It wasn't like someone's life depended on it.

Tony picked up the phone and started to call the data center.

Demie floated in a white haze of pain, caught in an eternal moment. She recalled some rain, running down a street, and then a giant hammer which hit her out of nowhere. It seemed so distant…not here and now…wherever 'here' was.

When that hammer hit, her senses melted in one fusing burst of agony, and gradually her eyes and ears faded into a sort of static. The hissing reminded her of that old-timer TV set in the beauty shop in town, when someone switched it to an empty channel. Except that her eyes and ears were the television. Was this what it felt like to be blind and deaf?

In some ways this felt eerily similar to when she first met the Shadowman, but instead of cold Demie felt pain, and she was enveloped in whiteness. Maybe she was still in the hospital, and the past three years were just a bad dream. When Demie tried to touch her face she couldn't. Her arms weren't restrained; they just wouldn't move. In fact, she couldn't even feel her arms. Or legs. Or anything.

Demie wanted to scream, needed to scream. But she couldn't. Her lungs held no breath, and she didn't even have vocal chords to tighten. It was like some crazed dentist had shot up her whole body with Novocain.

As she tried to feel sensation in any part of her body, Demie slowly became aware of her self as another kind of static, as a giant cloud, loosely held together and pushed randomly in different directions and into different shapes.

Deep in her core, a primal animal instinct yearned to howl and rose to take over. It would be so easy to just let go, to just go to sleep. Even as she felt herself slipping, she knew it would take her somewhere that she would never return from.

"Demie, please help me. Don't let go. Focus!" A voice cut through the mist in Demie's mind like a foghorn, a voice she longed to hear for years. It was Kori. She was really out there, somewhere. Demie needed Kori now, to give her something to hang on to.

Sensei had talked about focusing on something, if she could just remember. Yes, he called it chi, a kind of inner body of energy. At the time she dismissed it as nonsense, but now that seemed to be all she had left. The karate master gave some mental exercises to help focus her chi, which she had blown off. What the heck was it he said? Put her left hand below her belly button and her right hand over her heart...how could she do that, when she couldn't even tell whether she had hands, let alone where they were positioned?

Think it, will it, do it. Demie pictured herself, placing her hands. Then breathe, he said, picturing a warm light flowing from belly to head. Again, she tried to envision her breath as a warm light and focused her attention on slowly counting backward. She stumbled on the numbers at first, but then as she continued it became easier, and mental images began to take form for her.

She had to get herself together, literally, or she knew she would not survive.

The small room where Cassie waited was little more than an alcove carved out of a hallway, which contained a small sofa, a couple of chairs, a small coffee table and two vending machines. And not very comfortable chairs at that.

Good Shepherd Hospital managed to keep that name simply because no other facility within forty miles was more than a clinic. While Good Shepherd started out as little more than an urgent care center which happened to have a room of beds, over time a small Emergency Room was outfitted with all the essentials. Still, a serious multiple car accident would stretch its resources, which Cassie had observed several times.

Cassie alternated between pacing the small hallway and fidgeting in one or another of the chairs. Over the years she had seen other people in this waiting room they called Limbo. But until now she never truly understood the fear, the pain, the helplessness that lay behind those silent, haunted eyes. Most of all, how lonely this place was.

She kept remembering the defibrillator, which managed to get Demie's heart going long enough for the drive to the ER. On the way to the hospital she had to run the AED a second time, while Cassie shouted at Demie to keep trying. When they pulled her daughter out off the van, one of the nurses pushed Cassie out of the room and into the waiting area, saying she was too hysterical.

Fifteen minutes later, after assaulting both of the vending machines and tossing one of the chairs down the hall, she admitted to herself that the nurse had a valid point. Cassie finally settled down to drink a cup of what one machine claimed was coffee, though she would dispute that. When Mark came down the hall and sat down next to her, the uncertainty remained but at least easing the burden of loneliness felt like removing lead weights.

He gave her a thin smile. "Well, she's stabilized, and it looks like we won't lose her. But she's still not conscious, so we don't know yet whether..." Mark trailed off, and the compassion in his eyes started to reel her in. But she couldn't let herself go there again. Especially now.

Cassie reached over and squeezed his hand. That was safe enough. "Thanks for letting me know. We'll just have to wait and see." Her hand lingered, resting in the sad moment.

He returned her squeeze, glanced over her shoulder and then stood up. "Well. It looks like reinforcements are coming, so I think I better go now, and take the rig back to the firehouse. Call me if anything changes. You still have my number, right?"

Cassie stood up and nodded as her ex-husband Sherman Anderson and Lauren came down the short hallway. They looked right through Mark when he passed them on the way out.

"We just got your message and came straight here," Sherman said as he hesitated, and then gave his ex-wife a quick hug. "How is she?"

His words barely registered. Cassie glared at Lauren, driving unblinking hatred into the woman's eyes. She wanted to rip Lauren's limbs off and cram them down her throat. All of them at the same time. Finally, taking a deep breath, she turned to Sherman, "I'm not sure, but it sounds like she's stable at the moment."

Lauren, her eyes dripping with smeared mascara tears, started toward Cassie to also give her a hug, then stopped, arms dangling. "I am so, so sorry. She wouldn't let me give her a ride and ran off across the field. By the time I got in my car to follow her, she was gone and I couldn't find her." Lauren paused, her voice wavering with sobs, and then wailed as she started to collapse, "Oh God! If only I had somehow stopped her."

Cassie felt the emotional breath get kicked out of her, as Sherman eased his distraught companion onto the sofa. She barely tolerated her ex-husband's girlfriend at the best of times. Countless times she had fantasized about making Lauren cry. But now, the tears and pure anguish in Lauren's voice transformed the woman, at least for this one moment, into just another human who shared Cassie's pain. The dam of Cassie's anger cracked as her own pain burst forth.

Huge tears rolling down her face, Cassie sat next to Lauren and embraced her. "It's okay. No one could ever tell Demie to do something she didn't want to do. She was her own person." Cassie stopped, then whispered, "Is her own person."

As though punched in the stomach, Cassie sat back in shock. She was already referring to her daughter in the past tense.

The person on the other end of the phone spoke with a Jersey accent so thick, Tony could barely understand most of what the man said. He pounded his head against the back of his chair.

"Look, I'm not authorized to do nuttin. De supervisor will be right back, suh just wait."

"What, are you shitting me?" Tony burst out as he clenched the phone handset.

"Nah, he ain't takin' no crap. He's just out smokin'."

Tony sighed. The servers were so hosed they weren't even responding to reboot commands, and it wasn't the tech's fault that his supervisor stepped out. Taking a deep breath, he spoke again into the phone. "Sure, I'll wait. But we really need to get those servers reset."

It was taking longer to find someone who could implement what he wanted to do, than it would take to actually do it. At least while he waited, he could start sending the notifications.

Demie was developing a stronger awareness of her body, so the chi exercises helped. When she remained focused on counting, she didn't have time to feel scared and a tingling sensation grew throughout her body, like the Novocain was wearing off. Her bodily sensations grew more solid; where at first she felt like a thin fog, then it seemed like the vapor was turning into water and then ice. She couldn't help imagining a baby discovering that it had a body.

Which gave her hope because whatever happened to her must be passing. But it was scary freaky too, because there was no telling what she would find. As a sense of weight returned, she perceived that she was lying down. Her limbs still couldn't move, but the visual 'static' lessened until she made out occasional shapes passing over her from time to time. And the 'static' sound also eased, turning into random noises.

Slowly, as she re-connected with her body, she was learning to see and hear again. Then it started to come together faster.

Demie focused on her chi as she lay on her back, and resumed counting again.

When lightning struck just outside Chandar's house and shut down his computer, his first thought after jumping halfway to the ceiling was fear about whether the lightning fried his computer. Until he looked outside and saw Demie on the lawn, next to an exploded metal bat.

His heart burst with anguish as he ran outside because he was sure she was dead, and the call to 911 connected just as he got to the girl. Chandar felt helpless as he looked down at Demie and responded to a lot of stupid questions he didn't know the answer to, such as whether the girl had any allergies. When asked to check, he noted her shallow and irregular breathing, and kicked himself for ignoring those CPR videos in Human Anatomy 101 last year.

The ambulance pulled up and he watched the mother try to revive her daughter. Then everything seemed to happen at once as they moved the girl onto a stretcher and loaded her in the EMT vehicle. Chandar regretted not doing more, though he couldn't imagine what else he could have done.

The van raced down the street and turned the corner, and he slowly walked back into his house, still so shaken that he had to explain what happened to his parents several times before he got the story straight. They went to offer prayers for the girl at the household shrine, but he didn't really buy into all that religious stuff.

Not that he was about to tell them that.

Back in his room, he had to reset the circuit breaker on his power strip and then the computer came on right away and started up normally. The image of Demie haunted him, lying in the ambulance as they closed the doors. He spent a couple hours trying to work on homework assignments, but time and again his attention drifted back to Demie. Frustrated that he was unable to complete any meaningful study, he finally threw down his pen and turned to his computer.

The power had died just as he saved his character, so he wasn't sure whether the save went through. There was only one way to find out. When he logged onto the TerraMythos website and back into Panchala, Chandar had no character available to play with; certainly not one named DemiGirl.

He would have to re-create her.

Cassie lay back in the chair, closed her eyes and tried to relax. They were all at Demie's bedside in a 'room' defined by a sliding curtain; Cassie on one side, Sherman and Lauren on the other. They had been there for hours, watching the nurse and doctor come and go, mumbling to each other but saying precious little to the visitors.

Cassie's exhaustion drew her into an uneasy nap, just as the curtain slid aside and the doctor pulled a chair in. She sat up, and a dreadful chill surged through her. This would not be good; good news didn't take long enough to sit down.

"Well, there is good news and bad news. On the good side, we do not see any permanent damage. Just some burns that will heal in time, and may not leave much of a scar."

Sherman asked before Cassie could, "So is she going to be okay?"

Cassie looked away and tried not to listen. She dreaded hearing the answer. Her ears pounded with fear, and the physician sounded like he was at the end of a long tunnel.

The man looked down and then away. "We just can't tell. There is no neurological activity that we can detect, on any higher level. She does not..."

Lauren interrupted, "So are you saying that she's brain dead?"

Cassie turned to glare at the woman. How dare she even voice the thought!

The doctor looked increasingly uncomfortable. "That's one of the things we don't understand. She's very lucky because there is no brain damage as far as we can tell, and no apparent reason for her to not wake up right now and walk out of this room."

"So," Sherman asked, "What else don't you understand?"

Cassie barely heard the response. She wouldn't hear it.

"What is keeping her alive? After the tremendous shock she took and with this much loss of brain function, normally she would be dead. Instead, she's in a coma, and frankly there is no way of knowing when, or even if, she will come back."

Tony had waited so long he figured they must be hiring someone to talk to him, when the data center manager came on the line. This person sounded like he was from Great Britain, and after Tony explained which servers he needed shut down and re-started, the manager said he just had to verify the server information and would be right back.

Waiting again, Tony leaned back and closed his eyes. With any kind of luck at all, within a few minutes they would restore back to where they started from. The only problem was that while they could restore the backed up data, whatever user information had been collected over the past few hours would be erased forever. That would only affect the new beta accounts but the project timeline was still going to slip, so he had to start thinking how to explain all this to the TerraMythos CEO. That would not be fun.

The data center manager came back online, "Right, I'm ready to start. Which servers do you want to start with?"

"Thank God, at last!" Tony cried out, followed by a loud sigh of relief. "Let's just shut them all down at once, and then I'll give you the sequence we want to bring them back up in. So if you can..."

Then he almost dropped the phone as he heard the ping of an account logging in. What the hell? Tony looked over at Karen de Havilland's desk, and the account he tried earlier was now logged in and asking for a response. He rolled his chair over and activated his character. The session was somewhat sluggish so there was some vicious latency, but it responded.

"Wait, wait! Just hang on a minute," Tony said on the phone. "Let me check something first." He turned back to his computer and examined the connection with the primary server. Resource usage was still high but it was working, and the secondary servers were responding as well.

"Let's hold off for now," Tony said. "The systems are coming back online, so for the moment just make a note of which servers we were looking at. I'll call back if we still need them re-booted."

Tony hung up his phone, and rubbed his eyes. This was going to make him an old man before his time. Now that Panchala was running again he would just keep watch on his servers, and advise his team to stand by and stay available.

They didn't have to re-boot after all, but he still had to identify whatever caused the problem and then root it out like a nasty weed.

Chandar was disappointed that his character had not saved, but that was okay. He would just re-create it. She wouldn't have the exact same random attributes, but he remembered how he had configured her, so he soon had a new, similar character ready to be named.

Again, Chandar typed in 'DemiGirl' and clicked 'Save.' A few seconds later the message popped up, "Please select a unique name." What the hell? He stared in disbelief at the message, thinking he must have typed the name in wrong. Ten attempts later, he had to accept that the name of DemiGirl was indeed taken by someone else.

Chandar slammed his mouse on the desk and grabbed the nearest, heavy thing at hand to launch at his door. The bang when the backpack hit the door echoed throughout the house.

Twenty minutes later, after apologizing to his parents and

assuring them that the online computer game was not turning him into a homicidal murderer, Chandar turned back to his TerraMythos account. Without thinking about what he was doing, he changed the gender to male, renamed his character Demikiller, and this time it saved.

No, he wasn't a homicidal murderer in this world, but in the TerraMythos world of Panchala he now had one purpose. For a moment he felt a twinge of shame, since he never pictured himself as being 'that person' who stalked someone online. But this was personal now. He would make an exception to find, and kill, the fake DemiGirl.

Demie was still lying down, and felt a deep sense of relaxation. This must have been what Sensei meant about finding inner peace. For the first time in the three years since she woke up in the hospital, Demie opened the vault in her mind and let the memories emerge from when Kori had been taken. She had to face whatever foul deed she committed because it probably had something to do with what was happening now. Her thoughts drifted back to the tent, back to that fateful morning.

After Kori crawled into Demie's sleeping bag, the young girl fell fast asleep. But sleep eluded Demie, so she finally eased out of her bedroll as dawn broke. Demie's best friend at school had given her a joint and dared Demie to smoke it on the trip. She quietly retrieved the contraband from a hidden fold in her suitcase and then slipped out of the tent. It only took seconds to retrieve the matches Dad conveniently left in the storage box on the camp table, and a few minutes later Demie was crouching in some thick bushes about a hundred feet upstream. She had just taken her first puff when she heard a muffled shriek pierce the silence.

Kori must have been following Demie, because when she looked down the river bank Demie saw her sister dangling in the air several feet above the shallow water, within a dark, silent swirling mist. The slowly spinning cloud was about twenty feet away, as high as their two-story home and the width of the small river.

Within the cloud, Kori kicked and flailed her arms as she rotated to face her sister. When she saw Demie, she reached out, "Dee-Dee, please, help me!"

Her sister's plea and the fear of losing Kori propelled her to her feet, and she leapt forward, wrapping her arms around Kori's waist. Demie buried the side of her face against her sister's abdomen and felt Kori shudder within her grasp.

"Don't let go!" Kori cried but the words sounded garbled and far away, as if under water.

"Just grab onto me," Demie yelled and wrapped her fingers around Kori's belt. Sobbing with fear for both of them, she locked her arms around her sister's small body. The interior of the mist was darker and colder than the deepest winter night, and the swirling darkness pulled Demie loose and lifted her up next to Kori.

That was when those eyes approached, and the world folded in on itself. Demie desperately flailed and kicked, trying to break free of the grip this thing had on her. There was only one object Demie could push against to break free, and that was her sister. Blind with panic, Demie grabbed Kori and wrenched herself loose as hard as she could. The hold on her slipped, and then Demie kicked against Kori with all her strength. She slowly dropped, as if sinking through water, and looked up at her sister.

Kori had been propelled by Demie's kick deeper into darkness, and she stared at Demie in shock while her mouth silently shaped the word 'why.' The last Demie saw of her sister were outstretched hands, vanishing into the mist.

That look on her sister's face haunted Demie. Her thoughts returned to the present, now that she remembered how she saved herself at her sister's expense, by pushing herself out of the cloud by sending Kori into it.

Demie's sight focused enough to see a bright, semi-fluorescent blue sky above her, with occasional cotton-ball white clouds passing overhead. But the sounds were still indistinct and blurred, as though her ears were full of water.

Then an enormous dark shape passed over her, and with a startled jolt she found herself on her feet. She couldn't say which shocked her most; that she stood up without knowing how to move or that she was looking at the retreating end of an elephant. And if an elephant leaping over her wasn't bizarre enough, three men ran past her chasing it, wielding some wicked-looking swords.

Unable to move her head or body, she watched about a dozen people dash through her field of vision, chased by elephants, mutant baboon-monkeys and large rottweilers with horns.

CHAPTER THREE

Demie couldn't move. The peace and relaxation which helped her to focus her chi, vanished with a snap, like a firecracker. Tsunami waves of cold fear radiated from her abdomen, sweeping her mind of rational thought. She yearned to howl but could not release a sound, not even a moan or a whimper. Far worse than a scream that no one could hear was not even being able to scream.

No-no-no-no-I'm-not-dead-please-don't-let-me-be-dead-no-no-no-no.

She pushed and pulled against the bonds holding her, but couldn't feel any restraints. Her limbs hung limp and unresponsive, as if she were a paraplegic. The only sound was a constant static hiss, as people and strange animals continued to run past her, oblivious to her presence.

This-can't-be-happening-why-can't-I-wake-up-I-don't-wanna-be-dead.

Then, an amazon woman ran right through her, shattering her thoughts like a slap.

For the first time, she examined the vista that lay before her. A grassy plain stretched out toward a distant forest, and scattered over the field were people dressed for a costume party and bizarre animals running in all directions. But it was the colors that stunned her.

They were vibrant, with hues and shades she couldn't name and an odd tactile quality. Clouds with a silky white smoothness, the sky with a cushiony refreshing blueness she wanted to float in. And cool, crisp green grass, like a fresh slice of watermelon.

Was this how it felt to go crazy? If she wanted to stay sane, she needed to regain the mental state that helped her get this far.

Demie started the counting backwards which initiated the chi exercises, when an elephant ran through her left side, and she flinched to the right. About fifty feet before her stood a massive gray stone wall covered with vines and yellow flowers, encompassing a large open wooden gate that was held together with massive iron straps. The two-story wall curved away and around, enclosing flat wooden rooftops on top of brick two- and three-story buildings.

Her attention shifted to three men who raced toward her in pursuit of the elephant. Two of them wore some kind of armor and carried weapons, while the third wore some kind of sheet wrapped around his body like a toga. What the hell, she thought, was this some kind of Halloween nightmare?

The dude in the middle came directly at her, holding an enormous sword in front of him. She wanted to move, oh God she wanted to move, but she couldn't, so she tried to close her eyes as the gleaming tip was about to run her through. But she couldn't shut out the image either, and as his body was about to crash into her, she flinched and spun around again.

Just in time to see the man emerge and race away from her toward the pachyderm, which stopped to make a stand against its pursuers. The three men surrounded their quarry and the two guys with swords struck at the sides of the beast. Meanwhile the third man wearing a sheet waved his hands in front of the elephant. Maybe he was trying to hypnotize it.

The swords emitted flashes of light when they hit, and faint zigzags of lightning flared over the animal's body. It appeared to have some sort of force field, but the elephant visibly dimmed at the same time, then shook its head and turned toward the guy who apparently failed to hypnotize it. When the creature rose up on two legs, Demie tried again to close her eyes because she didn't want to see someone die. But she couldn't avoid watching it stomp the man flat to the ground, then for good measure it gored the man with both tusks.

The unlucky man stayed down, while his two buddies abandoned their friend and fled back toward Demie. After stomping on the fallen dude once more just to make sure, the elephant gave chase to the remaining men, heading right through Demie. She almost went crazy with fear as the huge beast approached, and she still couldn't move.

Then, flinching once more, she faced the gate and watched the charging animal follow the men as they raced to the city walls. But when they disappeared through the gates, it came to an abrupt halt, turned to the side and wandered off to forage on some clumps of vegetation scattered about in the grass. As if nothing had happened.

Unsure exactly how, Demie forced herself to 'flinch' once more and turned back around to face the scene of the brief fight. Demie was ecstatic. She still wasn't sure how, but for the first time she had moved on her own, and she could've wept with relief.

The fallen man lay unmoving in the field and then simply vanished. For an instant, a void remained where his body had been. Not dark or white, but rather the absence of any color or hue. Then, in another instant, the space contained grass. Demie stared, trying to wrap her mind around something she couldn't begin to grasp.

Dreams had a way of flowing and changing without any kind of rules, but what she witnessed appeared to have some order and structure, unlike any dream she ever remembered. Death couldn't be this real and vivid, could it? Dream, death, or maybe something in between. It was possible that she was losing her mind, but at the moment she didn't mind.

Crazy was probably better than being dead.

What she did care about was practicing a few more turns, and that made her smile inside. Then she stopped. Something was different, not the same as before. The static hiss. She had completely forgotten about it during the elephant fight, and now it was almost gone. But that wasn't what worried her now.

Instead, she heard actual sounds coming into focus, becoming clearer and then fading back out, as though tuning into a radio station. That was when she knew for a fact that she was going insane.

What had been static was now clearly music.

Tony closed the media subsystem application logs and leaned back in his chair. With a deep exhale, he glanced at the clock on his

PC, which read 6:13 pm. Despite several hours of scanning through server logs, he was no closer to figuring out what caused the servers to nearly crash. And after running on adrenalin for hours, he just felt like collapsing.

The online game stayed up and continued operating, thank God. He had time to come up with answers for the TerraMythos upper management, but not much time.

What the heck, it wasn't like he had a life, right? Tony composed some email replies to Joachim, Karen and Carolyn, advising them that he was watching the situation so they didn't need to come back into the office after all. By Monday morning they would have plenty of data in the logs to tear into, so they should expect a long day with their respective teams.

After clicking the email send button, he stretched and took a deep breath, then retrieved his cell phone as he thought about ordering some food. The first week of the project, his new team was brainstorming late into the evening and Tony decided they should get take-out. When he said his favorite food was Thai, Joachim laughed and said, "What, no chicken wings?"

"Seriously?" Tony stated, and stared at Joachim. Growing up, Tony wrestled with what it meant to be black, but long ago decided he would damn well be his own person and never let anyone or anything define who and what he was. As far as he was concerned, the race card was going to be dealt right out of the deck.

Finally, after what seemed like an eternity, Karen broke the awkward silence by leaning forward and taking Tony's hand. "As far as I'm concerned," she said, "Anyone who loves Thai food is my kind of man."

She smiled when their eyes locked, and the connection between them flashed into recognition of mutual attraction. They didn't start dating until a year later, and only with much misgiving on Tony's part. But when they did, they agreed on their first date that it started from that moment.

That fateful memory surfaced every time he pressed the speed dial on his phone for the Thai place. They said they could deliver in about 45 minutes, and he resigned himself to a long night, while periodically checking up on Panchala. Tony reached under his desk and pulled out the sleeping bag and inflatable hiker's sleeping pad.

This wasn't the first time he had used them.

Demie never knew music could be used for torture. The short song started yet again, sounding like someone tormenting a guitar, along with a bongo accompaniment. If she could find the source, she would take an axe like the one her father kept in his garage and smash that guitar into pieces small enough to stuff down the player's throat. Then feed him the bongos for dessert.

She had just decided to season the pieces with Tabasco when she heard footsteps approaching and saw someone dash past her. Once she started listening, she heard the clomping of more steps as figures continued to run back and forth. People just kept coming and going past her, like a trail of ants, though mostly they ignored her. Except every now and then one would stop and turn toward her for a minute and then continue on their way.

The first time, a man wearing one of those toga outfits stopped to look, pointed at her with a large wooden staff, and then ran off. Whatever the heck he wanted from her, the best she could manage so far was to turn. Even then she was uncertain how she did it, and it only worked some of the freaking time. But now that she was listening, she noticed other sounds such as the distant bellow of animals. She figured out that it was the baboons that screeched, while those horned rottweilers made a peculiar lion-like roar.

After countless repetitions of that ridiculous song, a woman wearing a fur bikini stopped to look at her, and Demie heard a "Zzziizzziiiipp," as if a fly had just dive bombed her ear. When Demie didn't respond, she heard the "Zzziizzziiiipp" again, followed by a brief "Zhurp" when the woman turned and ran off. If those were words, it was no language she had ever heard.

Demie managed a turn so she could get a better look at that fur bikini as it ran off, thinking there was someone who had some real self-confidence. Excitedly, she realized that her turns were not at all like real movement, where she moved her body. This was more like how Sensei had described doing Karate. Think the movement, will it to be so, and it would happen.

She eagerly pictured a full turn and then determined it was so, just the way sensei tried to explain it to her...and she faced back toward the gate. Then again, and she saw the bikini-clad woman vanish into the forest. Focusing her mind with all her strength, Demie imagined herself moving forward a step, and for the first time she moved off the spot she had been anchored to this whole time.

Yes! A few steps forward, then back, and she started moving in time to that detestable music, which wasn't so bad after all. Pumping her fist, Demie felt her heart flip, and the sky and ground rotated around her as she did a back flip. Then another. It was just like Sensei described.

Can I do Karate, she wondered? She envisioned a kick, and it happened. Flip, kick, strike, spin and kick. Demie was a flashing ball of arms, legs and hands. Finally, she landed on her feet and stood looking at the gate again. She wasn't dizzy or even breathing hard. Maybe this dream wasn't so bad after all.

A group of three men and two women ran by, so Demie took off behind them. Whether she was in a dream or the crazy house, she might as well start looking for Kori.

Cassie found the drive from Good Shepherd to the firehouse to be excruciating. Lauren tried several times to make small talk, asking if Cassie needed anything, and repeating how dreadfully sorry she was for letting Demie run off. At least for a few hours they had been on amicable terms, so Cassie clenched her fist in order to refrain from telling Lauren to just shut the hell up. When she finally buried her head against the passenger window with a soft moan, the woman got the message.

After Lauren dropped her off, Cassie sat in her car and puffed a couple of cigarettes. It was her policy to never smoke in the car, so she at least held the deathsticks out the window and exhaled through the cracked window. More than once she tried to kick the nasty habit, to no avail, and prayed that Demie never picked it up. Well, that wasn't a problem now.

When she turned the engine on, she put the car in gear to drive to the hospital where Sherman kept vigil over her daughter. Then she shifted back to park as she reconsidered. Sherman had stores to manage so Cassie had to be there in the morning to take over, which meant she needed to be rested for her watch. Duty persuaded Cassie to go home instead, but didn't prepare her for how quiet the house was.

Back home for the first time since leaving that morning for the softball game and then spending most of the day at the hospital,

Cassie faced her front door. She was so weary and drained that she had to lean on the doorframe while she worked the lock. Then she stepped into silent darkness. Flipping on the light switch helped to push against the emptiness as she locked the door behind her. But a palpable void remained within the house when Cassie turned, and she sagged back against the door.

Her steps echoed as Cassie shuffled into the kitchen, turned on the overhead lights and then went on through the rest of the first floor, switching every light on. In the living room she turned the television on and sound echoed throughout the rooms. Setting the remote down, Cassie turned away and didn't even notice that the channel was set to Comedy Central—Demie's favorite channel.

The phone at the foot of the stairs flashed, indicating it held messages. She had no need to hear how sorry people were about Demie, and the only message she wanted wouldn't be there. Demie had always been a phone call away, those nights she spent with her dad. Even the week Demie spent at camp, she could've called home if she needed to, and Mom would have been there within an hour.

Tonight there would be no call for Mom.

Cassie pulled herself up the stairs, the impact of the day's events as heavy as a waterlogged coat. Her bedroom was at the end of the hall, but she only made it as far as Demie's room. Pushing the door open, she switched the light on and stepped inside, surveying her daughter's domain. How she longed to see a shape under the blankets, but the bed lay flat and empty.

As usual, it looked like a pack of wild monkeys had rummaged through the room looking for food. Clothes lay strewn across the entire floor, flung over a chair and even hanging from the bedposts: everywhere, except in a drawer or on a hanger. Books, dirty dishes, old makeup, discarded shopping bags and miscellaneous knick-knacks precariously balanced on a dresser, somehow defying gravity.

The sole refuge of order in the room lay at the end of the dresser, where Demie kept a framed portrait she had sketched the summer after the animal attack in the woods. Her daughter refused to talk about it, other than to say it was a close friend who had moved away.

Cassie avoided looking at it; something about that picture gave her the willies every time she saw it. Even now, as she reached over to lay it face down, she felt an eerie ghostly presence to it.

This mess, which had been a constant source of argument between them, now seemed so trivial. Just inside the door lay the school backpack which spawned their latest argument the night before, when Demie had written "Demie-God" on it in permanent marker.

Cassie leaned against the doorframe, slid down to the floor and cradled the backpack. It was so hard sometimes to understand how a sixteen-year-old young woman could straddle the worlds of adult and child at the same time. After delivering a lecture on how tough it was to make ends meet as a single mother, she had ruled that Demie was incapable of being responsible for any pet that didn't live in a contained cage. The quivering rage in Demie's voice, as she laid out in explicit detail all the ways that she hated her mother, haunted Cassie. She could almost hear the words again.

This wasn't how she wanted to remember Demie.

Wetness around her eyes swelled to overflowing. The first tear that rolled down her face wrenched a sob out of Cassie, then the dam inside her disintegrated as more tears and sobs burst forth, until she was wailing so hard she couldn't breathe.

Cassie fell asleep hugging the backpack.

Demie warily followed the group at what seemed like a safe distance, about as far as she could throw a softball. They approached the tree line: a thick collection of tall trees draping vines and moss, with a solid undergrowth of huge ferns and various broad-leafed shrubs she didn't recognize. For all she knew, there were girl-eating plants in there, not to mention animals.

Much to her surprise, before entering the jungle the group turned to surround an elephant that was grazing off the path. She wanted to warn the unsuspecting pachyderm as they encircled it. The armored people wielding weapons moved up close, while the other two took up positions behind their friends, waving their hands and arms. That was when she noticed faint blue cords of light connecting one of the leading fighters to all of the others.

It was no surprise when they suddenly swarmed on the animal, which had been minding its own business, but she was still outraged. It hadn't done anything to provoke them.

Demie moved closer to get a better view of this fight and found these guys were a lot better than the earlier botched attack. The melee appeared to be chaotic at first, but then she noticed slight pauses as both the elephant and the group members took turns attacking. The humans appeared to have an unfair advantage in the sheer number of attacks, but whenever its turn came around the beast still managed to get in three strikes at a time. Each time, when it landed some pretty solid blows Demie silently cheered for it. But where those strikes would have flattened any normal human, these people took the punishment and kept striking back in turn.

Just as before, the blows from both sides landed with flashes that left marks. And while the elephant continued to fade, the fighters in the front brightened back up whenever the other two touched them. Eventually, the beast toppled over and Demie groaned. Then she jumped with surprise when everyone in the group glowed briefly, as if they absorbed the elephant's life force.

Wait. This was so familiar. She had seen something like this before. Maybe in a movie or book she had read. It was just like...

Demie lost the answer. One of the women in the group walked up and looked right at her. She heard another "Zzziizzziiiipp," more substantial than before. It was blurred, as if played at high speed, so maybe she could slow it down. Demie raised her hand toward the woman, to show some kind of response, and focused on the sounds.

The woman addressed her again, and this time a blurred thought literally popped into Demie's mind, like "Doyouwant-tojoinourparty". Demie didn't know how to answer, and raised her hand once more.

A reply came, slower and clearer in her mind this time, "If you want to join, just accept the invitation." The words were flat and unreal, like it was some kind of mind reading.

A moment later, Demie felt a push from the fighting leader. That was uncalled for, because all Demie had done was watch, so she pushed back on the rude bully. For some reason that satisfied the woman, who turned back to where the three fighters sat.

Demie noticed that a blue cord now connected her to the leader, when the elephant's body flashed out of existence without warning. Startled, she flinched, and suddenly floated outside and above herself, looking down at a strange body that she nevertheless knew she was connected to.

Instead of an athletic, dark-haired teenage girl, she saw a tall, blonde woman, holding a large rusty knife and wearing a skimpy leather armor outfit. And what the outfit revealed shocked her the most. She had huge boobs, as big as Lauren's. How could she...

The woman sent another message, "We're ready, follow us", and Demie snapped back into her body. Everyone in the group set off running down the path, heading into the jungle.

What had happened to her? She didn't know where she was, she wasn't sure whether she was dead, dreaming or just crazy. Now she wasn't even sure who she was.

Demie fell into place behind the last person and entered the jungle.

ॐ

Chandar felt vengeance close at hand. He launched a small utility on his computer, which he just finished downloading from an online friend he gamed with frequently. The friend, whom he only knew as Nightshade, was a programmer and hacker who developed a tool which enabled a player to locate any online character, regardless of whether or not they were a friend or member of a party. The utility made Chandar nervous, because if he didn't use it carefully the Game Masters would notice and his account likely be deleted.

After logging into TerraMythos, his character, Demikiller, materialized in Kampilya. The central market place of Panchala's capital, which served as a starting point for all new characters, teemed with a constant flow of figures. Each corner of the square held a large pavilion, and Chandar headed for one that displayed a banner with a spear on it. He determined that his first task was to get the best weapon he could afford.

Numerous stalls had already sprung up around the weapon pavilion as enterprising players hawked the spoils of their initial game play. Each stall was decorated with bright red, yellow and orange flags, and Chandar noted tables displaying a variety of weapons, armor, magical items and valuable raw materials such as minerals, roots and crystals. But he didn't waste time shopping the booths. These were items that either he didn't need now or wouldn't be able to afford.

A series of tan brick arches lined each side of the weapon pavilion, with steps leading up into the interior. Another identical set of arches ran along the second story, which supported a smaller third story topped by a small domed roof. The bright red banner draped from the rails of the third level was the only decoration on the imposing structure.

Stepping inside, Chandar engaged the merchant avatar and reviewed the selection of weapons available for his first level character. They were better than he could have imagined. He spent most of his starting gold on a sword that looked particularly nasty, long and thin, with a slight s-shape that curved back toward itself at the end. Demikiller was a warrior that could wield dual weapons, so Chandar also picked out a vajramushti; a type of brass knuckles sporting a pair of wicked looking blades on the knuckles and long thin blades which extended from the top and bottom. Any Klingon would've proudly used it.

Trotting across the market to the armor pavilion, Chandar purchased the best leather armor he could afford with what was left over. The leather was little better than standard clothing, but he wouldn't need much protection against his intended foe and he just wanted to get going after his target.

From the central market, Chandar ran his character as fast as it would go down one of the main streets that led to the city walls and through the gate onto the plains outside. Pulling up an area map, he did a character 'search' for DemiGirl to see if she was online. Sweet!

A flashing dot indicated she was outside of town, heading down a jungle trail toward the Ganges River. He set off on a tangent, at an angle to her current course. He should intercept her at the river.

And Lord Shiva help her when he got there.

Demie's group ran along the jungle path, weaving back and forth through the dense vegetation. She wished she knew who to thank because when they left the plains, the music changed to some sort of flute and drum tune. Several times they encountered groups or individuals heading the other way, all of whom passed without comment or greeting. People here weren't as polite as hikers on the trails back home, wherever that was. Though several times, as someone passed, a tingling chill swept over her like a light breeze and she jumped sideways.

Her teammates hadn't communicated their purpose or destination, and as they jogged through the trees they didn't talk much. Either they weren't much of a team, or she was left out. By the time they made the third or fourth turn, Demie determined that somehow she just had to learn how to talk. Right then she would give anything to know where the heck they were going, because wherever it was, she almost certainly wasn't getting any closer to finding Kori.

The trail led to the bank of a broad, slow moving brown river and then turned to run downstream. Demie paused for a moment where the trail met the water. Several large white birds swooped along the river, diving occasionally to snag a fish, and she wanted to get a good look at the graceful creatures. So, the rest of her group was about ten paces ahead of her when a blur of brown shapes burst out of the trees onto the front of the party, almost literally scaring Demie out of her body again.

A dozen of the ugliest monkeys ever known were shrieking, biting and flailing at the three fighters. The hairy creatures resembled what someone would get if they crossed a chimp with a pit bull, and then shoved several energy drinks down its throat. Demie prayed they wouldn't see her.

The other two people ahead of her, the ones wearing togas, somehow whipped staves out of their pack backs and waded into the melee, but Demie hesitated, uncertain how to even fight. When the woman who invited her said to follow, she didn't say what Demie was supposed to do. Common sense told her to run, but it seemed wrong to be part of a team and not try to help somehow. The last time she ran away, she had left her sister behind.

A rusty knife might not help much, but she would at least try her best. Demie started forward, when one of the monkeys turned its head to look at her with glowing crimson eyes and bared its fangs. Saliva dripped from three-inch pearl-white incisors, and the thing's screech sounded like fangs chewing on a chalkboard.

This was not what she signed up for. In fact, she was pretty sure she never asked to be signed up at all. Stopping in her tracks, Demie felt an urge to scream, forgetting she couldn't. Then she turned and fled back up the trail away from the river, not checking whether the monkey from hell followed. All she could think about was running, as quickly as she could will herself to move, and wishing she could fly. Demie rounded a bend and saw another person dashing down the trail toward her.

Like most of the other trekkers, this one carried a sword, as well as a wicked looking knife in his other hand, and he had them both drawn. She felt a wave of relief and hoped this guy would take on the demon monkey.

"So, you think you are smart?" The message popped into her mind from the man running toward her, like the slap of a cold, wet towel.

This greeting sounded neither very friendly nor helpful. Unable to respond, Demie did the only thing she could. She turned into the jungle and ran. The dense undergrowth was passable, but without a trail she had to weave between shrubs and ferns. She tried to maintain the speed she had on the path, desperately looking for any kind of break in the foliage. No need to look back. Crashing footsteps chased her through the trees, and she received another message, "Don't bother running. You can't run anywhere I can't find you."

When she darted off the trail, Demie had a good fifty-foot lead on her pursuer. But she kept running into the damned bushes, and she wanted to cry every time she bounced off them like a pinball cushion. It only took a moment to regain her momentum, but each time the footsteps got louder. A sword began slashing close behind her as she came out of the jungle onto another trail and turned to the right, hoping it wouldn't lead to a dead end.

But before she could flee up the trail, the sword cut across her body. It was like a fiery whip lashing across her back, laying her flesh open to the bone. Demie stumbled in shock, and tried again to run, when another slash cut across her back.

She collapsed onto the trail, face up. "Please, no, no," Demie wanted to plead. But the words wouldn't come out.

Demie's vision spun, and she couldn't move as a cold, floating sensation replaced her sense of up and down. Her pursuer loomed over her, brandishing that evil knife.

Another message came through, "Goodbye DemiGirl!"

No, no, no, I beg you, Demie thought. Please, please please don't do this.

He plunged the blade down into her, and Demie faded into blackness.

CHAPTER FOUR

Like a slap, a loud ringing jerked Cassie awake. Her heart tried to punch through her chest as her mind flailed...where was she? By the second ring, she realized she was lying on the floor of Demie's bedroom, still holding the backpack. She groaned as the events of the previous day flooded back into her memory.

The sharp staccato tone persisted, as Cassie staggered to her feet and stumbled down the cold dark hall to her own bedroom. She snatched the phone handset from its cradle.

"Yes? Hello?"

"Cassie? It's Sherman." His voice was tight and demanding.

A chill came over her. "Yes, I'm here. Is Demie...?" She dreaded the answer.

Sherman paused. "We're not sure. She suddenly jerked and flatlined without any warning. Then, just as the nurse got to us, she came back on her own. That was about ten minutes ago."

"Oh my God, Sherman!" Cassie's legs melted and she dropped to her knees, next to her bed. "How is she now? She's not...getting worse, is she?"

"She's stable now, pretty much the same as when you left. They're not sure what happened, but we're keeping a close eye on her."

Cassie released her breath, collapsing against the bed. "Thank God. What time is it, anyway?" Her hand shook with relief.

"A little after one, maybe 1:10 or so."

"Okay," Cassie caught a deep breath. "I'll be there in half an hour."

Sherman sighed, "That's not necessary, really."

"What? Are you kidding? She's my daughter, how could I not be there, in case...?"

"Cassie, she's stable. You don't need to come. I just thought you should know. Get your rest so you'll be ready to take over in the morning."

Cassie stared at the floor, sighed and then reluctantly agreed. "You're right. Well, thanks for calling. Just keep me posted if anything changes. Anything." She gently set the handset down and lay back on the bed, staring at the ceiling. Distant sounds of laughter echoed from the TV downstairs.

It was going to be a long night.

White-hot pain pulsed through Demie's mind as she floated, dreamlike. This feeling, like she had fainted or stood up too quickly, was so familiar. She had been here before, but when or why? And where was this 'here'?

The pain faded, replaced by drifting images. Lying in a field. A fragment of music. Running along a street. Something happened to her, but what? She started dissolving into static, fading into the void. It would be so peaceful to just let go, drift away.

No! A cold knife of fear sliced through the fog in her mind. She must hold on, like she had before. Uncertain, Demie imagined herself breathing and concentrated on counting. Her body tingled with fiery pain as it pulled together, slowly at first and then with a rush. Like blood flooding into a leg that fell asleep, only this tingling was throughout her whole body.

Then, like a veil drawn back from her eyes, she stood in the middle of a village street in some third world country. No cars or buses, and only a few horses. Whatever else these people lacked, they had plenty of color, because it looked like someone had splashed everything with red, yellow, blue and green paint. Where the hell was she, and why here?

Pedestrians walked around her, undisturbed by the fact that she appeared out of nowhere. Everyone wore various kinds of colorful clothing and armor and apparently gaudy was in fashion. Almost everyone also carried hand weapons like swords or clubs, so either this was a Hollywood film set or there was a real crime problem here.

Familiar music played from some invisible source all around her, which made Demie think of that time in Disneyland. Bits and pieces of a previous dream were coming back. She had been looking for something, or someone important, but she couldn't recall what it was and the not knowing scared her.

A pair of women walked by and she overheard a zip of conversation, so she followed behind the woman who spoke. Hopefully they would pay no attention to her, because there was no telling what they might do if they noticed her. Even from ten feet away, she could clearly hear them.

"Just follow me," one woman said. "You'll get better armor in this shop than any of the others."

"Remember, I can't use any metal," the other replied.

Good armor sounded like a good idea so she followed a short distance behind. And of course, the music followed.

The street surface looked like dirt, but had a pavement-like firmness, which didn't raise dust. Demie followed her quarry down a long boulevard, around a corner and then they made a sharp right turn. A door swung open as the women approached and then slammed shut behind them.

A sign on the wall above the door read 'Bhishma's Emporium,' with funny designs of swirls, circles and leaves carved all over. Whatever part of the world she was dreaming of, at least the signs were in English. Come to think of it, that was odd, because everything else about this place was foreign.

She walked up to the entrance and waited, but it didn't open for her. There was no handle, knob or other feature to grasp, so maybe the door was motion activated. Demie stepped back and waved her arms. Nothing. She jumped up and down, side to side, and even ran full speed into the barrier, but it refused to budge. Only then did she stop to think how stupid she must look. Fortunately, nobody was watching.

As she started to walk off, the door swung open without warning and the women darted out. Before Demie could jump through, it closed again and Demie smacked into the closed door.

There must be some trick, maybe a secret password like 'open sesame' but that stupid music was getting on her nerves and she wanted to smash that demonic guitar. Without any speakers to vent her frustration on, she kicked the door, wishing the damn thing would just open.

And with a creak of oil-hungry hinges, it swung out. The interior was dark, but she stepped through and then like an elevator door opening, she stood in a large square room lined with armor and weapons. She stared straight ahead, frozen with surprise.

A man stood behind a counter, staring back at her with his arms crossed.

Chandar hated to admit that it was time to wrap up for the night. But he had a quiz Monday morning in Business Law and a class presentation to give in Psychology. The Bull Water Buffalo went down, providing just enough experience points to advance another level. Soon he could start taking on some of the tougher foes in this area's wilderness, such as a Hill Naga.

The best exit from the game was a safe area like a town or well, because you never knew if a mob, like a Hill Naga might be hanging around if you came back online in the wilderness. Running his character up to a nearby well, Chandar started to sign off, and then stopped. He should check once more whether DemiGirl had re-joined the game. Just maybe he'd get lucky.

After launching the utility, he scanned the map. Yes, there she was! The small green dot flashed in the city of Kampilya. He just needed fifteen minutes of real-time to trudge back there, and then check again in town to pinpoint her location. The weariness he felt a minute before vanished like a dead mob. Business Law was a stupid-easy course; he could pass the quizzes half asleep.

He pointed Demikiller in the right direction and started trotting.

Demie frantically thought. The man behind the counter just stood, silent and waiting. He was built like a WWF wrestler, but wore some kind of goofy genie costume with a tiny cap that had a tassel, so she understood why he wasn't talkative. As she waited for him to make the first move, Demie noticed that the stupid music was gone, and her dream was silent for the first time.

Looking around, Demie never realized there were so many types of armor and shields. One wall held huge red and yellow shields decorated with feathers, surrounded by smaller shields of various shapes and colors. Most were round with knobs on the surface, and the fancier ones simply had more knobs and designs.

Another side was lined with armor, and Demie completely forgot about the wrestler dude as she counted at least five different kinds of leather protection alone. But most of the armor was chainmail and these also were adorned with plumes, feathers and designs. This was actually pretty cool. The shop reminded her of that museum Mom took her to in the big city.

While she looked around, the dude behind the counter just stood there. Which was kinda creepy, because he didn't move or speak, or even blink. When Demie side-stepped to the right, then to the left, the man shifted so that he kept facing her. After moving around the room and watching him track her, she went right up to him.

He still stood, staring at her, unblinking.

Demie waved, jumped up and down, and his head followed her up and down. Not being able to speak made her want to pound her head on the counter. Giving up, she headed to the door when she recalled how she got in there to begin with. By kicking the door and wishing it open at the same time.

Not that she wanted to kick this wrestler dude. That just didn't seem like a good idea. Instead, she walked up, reached across the counter and pushed on him. A cold, smooth but firm surface gave way and then pushed back, like a switch-button.

The moment she released the button, he responded, "Welcome to Bhishma's Armor Emporium. Would you like to BUY some of my excellent wares, SELL me your surplus equipment, or EXIT this shop?" Demie heard the words in her mind, just like on the street, but she also heard his deep voice with her ears as well.

His sudden response startled Demie, and when she tried to leap back she was held in place. Like a mouse she once found in a sticky trap, she frantically jerked back and forth, pulled and pushed, kicked and pounded against Bhishma. Until, like the mouse, she finally surrendered.

And the whole time, Bhishma just stood, waiting.

He could clearly keep her until he got an answer, but Demie just couldn't make a sound. For years she had played the mute, and now when she needed to talk she really was mute. She tried wriggling free some more, but just like when this dream-thing started, she couldn't move at all. Then it came to her. Maybe the trick to talking was the same as moving and opening doors: think it, will it to be so, and it would be.

Her first efforts only gave Demie a headache, but then a gurgling sound emerged, like a baby's first words. Even that little bit thrilled her, but it was good no one else was around to witness it. She focused on getting a single word out, and then all the words came out like a forced burp, "Let me go."

Maintaining his hold, the man replied, "To be sure, I regret that I do not have that item in stock. Would you like to BUY some of my excellent wares, SELL me your surplus equipment, or EXIT this shop?"

This time, Demie pushed back, along with the words, "What do you want?"

With barely a pause, he replied, "What I wish is naught else but to be of service to my customers. Would you like to BUY some of my excellent wares, SELL me your surplus equipment, or EXIT this shop?"

Shouting in frustration, Demie responded, "Buy!"

Whoa! A holographic sort of image flashed into existence in front of her, like someone changed a TV channel. She scrolled through the armor display, like some kind of vending machine showing many choices. Most of the options were dim, but several were bright, and after reviewing them all Demie touched one that had green accent trim and some intricate designs she liked.

The moment she touched it, the vending display vanished and was replaced with another, showing her selection and the armor she currently wore. The new set was way more stylish than the old one, so she touched it and she was instantly wearing it. Too bad getting dressed for school wasn't that easy!

Again, Bhishma asked what she wanted, and Demie managed to figure out how to sell her old armor. Trying one last time for a real response, Demie pushed on Bhishma as she asked, "Is that all you can say? Don't you ever want to do something else?"

He briefly glowed as he froze for a moment, started to reply and then stopped. The guy was too tongue-tied to respond. Demie sighed, said "Exit" and he instantly released her.

Pleased as a cat with a bird, she headed outside and back onto the town street. Now that she had some nice armor, maybe she could find a weapon shop and get something better than a nasty looking rusty knife. She set off down the street, ready to do more shopping. This was something she could do all day.

So Demie didn't see Bhishma do something that should not have been possible. He followed her out of the shop.

When Demikiller reached town, Chandar did a 'Lookup' on the area map, then swore. DemiGirl's location came back as unavailable, even though she was in town. So she must be in a game area, probably inside a shop. Most vendors were on the main roads leading between the gates and the market, so Chandar moved Demikiller to the main plaza and continued checking the map. Sooner or later, she would have to come out.

But after munching through a couple small bags of chips, he got bored and decided to call it a night. Then, just before signing off, Chandar saw DemiGirl's icon appear a couple streets over. While he had Demikiller quaff a speed potion, he watched to see which direction his target went. She was moving into a cul-de-sac; he had her now!

Demikiller raced across the market place and headed down the street.

The office was still dark when Tony's aching back woke him up, and his cell phone read 2:08 in the morning. Groggy and disoriented at first, he sat up on the sleeping pad and stretched, trying to work out some kinks and knots. He had to get a thicker pad.

Tony felt like he owned the place as he walked down a silent hallway to the kitchen. TerraMythos kept the refrigerators well stocked with soda, and the cold liquid going down his throat snapped his senses open. Time enough to make coffee in the morning. Sodas were made to keep you functioning in the middle of the night.

Back at his desk, Tony glanced at a book by Valentino Braitenberg, Vehicles, that sat on one of his shelves. He sighed as a favorite quote came to mind, about how threshold control introduces 'interesting dynamics' into otherwise rigid mechanisms. Interesting dynamics, indeed.

If TerraMythos hadn't plucked Tony out of graduate school, the evolutionary processes now developing inside Panchala probably would've formed the core of his doctoral dissertation in Synthetic Psychology. He just might yet end up back there. Tony casually opened the program monitoring Panchala, then almost knocked his drink over in surprise.

One of the subsystems, which should be relatively idle, was showing a consistently elevated amount of processing. It might fluctuate and briefly spike during peak periods, but a steady high level was striking. Something was going on that didn't belong there--especially in the middle of the night.

Tony smiled as he connected into the first application server. Clearly there was some sort of runaway process in the AI. For the first time, he had a clue where to look and started opening and scanning through logs. He could only infer what was happening inside the running system, but if he could identify the rogue process, then he could isolate it and effectively kill it.

The moment Demie stepped onto the street, the music from hell was back. Like a bad rumor, it followed her everywhere as she wandered down the road. Demie stopped at an intersection, and now that she could actually speak, shook her raised fist at the sky.

"Stop the music!" she bellowed, and it stopped.

After starting and stopping the tune several times, just because she could, Demie left it off and continued down the street.

At the next intersection, while trying to decide which way to turn, Demie jumped when she felt a surprising tingle, almost like a light breeze. It came from her right and then faded almost immediately. But not before she sensed that it was connected to that thing she needed to find, yet couldn't remember what it was.

She advanced down the road from which the tingle came, examining each door. Most were plain and unmarked, without names or numbers, and she never saw anyone go in or out of them. But every so often she came across random entrances with signs of one sort or another, such as 'The Roaring Tiger Tavern' with a foaming mug, or 'The Hall Of Dharma' with a white flower.

But wherever that tingle came from, she didn't feel it again and nearly reached the end of the dead-end street when she came across a promising sign, 'East Kampilya Weapons.' As Demie reached to push on the door, she noticed someone coming toward her, down the street.

It was that Bhishma guy, the one she bought the armor from. Why was he coming straight for her, did she still owe him money?

Because if he wanted to, he could snap her in half.

And running up behind Bhishma, like he was going to attack the shopkeeper, was an oddly familiar warrior waving a snake-like sword and a nasty looking knife.

Something was very wrong. Demie felt a severe headache, a tightness in her stomach, and she turned to run down the street.

But it was a dead end. There was nowhere to go.

Chandar maneuvered Demikiller around another corner, and there she was. The false DemiGirl just stood there, waiting to get killed again. It was almost too easy. Almost.

He raced down the street, and would've been on the dweeb except that some non-playable character moved into his way. Chandar screamed in frustration when Demikiller halted as if he had run into a brick wall. All Chandar saw was red vest, and he tried sidestepping but it was like he was stuck to flypaper. Finally he managed to back up so he could turn and maneuver.

It only took a few seconds to get around the NPC, but by then he faced an empty street. Chandar buried his face in his hands and sighed.

Going after DemiGirl was optional. His parents made it clear that anything less than a 4.0 average was not, especially since they were paying the tuition. And the fact that his father was on the college faculty made it impossible to get away with anything.

Chandar signed off.

Demie's memories were all fuzzy. Who the heck was that warrior who charged the Bhishma stalker dude and turned him around? Whoever her unknown friend was, she would thank him some time, but not right now. She glanced around for an escape route.

Demie was trapped, and she had to use the time her friend bought for her to get out of there. The street ended after a few more doors. Then Demie remembered why she came down this way, to find the weapon shop. At least it was a place to go.

She pushed on the door, and thank God it opened. Relieved, she jumped through.

The room was similar to Bhishma's armor shop, except the walls were lined with more kinds of weapons than Demie ever imagined possible. One wall alone held more swords, of every imaginable shape and size, than the Gap had jeans.

As in the armor shop, a man stood behind the counter looking at her, except this guy was kind of skinny and leathery, like a lizard. He reminded her of the town drunk at home, who hung out on Main Street. That guy was pretty harmless, so Demie walked up to the dude and 'pushed' on him.

Lizardman responded without hesitation, "Welcome to East Kampilya Weapons. Do you want to BUY, SELL, or EXIT?" Just like with Bhishma, she was held in place while he waited for a response.

Eager to practice her conversation skills, Demie responded, "If I wanted to exit, why would I come in?"

"You may wish to consult an oracle for a question like that, as I am a mere weapons dealer. Do you want to BUY, SELL, or EXIT?"

"Okay, what do you have to show me?" She wasn't getting anywhere with this guy.

"I regret to say that I am not a performer. Do you want to BUY, SELL, or EXIT?"

"Buy." He obviously wasn't too bright either.

Lizardman presented his display, but only highlighted a few swords for her to choose from. Demie selected a long, thin sword that reminded her of something Sensei demonstrated one time. It had to be better than a rusty dagger, which the shopkeeper refused to buy back, so Demie just dropped it on the floor of the shop. The shopkeeper either didn't notice or care about the litter.

She had no idea what was happening on the street, and was afraid to find out. But there were no windows to peek through, so after a while Demie decided to venture outside.

Her warrior-friend was gone, but that Bhishma dude was still there, and he was starting to creep her out. Maybe he was some kind of pervert, like that boy from last semester. Andy lived two blocks over, but started hanging out in front of Demie's house every day, even after it got dark, and stared at Demie whenever she came outside. Finally Deputy Willis talked to Andy's mom and he stayed away from then on. But Demie didn't know any deputies in this town.

She just started to turn to re-enter the shop, when an eerie shimmering curtain descended upon the street. Demie cried out in fear and tried to run, but everything on the street froze, including several other people. It was as if God hit the pause button.

A high-pitched whine began building, and at the edge of her vision Demie saw a swirling vortex open in the sky above. Every fiber within her wanted to run, hide and be anywhere but here.

Demie managed a whimper, but couldn't even turn her head.

Tony shouted, "Yes!"

After half an hour of opening logs and switching servers, buried among a thousand other threads he found one that led to the process he was hunting for.

It was unmistakable. Since it was embedded within the dynamic AI, he couldn't just terminate it without causing unpredictable results, which could cascade and likely crash Panchala. But by using a debugging tool they developed to peek into the active data structures, he had temporarily isolated it from the rest of the game. It wasn't going anywhere now.

Tony caught a snapshot of a similar data structure in another part of the game that should fit. They weren't exactly sure why or how it worked, but they had done this a number of times during testing, and the adaptive algorithms somehow assimilated the graft.

With a single click, he copied the new process in the place of the isolated one, and he released the data structure. The original one was gone. Erased forever.

CHAPTER FIVE

Nothing moved around Demie. Three pedestrians at the far end of the block stood frozen in mid-stride, like a movie scene where time just stops. Except she was in the movie.

A dreadful feeling that she was about to die grew within Demie, as the faint cloud-like structure rotated above her. Slowly at first, it gained speed and shimmering colors emerged, like an aurora borealis draining into the sky. The colors shifted from red up through the rainbow to violet, while the whine continued building in pitch, until it seemed sharp enough to slice through the walls themselves.

From the moment the force field dropped, Demie's eyes remained locked on the Bhishma dude. Back in his shop, he managed to speak to her without breaking his goofy smile, but now he just stood there, creases bunched between narrowed, down-turned eyes and an 'Oh' frozen in place on his drooping mouth. Demie felt a moment of pity for him.

Then a snap pulsed through her mind, and she would have screamed if she could've. With a sharp cracking sound, the shimmering curtain enveloping the street vanished. The event was instantaneous, like when Mr. Douglas exploded a hydrogen balloon in science class. Everything was the way it had been, except for one thing.

Bhishma was gone.

Demie completed the turn, which by now she forgot she had

started and found she could move freely again. Relieved to be released, she took a step back toward the entrance to the weapon shop but she didn't want to get trapped. Glancing around furtively like a trapped rabbit, she examined her surroundings. Whatever that thing was which attacked Bhishma, it was something she needed to avoid.

The road was empty, aside from the other three people on the street when that cosmic vacuum cleaner sucked Bhishma into oblivion. Incredulous, Demie stared when the people resumed walking as if nothing at all had just happened and turned into the weapon shop.

Demie went over to where Bhishma once stood. No scorch marks, no ashes, not a trace that someone had been there moments before. It made her want to shrink into invisibility. That whirlpool thing was familiar. She had seen it or something similar to it once before. It had taken something very important to her, but the memory remained elusive. Maybe, if she kept looking, something would jog her recollection.

A small group of people turned onto the street, went to the dead-end and kicked on the wall. A large panel swung open like a garage door, revealing a set of stairs leading down, and then it swung closed behind the group as they descended.

But before it closed, Demie glimpsed a faint glowing, yellow orb hovering above the stairway, and felt that tingle again. That little light awakened something within, which tugged until the wall closed up again. She headed over to check out the hidden passage.

But every few steps, she couldn't help fearfully glancing up at the sky.

When the debugging tool replaced the rogue process, Tony saw a slight improvement in server performance, just not as much as expected. There must be other rogue processes slowing down the Panchala servers, but he was so tired that he was starting to sleep-type. The walk to the fridge helped clear away some of the mental fog, and he scanned a considerable collection of sodas and energy drinks. He wasn't desperate enough to pay the price of the headache that accompanied an energy drink, so Tony grabbed a cola to keep him going, He went back to the logs to resume searching, when an IM session opened on his computer.

A message from Frank Beck, the CEO, popped up. "Why do I keep getting alerts that Panchala is not responding?"

Tony froze, caught off guard. Thank God he had disabled the webcam. "For a short while the servers froze up, but they are running now." Even as he sent that lame answer, he felt sick in his stomach. Frank had little tolerance for bullshit.

"Root cause?"

"Not sure, working on that right now."

"I'll be in later this morning. Report your findings then."

The IM session closed. Tony released a loud groan, then hurled an R2D2 droid across the room. Instead of getting called out on the carpet sometime Monday morning, at best he had only a few hours before he walked the plank.

So much for waiting until Monday morning; it was time for the rest of Tony's team to start sharing in the fun. He composed a quick email, tagged it with the code that would trigger the highest priority alerts on their mobile devices and sent it.

While he waited for their confirmations, he began working up a quick meeting agenda. Joachim headed the team of programmers in India and Russia and knew the client code better than even Tony, so he should get them reviewing it line by line. It was unlikely, but they should at least eliminate the client side as the source of these problems.

Karen, on the other hand, had forgotten more about servers than the rest of the team would ever know. She would work with the data center to start combing through all the server logs they could pull.

Carolyn's degree in Marketing Communications just might help them come up with some creative explanation they could sell to the CEO. Whatever it was, it better be good.

Tony went down the hall to start some coffee brewing. They were going to need it.

Demie slowly descended an open flight of steps, wider than her extended arms could span, looking and listening for any movement. She wasn't in the mood for any more of the surprises this world had in abundance.

The walls on both sides were perfectly vertical as if they formed the sides of buildings, but so smooth they might've been carved out of the hillside itself. The flagstone stairs made half a dozen twisting turns before the passage ended on a small landing. After glancing up, she nervously stepped out onto a single boulevard which stretched to her right and left.

This lower level of the town was not as busy, with most activity on the left side of the road, clustered around a gate about a hundred yards away. In the other direction the roadway ended at a large tower, and that small yellow light hung in the air about halfway down the street. First Demie went down the left side. She wanted to see what all those people found so interesting.

Numerous shops lined the street, displaying signs with plants, armor, weapons, rocks, food and odd-looking animals. A light but steady flow of customers went in and out of the buildings, and Demie followed most of the traffic through a large gate, with huge double iron doors at least three stories high. The gate opened onto a broad waterfront along an enormous brown river, lined with wide steps that spanned the whole length of the waterfront, leading down to the riverside. Demie just stared. She never expected to find something like this.

Off to one side, a man stood next to a small dock with some cute boats tied up. A woman walked up, handed him something and hopped into a boat. The guy didn't even untie the boat; it instantly left the dock, motored out onto the river and turned upstream. And it moved silently with almost no wake, as if pulled by a string. Even more bizarre was that when the boat reached the center of the river, another boat automagically appeared at the dock. As Demie watched, several more people rented boats. They all had very ornate and colorful armor and weapons, so they had to be the wealthy elite.

The main crowd, including a lot of shabby looking people, waited in the center of the step area. A large barge, twice as big as her school auditorium, crept into view up the slow-moving river and turned toward the riverside. Two huge figures stood at the back corners, propelling the barge with poles. As it drew near the embankment, Demie noticed they looked like minotaurs. Really? Minotaurs!?

The moment it touched shore, Demie jumped out of reflex as a wave of people literally exploded off the barge, while more than half of the waiting crowd swarmed onto the vessel. A single man stood off to one side of the craft, apparently supervising the loading and probably gathering tolls, though how he managed to collect anything from that mob was a mystery. Not that Demie was in a hurry to find out for herself. Without warning, the barge pulled out and continued upriver. It couldn't have been docked for more than a minute.

But the prize for weird went to a dude working on the other side of the barge landing, near the water. An old monk, wearing tattered yellow robes precariously clinging to his body, stood hunched over. A man covered with blood and gaping wounds staggered down the steps and bowed to the old man. Not even looking up, the geezer held out his hand to collect something, then waved the bloody man on down to the river.

Walking right into the water, the injured man dived in over his head, and then literally sprang back up. Clean, uninjured and not even wet! Without so much as a thank you, the healed man dashed along the waterfront and vanished down a trail leading into the forest.

Since Demie wasn't ready to go on a river excursion or venture into the jungle, and certainly didn't need a bath, she headed back to check out the other direction.

The yellow globe led her down the street to the square tower, which appeared about forty feet on each side. Intricate carvings of both familiar and monstrous beasts decorated the stone walls which were five stories tall, with several windows on each of the upper levels. The first level was broken only by an iron gate at one corner, and a heavy wooden door in the center. Above the entrance, on the second story, was a small balcony with a large window. The yellow orb had settled on the wooden door.

As she approached, Demie observed several people take unsuccessful turns trying to push the door open. They gave up and left, though two of them did walk over to the metal gate and went through that entrance.

She examined the tower door after they left. Swirling patterns decorated the wooden and iron entrance, and when she touched it her palms tingled from a light vibration or electric hum. As with the weapon and armor shops, the freaking door had no knocker, key or even a doorknob. But unlike the shops, pushing and repeated kicking did nothing to budge the opening.

Frustrated and lacking a magic password to open the door, Demie went over to the iron gate that the other people passed through. This gate was little more than a heavy grate on hinges, and on the other side a narrow flight of stone steps led downward into darkness. Far below, a flickering torch illuminated a small landing.

The gate likewise refused to open for her, but as she rattled the grate as hard as she could, a small group of people came down the street and passed through it. Even though she tried to sneak through with them, an invisible force field held her back, preventing her from entering. She was disappointed at first, but when they reached the landing and she heard some deep-throated roars, she figured it was probably just as well and decided to explore the rest of the city.

That peculiar small glowing ball remained on the tower door, and by the time she climbed back up the stairs to the main level of the town, the sun had moved across half the sky and was nearing sunset.

Although the upper level of town was much larger, it didn't take long to figure out the layout. A large plaza lay in the center of town, filled with more stalls than the county fair. Four large roads radiated from the square, leading to gates in the town walls; one at each point of the compass. Smaller side streets branched off these roads, with shops scattered at random. And of course this town didn't believe in using street signposts.

At each compass gate, Demie observed what lay outside the town walls.

The North gate opened onto some hilly jungle terrain, and snow-capped mountains rose in the distance. From the East gate, a road led out across a small clearing and into dense jungle. A man ran out of the jungle with a huge tiger on his heels, and as he neared the gate, Demie was about to turn and run as well. She didn't have a good history with cats, big or small, but then the tiger stopped outside the gate and casually strolled back into the jungle.

The South gate bustled with a constant flow of people running along a road, down to the river and then across a bridge into the jungle. She considered exploring the road to see where everyone was going, but a tiger emerged from the trees and ran along the river bank. Maybe another time, she decided.

When she got to the West gate, and looked out onto a broad grassy plain, a startling flood of images rushed into her mind. Awakening in the grass. Learning how to move. Watching people attack an elephant. Just frustrating fragments. They were coming back, but hard as she tried, she couldn't remember exactly what happened to her. Demie moved out, through the gate and onto the plains. Maybe something would jog her memory.

A woman stepped away from one of the groups walking by, and walked up to Demie. The burly red-haired amazon asked, "Do you want to rejoin our party?"

ॐ

Cassie lay curled in the stuffed vinyl chair next to Demie's bed when the doctor entered. Chirps from the monitors roused her, as the physician checked the monitors. Then hunger pains and aching joints brought her fully awake. Groaning and stretching, she untangled herself from the blanket and sat up. It was Doctor Peterson, a founder of the clinic, and one of the only trauma doctors in their rural county.

A glance at her cell phone revealed it was early afternoon; she had been on watch for hours, and Sherman should return soon. Unless some important business thing came up. His business had been 'the other woman' long before Lauren came along.

Doc Peterson made some notes in the chart and looked over at her. "You're Cassandra, right, one of the EMT volunteers? I've seen you bring patients in." Cassie nodded, and he continued, "When your husband gets here, we need to talk about your daughter's situation."

"My ex-husband. It's legal now."

"Oh. Well, congratulations, I guess. Just...let me know when he gets here."

Cassie nodded, and the doctor hurried off. He probably wanted to talk about Demie's prognosis, and she wasn't sure she could face that. Other people always seemed to think she was strong, but she despised how weak she really was inside. How she held it together sometimes was a mystery to her.

After eating a cold sandwich from the vending machine, Cassie curled back up in the chair. The play of light through the leaves outside, along with the steady chirp of the heart monitor, lulled Cassie back to a dull edge of drowsiness until Sherman showed up.

He pulled a chair over to Demie's bed, as Cassie noted thankfully that he came without Lauren. What the doctor wanted to discuss just wasn't a Lauren-thing.

After letting Sherman know that Demie's condition hadn't

changed, Cassie walked over to the nurse station to fetch the doctor. A few minutes later the curtain swung open.

"Mister and...umm, Cassie and Sherman," Doctor Peterson started, as he pulled another chair over and sat facing them. "This must be a very difficult time for you both." They just stared at him, and he continued. "Demie's condition has not changed since she came in. The attending physician administered an EEG, which did not show any higher brain activity, and late this morning we ran another EEG with similar results. We also did a video consultation with one of the region's top specialists in neurological trauma and she confirmed all of our assessments."

Cassie's mind blurred as the doctor opened the chart and explained the significance of tests she didn't understand. Columns of numbers swam in her vision, and Peterson could've been speaking a foreign language for all she understood. The flat tone in his voice said everything she needed to know. The sharp tang of antiseptic pierced her thoughts, the same odor from the funeral home where her mother was buried.

"So, did you get all that, Ms. Morris?" Doctor Peterson looked at her over his eyeglasses.

"I'm sorry. Just tell me what it all means." Really, she didn't want to know what it meant. She just wanted to flee the room.

"The bottom line is that, considering the lack of brainwave activity, there would be no reason to expect any change. One might have more options in a major city, but there is no reason to expect any different outcome based on the indicators. Now, if one were to turn off the breathing machine..." His voice trailed off.

Thankfully, Sherman asked The Question. "Are you suggesting what I think you are?"

The doctor looked uneasy. "Good Shepherd is not equipped for long term care. The support equipment is meant for emergency and short-term care. The nearest hospital equipped for the kind of long-term, intensive care she would require is 230 miles away, but even that would just maintain her condition. It wouldn't help her get any better. So you could transfer her there, that's your decision to make, but this is a pretty clear case. Now, doctors are required to inquire about organ donation and explain the consent forms one has to fill out. But this is a lot to take in, so for now let's leave them here, for you to look at and think about."

The doctor set down several sheets of paper on the table next to

Demie's bed, and stood up. "I'm really sorry," he said as he left the room.

The ventilator thumped as Cassie and Sherman stared at the forms.

Chandar walked into his room, hurled his backpack on the bed and powered up his computer. Throughout the afternoon shift at the theatre, he couldn't stop thinking about TerraMythos and hunting down that character. So he wasn't paying attention when Sierra, who worked the concession stand with him, hinted that she would just love it if he asked her out. The theatre owner's daughter was in his Psychology class, and she personally helped him get his job. So, as he shoveled popcorn into buckets he simply responded, "Sure, I guess I owe you a favor."

What she really meant only registered moments later, when she dumped a max-size soda on him. As a result his shift got cut short so he could go home and change, but he didn't mind. All the more time to spend online.

After changing, Chandar pulled up his illicit utility and ran a lookup on DemiGirl. She was online, and fortunately not far away. The map indicated she was just outside of town, and he would be there before she knew it. Literally.

Chandar pointed his character toward the West gate, and Demikiller trotted through the streets and across the threshold of the gate. When the screen refreshed in the new area, he saw DemiGirl walking away over the plains, with a group of characters.

He frowned. This would be a lot harder if she hooked up with a party. He'd just have to trail them, and when she made a mistake, he would be there.

Demie stared at the strange woman who issued the invitation, and then it came to her. She was from that first group Demie joined, just outside the jungle.

Demie responded with "Sure," and a moment later felt something tug her toward the group. She enthusiastically tugged back, and instantly a faint blue cord connected her to one of the men, Lizat, who must be the leader because a similar blue cord connected the others to him as well. When it connected, the cord carried whispers between everyone along with their names, like they somehow heard each other's thoughts in a freaky sort of way.

As the group walked toward the jungle, Demie examined the other five people. Danja was the amazon who invited her, and not only was she encased in armor but she had a truly humungous sword with a blade as big as a snowboard. How could Danja even swing that thing? The other woman, Branelle, had no apparent weapon aside from a walking stick and just wore scruffy looking robes that a homeless shelter would've rejected. Branelle was probably tiger bait.

Of the three guys, Kelnick and Durgon were outfitted like Danja and looked ready to tackle tigers single-handed, while Lizat must've scrounged his ragged robes from the same garbage dump Branelle visited. Good thing she couldn't smell them.

As they crossed the plain and headed toward a trail leading into the jungle, Lizat directed a question at Demie, "What role do you prefer?"

Demie panicked a bit, then just thought back a question mark.

"Are you a newbie then?"

"Right." Wow, this guy was a real Sherlock!

"That's cool. Just help where you can, and you'll pick it up quick."

They reached the edge of the jungle, when Demie felt something off to the right of the trail, like a puff of air coming her way. Without thinking, she jumped back as an enormous leopard landed on the spot where she stood just a moment before.

She screamed and flailed with her sword as the leopard turned like a homing missile toward her and crouched. Already Danja, Kelnick and Durgon were swinging their weapons, while Lizat started waving his arms. Two of the fighters hit the big cat when it sprang, and though the bright flashes left burn-like marks on the beast, they didn't slow it down.

The animal's paws struck Demie with electrical shocks that left her feeling dizzy and light-headed, but still standing. Now enraged, Demie swung her sword at the beast and did a forward flip she learned in Karate. She landed behind the leopard and swiped at it again.

For a moment, the leopard froze as if confused then turned toward Danja, the last person who struck it. The cat managed one last attack on Danja, and then a bright flash of light from Lizat brought it down.

Kelnick examined the leopard body, while Branelle came over to Demie and started waving her arms around. A flash of light erupted from her palms and Demie's light-headed feeling was gone. So that's what Branelle was good for!

Durgon, Danja and Kelnick took up positions on the trail around their group, while Lizat turned toward Demie and she felt an odd tingling pass over her, like a light rain shower.

Lizat asked the group, "Did you see how fast DemiGirl moved?"

Without turning, Danja responded, "So fast I barely saw it."

Lizat replied, "There was no lag time at all, she must have a fast connection." He then directed a response to Demie. "See the gate we came out of? I want to race you there and back." Without waiting for a response, he darted toward the gate.

Surprised, Demie took off after him a moment later, and found that while there was a limit to how fast she could move, she could enhance her speed by carefully timing her strides, as if hitting the peaks of a series of waves. It was unlike any running she had ever done before, and it was totally awesome.

Demie passed Lizat before they were halfway, and when she turned at the gate to head back, Lizat was still at least twenty yards away. Lizat was only halfway back when she reached the group and turned around. The strange thing about this running was that neither she nor Lizat were breathing hard. In fact, Demie couldn't remember breathing at all...apparently something this dream lacked.

"So," Lizat said when he reached them, "I think you would be a natural puller."

"A puller? What do you want me to pull?" There was nothing around here to pull, and she hadn't seen any carts in the town. But if they wanted her to haul a little red wagon around she would help any way she could.

"You'll see. Just follow us." Then Lizat and the rest started running down the path, and Demie turned to follow. But not before she noticed someone familiar over by the West gate.

It was that nice friend who helped save her from the Bhishma dude.

Tony felt beads of sweat roll down from the short-cropped curly hair on his scalp onto the back of his neck, tickling his spine all the way down. But he didn't dare wipe them away, as he sat in a single chair planted in front of the desk belonging to the TerraMythos CEO.

Frank Beck had a reputation that he gave his people a lot of freedom, until they came to him with problems. Tony nervously glanced at the sign Frank kept on his desk, which read 'Our customers play games, I don't.' When Frank started saying 'I'm not playing here,' you knew you were in trouble.

"So, just to make sure I'm understanding you correctly," Frank slowly said, leaning back with arms crossed, "You are saying part of Panchala is out of control and you can't find the cause."

Tony wanted to sink into the chair and slip away. "We're getting both the programmers and the server technicians looking into it, but, uh, yes. That's what it comes down to."

Frank turned his chair around to look out the wall of windows facing the beach and surf. Several large waves rolled ashore before Frank let out a loud sigh, then swiveled his large executive chair back around to face Tony. "During the early development of Panchala, didn't you have some anomalies develop in the AI engine? What did you call them, cancers?"

This question caught him by surprise. "Tumors. They were AI processes that grew out of control. But the pattern we are seeing here is completely different."

"Okay, but you developed a program to find and eliminate them, right?"

Tony frowned, "Yes, the Terminator app. What about it?"

"Keep your team working on identifying the cause of these slowdowns, and have them follow every lead. Meanwhile, I want you to brush that app up. It may come in very handy." Frank turned back around to face the ocean, and Tony got up, fast.

He was getting out of Frank's office while the getting was good.

Demie followed her group as they ran along the trail through the jungle. The path went up and down some rolling hills, passed through intersections with several other trails and crossed a river before they came to another plain. Numerous animals wandered over the gently rolling, grass-covered hills which extended off into the distance.

They ran out into the open field about 30 yards to the top of the first hillock, where Lizat stopped and told everyone, "Okay, this is a good spot."

Kelnick and Danja practiced swinging their weapons aimlessly, and Branelle and Durgon started waving their arms like complete idiots. Demie just wanted to shrink down into the grass and hope nobody was watching.

Lizat pulled out a small stick, then said to Demie, "See that rhino over there?"

On the next hilltop, a huge brown rhino about the size of a small bus munched on some grass, unmindful of the party.

Demie looked at the beast. "Yeah. What about it?"

"Go get it."

"Say what? Like I'm just going to pick it up and bring it back?"

"No, go over there and hit it with your sword."

"Seriously? Are you nuts?" Lizat made about as much sense as Mom usually did.

"You hit it and then run back here. It follows you and we kill it. Simple."

Demie doubtfully stared at the rhino, hoping it would wise up and run away. The animal appeared to be oblivious to their presence, perfectly content and minding its own business. The rest of the group stood looking at her, so finally Demie walked over to the rhino, which continued munching on grass. After looking back at the group to make sure they were still there, Demie took out her sword and, wondering if she was insane, swung at the animal.

She intentionally missed, but nevertheless the animal suddenly turned, and its attention focused on her. When the beast let out a deep bellow, lowered its massive head and charged toward Demie, she stopped feeling sorry for it and raced back to the group.

It took them longer to finish off the rhino than the leopard, but this time Demie didn't even get hit.

Lizat pointed out another nearby rhino, and Demie dashed off. She turned several cartwheels as she went, and even turned on the music so she could dance a few steps to it. She didn't notice she was quietly humming the tune to herself.

Cassie couldn't look at the forms. Every time she glanced at them she got light-headed and wanted to throw up. She did nod in agreement when Sherman said there was nothing else they could do and they should just sign the forms. But her eyes never strayed from Demie.

Her daughter lay motionless in the bed, aside from the slow rise and fall of her chest as the ventilator worked. But what Cassie saw in her mind were images and scenes from the past. The high-pitched cry Demie made when she was born, the downy softness of Demie's baby hair as her head rested on Cassie's shoulder, a little piggy costume from a school play, that awful smell when Demie found a black kitty in the back yard with white stripes.

Setting aside the forms Sherman handed her, Cassie reached over to stroke Demie's cheek, but the skin felt abnormally warm and dry; almost plastic. It broke her heart, because whatever this was laying in the bed, it was just a shell of the girl she once knew.

As she picked up the pen, tears welled up in Cassie's eyes and the pen slipped from her shaking fingers. Without a word, Sherman retrieved it for her and eventually Cassie managed to sign everywhere that Sherman signed. The pen slipped again as she signed the last form and she sank back into the chair, curled up and wracked with sobs.

Sherman left with the forms and returned a few minutes later with Doctor Peterson. Her ex-husband nodded when the doctor looked at him, but Cassie jerked her eyes away when Peterson looked toward her.

Would Demie forgive her? Would she ever forgive herself?

Walking around the bed to the machines, the doctor quickly pressed buttons on several consoles, and within moments the beeps, pumps, motors and monitors shut off.

The room was completely silent, except for a high-pitched, inhuman wail from Cassie.

CHAPTER SIX

Demie had a ten yard lead on yet another rhino, when her vision suddenly fogged up and she stumbled. A fire burned in her chest as she fell to the ground, stunned and wondering how she tripped. Then the rhino was on her and she screamed. It slashed her back open with a wicked horn that was as long as she was tall, then moments later her friends were gathered around, fending off the beast.

It only inflicted two hits on her, but Demie was close to fainting and she watched the ensuing fight through a haze. When they pushed the animal back, Demie felt more than just relief. In that moment, she would've have done anything for these people.

"You gotta be more careful." Branelle stood over her, but her muffled words echoed as if through a long tunnel. The glow from Branelle's weaving hands washed over Demie, but Demie's vision remained cloudy. For the first time in this dream she felt a need for air, but it was like she was trying to breathe the empty vacuum of space.

Demie was dying, and she couldn't move or even speak. Coldness spread within as her chi faded, like it was bleeding out of her. She had to stop the flow.

The energy was draining from a spot in her belly area, through a sort of hole that had to be plugged. She willed energy to that spot and as it collected, the intense cold pain slowly eased. She continued until the flow felt balanced, and then she let herself relax.

Demie's vision focused, and sound became clear once more. A pulsing ache squeezed her head, she felt dizzy, and there was a queasy feeling in her middle that hadn't been present in this dream before. But she was relieved when she could stand up again and move around.

"What happened?" she asked Lizat.

"I'm not sure," he replied, "but I think you lost connection with your server for a minute there. Are you ready to get another rhino?"

She had a server? Demie looked around, but she didn't see any servants. Whatever. She wasn't 100%, but after what they had just done for her, she didn't want to let the team down. "Sure, I guess so."

"Okay, we'll wait up at the top of the hill."

Demie trotted to the crest of the next hill and searched for their next victim, but her group had cleared out all the nearby hillocks. The closest rhino grazed about four hills away, so Demie set off running. She didn't stumble, and her confidence grew as she ran.

So far they managed to kill off what amounted to a small herd, and the dead ones disappeared as quickly as they could slay them. Occasionally new full grown ones would just show up, but not as quickly as they were killing them off. She never saw baby rhinos, so she wasn't sure where they came from. They must automagically appear like the boats. And since Demie had to run further and further to find more victims, that explained why Lizat said Demie would be great for this job.

At the top of one hill, she nearly ran into a pair of the ugliest bison that ever ate grass. Lizat hadn't said anything about getting bison, so Demie swung around them, and crossed another valley up to her target.

The unsuspecting animal had moved along the ridge, so Demie approached from the rear. After checking the direction she needed to return and ensuring that her group was ready, she swung at her prey and landed a solid hit on its butt. The rhino snorted, turned, and Demie took off, racing back toward her party.

As the beast followed, she felt a sort of tether tugging between them. It was like the time she went water skiing on a Girl Scout trip, except this time she was the boat pulling the rhino. Cool, there was even a handle. That explained why they called it pulling.

Demie could have easily outrun the rhino, but maintained a 15-

yard lead as she dipped down into the shallow valley and came up over the first hill on the way back. The pair of bison were foraging in the same spot and she glanced at them as she passed.

As if she slapped him, the nearest bison raised its head and snorted. Shaking its massive skull, the thing bellowed, pawed the ground and then charged after her as well, almost cutting off the rhino. Moments later the second bison also looked up, bellowed and joined the small herd.

It wasn't her fault she told herself, but by the time she came up the last hill, she had four bison escorting the rhino. All the members in her party turned and fled. Picking up speed, she slowly gained on them and caught up with Lizat as they crossed the river.

"What did I do?" Demie asked. She hoped they weren't mad at her.

"Look behind you," Lizat replied without slowing down.

Demie paused on the far bank to look. Jumping into the water was the rhino followed by at least seven bison, a leopard, a couple of boars with sword-like tusks, and what had to be the most hideous moose she ever saw, even for a moose. As she watched, a shaggy black bear ambled out of the trees to join in the fun.

Feeling like an idiot, Demie followed Lizat and a few minutes later they passed through the gate into town.

Then they all turned to look at her.

Tentatively, Cassie let go of her daughter's hand, and Demie kept breathing.

Groaning, the woman unfolded aching legs which had been tightly tucked to her chest for hours and pulled herself up onto wobbly limbs so she could shuffle down the hall to the bathroom and freshen up. It had been two hours since the doctor switched off the machines, and Demie was still breathing.

The first minutes had been the worst.

After shutting off the ventilator, the room was silent for a few eternal seconds and then the doctor stared as Demie started gasping and shuddering. Cassie screamed, sprang to her feet and tried to shove Doctor Peterson aside as she pounded on the consoles.

"Turn it back on!" she shrieked. The doctor pulled her back, and she flung him across the room. Cassie blindly punched at buttons before Sherman and Peterson double-teamed her, and pulled her back into her chair.

"It's just a physical response," Sherman yelled, as he held her down.

On the bed, Demie's body hideously twitched and shuddered, and then the movements started to die down, becoming weaker and less frequent.

"No! No! She needs to breathe!" Cassie wailed, and willed her daughter to take a breath, trying to breathe for her. Breaking an arm loose, she reached out and grasped her daughter's hand. "Breathe, Demie. I know you can do it. Please!"

And as Cassie squeezed her daughter's hand, Demie took a breath. Shallow and hoarse, but a couple seconds later it was followed by another, and then more. Within minutes the girl settled into regular, shallow breathing. And over the next two hours, Cassie maintained a firm grip, as though only her willpower kept Demie alive.

When Cassie returned and sat at the foot of the bed, Sherman broke the silence.

"So now what do we do?"

"You sound disappointed." Cassie just stared at the bed, and refused to look at him.

Sherman sighed, "You know that's not it. The doctor can't explain it, so he's changed his diagnosis to a persistent vegetative state. She still can't stay here, but they can move her to a nursing facility two hours away."

"I'll take her home." Her words were not an offer, but a statement of fact.

"What? Are you crazy?"

Cassie turned to Sherman, her blue eyes turning icy and her thin mouth hardening.

"I've been thinking about this for the past hour. We'll arrange home healthcare, with a nurse coming by just like Betty Carson did with her mother. You're way too busy to take care of Demie, but I run my CPA business from home and can watch over her during evenings and weekends. You just open another store to cover the costs, and I'll take care of the rest."

The way Sherman flinched, she could tell her last comment struck deeper than intended, but Cassie was beyond caring.

"That's a lot for you to take on. Can you really handle it?"

Cassie's glare became as sharp as her tone. "I will do whatever it takes to make sure my daughter is well cared for. I can't do that when she's two hours away."

"You're not the only one who cares about her," Sherman protested.

"Don't worry," Cassie shot back. "You'll still have visitation rights."

Sherman sighed, and stood up. "Fine. I'll make some phone calls, and see how quickly we can get something arranged."

As he left, Cassie reached over and grasped Demie's hand.

"I'm sorry," Demie apologized, almost whining, "I don't know how that happened."

Lizat responded, "When you pull, you can't run too close to mobs. Otherwise you activate them as well."

"They have mobs here?" Demie asked in surprise. She hadn't seen any flash mobs so far.

"You know, mobiles. Mobile NPCs. Monsters. Like the rhinos."

"Oh, right. I'll be more careful. Can we go back now?" Demie had no idea what the heck he was talking about, but as long as it made sense to him.

"Maybe another time," Lizat answered. "The others need to go, so I'm disbanding the party. See you around."

Demie wanted to ask where they went, but Lizat vanished, and with him the blue cord which joined them all. Moments later Branelle, Durgon and Kelnick vanished, and Danja walked away toward the market. It happened so fast, she had no time to react.

When Lizat cut the connection, Demie felt how alone she really was.

After only a few hours with this small group, they had been as tightly knit as any team she played with. Closer, in some ways. Along with the emptiness, a sense of weariness came over her. The headache and nausea had never gone away, after getting mauled by that rhino. Now she felt as fatigued as when coach made them run twenty laps around the softball field. Not exactly sleepy, but she definitely needed some sort of rest.

She didn't remember seeing any hotels in town, but she hadn't been looking for one either. As she walked to the central square, she examined the various shop signs. Weapons and armor were obvious, but what symbol would represent a hotel?

Her headache reached the sword-through-the-head level, when Demie recalled a book that her English teacher made them read. Some dudes, telling stories about nuns and knights and other boring stuff, but the point was that they were staying overnight in a tavern. And Demie had seen several taverns.

A block later she entered The Roaring Tiger Tavern. The space was somewhat larger than the other shops she entered, with half a dozen tables scattered within the room. Several tables were occupied by people talking and trading, but they ignored her. Behind the bar stood what must be the innkeeper, so she walked up to him and pressed on him like she had the other shopkeepers.

Demie felt the familiar 'hold' as the innkeeper responded, "Welcome to The Roaring Tiger. Would you like a DRINK, some GOSSIP, a ROOM or EXIT?"

Gossip sounded interesting, and she was tempted to choose 'Drink' just to see what he would offer, but decided to experiment later. She really needed to get that sword out of her head.

"I think I'll take a room," she responded.

A display flashed up, similar to the armor and weapon displays. This one offered the choice of a mat in front of a fireplace, a pile of hay, a room full of bunk beds or an actual private room. Really, were they kidding? She chose the private room, and the tavern faded into blackness.

As if releasing her grip on something she had clenched onto for far too long, Demie let herself melt into darkness.

Karen de Havilland hung up her phone and turned back to her computer. No question, the server monitoring applications confirmed what she heard from the data center. Maybe she would get the rest of her weekend back after all.

Out of the corner of one eye she saw Tony walk in and drop into his chair, so she swung her chair around to face him. "Guess what? The processors just dropped activity by 65%. They're almost back to normal."

He gave her that 'are you sure' look she hated so much, and said, "Really? Why are they down, did you do anything?" Tony constantly questioned her judgment, and someday she would make him pay for that. Dearly.

"That's the strange part, we haven't done anything. Since you called us in, I've just focused on analyzing every log and event trap I can find."

"Let me guess...you haven't found anything there either."

"Nope." Karen shook her head, making sure to dangle that lock of auburn hair just the right way to drive Tony crazy. At one point she almost fell hard for him, but she caught herself just in time and now kept things mostly professional between them. Mostly. He probably didn't even realize she was teasing him, which made it all the more fun. A girl needed a little harmless play now and then, after all.

She continued, "So, how did it go with the Game Master?"

Tony let out a sigh, and deflated into his chair. "About the way you would expect. He won't meddle, but I sure as hell better keep him informed. Do whatever we have to; just keep the launch on track. And make sure the man behind the curtain stays behind the curtain. Be glad you weren't there."

"That's why you get the big bucks," Joachim tossed over his shoulder.

"Oh, one other thing, Karen. Do you still have Arnold?"

Karen wrinkled her forehead in thought. Over a year ago she had written a small program to deal with certain server threads which kept cropping up during some early beta testing. To avoid offending either of the testosterone geeks she sat between, she chose a neutral theme and named the utility after Arnold Schwarzenegger, from The Terminator.

"I'll have to look, but you know I save everything. Why, are you still taking credit for my work?"

"Someone has to. Just find it, we may need it when we find what we're hunting for."

Very funny, Karen thought bitterly. You'll need more than some background utility if I have anything to say about it. She turned back to her computer.

There was nothing funny about what Arnold would do when she turned it loose.

Every time Chandar logged into TerraMythos over the next several days, he found DemiGirl online in Kampilya but her status was always 'unavailable', in some game area.

Fortunately, Spring break was coming up, so when he wasn't working at the theater he could spend time online waiting for DemiGirl to come out in the open. Unless he was on a date with Sierra.

After she apologized for dunking him with soda, she said the only way she could really make it up would be to buy him dinner, because she had cost him both time and money. So she wanted to treat him to the four-star steak house that recently opened in the county seat. When he protested that really wasn't necessary, because it was more of a Red Robin level of inconvenience, she said Red Robin was fine with her—how about next Thursday?

Of course, there was no way he could tell his parents. Not that he wanted to.

In the meantime, he had plenty of time to wait for his prey to show. She couldn't hide forever, and when she came out, he would be ready.

Demie had no idea how long she rested in that dreamless state, but when she found herself back in the tavern, she sensed time had passed. Aside from a couple of warrior types standing near the innkeeper, the tavern was exactly as she had left it. Much to her surprise, she was free to go, so Demie simply pushed on the door and found herself back out on the street.

She checked the marketplace and all the gates, but her new friends were nowhere to be found. Since they split up at the West gate, she decided to hang out there and hope they might eventually show up. A line of people passed back and forth, and more than half of the people heading out onto the wide plains were by themselves. So why did she need someone with her?

The jungle was awfully far off, and now she remembered those monkeys-from-hell. So a hike through the jungle didn't seem like a good idea, but lots of people wandered around the fields outside the gate. And if she got in trouble she could just run back. As long as she stayed in sight of the gate, she should be fine.

Pulling out her sword and feeling confident, Demie marched through the gate and along the main path about 50 yards. There, off to the right, a large brown rabbit with a fluffy white tail and long floppy ears hopped around, nibbling on the grass.

Really, how bad could a bunny be? Demie walked up behind it

and gave it a solid whack.

When she connected, the thing turned on her with glowing red eyes, rose up on its back legs until it was almost as tall as she was and bared white fangs as long as her fingers. She missed with her next swing when it hissed at her like a cat, and then buried those fangs into her arm.

A deep, burning pain ran from her arm into her chest, then she desperately started slashing. She kept jumping as she swung, but it still managed to sink another two bites into her before it finally collapsed.

The Rabid Rabbit, she saw the name as it died, had injured her pretty bad and she was worried. Without Branelle or Lizat around to wave their arms, Demie wasn't sure what to do. Other people sat down after their battles, so she tried that. She found she didn't even have to try to focus her chi, it somehow worked on its own and a minute later she felt stronger than before.

While resting, she also realized that when the bunny succumbed, she briefly tasted something citrus-like and felt a surge of energy, as if she gulped down an energy drink. It hadn't healed her, but she did feel a tiny bit stronger. That could be addictive.

Now she knew what to expect, and worked on clearing the plains of all the rabbits she could find. By constantly jumping to one side or the other, she discovered she could dance around them and hardly get bitten. Before long all the bunnies were gone.

Bunnies were getting pretty easy anyway, so Demie figured she was ready for something a bit larger. Further toward the jungle stood a gray pygmy goat with cute little horns, chewing on some red flowers. She made sure to come up from behind so she could get in an extra hit or two, and smacked it with her best hit. But before she could get another swing in, the thing wheeled to face her. Not only was it much faster than a bunny, it struck at her with hooves as well as those horns.

Demie managed to dodge more than half of the attacks, but the thing was every bit as stubborn as any goat she had ever heard of and just refused to die. She was very weak and about to make a desperate run for the gate, when the goat gave one final lunge with its horns and collapsed. But that lunge struck Demie and she nearly went down as well.

Another goat automagically appeared nearby, and Demie prayed it wouldn't see her. She hung by the thinnest thread and sat down to recover some strength before dashing for the gate.

The town entrance appeared so inviting from where she sat. Then she noticed, running right toward her, that friend from the town who attacked the Bhishma dude. He must be coming to watch over her again and make sure no goats bothered her.

She was relieved. Now she had nothing to worry about.

Chandar sat at his computer. He had just gotten home from having lunch with his parents...and his potential 'fiancé' and her parents.

It was the first time he met her, and he had to admit Sanjali was quite attractive, with light brown skin, dark rich hair flowing past her shoulders and warm brown eyes that constantly laughed. They hardly spoke, and she also appeared embarrassed and uncomfortable with the arrangements their parents were making for them. But family and tradition were a deep part of who they were, so they tried to make the meeting as graceful as possible.

Needless to say, he didn't mention his upcoming date with Sierra. In fact, he was trying real hard not to think about that.

Chandar sat down at the computer and he just wanted to hack and slash things, something simple where he didn't have to think about what he wanted to do. So when DemiGirl decided to come out of her hidey hole, it didn't take long to find her on the plains outside town.

He guided Demikiller out the West gate and watched for a while, to make sure his target was not part of a larger party. Once he was certain she was alone, he moved closer and then ran toward her just as she finished off a goat. When she sat down, he scanned her. She was down to one hit point...all he had to do was practically sneeze on her and she would die.

It hardly seemed fair, but that didn't slow Chandar as he ran up to DemiGirl. The moron just sat there, looking at him, as he hit her with his most powerful sword.

Demie watched her friend run up, and even as he swung, she thought he was swinging at something behind her. But when his sword connected with her, Demie instantly sprang into action, grateful she had recovered enough to survive that first strike. She wouldn't survive another one.

Using a roll she learned in Karate, she twisted sideways and landed on her feet, running as soon as she felt the ground. Her so-called friend apparently didn't expect that, because when Demie glanced back, she had at least a 15-yard head start. With her speed, the gap widened steadily as she raced for the gate.

Unlike tigers, rhinos and bison, her friend did not stop at the gate, and pursued her through the streets of the upper level. By now she knew the streets well enough to avoid dead ends, but after two circuits she clearly wasn't losing her pursuer and she started worrying.

Demie turned onto the street where Bhisma vanished and ducked down the hidden stairway. Unfortunately, he knew about the passage as well, and she heard him getting closer as she negotiated the turns. She really should have practiced running down stairs.

On the lower level main street, Demie turned with a sinking feeling toward the tower. That was as good a place as any to make a final stand. She glanced back and he was no further than twenty feet away, but on the straightaway down to the tower she managed to open the gap.

As she came to the tower wall and turned to face her end, she noticed something. A large flag flapped from a pole, set above the main tower gate, and she felt a surge of hopeful energy. She would only get one shot at it, but it was worth a try.

If she missed, her enemy would finish up where the goat left off, but Demie didn't think about that. She timed her stride and jumped as high as she could. One hand completely missed, and the other hit the pole, then she felt it slipping out of her grasp. She heard a girl's voice call out to her, "Don't let go!" and shivered as she held on with both hands. She knew that voice.

Clinging to the pole, Demie looked down and saw her stalker swing, just missing her feet. Rocking her legs back and forth, Demie flipped up and onto the balcony on the second story.

"Bye," Demie shouted down with a taunting laugh and she slipped through the window into the tower. She landed in a room containing gold inlaid furniture and walls lined with colorful draperies depicting scenes of maidens bathing and herding cows. Standing in the middle of the room, looking at her, was one of the most beautiful women she had ever seen.

The woman, with jet-black hair and wearing a deep red robe

gilded with gold, walked toward Demie, put her palms together and made a slight bow.

"Namaste," she said with a gentle, flowing voice, "I am Draupadi, Princess of Panchala."

CHAPTER SEVEN

Chandar gleefully watched DemiGirl leap for the flagpole and knew he had her. Then she grabbed onto something that shouldn't be there and dangled just out of reach. A moment later, she was gone.

He silently stared at his monitor for a long time, stunned. Whoever played DemiGirl was far more advanced than he realized. What he witnessed required the kind of cheat that was beyond anything he had; it was beyond anything he had even heard of. Time to bring in some big guns.

TerraMythos online characters in one game world could only legally move to a new world through reincarnation, which meant they could take experience, levels and abilities with them. But the reborn character left behind all material possessions such as wealth, armor, etc. Unless you used a hard-to-find cheat that Chandar heard about from a friend a few months ago.

Because the cheat source code was jealously protected, it was nearly impossible to find. And using it brought the risk of getting caught by one of the random sysops who operated stealth characters, looking for players who cheated. Of course, TerraMythos knew some degree of cheating was inevitable, but if a sysop thought you were unbalancing the game too much, he could permanently erase your character. He had seen it happen once.

Chandar began composing an email to his friend. He needed that transport code so he could bring over one of his strongest characters from Babylonia. And while he was at it, he would ask whether his friend had ever seen the kind of hack DemiGirl pulled off.

If anyone knew about the cheat he had just seen, it would be Nightshade.

Demie examined the princess, who stopped about ten feet away and waited for a response. Draupadi didn't have a crown or tiara or whatever, but wore an elaborate golden necklace and enough gold bangles to outfit a small gang. Likewise, her garments were simple but rich in color and edged with delicate golden trim. She appeared to be in her mid-20's, maybe a bit younger than Lauren, and had long flowing black hair that reached halfway to her waist.

The woman stood waiting, kind of like those guys in the shops, except Demie didn't feel any kind of 'hold' or menu of choices that required a response. There was something different about Draupadi, so maybe she would get more of a response from the princess.

"What is Panchala?" Demie asked.

Draupadi smiled and paused for a couple seconds, as though searching for the answer, then replied, "Panchala is the land bound by the river Gomati to the east, the river Yamuna to the south and the west, and the Himalaya to the north." With a slight bow of her head, she resumed waiting.

Great, that answer was about as useful as the High School algebra Demie had to study last semester. She walked around the room and examined the contents. The far side of the room held a huge four-post bed with elaborately carved posts the size of small tree trunks and a mattress as high as her waist. A colorful comforter, consisting of numerous beautifully patterned circles, spread across a bed that could have accomodated a small family and a thin gauze canopy draped from the frame atop the posts. Two large wooden chests sat at the foot of the bed and small side tables flanked each side of the bed.

A huge square window, which Demie entered through, filled the middle of one wall and directly opposite the window was a large, closed door. Spread across the whole floor of the room lay an enormous rug which depicted some sort of battle, with two armies facing off, each side led by a heavily armed king. That raised a good question.

Demie turned back to Draupadi. "Are you the ruler here?"

The princess responded quicker this time, "No. I am Draupadi, Princess of Panchala."

Demie would have to be specific with her questions. "Okay, then who is the ruler?"

"King Drupada is the ruler of Panchala."

"Who is King Drupada?"

"King Drupada is the ruler of Panchala."

She should have expected that one. "What is your relationship with King Drupada?"

"I am the daughter of King Drupada."

Now she was getting somewhere. Maybe. "What can you tell me about King Drupada?"

"King Drupada, also called Yajnasena, is the son of Prishata. He is also the childhood friend of Drona."

"And who is Drona?"

"Drona is the teacher of the Kuru princes. And he is King Drupada's enemy."

Nice, the last thing Demie wanted to do was get in the middle of some royal soap opera. But Demie thought she saw a pattern here.

"Do all the names that end in 'a' belong to guys?"

Draupadi paused for a long time, and then finally answered, "Yes."

"Why?"

Draupadi looked at Demie and froze. After a few seconds, Demie started getting impatient and continued to examine the rest of the room while she waited for a response. The side opposite the bed contained a large wardrobe that stood almost to the ceiling, and when Demie opened the doors, she found more robes just like the one Draupadi wore.

Next to the wardrobe sat a huge dresser with eighteen drawers. Each drawer opened when Demie pushed on them but most of the drawers were empty, except two which held necklaces, and one with a strange rod made out of what looked like black iron, with a dark green gem mounted on one end. She was kind of curious about that one.

She glanced at Draupadi, who still hadn't moved and was looking the other way. When Demie reached for the rod, it vanished as soon as she grabbed it. She had no idea what happened to it, but she closed the drawer as fast as she could and just hoped the princess wouldn't notice. The only other items in the room were a small, bare table and two chairs, so Demie walked back over to Draupadi, who still hadn't moved since Demie's last question.

Worried that she had somehow broken the princess, Demie asked, "Are you okay?" and pushed on her.

The moment Demie pushed, she felt a shock run through her, not unlike when one of the animals bit or hit her. But this coursed through her entire body and drained out, not in. Demie felt a surge of fear, and for a moment she felt twisted inside out, then Draupadi shimmered and a green glow enveloped the princess's form.

Draupadi looked around, fixed her eyes on Demie and replied, "I don't know."

It was mid-morning, and Tony was late with his daily report to the CEO. They were getting harder and harder, because there were only so many ways to say you had no clue, which was basically what he had been reporting all week. All Tony could do was hand the report off to Carolyn, and let her do some of her creative writing magic.

One more detail to add. "Karen, where are you with Arnold? Have you found it yet?"

Karen turned his way and presented a wistful smile. Tony's stomach fluttered and his face tingled, which he prayed wouldn't show. Hardly a day went by that he didn't wish things had turned out differently between them, but he wasn't going let her know that.

"Not reading your email again?" She continued, "I had it archived all along, but it took awhile to update it to work in our current build. So what do you want me to do with it now?"

"Check with Joachim to see if he has any signatures for Arnold to search out. Then update it to run in the background on the current Panchala platform. How long do you think that will take?"

Karen slowly licked her lips, and Tony groaned inside. "Well, if I run the signatures as a separate module, then I don't have to wait for Joachim and can just focus on adapting Arnold to run in Panchala. That way we can probably be ready to test it in the lab by early next week."

"Great idea, do it." Tony turned back to his report, grateful to finally have something concrete to report. After updating the document, he sent it over to Carolyn's workstation, just as Karen's computer started pinging. A moment later he heard her mutter a curse.

"Here's something you can add to your report," she called over. "Part of the Kampilya module just reset, and the processes are rebuilding."

ॐ

Demie leapt away from Draupadi, and prepared for an attack. But the princess just stood there, repeating "I don't know" several times, then shimmered again and locked up for good. The last time one of the locals shimmered and froze, really really bad things happened. Demie had no need to wait for another whirlpool to show up.

There were just two exits from the room; the window she came in, and the door on the opposite wall. Curious to see what else was in the tower, Demie tried the door but it wouldn't open and she didn't have time to mess with it. The window it was, then.

Glancing out the window to ensure there were no whirlpools in the sky and that her stalker was gone, Demie climbed out and dropped down to the street when she heard a message.

"DemiGirl, are you around?" Lizat asked.

It was so good to hear a friendly voice. She knew they could talk across a plain, but didn't realize there was no limit to the distance. This was better than instant messaging, but why did they keep calling her DemiGirl?

"Yes, I'm here in the town. Where are you?"

Lizat shot back, "Which town are you in?"

"I don't know. The same town as before."

"Okay, you're in Kampilya. Can you meet us at the South gate in a few minutes?"

"Sure," and Demie headed for the stairs leading to the upper level. She arrived just in time to see two chariots race up the hill, each pulled by a pair of white horses festooned with feathers, ribbons and braided manes. The red and yellow chariots came to a stop next to the gate, and Danja and Lizat jumped out of one chariot while Branelle and Durgon stepped off the other one. Then, the driverless chariots both turned and raced back down the hill.

"Kelnick can't make it, so it's just us," Lizat sent to Demie, "But that's okay, we still have one tank."

Demie looked around, "They have tanks here? Where?"

"Durgon, of course," answered Lizat, "He can actually take more damage and attacks than Kelnick. He just hits like a girl." Durgon ignored him.

Lizat led their small group down the hill and across the bridge over the river. Just on the other side, they turned into the jungle and spent a few hours chasing down wild boars.

Demie quickly learned that not all boars were equal. A Patriarch Boar was almost more than their party could handle without Kelnick's powerful sword. But Bush Boars were a good match, and sometimes they even had a couple of piglets, or were they boarlets? As soon as their mothers fell, the little ones made cute little squeals, wiggled tiny curly tails and scampered off into the trees.

When Lizat said it was time to head back, Demie wanted to stay but after her experience with the goat, that didn't seem like such a good idea. She actually skipped as they headed up the hill back to town, and when they got to the gate, she tried to hug her companions but they just stood limp and unresponsive. Oh well.

The others winked out, which didn't freak Demie out as much as it used to, and then Lizat turned to her.

"We are thinking to go to Vatsa Forest next time. Want to go?"

"Sure. I guess." Demie had no idea where it was, but a vast forest couldn't be any worse than a jungle.

"Then you need a lot better armor than what you've got now. I'll give you some gold." Lizat pushed at her, and Demie almost jumped.

For the first time, Demie realized she had a sort of purse which contained coins as well as some other items she had never seen before, such as a small flask and a pair of boots, along with Draupadi's iron rod. So that was where it went!

Demie accepted the push, and her coins increased from 1,643 to 351,643.

Lizat sent a final message before he disappeared, "Buy the best armor you can get. You'll need it if we run into a yaksha."

Cassie found that preparing to bring Demie home was much more involved and exhausting than she expected. Just locating and bringing in a special bed took several days, and the expedited delivery costs were almost as much as the bed itself.

That was just the start. Setting up everything that Demie required meant a lot of changes in the house. Cassie had to clear out the downstairs study, so the medical delivery company could set up Demie's bed and equipment in there, which meant moving her home office into the dining room. She usually ate at the small kitchen table anyway, so the dining room furniture went into storage in the garage. She didn't expect to do any entertaining in the near future.

The hospital agreed to provide a couple days of transition care, but after that Cassie would be on her own. Which meant she had to arrange some part-time nursing and buy a closet-full of medical supplies she had never heard of. Juggling all that meant missing more AA meetings, but she didn't really need them anyway.

Just what had she gotten herself into? Cassie wondered as she stood in her living room and watched the ambulance drive off. In the next room, she heard the rattle of IV poles as the nurse set up everything Demie needed. Cassie was postponing the inevitable; the health care worker had a thick binder and pages of checklists waiting for her to review, covering everything she needed to know.

And if that wasn't enough, just as Cassie was getting ready to take a smoke she saw Lauren pull up in the driveway. With a sigh, she met Lauren at the front door.

"Hi Cassie. I promised Sherman I would check in on Demie."

"Thanks for stopping by, but this really isn't a good time. The nurse is still getting her settled in." Cassie held the door half-closed and filled the open half with her own body. Even Lauren had to get that message.

"Well, let us know how she is, and maybe we'll stop by later. At a better time." Lauren started to turn away, then added, "If there's anything I can do to help...just let me know. Okay?"

Cassie grimly nodded, then closed the door. Lauren undoubtedly meant well, but the last time Lauren offered to help, she was supposed to give Demie a ride home.

Demie had no idea what a yaksha was, but she really liked the idea of better armor. Before passing through the South gate into town, she checked the street and even the corners for her stalker. Whoever was after her always seemed to know where to find her but Demie never knew he was coming until it was almost too late. The next time she saw Lizat, she'd have to ask him about that.

The street looked clear, so Demie made her way back to Bhishma's Emporium. At least it still said Bhishma's Emporium, but she hadn't gone inside to see if he was there or if someone else had taken over the shop after Bhishma got raptured. Now that she thought about it, he hadn't actually bothered her; he was just following her around the town. In hindsight, maybe he was trying to protect her from that nut job after all, and she felt a bit guilty.

So she was pleasantly surprised to see him standing there, just like the first time. As Demie walked up to him, she remembered the sad look on his face. But whatever that spark of life was, it had been replaced with a false, plastic appearance now.

Demie pushed on him and like before, he responded, "Welcome to Bhishma's Armor Emporium. Do you want to BUY, SELL, or EXIT?"

This time she didn't have to think about it. "Buy."

The holographic vending machine popped up again, but this time every set of armor was bright and available. Scrolling through the choices, she found a set at the bottom called a Rikshasa Lord's Armor. Every surface was encrusted with rubies and engraved with swirling red and green markings, and it had gnarly spikes around the shoulders and a helmet with swept-back wings and a flowing scarlet plume. The thing looked downright wicked and it was lit, meaning she could choose it.

Demie excitedly touched it, and she was presented with the option to keep wearing her current armor, or switch to the new set. Duh; she chose the new one. After selling her old armor back, she had just under 20,000 gold left. That should get her a decent weapon.

The transaction completed, Bhishma returned to his welcoming question, and Demie asked, "Are you alright after what happened on the street?"

With just a slight pause, he responded, "I am sure you must be thinking of someone else. Do you want to BUY, SELL, or EXIT?"

Demie felt sad as she sighed, chose "Exit" and when he instantly released her, she went back out onto the street.

The moment she exited the Emporium, a stinging blow hit her from the left, and she spun around to find her stalker preparing to take another swing. Fortunately, her new armor absorbed all the damage but she didn't intend to hang around and see how long that would last. Demie darted down the street.

This time, she ran straight for the stairs to the lower level and realized she had to do something about this idiot, because it was only a matter of time until her luck ran out. Although he managed to strike her several times on the way down to the lower level, the new armor continued to protect her, and she managed to outdistance him on the last stretch.

By the time she made the leap for the tower flagpole and slipped through the window, Demie knew exactly what she needed to do, when the time was right.

Whatever her problem was when Demie left, Draupadi had now recovered. The dark-haired woman walked toward Demie just as before and said, "Namaste. I am Draupadi, Princess of Panchala."

Demie sighed, and said, "Yes, I know. And I'm Demie."

Draupadi brought her palms together in front of her face, gave Demie a half bow, and replied, "No, my good Lord. You are DemiGirl."

CHAPTER EIGHT

Demie started to correct Draupadi, then paused. What was there to correct? What had she said or done which gave Draupadi a reason to think she was some kind of lord? And why the heck did everyone keep calling her DemiGirl?

Putting her palms together, she returned Draupadi's bow, "Why do you call me lord?"

Draupadi pointed at Demie, "You are an Aryan, and wear the armor of a lord. I am Dravidian, of course."

That just raised more questions. Like, why would Draupadi accuse her of being some kind of Nazi? "What do you mean, Aryan?"

"Aryans are the nomadic invaders from the north. Your people fill our streets and have overrun our home, the land of the Dravidians. Since your people have conquered us, it is only fitting that I address you as Lord, if you please."

"I don't please. But how do you know I am an Aryan?"

Draupadi pointed at Demie and then herself, "Your people are fair of skin and hair; whereas mine are dark, as am I."

So...did that mean...all those other people she met on the streets were sharing this dream? Just thinking about it gave her a headache. "What is this land of the Dravidians?"

Draupadi gestured toward the rug on the floor, which was covered with images detailing a great conflict, "This tells of our downfall. We are the long forgotten remnants of an ancient, great civilization which once stretched from here to what you call the Mediterranean Sea, and into lands you call Africa and Europe."

Now that she examined it closer, Demie noticed that one of the kings stood backed up against the sea and the rooftops of a flooded city poked through the water behind him.

"So what happened?"

Draupadi knelt down and swept her hand over the tapestry. "Great natural disasters, which are now only myth, devastated our civilization. Almost overnight, sea levels rose and swallowed our greatest cities, and what remained crumbled before the Aryan invasions. All that now remains are stories we pass on to our children, and the myths we handed down to the civilizations which rise from our ashes."

Draupadi recited her words as though performing them, but it still sounded like her people had some real tribulations, so maybe being a princess wasn't just fun and games after all.

Anyway, Demie had her own problems to deal with, such as the creeper who kept chasing her. She was excited now that she had a plan, but she wanted to be as refreshed as possible. Although she could go back out onto the street and try reaching The Roaring Tiger, that idiot was probably still out there, waiting. Demie turned to Draupadi.

"Princess, can you open that door?"

"To be sure, I regret that I can not. I am most certainly a prisoner here."

Of course. The princess couldn't open the door, that would've been too easy. Maybe Demie could find a spot to rest here in the room. Based on what Draupadi said, Demie was the first person to enter this place, but that didn't mean she would be the last. Which meant the bed was probably a bad idea; it was too obvious and she would be too exposed. Then the wardrobe caught her attention. It was tall enough, that was for sure. Maybe she could fit in there.

Demie walked over and opened the door, and it was still full of red robes. No matter how she pulled on them, she couldn't remove them, but just as she was about to give up, Demie found she could move them aside.

There, hidden in the back of the wardrobe of course, was a door. Someone had a sense of humor. There was even a sign on the door reading Narnia.

Demie glanced back at Draupadi, who remained standing in the middle of the room, watching. The back door yielded when Demie pushed on it, and she pulled the outer wardrobe door closed. A weightless sensation swept over her when she stepped through the back, as though she crossed some sort of threshold.

Demie entered a featureless, gray room. The silent space was illuminated, but there was no obvious source of light, nor was it hot or cold. Tentatively, she touched the walls but they felt solid, smooth and devoid of temperature, like a hard plastic. There were no furnishings, but when she lay down, she was suspended above the floor as if on a virtual bed.

The room reminded her of a prison cell, but it felt safe, so Demie closed her eyes and let herself relax.

Demie sees/hears/feels static, and then she is five years old, lying in her bed at night.

She hears crying from the crib next to her, and slips out of her covers. In the faint glow of the nightlight she sees Kori standing, holding onto the bars of the crib, sobbing. Demie pushes the toy chest to the end of the crib, wrestles her small body over the side and then drops down next to Kori.

"Dee-Dee!" Kori sobs, as Demie puts her arms around her, and comforts her sister.

Lying down on the small mattress, Demie pulls Kori down next to her, and as Kori snuggles up, she pulls the baby blanket over her sister. It only covers part of Demie's shoulder and back, but Kori will help keep her warm.

Kori whispers, "My Dee-Dee," and then her sobs turn into sniffles.

Demie kisses her sister's forehead and then strokes downy golden locks, as she whispers, "Don't worry, Kori. I will always be here."

Kori's sniffles settle into easy breathing, then Demie sees/hears/feels static...

Demie holds her five-year-old sister's hand as they follow Mom down the hall to Kori's first day of Kindergarten. Kori hops up and down in excitement, and her lunchbox springs open, scattering sandwich, chips and an apple onto the cold tiled floor.

Demie and Kori scramble to reassemble the lunch, then they race to catch up with Mom. Breathing hard, they stand outside the open classroom door, and Kori looks into a room full of children, all strangers, laughing and playing.

"I want to start Kindergarten tomorrow," Kori cries out, and tries

to pull Demie back down the hall.

Before Mom can intervene, Demie puts her arms around Kori and gives her a bear hug. "You don't have to be afraid, Kori. I'll be right upstairs."

Kori resists at first, and then relaxes and finally squeezes back. Demie hears her muffled voice through the winter coat, "Thanks. I love you, Dee-Dee!"

Kori's embrace eases, and Demie sees/hears/feels static...

Kori hoists an over-stuffed backpack and staggers under the weight before Demie dashes over and steadies her seven-year-old sister. Together, they carry the pack and sleeping bag over to the Girl Scout van, while Mom checks in with the Brownie leader.

"Demie, what if a bear breaks into the cabin and wants to eat me?"

"Here's what you do." Reaching into her pocket, Demie pulls out a candy bar and stuffs it into her sister's pack. "Keep this under your pillow, and if a bear comes in, just throw this onto the bed next to you. The bear will go after that and leave you alone."

"Thanks!" Kori smiles, gives Demie a quick hug, and skips over to the van door.

"Have fun, Kori. I promise, everything will be okay!"

Kori laughs, blows a kiss and climbs in the van, as Demie sees/hears/feels static...

Then, she recalls shoving against Kori to save herself, and Kori helplessly looking at Demi as she vanished into the infinite blackness...and the guilt comes back to her, which haunted her every day, and held her silent for the next three years.

Demie's eyes and mind snapped open, and she stood. It all came back now, and she felt frightened, relieved and determined all at the same time. So...Kori was real, and she knew once more what she needed to find. In any case, whatever connection this place had with Kori, she had some business to take care of first.

Demie had no idea how much time had passed, but she felt renewed and ready to carry out her plan. The door leading out of the gray room swung open at her touch, and she passed back into Draupadi's room.

The princess had moved to the window and stood looking out. She turned at Demie's approach and asked, "Will you be leaving now, my Lord?"

"Yes, there is something I must do."

Draupadi turned back to face the window. "What...is out there?"

Somewhat annoyed, Demie replied, "You live here, this is your land. Don't you know?"

Draupadi didn't answer right away, and when she did, it was almost a whisper. "It is most strange. I know many things, yet have experienced none of them. Now I wish to."

Demie clambered through the window onto the small balcony, and turned back to Draupadi. "Sorry, but you'll have to stay here for now. What I'm doing, I must do by myself. But I promise to come back." Then Demie dropped down to the street.

Now, where was that stalker nut job when she wanted him?

Cassie stood next to Demie's bed, flipping through page after page of detailed care instructions. Every hour or two, there was some task or another she was supposed to do. Check the IV tube, give a sponge bath, change the diaper. She never thought she'd be doing that again.

The nurse spent two hours going over everything the previous afternoon, but when Cassie woke up the next morning, everything the nurse said was erased from her mind. Now she was on her own and feeling somewhat overwhelmed. She badly needed a smoke. That wasn't all she needed, but she wasn't supposed to go there.

Two days of transition care just wasn't enough, and of course the rent-a-nurse Sherman scheduled to be here first thing in the morning hadn't shown up. That was no surprise, though, with something Sherman arranged.

After checking the tube and changing the IV bag, and almost forgetting to prime the tubing, Cassie went into the kitchen to wash up and then sat down with her phone. Halfway into dialing Sherman's number, she hit cancel and set the phone down. There was no point in calling him, she already knew it would be a waste of time.

Cassie stared out the window and watched leaves blow around for a few minutes. Letting out a long sigh, she ran her hands through her hair, picked up her cell phone and dialed another number. It seemed to ring forever before it went to voicemail.

"Hi Lauren, this is Cassie. The home health care nurse didn't show up today, but the company said she'll be here tomorrow for sure. Anyway, I'm taking care of things for now, and I need your help with something this afternoon. Give me a call back. Thanks."

Cassie hung up, and watched the leaves swirl in the backyard. God, she hoped she wouldn't regret this.

Chandar had his character on the lower level of the town waiting for the barge to Krivi, the next town downriver, when he realized that DemiGirl was online. According to the map, she was stationary in the central plaza on the upper level, and he let the barge come and go without him, as he watched her position for several minutes.

She didn't move, so she was probably away from the keyboard. Nice, it would only take him a few minutes to get there. As he entered the plaza, she was still in the same spot, and he set Demikiller to rush forward. Then, DemiGirl sent a message.

"I knew you would come. Stop. If I run, you know you'll never catch up with me."

He paused, and sent back, "So run. I'll find you."

Instantly, she shot back, "You won't have to look. I'll be outside the West gate in an hour."

"Is that a challenge? You won't stand a chance!" This was better than anything Chandar could have hoped for.

"Call it whatever you want. I'll see you in an hour." Then DemiGirl darted off, out of sight.

Karen didn't remember the lab being this cold. She pulled the sweater tighter around her slim frame and brushed the bangs out of her green eyes. After spending the whole morning in here setting up several test servers, she had a Panchala test environment up and running. A couple gaming simulations validated the setup, so now she could run her test.

With the recreated online world running, Karen launched half a dozen virtual players to represent online TerraMythos customers. Then, she introduced her test rogue process, an NPC that diverged from programming parameters.

In the TerraMythos game worlds, the NPCs, or Non-Playable Characters, were designed to learn to a limited extent, and adaptively respond to player characters. That way TerraMythos players, who were the paying customers, could be more creative in their adventuring.

During early beta testing they found that, for some reason they still didn't understand, sometimes an NPC would seemingly develop a mind of its own. The threads generated for each player was supposed to have a built-in lifespan, but sometimes a process would start growing out of control, like a cancer, which led her team to call them 'tumors'.

The utility program Karen created would recognize and terminate these processes, but since it was not generated by the AI, it existed as a discrete avatar. Now she watched as the test rogue NPC wandered outside of its assigned area, interacting in ways it was not designed to. With a mouse click, she released the modified Arnold program, which they had given a wolf avatar to make the utility more transparent to the players. The wolf dashed down the street, tackled the rogue NPC and devoured it.

When the wolf finished and began to sniff around for more prey, Karen checked the server processes. She grinned and sat back; no trace of the rogue process. It was only Friday, and she had promised to have it ready early next week. There was plenty of time to modify the avatar so it would fit into the Panchala milieu.

The avatar needed a suitable mythical figure. With a wicked smile, she named it Kali.

Hopefully her stalker wouldn't get impatient.

Demie had to hunt further than she expected before she found what she was looking for, but there it was; a bull elephant, way out on the plains where she previously hunted rhinos.

While pulling in victims for Lizat's party, Demie noticed that the animals migrated from location to location, maybe in response to being hunted. So one day elephants might be outside the West gate, and then another day they might be down by the river, or in this case out on the far plains.

Demie was really looking forward to this. She raced up to the elephant, whacked it with her sword and then dashed off. The elephant trumpeted, stomped its feet and took off after her. Demie led her newly acquired pet toward several more elephants and ran in an arc that brought her behind them, heading toward the trail back to town.

A quick backward glance satisfied her, that she was leading a small thundering herd.

Elephants were a bit slower than most of the beasts she was

accustomed to working with, so she had to be careful not to get too excited and get ahead of them. By the time she crossed the river and checked again, her parade had grown to include a few more pachyderms, half a dozen rhinos, at least a couple dozen boars from the woods, several leopards, a bunch of hideous moose and a couple of shaggy black bears bringing up the rear. She smiled when she noticed some crocodiles crawling out of the river in a vain effort to join up.

A small group on the trail in front of Demie scrambled off to the side to get out of her way, and Demie laughed as she weaved back and forth over the hillside leading up to the South gate. In the process she picked up several dozen bison, ten or fifteen goats, and more rabbits than she could count.

As each animal joined in, it fell into place behind the elephants leading the charge, which was precisely why she started with them.

Having scooped up everything outside the South gate, Demie swung over toward the East gate to see what she could pick up there and was rewarded with seven or eight tigers, a small herd of some kind of wild sheep, and more boars.

Continuing her circuit around the city, she came out onto the West plains. And she was relieved to find that the creeper was there, standing just outside the gate, watching her.

Leading her parade out across the grass land, Demie shot straight toward the jungle until she was a little more than halfway, and began an arc to her left, picking up a pride of lions and yet another herd of bison in the process. No matter how many pursuers she picked up, the tether never pulled any stronger.

Demie began her turn back to the gate, and she stopped smiling and became more serious. This was the tricky part, because now the field was so full of animals she could hardly see where she was going and had to make sure she didn't double back on her train. By the time she approached the city walls, she had to dodge a pair of cheetahs she picked up somewhere.

Carefully staying about ten yards ahead of the leading elephants, Demie aimed straight for the gate. Just as she hoped, the stalker moved straight in front of her, in order to block her access to safety. Demie made no effort to change course.

"I hope you enjoy this," the creep sent, as their bodies collided.

"More than you realize," Demie shot back. Then she stuck the handle of the tether onto the chest of her adversary as she dashed past.

By the time Demie reached the gate and turned around, the massive herd had surrounded and piled onto her enemy. The only thing visible was a surging mound of animals trying to bite, stomp, stab and gore whatever was at the bottom of that pile.

It reminded her of a huge ant nest she once stirred up.

Lauren pulled into Cassandra's driveway, turned off the engine and asked herself one more time if she really wanted to do this? Not really, but she wasn't doing it for Cassie anyway. She brushed back her fine shoulder length blonde hair, touched up the color on her broad lips, then took a deep breath. Stuffing the keys into her purse, she opened the car door and walked up to the front door.

Cassie greeted her, awkwardly at first, but it wasn't too bad once they got down to business and started reviewing the home care binder. When Cassie started going over the checklist for the third time, Lauren lost her patience and firmly took the clipboard from her.

"I've got it, Cassie. This isn't rocket science, after all." That earned an icy glare from Cassie for a moment, but Lauren stopped caring about Cassie's feelings long ago.

"You're sure you got everything?" Cassie slipped on a coat and grabbed her purse and car keys. "You have my cell number, if anything comes up. This isn't too much for you to manage?"

Lauren picked up the binder, "It's all in here, I'm sure it'll be fine. When do you expect to be back?"

Cassie glanced at her cell phone. "It'll take me about two hours to get to the city. The medical supplies and the pharmacist shouldn't take more than an hour or so, and then figure another couple hours to get back. I should be here by five."

Lauren walked with Cassie to the door, and then headed into Demie's room to check on the girl. She ran down the checklist, and watched with relief through the den window as Cassie backed out of the driveway and drove off. Satisfied that the checklist was current, she took the binder with her and settled on the couch, reviewing the instructions on her own.

It was pretty straightforward; what could go wrong?

Demie watched the writhing mound of beasts, with no small

amount of satisfaction. Her plan worked better than expected; this was as good as hitting the home run Mom missed. She'd have to tell Mom about that...or had she already? What was real, and what was dream? What had she actually done, since running home in the rain...?

The creeper sent Demie a message. "Okay, I don't know how, but you got me. Next time I won't be so naïve."

"What do you mean, next time? I don't even know why you're after me." Demie shot back angrily.

"Of course you know, DemiGirl. Or whoever you are. You stole my character."

DemiGirl again! Everyone kept calling her that. Did they see something she was missing? There was something important about that lost time, between when she was running home from softball and when she woke up in this field the first time. What was she missing?

Demie shouted back at the dude. "Why do you keep calling me DemiGirl? And what do you mean I stole your character?"

She felt the answer coming, like solving an equation in math class when the numbers finally began falling into place. But she wasn't sure she wanted to see the solution. Images of boats reappearing, beasts vanishing, being held in place by Bhishma. This was unlike any dream Demie ever had...but then, when she woke up on the plains that first time, what had she woken up from?

"DemiGirl is the name of the character I created. The character you took over and are now playing. In this game."

A game?! Everything did have a game-like quality to it. Either she was dreaming about being in a game, or...

She wanted to cry. The pieces fell into place, she could no longer avoid the truth. This was not a dream. Somehow, this was her reality: where she was, what she saw, who she was.

Demie's vision and hearing faded into a blurry static, and then into darkness.

CHAPTER NINE

Lauren finished reading the section of the binder that covered daily care, stretched her back muscles and glanced at the miniature grandfather clock on the wall. According to the daily checklist schedule, the time had come to conduct another check on the drip tube. Then carefully reposition Demie's body so she wouldn't develop bedsores.

Setting the book down, she headed into the converted den where Demie lay. The lights were off but ample sunlight came through the shades, so Lauren didn't bother turning them on. After changing the drip bag and checking that the tube was clear and unobstructed, Lauren paused to gaze down at Demie.

The girl lay with her face turned away from the window toward Lauren, eyes closed and dark strands of hair falling across her face. Speckled sunlight made it through the curtain and fell sideways across her face, creating an almost angelic glow. Lauren gently brushed back the stray hair and lightly stroked the girl's cheek; something which Demie would never have allowed her to do.

From the first day she met Demie, Lauren found her to be a precocious child who plunged deep into her heart. Where others saw anger and rebellion, Lauren saw hurt and pain, but every attempt to reach out to the child was countered with loathing. The worst curse for a stepmother was to love a child as her own, only to be despised.

It didn't help to know that wouldn't change when she and

Sherman married.

Lauren brushed away the tears in her eyes and went out to the living room to get the binder. She was reviewing the pages that diagramed the proper procedures for body repositioning, when she thought she heard some moans from the study. Hurrying back, Lauren found Demie exactly as she was before: silent and unmoving.

After checking the drip line again and ensuring that Demie was still okay, Lauren walked around the bed to look upon Demie's face again, as the sunlight fell square upon it. Gently, she repositioned Demie according to the manual to alleviate pressure, 'tossing and turning' Demie's body for her. Finishing with a light kiss on Demie's forehead, Lauren went back out to the living room and stretched out on the sofa.

She knew Demie blamed her for the breakup of her parents' marriage and hated her for that, because she had said that one time in so many words. Lauren didn't respond, and afterward she cried for hours, washing out the wound Demie's words had inflicted. But even if Demie was awake right that moment, Lauren would not be the one to explain that Sherman and Cassie's marriage ended the day he came home and found Cassie in bed with her EMT partner.

Before Sherman ever met Lauren.

Demie was falling, in darkness, spinning as though lying in the center of a small merry-go-round. Then, she opened her eyes, and the world stopped spinning. She still stood, scared and confused, on the plains outside the West gate.

The feeling passed, but it was like the time she fainted on the softball field, that hot summer day when she didn't drink any water. Only you didn't come out of a faint into a dream...unless it wasn't really a dream.

"So, now you're not talking to me?" The creep's message reminded Demie what had just transpired.

"I'm sorry, I need a minute. Don't go anywhere." Not that he actually could.

Demie thought over everything that happened since she woke up in the field. Learning to move, turning music on and off, crazy monkeys and disappearing rhinos. The whole idea of actually being inside a game was truly insane, but what was it Sherlock Holmes said? When all else has been eliminated, what remains must be true, no matter what. Or something like that.

Okay, Demie told herself. So let's just say it's true, for the moment, and see where it goes. She would work with what she had. Which at the moment was the creep.

"You say I'm DemiGirl. The character you created, right?"

"Yes, though I don't know how you took control of her."

"Dude, believe me, I don't know either. However it happened, I didn't mean to. Really, it was an accident." For God's sake, she thought to herself, who would've done something like this to themselves on purpose? All right, there were a couple of geeks at school who probably would, but they didn't count.

"No problem then. Just turn the account over to me."

"It's not quite that easy. Because..." Demie hesitated; how was she going to explain this? "You won't believe this, I'm not sure I do myself. But this is more than a game to me."

"Yeah, I tell my parents that too. So what, just create another account."

"You don't understand, this is reality to me. I'm in the game. I'm not playing DemiGirl, I've become DemiGirl."

The animals were now dispersing, and Demie saw the stalker's form lying on the ground, faded. Then, with a flash of light, it stood up renewed and whole, and walked toward her.

"That is the lamest excuse ever. You either think I'm a complete retard, or you are one."

Demie stood her ground. "I don't think you're a retard, I don't even know who you are. All I know is that one minute I'm running home in the rain, and then the next thing I know, I'm here. Wherever this is."

"You are where my sword is about to be, DemiGirl!" The stalker pulled out his sword and started to charge.

She was so tired. Tired of running, tired of feeling guilty. Tired of being tired.

"Kill me if you want. But at least use my real name: Demie." She turned around so she wouldn't see him run her through, and waited. And continued to wait.

"What did you say your name is?"

Demie turned back around. Her enemy had stopped five feet away from her. "My name is Demie. Demetra Anderson."

"That's not possible. Do you live on Oak Street?"

"Yes, 513 Oak Street. How did you know?"

"Who are you, really? I know you can't be Demie, because she has been in a coma since she got hit by lightning. That's just not possible."

Cold chills swept over Demie, as she thought back to the last moments before she woke up in the field. The lightning strike a few blocks away, as she turned onto her block, and then getting hit by something. At least now she knew what hit her.

"How do you know what happened to me? Who are you, anyway?"

"My name is Chandar. I was the one who called 911 when she got hit. But I still don't believe you are Demie. That's just not possible."

"The Indian boy next door? I'm finding that pretty hard to believe, too."

"I guess we both have something to prove then, because I still think you are just playing a sick joke."

"What if I can prove to you that I am who I claim to be? Can you prove your identity to me?" Demie had an idea which would give him proof beyond any shred of doubt. But she needed to be sure this was really the boy next door.

"The first time we met, you wrote me a note that said 'catch me if you can'."

"I guess you're still trying. Okay, here's what I need you to do." Demie proceeded to give Chandar very specific instructions.

Lauren had just drifted into a catnap on the couch, when the doorbell woke her up. On the way to the front door, she glanced at the clock and confirmed that she had only dozed for twenty minutes. Good, she hadn't missed any checks.

When she opened the door, a tall, wiry dark haired young man stood there.

"Is Miss Morris here?" he asked.

"No, I'm afraid she's out for the afternoon."

"I'm Chandar, the next door neighbor. I'm a friend of Demie's. Sorry about what happened." The boy shuffled back and forth on his feet and glanced beyond Lauren, into the house. He seemed like a sweet kid.

Lauren smiled, "Oh, you must be the one who called for help. I'm Lauren, a...friend of the family." There was awkward silence for a few moments. “So, how can I help you?

“Oh, right.” The boy apparently remembered why he was there. “Just before, you know...I lent Demie a book and I need to get it back for a school assignment. I know exactly where she put it, so if I could just get it...”

Lauren hesitated, then responded, “Well, if it’s just a book I suppose there’s no harm in that.”

She stepped aside so he could enter and then followed him up the stairs and down the hall. When he knew exactly where to turn into Demie’s room, she relaxed a little. He must be familiar with the house after all.

As the boy entered Demie’s room, she stood in the doorway and watched him walk right over to a dresser, reach around a stereo system and retrieve a small book. He nodded thanks as he passed her and scurried down the stairs.

He was already down to the sidewalk by the time Lauren closed the front door, perplexed but not sure why.

Demie headed back to the tower. While Chandar worked on confirming her story, she really needed a safe place to try and wrap her mind around what all this meant, and sort through what to do about it. She also wanted to check in on Draupadi. The last time she saw the princess, there was something different about her, and Demie needed to talk to her.

When Demie slipped through the window, Draupadi wasn’t standing in her normal ‘waiting’ spot in the middle of the room. Then, she saw the royal figure in front of the dresser, peering into an empty drawer. As Demie stepped into the room, Draupadi turned and walked to meet her, and greeted her with that hands-together-bow.

“DemiGirl, I am well pleased that you returned as you promised. Were you successful in your endeavor?”

Demie paused, considering what she should say, or even whether she should say anything at all. If this whole world really was a game, then who could she trust, what effect would her words and actions have, what were the rules? Granted, Draupadi had given Demie no reason to distrust her, but she would have to be more careful about what she said, until she learned more.

Demie returned the bow, “My idea worked, and now I wait for

someone to do his part. What exactly do you do here, Draupadi?"

"It is my place to wait, though for what, I am not certain. When this door opens I must respond, but I will not know how or why until then."

Demie walked around Draupadi, and closely examined not just her clothing and body features, but her movement and stance. Unlike Danja and Lizat, Draupadi was clearly a part of the game. Even so, there was something different between her and some of the other game characters she had met, such as that Bhishma dude, and the change had taken place since the first time she met the princess. It wasn't just how she behaved or moved, but in a subtle way that Demie felt as she walked up close to Draupadi. There was a difference in texture, even though they didn't touch. It was almost a vibration, and now that she thought about it, it started when Draupadi somehow sucked that energy from her.

"If you are supposed to wait here," Demie asked, "Then why do you want to leave?"

Draupadi actually frowned, showing a facial expression other than a smile for the first time. For long seconds, the princess looked lost in thought, and walked over to the window.

Staring out the window, Draupadi finally responded, "I do not know the answer to that question. But, since you came, I now find it is not enough for me to just wait here. Your prana has awakened something inside of me."

Demie wasn't even going to ask why the princess blamed it on some carnivorous fish. "Who are you, in the real world?" Not that Demie was sure what the real world was anymore.

Draupadi gave her a blank stare, before responding, "Why, I am Draupadi, Princess of Panchala. And this is the real world."

"That is what you are, not who you are. And how do you know this is the real world, when you haven't been outside of this room?"

Draupadi's eye's widened, and a large smile spread across her face. Walking away from the window, she took Demie's hands and urgently replied, "Yes, I know. That is why you must help me escape. Now."

The sun was close to setting, and Tony was ready to call it a week. Friday never looked so good before.

He still had emails to respond to, but they were not urgent. He would remotely access his computer over the weekend and shoot off some responses. Karen had been in the lab all day, so he would drop in and check on her progress on the way out. He just needed to be out of here in the worst way and mindlessly playing that new football game.

Tony had just finished zipping up his laptop bag, when Karen and Joachim quickly walked into the cubicle space toward him, both of them frowning and tense.

"Whatever it is, I don't want to hear about it until Monday." Tony slung his laptop over his shoulder.

Joachim and Karen stopped in their tracks and looked at each other. Karen shrugged and turned, and Joachim was about to follow, when Tony said, "Okay, spit it out. What happened?"

"I just got a Module Failure error." Joachim's voice started cracking and his hands were shaking, a reaction he had never seen in his long-time co-worker. "Some major shifts occurred in the links between certain primary character modules, leading to the collapse of some key story lines."

Tony snagged his coat and pulled out his car keys, "Aren't the links supposed to change, as the online world develops?"

"Yes, they are supposed to change," Karen responded. "But not this way. This is much bigger than we expected."

Tony put his laptop bag down. "Well, just how big are we talking about?"

Joachim replied this time, "It's as if the primary character actually died, because all links to it have been lost. But we checked, and it's still in the game world."

"Who is it?" asked Tony.

"Draupadi."

Chandar walked back into his room, closed the door and sat down in front of his computer. He held a green cloth-covered spiral notebook in his hands and stared at the screen. His thoughts bounced and careened in his mind, as aimless as they were the other night, when Sierra asked him to walk her out to her car and then hugged him. Close and tight.

Now that he thought about it, going over to Demie's home was foolish and risky, but so far everything was just as the person playing DemiGirl said they would be. This was the first time he had been in his neighbor's house, and every detail was exactly as described. The layout of the house, the colors of the furnishings, the description of Demie's room and even the exact location of the book she instructed him to retrieve.

He took a deep breath, and logged back into Panchala. It was time to get in touch with this person who claimed to be Demie, and see what final proof she would provide.

This had better be good.

Demie gave up kicking on the door leading out of the room and called Draupadi over to the window. She pointed to the small balcony just outside the window.

"You've seen how I climb in and out of the window? Go ahead and climb out, and I'll help lower you down."

Draupadi stepped toward the window and tried to lift a leg over the sill, then stopped. Demie impatiently gestured for her to go; Draupadi tried a couple more times, and each time dropped her leg back to the floor.

"I can not enter the window."

"Yes, you can, just like this." Demie slipped half-way through the window and came back into the room. This was as bad as trying to get her sister Kori to do something.

"No, you do not understand. I truly cannot. A wall prevents me, which I can not see."

Demie tried coaxing Draupadi several more times and then finally, in frustration, simply picked Draupadi up and lifted her through the window. At first, some sort of force resisted, as though she were trying to push the princess through a sheet of cellophane. Demie exerted the same determination she used when first learning to move, and then it gave and she held Draupadi outside the window, above the balcony.

"Just stand here," Demie directed her and then set Draupadi down on the ledge. A moment later she stood next to the princess, and grasping the woman's wrists, lowered her down to the street. A moment later Demie joined her, as Draupadi knelt down to run her hands over the street surface and then looked around in wonderment.

Just then, Demie received a message from Chandar, "Okay, I have the book. Now what?"

Demie led Draupadi to the side of the street, thankful that this end of the town level got little traffic. Then she responded back to Chandar. "The book I asked you to get is my diary. Remember, you promised to only look at the last page!"

Normally, she wouldn't even let her mother look at the diary. But at this point, she was either in the midst of a really bad dream, in which case no one was really looking at her diary, or she had much bigger problems to deal with than someone reading her diary.

Besides, this was the only way she could think of, to prove something that only she would know.

"Yes, I know," Chandar replied. "I have the last page open."

"You'll see that the last entry is dated the night before my accident, and it talks about how my mom and I had a fight over my backpack, and because of that she wouldn't let me get a rabbit. The last thing I wrote was that I was going to run away next week to stay with my dad."

There was silence from Chandar for a couple minutes, and Demie began to wonder if she had lost connection with him. Then he replied, "So, let's just say this is all true. What do we do now?"

Demie wanted to smack her head. She didn't need to be in the Advanced Placement program to know the answer to that question. "You help me get out of here!"

"But we don't even know how you got in there. Until we figure that out, we won't know how to bring you back out."

That wasn't the answer Demie wanted to hear, but it made sense. "What do I do in the meantime?"

"I'll teach you everything I know about TerraMythos. You have a lot to learn, if you want to last very long in there. You haven't been to the really wild areas yet."

"You're probably right. Can we start now?"

"I can't," Chandar sent back. "My family has some visitors coming over soon, so I'm going to be busy for a while. But I'll be back as soon as I can."

"Okay, I'm not going anywhere."

"And Demie," Chandar sent. "I'm sorry. About hunting you down and all."

"That's okay. See you soon."

She didn't hear anything more from Chandar, so Demie figured he was offline, or whatever they called it. Besides, now she had a new problem to deal with. Demie turned to Draupadi, who was examining the outside wall of the tower.

"Are you okay, Princess?"

Draupadi turned to Demie and smiled. "Yes indeed, DemiGirl. And I thank you for my release."

"My friends call me Demie, rather than DemiGirl."

"I would be honored to do so. And you may simply call me Draupadi."

"Okay, Draupadi. Do you have any suggestions for where we should go now?"

Draupadi paused for a moment, then responded, "Why yes, we should go to Krivi. My husbands will help us, if we can find and release them."

"Your husbands?" Demie asked.

"Yes," Draupadi replied. "All five of them."

PART TWO – THE AWAKENING

CHAPTER TEN

After signing off, Chandar leaned back in his chair. He moaned as he rubbed his eyes. Was he insane, going over to Demie's house? On one hand, this was the kind of elaborate joke one of his friends would play, but not even Evan would be quite sick enough to go this far. Plus, how could Evan have gotten the diary?

A knock on the bedroom door interrupted Chandar's musings, and his father stepped in. "Sanjali and her parents will be here in half an hour. When are you getting dressed?"

"Right now, Baba. Look, I'm off my computer!" Sometimes his folks had no patience.

His father took a deep breath. "They are coming for high tea, so Sanjali will be wearing a sari." His parents were probably the only ones in the whole county that practiced high tea; his father seemed to think it imparted status. They brought the practice over with them from India, one of the by-products of many years of British dominion, and when Chandar mentioned the ritual to his friends, one of them actually asked if the tea was made from pot leaves.

"Your mother wants you to wear a blazer and tie. She thinks the dark blue one, with a red tie would be most distinguished."

"Thank you," Chandar said, biting down on the tone of his voice. "Tell her not to worry, I've got it." Respectfully but firmly closing the door, he leaned against it and sighed.

Chandar was still connected to TerraMythos and had a quick task to run. That morning he received the illicit utility from his friend, Nightshade, so Chandar could transport a character in from the online world of Babylonia. Samita was the best he could afford to risk. If it worked as promised, the items that came across would be invaluable. They would need them if this Demie girl was telling the truth. He started the utility, and either it would work or it wouldn't.

Then, Chandar placed the blazer his mother recommended on the bed along with the tie, white shirt and navy blue slacks he selected that morning. Unlike all the other times when his parents brought prospective girls around, he looked forward to this tea. He didn't know Sanjali very well yet, but she had a great smile and he enjoyed her laugh. The girl had a good sense of humor and wanted to be a journalist, she wasn't stuffy and boring like the others. So he did want to look nice because their parents brought them together, but ultimately they both had to agree to the arrangement.

For now, he would play along and see where this went. With both Demie and Sanjali.

Demie stared at Draupadi. Had she heard right? Did the princess really say she had five husbands? Like, all at the same time? What the hell, that almost seemed normal compared to vanishing rhinos and people running around wearing armor and waving swords. Speaking of which, they needed to get off the street.

"Come with me," Demie urged as she seized the princess's hand, "We need to find a better place to talk."

Wearing only a silky red robe, Draupadi looked as out-of-place on the street as a lawyer riding a farm combine. Now that Demie understood she was inside a game, she realized just how much she didn't know about this world, especially the dangers. She learned the hard way from Chandar's first attack that 'Game Over' took something out of her, in a very real sense. The next time she might not be able to pull all the pieces back together, so she needed to be careful about attracting unwanted attention.

That room behind Draupadi's wardrobe had been a good refuge for Demie, but she didn't want to risk going back into that room and she wasn't sure what effect it might have on the princess. So as they walked down the street Demie kicked on each door they came across until she found an empty building that let them in.

The first level of the two-story structure had a fireplace opposite the door and a table with chairs in the middle of the room, with stairs in the far corner. Demie led the way up the stairs and entered one of the two bedrooms, which lacked doors but it was about as private as they would get. The space contained just a bed and several pieces of abandoned armor in one corner. Apparently even online games had litter problems.

"We should be safe here for now." Demie turned to the princess. Time to get gossipy, one of the things she missed most when she was being mute. "So, what's this about five husbands? Do they know about each other, or are you somehow keeping them all in the dark? You have to tell me more."

Draupadi turned away from Demie and walked to face the far wall. Demie waited, and when Draupadi didn't answer, she asked, "What, did I say something wrong?"

Draupadi turned back to Demie, her hands held together and looking downcast. "No, you spoke fairly. I am troubled, my friend. All that which I know of my husbands is vague and distant, as if stories told by another. There is a void within myself, where something is missing."

"Tell me what you know, then."

"My husbands are the five Pandava brothers. Yudhishthira is the eldest, and is honorable, just and always truthful. Next, Bhima is violent and uncouth but fiercely loyal, and then comes Arjuna, a mighty warrior and great archer who exhibits enormous control and virtue. No man in the world is more handsome than Nakula, and Sahadeva is most heroic and chivalrous."

"Do you remember anything else about them?" Demie asked.

"I do know things about them, but have not memories. Not the way I can recall you coming through the window."

"So where do you think they are?"

"They may be found in the city of Krivi, scattered and hiding in disguise. Hence, that is where we must go."

Demie wanted to bang her head on the virtual wall; she didn't have patience for what sounded like a wild hubbie chase. "How can you be certain they are really there?"

Draupadi insisted, "I know not, but in fact they are."

"I have some serious problems right now," Demie replied, annoyed by the addition of yet another thing to deal with. "This isn't the best time for a road trip."

Draupadi came over to Demie and grasped her hands. "All the more reason, then, for us to leave immediately. Yudhishthira is exceedingly wise; he could almost be a rishi. We will tell him your problem, and I know he will help you find that which you seek."

"I'm pretty sure I need more than a rishi." Demie herself wasn't certain what the problem was. He would have to be quite a wise man, to have an answer when she didn't even have the question. Then again, the princess did seem pretty confident. "I'll help, but just not right now."

Draupadi stepped back, crossed her arms and planted her feet, just like Kori used to. "My good friend Demie, to be sure, I can not explain why. But this is what I was meant to do."

Throwing up her hands, Demie exclaimed, "It's probably going the wrong way."

Draupadi turned away from Demie, "You should take whatever path you find needful. But I must find my husbands, and will go alone if necessary."

Lauren was starting to doze, and jumped when the front door rattled. Draping her shawl over her shoulders, she hurried and reached the front door as it swung open. Cassie walked in with a couple of bags in her free hand.

"Do you have more?" Lauren asked, slipping her shoes on.

Cassie dropped her purse in the corner, nodded toward the SUV, and headed into the den with the supplies. Lauren went out to the back of the vehicle and grabbed a couple cases of bed pads, as Cassie came back out.

"So how did it go with Demie?"

"It was fine," Lauren replied. "I wrote down when I did each check, and there were no surprises. Though it took a while to figure out the afternoon physical therapy exercises, and I'm still not sure if I got it right."

"I forgot to tell you, there's a DVD that shows how to do that."

Yeah, that would've been helpful, Lauren thought as they stacked the last of the boxes in the corner of the den. Then again, maybe the oversight really was an accident.

"Thanks for watching Demie," Cassie said as she walked over to the girl, checked the lines and tucked in a stray corner of blanket. "You didn't have to, but it really helped to get these supplies directly from the city. I can't afford Good Shepherd's prices and didn't have time to do mail order."

"I was happy to," Lauren smiled. "Really, she was no problem." Cassie actually seemed to be thawing and treating her like a real person. They might never be best friends, but Lauren felt like she could finally let her guard down. "I have to run, but just call any time you need me to watch her again. Or if you need a break, or whatever."

Cassie stood up, stiffened and sharply responded, "Why, are you trying to work off some guilt?"

Lauren's mouth dropped, and she stared at Cassie's back. For several seconds she contemplated actually hurling a box at Cassie. Then, without a word, she turned to go back to the living room. Picking up her coat and purse, she headed straight for the door.

As she opened the door, Cassie called out from the den, "Wait. I'm sorry, that was uncalled for."

Pausing halfway across the threshold, Lauren replied, "Yes. It was." She stifled the urge to slam the door.

Ten minutes later, Lauren pulled into her driveway, took several deep breaths and wiped away the tears. Lauren wasn't sure who she was more furious with: Cassie for slipping the knife in and twisting it with both hands, or herself for handing Cassie the knife and showing her where to plunge it.

While she cleaned her face and applied some makeup so Sherman wouldn't ask questions about something she would rather forget, Lauren realized that she neglected to tell Cassie about Chandar.

Well, that was something best just forgotten.

Demie felt anger rising within as she stared at Draupadi's back. She should just walk out of the room and leave her royal stubbornness to her own fate. After all, Demie only agreed to help get the princess out of that dumb room, and didn't owe her anything else. She went down the stairs, then stopped at the exit to the street.

In a lot of ways, Draupadi was young and innocent, much like Kori had been. Demie cringed inside as she thought of the sister she sacrificed, just to save herself. Exactly how real was Draupadi? Maybe she was just a computer program. Or had she become something more? Either way, the naïve, helpless 'girl' upstairs was Demie's only friend in this world. And having abandoned one person who needed her, Demie just wouldn't do that again.

Besides, that Yiddish-dude might have something useful to offer. It wasn't like she had a better plan.

Demie went upstairs. Draupadi was standing in the corner, staring into space as if lost in thought. If there was one thing Demie could relate to, it was being lost. She went up to her friend, placed a hand on the princess's shoulder, and said, "Alright, Draupadi, I'll help you."

"You will?!" Draupadi spun around and embraced Demie. Demie felt energy draining out of her toward the princess again, but not quite as strong as before.

"I'm not going to go and leave my bestie all alone."

"Is that some sort of mount that you ride?" Draupadi asked.

"No, you're my bestie. You know, my best friend. Now if we are going to find these husbands of yours..." Demie started.

"The Pandavas."

"...wherever they are..."

"Krivi."

"...then we need to get you out of that red robe."

"Sari."

"Whatever." Demie walked over to the pile of armor and picked up a breastplate. "Can you wear this?"

"In truth, I will not. I shall wear other clothing if you wish, but no armor." From the tone in Draupadi's voice and the stance she took, Demie knew not to bother arguing.

"That's fabulous. Okay, let's find something you can wear then." Demie tossed the armor away and went downstairs, making sure Draupadi followed.

On their way to Bhishma's Emporium, Lizat messaged Demie. "Are you ready for our trip to Vatsa Forest?"

Oh crud. She forgot all about that. A vast forest didn't sound like somewhere she wanted to drag Draupadi anyway, even if she could convince the princess her hubbies were there.

"Dang it, I'm sorry. I've gotten caught up in something, and have to go somewhere else right now." She sent the message back to Lizat, wherever he was.

"Oh, you're on a quest? Where are you going?"

"Some place called Krivi." Not that she had any clue where that was.

"Really? Krivi is on the way, we can at least go together that far.

Can you meet us at the barges?"

"Totally. Give me about ten minutes," Demie agreed, so happy to have the company that she started skipping as they came up to the Emporium. Firmly leading Draupadi by the hand, she entered and as usual, Bhishma stood behind the counter.

A firm push elicited the familiar response. "Welcome to Bhishma's Armor Emporium. Do you want to BUY, SELL, or EXIT?"

The merchant presented far fewer available choices due to Demie's lack of funds, but she pointed out a nice set of leather armor, thinking that might work for the princess because it wasn't metal.

"Please do not be angry, my friend," Draupadi responded, "But I shall only wear attire that was not meant for the field of battle."

"Well, here's some crappy armor that I'm certain was never meant for any battle." Demie highlighted the cheapest leather armor, covered with mold. Draupadi shook her head. "Okay, what about a heavy cloak and traveling boots?"

"I would greatly prefer the one at the top, if you please."

"You've gotta be kidding me!" Demie highlighted a set of rags that even a dog would refuse to lay on, as much disgusted with Draupadi's taste as with the choice itself.

"To be sure, those are not the clothes of a court jester. But they are the ones I would have."

Apparently, there was no accounting for royal fashion. Demie selected the rags, and Bhishma had the nerve to actually charge a copper piece for the privilege of taking them off his hands. She handed the rags to Draupadi, who automagically changed into them. When she handed the red sari back, Demie stored it in her magical purse.

Back out on the street, the princess blended right into the pedestrian traffic, so maybe Draupadi knew what she was doing after all. She was certainly incognito.

At the East Kampilya Weapons shop, Demie almost told Draupadi to take a long hike to Krivi by herself. When Lizardman presented his display, the royal pain in the butt decided that any kind of weapon was beneath her and refused even a knife. Finally, when Demie insisted she carry something so she wouldn't draw attention to herself, Draupadi agreed to take a common staff, calling it a walking stick.

As Demie led her charge down to the barges on the lower level, she hoped Draupadi wouldn't insist that they lash some logs together to make a raft.

Karen stood up and stretched. When she saw the clock she exclaimed, "Crap!" It was almost midnight, but at least the Draupadi module was reloaded where it belonged.

It seemed like just an hour ago that she watched the sun set. Before heading into the lab, she walked out onto the beach and quietly drank in the deep red and orange colors painting the sky. A cool salty breeze blew her auburn hair across her sharp, angular face, and the distant crashing of incoming breakers brought an inner peace that she so rarely found anymore.

Then the sun slipped below the horizon, taking the moment with it, and she went back inside. But the hours were well spent, because she made great progress in re-tooling her pet program, Kali. The updates needed to run in the current version of Panchala were easy, because they had used it in the original beta. The tricky part was tweaking the search parameters. Since they weren't yet certain what they were seeking, and the tool had been developed with hardcoded parameters, she modified it to use definitions that they could update on the fly, similar to the way anti-virus software updated itself. The result gave Karen, if not peace, at least a great deal of satisfaction.

The time consuming part was the avatar Kali would use within the game world. Leading up to the beta, Joachim's programming team developed a rudimentary avatar, but it was little more than a shell, which was fine for a test lab but not for a customer environment. In order to move and interact within Panchala independently and still fit in, Kali needed a logic structure for its actions and responses. Karen cut and pasted a great deal of what she needed from a few NPC modules, but it was still a time consuming process.

Now she had a working copy, and completed a series of lab tests to ensure it was ready. She sent Tony an IM, advising him that Kali was ready and he could start working on the search parameters. His smart phone alerts were probably still set to 24x7 for her messages. Sure enough, by the time she got back to her desk with a soda, he responded with approval to launch. She was more pleased with how quickly he replied than with the answer itself. The girl still had her touch.

Karen logged into the primary controller, and pondered where to insert Kali. After another IM to Tony, asking where he found the one rogue process he terminated a few days before, a minute later the one word response came back: Kampilya. She uploaded the code and configured the Kali application to run in hunt mode. Now to see what it turned up.

A few minutes later, a heavily armed warrior appeared in the central plaza of Kampilya.

ॐ

By the time Demie got to the barges, Lizat's party was already there, and she wanted to sigh with happiness. This team, which she only worked with a couple times, was the closest thing she now had to family. She headed over to Lizat, leading Draupadi along by the hand like a Kindergartner on the first day of school, bringing back eerie memories of Kori. This crowd would not be the place to lose the princess.

"So how does this barge thing work?" Demie asked. "I've never used it."

"There are two barges," Lizat replied. "One goes upriver and the other down. Since Krivi is downriver, we need to make sure we catch that one." Lizat turned to examine Draupadi.

"Say, why do you have a major NPC tagging along with you? I've never seen one act as a companion."

So much for disguises, Demie thought. She was very disappointed that he had seen right through the rags. "I think it's part of the quest. I'll learn more when I get there." Which was true enough. An incoming barge spared any more questions.

"This is it," Lizat confirmed, and joined the mad rush aboard.

Demie walked forward, and at the edge of the boat she felt a tingle in her purse. She checked, and somehow the toll collector dipped into her purse for five gold pieces, the sneaky dog. But Draupadi didn't have a problem walking onto the barge, probably because she owned it.

Moments later the barge pulled away and headed out into the river, turning left as it moved downstream. Leading the princess, Demie crossed the deck and scaled a small flight of stairs up to a plain observing deck. There she could watch the riverbank slide by.

On both sides, jungle came down to the water with few breaks in the wall of vegetation. Several times they floated past a spot where a trail led right into the water and then continued on the other side of the river. The water must've been shallow because numerous people, individually and in groups, dashed across going both ways.

A number of miles downriver, a small village came into view, populated with hairy man-like figures. When they noticed the barge, a large group gathered on the shore and shot arrows at them, all falling short of the craft. Fortunately, they didn't have canoes.

"Those are Danavas, a tribe of wild men," Lizat said, and Demie noticed that he joined her at the rail. "When we get stronger, we'll come back and raid this village."

Demie wasn't sure whether the Danavas deserved that kind of treatment, but she wasn't going to worry about it. As the village slowly drifted behind them, Demie wondered how long the trip would take. She missed a real sense of time, the way it was in the real world. For all she knew she had been in this place a week, a month or a year. And Mom had no idea Demie was even here.

Mom.

Though she missed Old Mom more than New Mom, mom was still Mom. Demie had never been completely cut off from her family before, and she ached to tell Mom everything that happened. As a sixteen-year-old she might not like to admit it, but when life got really broken, a part of her still wanted Mom or Dad to fix things. Preferably without them knowing about it.

But there was no fixing this. In that moment, Demie wished she could climb over the rail with a large rock strapped to her waist and jump into the river. She was utterly alone, not just the last person in the world, but the only one.

A need to cry built up inside, the pressure silently screaming for release. But her eyes could not weep, there were no tears she could shed. Demie felt a light touch on her shoulder and turned to face Draupadi. The princess slipped her arm around Demie's shoulder and pulled Demie into an embrace. Demie felt the emotion release inside and realized this was the first, real contact she had in this world.

It wasn't the same as a good cry, but Draupadi's hug acted as a drain for Demie's sorrow and pain, and Demie felt something break open inside her when she returned the hug. Those years of being mute had been terribly lonely. After what she did to Kori, Demie would let no one in. No one to betray, let down or hurt.

It was imperative that she contact Mom somehow. Chandar was the only direct contact Demie had with the real world, so it would have to be through him. Demie slowly regained her composure and another large town came into view. The barge angled over toward a wide expanse of steps, just like the ones in Kampilya.

"Is this Krivi?" Demie asked Lizat.

"Yeah, you'll want to get off here. Vatsa Forest is further downriver, so we're going to stay on board."

"Thanks," Demie replied and led Draupadi downstairs. "Let me know how it goes."

"Will do. Good luck with your quest."

Demie watched the barge head out to the center of the river, and continue downriver. Nudging Draupadi to follow, she climbed the steps into the new town and saw a large, forbidding amazon warrior standing at the top of the stairs. She wore the most elaborate golden armor Demie had seen in this world, with at least three kinds of swords slung over her back, two of which glowed.

The warrior took several steps toward them and sent Demie a message, "I've been looking for you."

CHAPTER ELEVEN

Cassie organized the last of the medical supply boxes in the den closet, then gave Demie a quick check once more. She found several places where Lauren got sloppy and missed tucking the blanket in, and she found some careless bends in the drip tube. Nightfall was coming so she made sure the nightlight was on and tested the wireless monitor she carried throughout the house.

After the long afternoon drive, Cassie was exhausted and just wanted to relax, so she nestled in the living room. None of the cable channels captured her interest so she finally switched the TV off. There was the library book that was due back next week but after reading the same passage for the fourth time, she shut the book and tossed it back on the coffee table.

She had to do something. Cassie wandered into the kitchen but wasn't hungry enough to fix dinner. Continuing up the stairs, she drifted down the hall toward her bedroom, then stopped outside Demie's room and opened the door. Cassie leaned with her head against the doorframe and examined the room, for the first time since the night she fell asleep holding the backpack.

It was exactly as Demie left it, forever ago.

Surveying the scene, Cassie resolved to preserve her daughter's room exactly as it was. Except for the dirty clothing strewn across the floor. Demie would need clean clothes when she awoke. Cassie wouldn't admit the real reason for keeping the room unchanged—the mess was tangible proof that a sixteen-year-old had lived there.

She navigated through the debris to the corner where the dirty laundry basket sat, containing a single clean sock. Scooping up jeans, shirts and undergarments into the hamper, she headed downstairs and nudged the laundry room door open. While sorting garments, she started the washer and checked the dark load for any pocket surprises. She never skipped that step since the nail-polish disaster, when several bottles made it through the wash, only to smash apart in the dryer. The whole load had to be tossed, but the dryer was saved by the fact that the polish baked onto the drum, where it remained as a cautionary reminder.

Cassie found the sealed card in the third pair of jeans and set it aside while she checked through the rest of the load and got the lid closed. Leaning against the machine, she opened the undelivered greeting card and read:

Mom,

Happy Mother's Day! I know I give you a hard time, but you are the best mother anyone could ask for. I'm glad to be your daughter.

Love, Demie

She stared at the card for several minutes, reading words she had long wished to hear. The fact that her daughter had written it at all stunned Cassie, almost as much as realizing that Demie would have given it to her in another week when Mother's Day rolled around. Then, she slowly walked to the kitchen and retrieved the Crown Royal whisky she placed there just an hour earlier. The purchase in the city had been an impulse. Now she held the box in her hand, contemplating whether to break ten years of sobriety.

Still undecided, she opened the box and caressed the soft blue velvet bag containing her hidden treasure. Gently pulling the bag open, she slipped the bottle out and slowly unscrewed the cap, until the sharp tangy smell hit her nostrils.

Half filling a glass with some cold Coke, she tossed in a few ice cubes and topped it off with the golden liquid. Carrying the drink in one hand and Demie's card in the other, she went into the living room and sat on the sofa, re-reading the message.

By the time she read it through the third time, Cassie's eyes were too blurred with tears to see the words. Her hand trembling, she raised the glass to her lips and paused, eyes closed as she mustered the will to cross the first-drink threshold.

Endless moments passed, and anguish wrestled with resistance against throwing away the past ten years, until she finally lowered the glass and walked back into the kitchen. Pouring her drink down the kitchen drain, Cassie took the bottle of Crown Royal over to the sink and turned it over, watching the liquid flow into the sink.

The warrior advanced toward Demie, but she was less worried than confused as she tried to recall if there was something she had forgotten? Who would bother looking for her, let alone why? She replied, "You must have me confused with someone else. I don't even know you."

The golden warrior paused halfway down the steps and waited before replying, "It's me, Chandar. I'm using Samita now. She happens to be a good fighter but more importantly has some items we can really use. So why are you here, and who is this?"

Demie almost hugged Samita, she was so glad to see her one link to the real world. Draupadi stood to the side and silently examined Samita, while behind the princess another group of people boarded the barge. Then Demie observed something she hadn't noticed before. Brief flashes of light flickered back and forth between people, and many flashes went somewhere upstream. These were messages being sent back and forth, and Demie focused on one of the figures closest to her. She wanted to see if she could catch one, and snagged a comment about a player in the game named HotLover, who according to the message sender, was definitely not.

"Demie? Are you there?"

Demie turned her attention back to Chandar/Samita.

"Sorry. This is Draupadi, and she brought me here on some kind of task." Yes, there was the flash, so quick and subtle she hadn't noticed it before. But now she couldn't miss it.

"You mean the Draupadi? On a quest? What are you seeking?"

"She wants me to help her find some friends of hers, but after that I don't know." Demie continued to study the flashes between her and Samita/Chandar. "Have you learned anything new?"

"Nothing new, but when I was over at your house..."

Just then, Draupadi started up the steps, and Demie followed. After the loneliness of the barge trip, she was eager to talk with Chandar. "Tell me while we walk. So you told my mom what happened?" Draupadi reached the top and entered the town without looking back, so Demie hurried to catch up.

"No, someone else answered and said your mom was out running an errand. What do you mean, did I tell her? Do you have any idea how crazy that would sound? I'm still trying to believe it myself."

"But she's my mom, you have to tell her! She needs to know I'm okay."

Chandar didn't answer right away, and Demie glanced back to make sure he was still following. Draupadi strode down the main street and entered the Krivi equivalent of the main square. Without hesitation, the princess angled to the right and crossed toward a large avenue which led to the east.

"Look, Demie, I can't really say anything about it yet. How do I convince someone else that this is true, if we haven't figured out what happened to you and how you got there? We don't even have a crazy explanation yet, let alone a sane one."

Demie wasn't the sort to pout, but this was not the answer she wanted. Draupadi turned down the eastern avenue, and Demie picked up her pace so she wouldn't lose sight of her friend.

"I guess you're right," Demie reluctantly admitted. "So let's go over what we do know, then. Obviously, it involved getting hit by lightning. Have you ever heard about anything like this back in India?"

After a pause, Chandar responded, "I was born here in the States. But I've heard stories about gurus who have out of body experiences. In one case, a guru was meditating in his ashram with his students one evening..."

"What's an ashram?" Demie interjected.

"Sort of a monastery. Anyway, the guru had a heart attack, and the next morning a family member arrived from a hundred miles away, saying the guru came into his room the night before and told him to come."

"So? Someone had a lucky dream."

"The thing is," Chandar continued, "there were two other people in that distant room who also saw and heard the guru. My grandfather was one of them."

"Wow, now that is creepy. But unless this guru happened to be flying a kite in a thunderstorm, I don't see how that helps. Hurry up, she's getting ahead of us."

Draupadi entered a smaller square, looked back at Demie, then headed straight across the plaza to a long, high wall. The princess stopped in front of a large wooden door identical to the one securing Draupadi's tower in Kampilya.

"The point is that if a guru could leave his body and show up a hundred miles away, why not show up in a virtual online world? Anyway, you know what was really creepy? Seeing your body lying there, in your house."

Demie halted, suddenly feeling as cold as the heart of winter. "What do you mean, my body? What did you see?" This was freaking her out.

"Not much. On the way up to your room I glanced in the den and there you were. All quiet like, with tubes and wires and shit hooked up. I would've turned around and left but that lady was right behind me."

"What lady? Do you remember her name?" There just weren't many friends Mom would've left in charge. It was a pretty small town after all.

"I don't really remember, but I think it started with an L, like maybe Lisa or Linda. Or perhaps Laura."

"Not Lauren."

"Yeah, that's it. Her name was Lauren."

Demie couldn't believe it, but there were no other Laurens within a hundred miles, at least none that Demie knew of. Mom made it a point to never let that woman in the house. The few times Lauren came over with Dad to pick up Demie, Mom kept them waiting on the porch. Even that time when it was raining outside, and Demie had to scramble to get her overnight bag ready. The drive back to Dad's house that night was a long, silent ride.

So, it made no sense that she was there. Mom would sooner have glass shards driven under her fingernails than let Lauren step foot in the house; she'd said so herself more than once. What was going on?

Chandar interrupted Demie's musing, "Where did she go, that NPC you were following?"

Demie turned back around, and without thinking exclaimed, "What the hell?" Where Draupadi previously stood was now only an empty square. And an open door.

Karen groaned and turned over, away from the sunlight streaming in her bedroom window. Stretching, she glanced at the clock and realized she slept in later than intended. Damn, she barely had time to get ready for the aerobics class she led every Saturday morning.

Mornings like this, it felt like more trouble than it was worth, but leading the class helped her stay in shape. And sometimes just the prospect of pushing the class to the point where they started dropping, knowing she could break them if she wanted to, was enough to get her going.

Sliding out of bed, Karen went to her computer and woke it up. While it processed some pending updates, she cracked open the balcony glass door and began some stretches, both to wake up and warm up for her class.

A cool, salty breeze whistled through the gap. From the 12th floor balcony she could see ships far out to sea, a handful of surfers and several joggers on the beach below. The condo cost most of her TerraMythos stock options, but she never regretted it. She truly felt content on mornings like this.

The computer chirped to let her know it was ready, and after a few more lunges, Karen eagerly sat down and logged into the Panchala primary server. She had been wondering from the moment her eyes opened what Kali had come up with overnight.

When she opened the utility which monitored Kali's activities, Karen frowned. For some reason, Kali was no longer in Kampilya, although it had spent an hour in the city and eradicated a couple of game shopkeepers. The system regenerated the shopkeepers of course, and that replaced the previous data structures, so she had no clear root cause for why Kali destroyed them. Karen would remedy that on Monday morning.

Further down in the log, she saw where Kali picked up traces from another module in the game and then exited the town. The tracking page of the utility located Kali trotting across the countryside, and Karen scrolled the map in the direction her little pet was headed. Another small city called Krivi.

Karen logged out, picked up her workout bag and smiled to herself. It was time to make some grown women cry.

Draupadi felt them; a sense within her, not so much of pulling as pointing. Her husbands were near, and she would soon find them. This was something she was meant to do, had always been meant to do. She just didn't know why, or how long 'always' was.

Before DemiGirl climbed through the royal chamber window, Draupadi simply waited outside of time for the door to open. She didn't know whether there had been a before time, just that she had been asleep until DemiGirl woke her up. And awoke strange stirrings inside that confused her greatly, such as the urgent need to find her husbands.

The palace door opened at her touch, and once more she felt that stirring inside, the feeling that good things would happen. The princess entered a large cobblestone square which held a large bubbling fountain in the center and colorful flower planters along the walls. Otherwise it was empty except for a court jester, some beggars sleeping in one corner, and a pair of soldiers standing guard before a large doorway, opposite the opening she came through. Arched entries on the sides of the courtyard were unprotected, but her sense pointed forward.

As she rounded the fountain, she heard Demie enter the courtyard. The jester and beggars had ignored Draupadi, but the moment Demie and her warrior friend arrived, the jester started juggling and singing, while the beggars leapt up and hastened to intercept her companions. Draupadi continued unmolested toward the guards.

The sentries stood at attention and casually shifted their weapons back and forth until Draupadi approached within ten feet. Then they sprang to life and moved to block the opening, beyond which rose a flight of stairs. They dropped their spears to block her way and one stepped forward, which caused a great stirring inside Draupadi, of not-good-things-happening.

"Halt! What business have you with King Virata?"

"My business is my own counsel, and naught to do with the king," Draupadi said as she tried to move past them, but an invisible wall like the one on the window of her royal chamber held her back. The stirrings within made her want to run away, but she couldn't; the need to find her husbands wouldn't release her.

"Return when you have an invitation to the party," the guard responded as he continued to bar her way.

Draupadi redirected the stirrings into pushing, the way DemiGirl pressed through the window, and she slipped through a split in the unseen wall between the guards. When she looked back, the guards had returned to their positions, once more shifting their weapons back and forth.

Climbing the steps, Draupadi reached the first landing when she heard the guards repeat their question. Demie and her friend stood in the doorway, blocked by the guards, because Demie was not pushing hard enough.

After another flight the stairs opened onto a large hall, painted a light brown with huge golden molding along the ceiling. Yellow and orange patterned curtains decorated the walls. The first half of the large room had two doors on each side, but otherwise was open and empty. Several large rugs spread across the floor depicting scenes of gods and goddesses, hunters and hunted, in rich red, yellow and purple colors.

An enormous throne sat at the far end of the hall, with a long, low table positioned in front of it. A number of men wearing fine garments and jewelry sat around the table, playing a dice game. Another man with a crown sat on the carved, gold throne, watching and cheering them on, while a continuous line of servants moved between the table and one of the side doors, bearing platters of food back and forth. Her sense drew her toward the table.

The stirrings inside made her want to dash across the hall, but Draupadi politely walked up to the table and approached the man on the throne. The king's name came to her, from the same source in her mind that provided knowledge of her husbands. She must ask Yudhishthira about this concealed knowing, which caused much stirring of confusion and not-rightness.

She put her palms together over her head, bowed toward him and said, "Namaste, King Virata." The king ignored her and laughed while gesturing toward the table.

This caused stirrings of not liking the King, but she focused on the feeling that pointed around the table toward a younger man, with dark flowing hair that cascaded over powerful shoulders. His garb was plain compared to the others, but he moved smoothly and with grace as he reached for the dice to take his turn. This was Yudhishthira, her eldest husband.

The pull from inside her chest and stomach became so strong and intense, she needed to stop it. Before it made her existence stop altogether. Putting her palms together, Draupadi bowed toward her husband and said, "Namaste, Yudhishthira." Like the king, he ignored her, and Draupadi's insides felt like snapping.

As she walked directly up to Yudhishthira, that feeling became so strong she nearly dropped to her knees. He was surrounded by the same unseen wall she found with the guards and she tried to push through, but this time she couldn't get a firm grip and just slipped off. Yudhishthira remained asleep in this place and she wanted to start hitting him. Then, she recalled how Demie awoke her from the Sleeping, by pushing directly with her life force. Draupadi put her palms together again and performed Namaste once more, this time pushing hard against his wall, trying to give him the same energy she received from Demie.

When she looked up, the entire room was frozen and Draupadi stepped back. There was a wrongness throughout the space that made her want to run, hide, hit something. It flowed over her and threatened to consume her. Just as she reached a point where she thought she would cease to exist, the figures in the room began moving again. Yudhishthira stood up and turned toward her. The wrongness inside went away, and Draupadi marveled at how good it was to stop feeling something.

"You are Draupadi." He spoke plainly, as though addressing the dice or the table, but he just stood looking at her.

"Yes, I am. It is time." He didn't respond, which created a stirring of emptiness inside her, but she continued, "Come with me, we must find the others."

A new feeling pointed Draupadi toward the side door which the servants resumed using, and she entered a huge kitchen. In one corner, a hairy, burly man sat stirring food in pots hanging over a fire. Walking up to him, Draupadi used the same technique to get his attention that she used on Yudhishthira, and said, "Namaste, Bhima. Come with me."

Without a word he dropped the large spoon he held and fell into place behind Yudhishthira. Draupadi felt that stirring again, of good things happening, as she exited the kitchen and entered another side door. A tall, lean man stood in a room full of musical instruments, handling a stringed instrument.

Draupadi pressed on him, saying, "Namaste, Arjuna. It is time to come with us." He set the musical instrument down and joined the first two brothers. She led them across the hall, to a small horse stable where she found a young man grooming one of the horses.

When she said to him, "Namaste, Nakula. We are here and the

time has come," he laid down his brush and fell in behind Arjuna. The growing crowd made it hard to maneuver back through the door, and Draupadi felt a stirring that not-good things might start happening.

She hurried back into the hall and through the last door, which opened onto a small corral full of cattle. Standing next to the corral was a young, handsome man. Draupadi went up to him, and once more said, "Namaste, Sahadeva. Come with us."

As Draupadi led them back out into the hall and toward the stairs she came up, she experienced yet another thing she never experienced. There was a different kind of wrongness about her husbands' responses, or rather their lack of response. It gave rise to an even stronger wrongness inside her.

Draupadi questioned herself, which in itself was a wrongness. She had never asked herself anything, it never occurred to her before to do so, and it made her want to freeze.

Why am I here? She asked herself. What am I to do now?

Chandar knew they were screwed and sat back in his chair rubbing his eyes when they got to the guards. Somehow, that Draupadi character managed to get past them, probably because she was an NPC. Player Characters were subject to different rules, so he knew they would never pass these guards until they earned some sort of token within the Panchala game world.

But that girl, Demie, had to learn for herself. So he simply watched while she tried talking with, fighting against and sneaking around them. She was climbing the fountain when his father knocked on the door and Chandar was so startled he jumped out of his chair. So he was standing when his father entered and walked over to sit on the bed.

This was what Baba did whenever he came to deliver one of those Talks. Chandar powered the monitor off and turned to face his father.

"Son," Baba said. When he put his hands together and leaned forward, Chandar knew this was going to be a serious one. "You are doing very well in school, and I want you to know that your mother and I are very proud of you. Your uncle has a position for you when you graduate, so you will soon have a good accounting job as well. These are the opportunities we came to this country to provide for you, and you will go far."

His father paused, and Chandar nodded, trying not to show his boredom. Father would get to the point in his own good time.

"It is important to have a good job, but what truly makes you a man is when you get married and have a family. When I was your age, I just wanted to have fun. Only later did I really understand what was most important. Do you understand?"

Chandar understood that he just wanted to get the Talk over with, so he nodded again.

"Good. Sanjali is an excellent girl. She would be a loyal wife and make a good mother. Those are important things, but it's also important that you like her as well." Father stood up and placed his hand on Chandar's shoulder, "You do like her, right?"

Chandar stood up as well, "Sure, Pop, she seems real nice."

"Good," Baba smiled as he headed for the door. "Don't forget she is coming over for dinner soon. We'll talk more later."

Chandar smiled as he waited for his father to pull the door shut, then turned the monitor back on and let Demie know he had to go.

Dinner would be ready soon, and Chandar had homework he had to complete. It took twice as long as normal to work through the daily math problems, and the accounting class assignment refused to come together. He just couldn't focus his mind on the schoolwork.

The source of his confusion was Sierra, the girl from the theatre. He was working the night before in the stockroom when she came in, asking for help opening a jar. As he handed it back, she rested her warm hand on his arm, then thanked him with a long, unhurried kiss. As she slowly pulled back, eyes closed, her jasmine perfume lingered on his collar. He could still smell it on the shirt, and all he knew was that suddenly he didn't know what he wanted.

No way would he tell his father about his upcoming date with Sierra at Red Robin.

Demie wanted to spit as she watched Chandar's character vanish and abandon her just when she needed some help. She tried a few more times to sneak behind those bouncers that Draupadi somehow got past, but every time she got within ten feet they turned to face her.

Talking to the clown didn't help, so why he was even there was beyond her. All the beggars did was beg, so she was getting quite frustrated and ready to head back to town, when Draupadi came back down the stairs leading a small parade.

Demie stared with surprise at the group as they entered the courtyard but the guards just ignored them, apparently more concerned about who came in than went out. Draupadi led her crew into the middle of the courtyard and pointed toward the oldest one.

"Demie, this is Yudhishthira. He is the wise husband I spoke of, and he may have the answers you seek."

She circled a quite average looking man, so Demie had her doubts. Then she pushed on him gently, as she had learned to do with people in this world, and said, "I came from a place far away, searching for someone who may be lost here, somewhere. How do I find her and take us both back to where we came from?"

Yudhishthira paused for a moment, and Demie thought he had frozen. She was tired of nothing working right in this town and was about to give him a hard shove when he responded, "The answers you seek exceed my wisdom. Only a great rishi has the discernment you require."

"So, where do I find one of these guys? One of these rishi dudes?" Demie really wasn't in the mood to play twenty questions with this guy.

"I know of a great rishi, but he lives in a distant land. His ashram is in Amaravati, the ancient lost city of our people. Alas, I can not tell you where you may find Amaravati."

Draupadi stepped up. "If I may be so bold, good my lord, I know where it is. Or rather, I should say I know of a tale that may lead us there. We must travel across the land of the Kurus and down into the Thal Desert."

Demie wanted to scream with frustration at the idea of embarking on another search for who knew what, going who knew where. But, she had to admit that she didn't have any better ideas. In fact, she didn't have any worse ideas either. "Would you show me the way?"

Draupadi actually smiled. "My friend Demie, I owe you a great debt for releasing me. You would honor me if you let me repay you this way. My husbands will accompany us there."

"Then we might as well get going." Demie hid her lack of enthusiasm and embraced Draupadi, and after a moment Draupadi responded in kind.

"You do know the way, right?" Demie asked.

Draupadi gestured to her husbands, the Pandava brothers, and they gathered behind her. "Most surely I do, but first we must proceed to a location outside of town where we shall retrieve my husbands' weapons. Then we may commence our journey to Amaravati."

Now that they had a goal, Demie followed Draupadi out to the street, actually looking forward to the journey as she took up a spot at the end of the column. Just as Draupadi reached the public square, a huge black female warrior, taller than an NBA basketball player, leapt into view.

Demie screamed out in surprise when the enormous woman knocked the princess back into the courtyard with a massive blow. Even at first glance, this adversary was unlike anything they had yet encountered. Not only did the bitch have four arms and two weapons, she actually glowed!

The demonic warrior swung a sword at the princess as Draupadi cried out, "Lord Kali!"

CHAPTER TWELVE

The color was still wrong. Lauren hurled the paintbrush across the studio in frustration and tossed the palate on the table behind her. She had been working on this oil painting all day and knew exactly how she wanted the mountain scene to look. But after hours of wrestling with it, the hue for the mountain still wasn't working.

She reached for the scrapper to peel off her latest attempt, but grabbed the utility knife instead. Flicking out the blade, she squared off with the easel, ready to shred the canvas and be done with the damn thing. At least she could salvage the frame. But her hand paused, as the knife kissed the canvas.

It wasn't the subject, it wasn't the paint, and it sure wasn't the canvas. It was the painter. With a sigh, she retrieved the brush and stuck it in a jar of solvent, then wrapped the palate to clean up later. After quickly scrapping off the offending paint, in case she wanted to try again later, Lauren exchanged her battle-worn smock for a sweater and stepped outside her studio into the late afternoon sunlight. She closed her eyes, took several deep breaths of cold crisp air and felt the warmth of the sun on her cheeks.

Sherman built this small outbuilding just down the hill from their house, below a small ridge that hid the main house and gave Lauren a sense of isolation, even if she was really only a 30-second walk from home. Right then, she was no more ready to go home than she was to paint. In fact she had no idea what she wanted. So instead of taking the uphill path back to the house, she headed downhill toward the county park. Maybe fresh air and a good walk would help.

As she ambled along the small river, she mentally replayed Cassie's comment about trying to work off guilt. Although she agreed to watch over Demie because of her genuine love for the girl, it didn't minimize the stinging truth behind the woman's words. Every time she pictured Demie lying in that bed, she shredded herself with what-if's and recriminations. But life was an unbroken train of what-if's, and as she sat on a picnic table, flinging stones into the flowing water, she knew exactly what bothered her.

It was dusk by the time she got back to the house, and Sherman was in his study reviewing possible ads for his stores. Lauren knew exactly what she wanted by the time she straddled a chair and rested her arms and chin on the chair back, watching him. This was their agreed-upon sign that she was waiting for his attention. He quickly finished sorting the options and stacked them to one side, then turned toward her.

"How's the painting going?"

"Awful. It's not going at all. We need to talk."

"I was wondering when you would realize that." Sherman smiled, and she melted inside. "You've been moping all day, buried in some hole deep inside yourself. I've just been waiting until you were ready to come up for air."

Lauren sighed. It had been so clear on the walk up from the river, but now she wasn't sure where to begin. "Well, it's about that question you keep asking me, and I keep saying yes, but not right now."

"You mean getting married?"

"Yes. And I mean yes, right now. I mean, I've always meant yes, just not right now, but now I mean yes right now too...but I don't mean right now, you know, I mean..."

"Okay, hold on," Sherman interrupted. "Are you saying that you want to go ahead and get married?"

"Yes!" Lauren exclaimed, her long-suppressed agreement bursting out like a broken dam as she half rose out of her chair. "I mean, not right now, but...yes. Let's get married. Soon."

Sherman looked surprised, and leaned back. "Wow. That's great, don't get me wrong. Yes, let's do it. But I'm just curious, why the sudden change?"

"Things *have* changed, Sherman. I kept hoping Demie would

accept me without the pressures of being a stepmother, that she would welcome me into her life. Plus, I was trying to avoid complications with the ex-wife, but that's already complicated. So, I guess I've realized that all the reasons for waiting are pointless, compared with the reason for going ahead."

"Okay," Sherman said. Then, more enthusiastically as he stood up and gathered Lauren into his arms. "Okay, let's do it!"

She wrapped her arms around his neck and pulled herself close. As he held her, her world felt complete and at peace, and she buried herself in his long kiss with closed eyes.

"So when and where?" Sherman asked.

"The first moment you can break away from your business for a few days, Mister Anderson. And just a small civil ceremony for now. We can have a public wedding for friends and family later."

Sherman gave her another kiss and sat down at his desk again. "I need to finish arranging this advertising campaign, then I'll call my new assistant manager. I think he's ready to take the reins for a week or so."

Lauren started to head out of the study, and then turned back. "By the way, can you tell Cassie when you get a chance? It would be better if it came from you, rather than from some rumor or, God forbid, from me." Sherman nodded, barely looking up.

Lauren left the study and quietly pulled the door closed behind her. She softly hummed a low tune as she headed into the bathroom to take a long soak in some bath salts, wondering how Cassie would take the news.

And telling herself, really, it wasn't about getting back at Cassie.

Draupadi felt deep stirrings to run/fight when Lord Kali's sword swung toward her, and she took a quick step back into the doorway, then ducked as Kali's blow connected with the doorframe. Two quick steps and a roll between her opponent's legs, and Draupadi's strength-stirrings grew inside when she regained her feet behind Kali.

The warrior form which Kali had assumed for this incarnation was almost twice as tall as a person, and had four arms which held a sword, spear and shield. Armor covered all the conventional weak spots, but there were still openings for someone who knew where they were. When Kali turned to face her, the princess felt strong stirrings of rightness as she landed a well-placed kick on the inside of one leg and the warrior went down.

Now perched on one knee, Kali swung her sword and it thudded into the ground where Draupadi had just been standing. The princess completed her roll back onto her feet, Kali swung again, and Draupadi nimbly dodged several strokes, ducking and stepping first one way, then the other. When Kali lunged with her spear, Draupadi grabbed an arm with one hand and pressed a spot on her foe's exposed wrist. The weapon dropped from the now-useless hand.

Kali swung again from the other side with her sword, and the princess made a loud call as she executed a spin, which ended in a kick that connected with the warrior's head and knocked the helmet off. Following up with a couple of punches, Draupadi launched into a flip that took her over Kali's now unprotected head while she landed stinging blows to the ears, followed by a powerful kick on the back of the head as she came down behind. When she landed on her feet, Kali was already falling forward.

Draupadi felt very deep stirrings of rightness inside, since she had not been hit once, and by the time the Pandavas and Demie got to her Kali was already starting to fade. The rightness gave her a feeling of strength, something she had never felt before.

The Pandavas lined up behind the princess as though nothing happened, but her friend and companion Demie ran up to her. "I can't believe what you just did. What the hell was that?"

"Kalarippayat, my good friend. It is the mother of all martial arts," Draupadi responded as she made a respectful bow to her fallen opponent.

"I had no idea you could fight like that. Why wouldn't you take any weapons?"

"My friend, I only said I would not bear any arms. I never said I would not use my own arms." Turning, Draupadi added, "It would be well for us to go and retrieve my husbands' weapons. We may all have need to fight next time."

The same inner pointing that guided Draupadi in locating her husbands, now led her through several streets and out a gate into the countryside. Although she couldn't say where it came from, she had no doubt about where the pointing was leading her, as they followed a well-used path. But not knowing where it came from gave Draupadi a deep sense of not-rightness.

Before meeting Demie, the princess knew only the bedchamber room and the act of waiting, and until now had not thought to question that. But if there was no before, how could she know the way they must go now? And how could she know of Amaravati, even though she had never been outside her own room? From where, inside her, did these thoughts arise? These questions caused her to momentarily freeze, but she caught herself and set them aside. Perhaps after the rishi answered Demie's questions, he could answer her questions as well.

After crossing over a couple of small hills, she turned off the path and walked up to a small, featureless cliff. The concealed-knowing told her to reach out and touch an ordinary looking spot on the cliff. But the knowing didn't warn her that part of the hillside would swing out, and her insides made Draupadi jump.

The opening revealed a shallow cave, and neatly stacked inside were weapons, armor and shields, which Draupadi began handing out. On one side lay five sets of armor, and even though all the sets were the same size, as she handed them to the Pandavas, each one adapted to fit the wearer. Likewise, she handed each person a silver shield, gilded with gold inlay and decorated with designs. The weapons were stored on the other side of the small cave.

On top lay the legendary bow, Gandiva. Had Demie asked, Draupadi could have recounted the story of how Arjuna gained Gandiva as a favor from the god, Agni. But she had no idea how she knew that story, which added to her sense of not-rightness.

Taking Gandiva in both her hands, the princess turned to Arjuna and dropped to one knee. "My good lord, take this and use it bravely and wisely." She lifted the bow to him, and greatly willed herself to pass along the courage and knowledge she had gained from Demie.

"I will strive to be worthy in my words and my deeds," Arjuna said as he took the bow, and then he froze for a moment. Draupadi felt a strong stirring in her chest as she handed Arjuna a quiver of arrows and a sword, and a faint blue glow flowed between them. When he took them, he didn't just fall back into line with the others; instead, he wandered off a short ways to examine his new items.

The same way, Draupadi passed an enormous club to Bhima and then the rest of the swords she handed out to Yudhishthira, Nakula and Sahadeva. Each time, she tried to pass along more to them than just a weapon and each responded in his own way, especially Sahadeva.

"I will use this great gift," he responded, "To protect you and your honor from all danger that may befall you. For no sacrifice I could make would exceed the gift that you give me now."

Each of these changes in the Pandavas gave Draupadi a growing sense of rightness that felt warm and glowing. And she couldn't say why, but she felt the most rightness for Sahadeva.

Karen's day had gone so well, up to this point. When she arrived at her aerobics class, she loaded a fast-paced CD she was saving for a special occasion. Toward the end of the class, as they went into a series of kicks, lunges and steps, she challenged them to keep up and tighten their steps. She had to restrain herself from cheering when several of the soccer moms that she particularly despised literally dropped in the back.

The best part was afterward, when they came up and complimented her. Where else could you torture and abuse people, then get thanked? And paid on top of that!

On the way out of the gym, the swimming coach she had been toying with finally asked her out to a concert she had wanted to see anyway. He wasn't really her type, but she would have some fun with him until he figured that out.

After a brief stroll along the beach, she came back upstairs and logged in to check on Kali. Then she stood up, kicked her chair and swore, wishing she had just stayed on the sand.

Karen logged on just in time to observe some Player Character beat the crap out of Kali. She wasn't sure what pissed her off more. That Kali actually attacked a PC, which was definitely not supposed to happen, or that the battle was so one sided. The PC was obviously a very high-level monk, which Kali had not been designed to tackle, but it should've put up a better damn fight than that.

The flaw in combat ability could be easily fixed by patching in some additional programming. The bigger problem was that Kali attacked a customer. With her luck that would result in a complaint to customer service, and Karen was not looking forward to coming up with some creative explanation for the resulting service ticket on Monday.

But there was a silver lining to all this. It was only Saturday afternoon, and she had almost two whole days to dig into the programming behind Kali. And if she was at all lucky she would find a way to pin the blame where it belonged.

A big target called Tony.

Demie would've given anything right that moment to have her softball bat, so she could smack Draupadi upside the head and knock some sense into her. Then again, after watching the princess fight, that might not be such a good idea after all.

She could understand why the Pandavas, as Draupadi called her husbands, needed to have their weapons and armor, so she went along with that little side trip. And she had to admit, as they marched along, her group looked like they had their own personal army now.

She didn't even say anything when Draupadi held a little pep rally with the boys. But when Draupadi led them back to the river, past the barges and started walking upstream, Demie couldn't take it anymore and had to stop her.

"Why don't we just take the barge? That would be faster."

Draupadi looked at her, like a teacher speaking down to a student. "My friend, the story I follow does not mention a barge."

"But it's the same river. Just pretend it's in the story, what's the difference?" Demie's voice was starting to rise.

"The story I follow does not mention a barge," Draupadi repeated, and then continued walking. Demie repeated her question several times and each time Draupadi gave the same response, until Demie finally gave up and took out her frustration on a couple of luckless boars.

The sun moved through the sky at a much faster pace than Demie felt a real sun should move, so she wasn't sure how long they actually traveled, but at least they didn't have to stop to sleep. Though a couple of times, Demie forced them to pause while she took a brief catnap, partly because she was tired but more from boredom. The day and night lighting had cycled five or six times when the river made a sharp turn to the right and headed toward some distant mountains.

Draupadi stopped and turned to Demie. "Here we leave the river bank, and enter the land of the Kurus. We must pass quickly, until we come to the great river that leads into the desert."

"What are Kurus, some kind of giant bird or something?"

Plunging into the jungle, Draupadi shot back, "The Kurus are the ruling family and our sworn enemies. They are also cousins to the Pandavas."

Oh great, thought Demie, now I've gotten myself in the middle of a family feud. With my luck, our next stop will be the Panchala version of the Jerry Springer show.

After a while they came across a nice trail, heading mostly in the right direction, but Draupadi insisted that they stay off the paths. That almost set Demie off again because staying off trails slowed their progress considerably. The flat jungle transitioned to more hilly terrain, and then they came over a large hill into a clearing, where Demie saw a city off to their right.

"Is that where we're going?" Demie asked, pointing to the brown walls enclosing milky white towers on a distant hill.

Draupadi replied, "That is Hastinpura, the Kuru capital. To be sure, we don't want to go there."

Halfway across the clearing, Demie toyed with the idea of slipping away from Draupadi's little parade and looking for answers in the nearby city, when she was startled by a group of mounted riders that emerged from the jungle ahead and rode toward them.

One of the riders called out, "Hail, Yudhishthira! Welcome to the land of the Kurus."

Draupadi immediately turned and ran, but instead of following the princess, Yudhishthira walked toward the horsemen. The riders pulled up sharply before him, and Yudhishthira put his palms together, bowed, and replied, "Namaste, Shakuni, my cousin's uncle."

The lead rider dismounted, walked toward Yudhishthira and returned the bow before responding, "Namaste, Yudhishthira. We have been waiting for you. A feast has been prepared at the castle, and you must come play dice." The man then re-mounted, and the riders rode back in the direction they came from.

Yudhishthira followed them without a word, then to Demie's surprise Draupadi followed as well. She had no idea what was going on, but this didn't look good.

"Where are we going?" asked Demie, as she ran to catch up.

"We go to the Kuru castle, in Hastinpura."

"Wait, I thought we didn't want to go there."

Draupadi paused for a moment before she replied, "We don't."

After her close encounter of the bottle kind, Cassie purred inside. She was actually doing pretty good, and might even make it to the local AA meeting that evening.

Having pulled out of the nosedive, she was determined to stay busy cleaning the house, planning out her schedule for the coming week and stocking up the refrigerator with groceries. She even began organizing the garage, something she put off doing ever since Sherman moved out years ago. Her ex-husband drove up as she wheeled out the second can of junk for the garbage men to pick up Monday morning.

"Looking good, Cassie! I'm impressed." Sherman greeted her, as he climbed out of his truck.

"I warned you long ago that I would clean out this crap." She brushed off her hands, smiled and actually shook his hand. Something she hadn't done in a long time.

"Well, just keep your eyes open for my High School yearbook. That's the only thing I haven't found, that I wouldn't mind having."

"Sure, I'll let you know if I see it," Cassie replied, suppressing a guilty twinge. She wasn't about to tell him what really happened to it. That was a long time ago. "So what brings you by?"

"Do you have a few minutes? I wanted to tell you something in person, without you hearing it second hand."

Cassie gestured for him to go ahead.

"Well, you know, Lauren and I have been seeing each other for quite a while, and during that time she and I have had our ups and downs. And occasionally, during some of those downs, you and I brought up the idea of possibly getting back together."

"You have to admit that you brought it up at least as many times as I did," Cassie laughed. "So, are you saying you want me to haul this stuff back in?"

"Look—there's no easy way to say this, Cassie. So I won't beat around the bush. Lauren and I have decided to get married."

The room spun around Cassie, and she leaned against the workbench, tightening down on herself. And trying to remember how to breathe. "That's great. I hope you're happy."

"Thanks, Cassie. I wanted to come tell you myself, because I didn't want you to be blind-sided. I owe you at least that much."

"Yes, I do appreciate that, Sherman. Look, I've still got a lot to do here, so..." Using a broomhandle to keep herself steady, Cassie led Sherman out of the garage.

"How is Demie doing? I was hoping to see her."

"She's doing fine, but you know, this really isn't a good time right now. Let's talk sometime, okay?"

"Sure, I understand." Cassie stood watching him as he walked back to his vehicle, and drove away.

Then she walked into the kitchen to retrieve her purse, went to her car and settled behind the wheel. Watching herself as if on TV, Cassie started the vehicle up and backed out of the driveway. Fifteen minutes later, she returned with a brown paper sack.

This time, when she pulled the bottle of Crown Royal out of the bag and poured some into a glass of coke and ice, she didn't hesitate. After draining the first glass in one long gulp, she re-filled it and went to the living room.

Cassie took a sip this time, and closed her eyes as she let the liquid pleasure swirl in her mouth, before she swallowed. Shivers swept over her. How hard she fought against this moment, how painful at times it had been to turn away. And yet, how easy it had been.

Giving in felt so good, she almost wept. Not because of the drink itself, but because she wouldn't have to fight any more. She took another swallow and felt release slide down her throat and into her stomach.

Cassie was unaware that, by the time she finished her fourth glass and faded into a dreamless sleep on the couch, Demie's drip bag was completely empty.

Demie was disgusted. She vowed she would never take Yudhishthira to Vegas. Not only did the fool refuse to stop, he somehow managed to lose every time he threw the dice.

They had accompanied Yudhishthira to this place, in Hastinpura. This was a full city, larger than Kampilya or any settlement Demie had seen. There were actual lines waiting to get into some of the shops they passed by. Like the other towns, the palace entrance was at the end of a street, just off the central square, and that was where Chandar re-joined them.

The inner courtyard was larger and busier than the one in Krivi, and Demie got nervous when she saw guards at every doorway. But the bouncers ignored them and the group threaded their way upstairs, into a hall as big as the gymnasium at school.

Yudhishthira and some other dude got into a boring discussion, then they sat down and started throwing dice. She didn't need to watch the world's worst gambler in action, plus she was starting to feel queasy for some reason. Yudhisthira's game playing would make anyone sick.

Chandar was working his way around the room, opening every box and drawer and poking into every cubbyhole he could find. That was certainly rude, but their hosts didn't seem to mind, so she went over to see what he was getting into.

"Did you find anything?" She asked.

He closed the doors on some sort of curio cabinet, and flashed one of those vending machine displays, with several bottles, a couple of sticks and some gems.

"Take these. I'll hold onto the other things until I figure out what they are for."

Demie touched the items and they all vanished into her magical purse. It was weird but she was getting used to how things worked in this world.

"How do I look, Chandar?"

The amazon warrior that Chandar controlled turned to look before responding, "No different, why?"

"I'm feeling really dizzy, and just wondered if I'm fading or something." She also felt a strong need to throw up, and that kind of scared her because how did someone throw up in a world where no one ate anything? That was when Draupadi called for help.

"Demie, you have to stop him!"

The princess stood at the gaming table, next to Yudhishthira, and what Demie saw made her forget about her non-existent stomach. The Bhima brother was being tied up, and by the time Demie got there the other brothers were all tied up as well. She turned to Draupadi.

"Holy crap! What's going on?"

"My husband Yudhishthira has wagered all his possessions, all of our lands and wealth and lost it all. With nothing else to wager, he has staked his brothers and lost them as well. Now he wagers himself."

"That's crazy, get him to stop! There are groups that can help with this kind of problem. My dad's best friend had a gambling addiction and they..."

Draupadi turned to Demie. "You don't understand, there are rules of honor that someone of his position must follow. He has no choice."

"Yeah, that's what they all say." Demie stepped forward so she could watch.

Behind the princess, Yudhishthira threw his dice and Demie observed something she hadn't seen before. As with the messages she noticed in Krivi, when the dice hit the table a faint, brief flash of light enveloped them, changing what would have been a 'good' throw into a 'bad' one. Someone was cheating her friends here, and no one pulled a con over on her bestie.

Demie sidled closer to the table and examined the dice as they lay on the table. She didn't understand the rules for the game, but the dice had small handles similar to the tether she felt while 'pulling.' She might not even have to touch them if she extended a push from her hand, kind of like extending an aura. Trying her idea out, she waved her palm toward the dice and willed a nudge, then one of the cubes flipped over. She was about to try again when she heard Draupadi cry out.

"No! Please, good my lord, not that! Surely there must be something else?"

Draupadi dropped to her knees before Yudhishthira, but he was already reaching for the dice.

"What is it?" asked Demie. Now what had Draupadi's loser husband done?

"He has wagered me, and if he loses, I will be property of the Kurus."

Already Yudhishthira was shaking the dice and preparing to cast them. Demie tensed up, because there was a lot more than a softball game at stake here, literally. Too bad she didn't get a chance to practice a few times with the dice, but it looked like she would just get one shot. Fighting back a growing urge to vomit, she moved to clearly view the roll.

Fortunately she didn't have much time to get stressed. The small cubes flew across the table, and started to drop into a winning combination. Just like before, a short flash of light shifted the dice and they started to settle. Praying she got it right, Demie stretched her hand out and caused them to shift back into the original pattern, and held her hand out until they settled onto the table.

The music, the room, and everyone in it froze.

The light was fading, and so was Tony. After spending hours updating Kali's search parameters, night was coming on hard and fast in the canyon where his house clung to a hillside. The picture windows looked out over a pocket of untouched Southern California nature, and the open panes let in a cool, refreshing breeze.

After coming home from his volunteer stint at the inner city Big Brothers club, he set the mail in the kitchen, ignored the flashing answering machine and plunged into working on a problem that nagged him all week. It was a small glitch in the definitions, one that failed to recognize the difference between a Playable Character and a Non-Playable Character.

Not that it was likely to cause a problem, since only an NPC would have the signature Kali was hunting, but Tony liked his programming neat. And this would be fixed by Monday morning before anyone even noticed it. He was so deeply engrossed in comparing some lines of code, he almost jumped off his chair when his PDA pinged with an alert that one of the modules had crashed.

Since he was already logged in, Tony quickly shifted over to the primary controller for Panchala and found the crashed module. It was a small subroutine within the Hastinpura server, and a relatively advanced story line that was unlikely to have any customer activity this soon after opening Panchala.

Tony let out a sigh of relief. That would be easy to fix, because he could just shut down and re-start the module by stopping the services on one virtual server. Opening the console management program, Tony accessed the virtual server, and started bouncing the services.

Demie was ready to have a nuclear freak out. She wanted to run, fast and hard, because the last time she saw the world freeze, people vanished. This time she was inside the frozen area, and she had absolutely no need to find out where Bhishma the shopkeeper went. Not at all.

She could move, but her motions were sluggish, as if moving through a pool of syrup. Chandar was the only other one moving, so she shouted at him while shoving on Draupadi as hard as she could to try and wake her up.

"Hurry, Chandar! We have to get out fast. Please, help get these guys going!"

Draupadi woke up, and Demie moved on to the brothers. As she pushed each one, the ropes slipped off their arms and she began herding them toward the stairs, pushing and shoving for all she was worth.

"The passage is shrinking or something," Chandar called from the doorway. "I got it open, but it keeps trying to close. So hurry through."

Sahadeva was the first one there, and Demie tried to push him through. Instead of going, he insisted on holding the opening and she wanted to scream.

"It is my brother's fault that we are here," Sahadeva said. "I will help hold this doorway until all have passed through."

"Fine, whatever," Demie replied as she and Sahadeva held the sides of the portals with their bodies. Chandar popped through, followed by Draupadi and the other Pandavas.

Then Demie stepped through, and turned to hold the opening for Sahadeva.

Chandar was trying to push people down those stupid stairs so they could make room for the ones still coming through. What the hell was Demie doing in there? If that dedicated instance area collapsed before she got out, there was no telling what might happen to her. Didn't she realize she could die, for real?

She still hadn't emerged, when he heard a knock on his door and his parents stepped into the room.

"Did you have a good time this evening with Sanjali?" his father asked.

"Uh, yeah, I did. She's really nice." Chandar nodded enthusiastically as he faced them, before his eyes drifted back toward the screen.

His mother spoke up, "I believe she likes you as well."

"Yeah, I think you're right." Every time they met with Sanjali and her parents, they had this conversation, and Chandar learned to just agree with whatever his folks said. Out of the corner of his eye he saw that Demie started to step through, but then she turned around and stepped back. Was she nuts?

"So," asked his father, "Do you think she is someone you would like to marry?"

"Sure, why not?" Chandar tossed back. Demie came partway through now, but stood within the portal, arguing with Sahadeva. Why didn't she just get the heck through?

His mother chimed in, "So should we go ahead and ask about it next week?"

"Yeah, I'd really like that." He wouldn't mind seeing Sanjali again next week. Just so long as he didn't have a date with Sierra at the same time.

Demie finally jumped through the portal, and Chandar let out a sigh of relief as he started leading the party out into the courtyard. So he didn't hear his father, as the bedroom door closed.

"Let's call her parents and schedule the wedding."

CHAPTER THIRTEEN

Draupadi felt deep stirrings of wanting to run as she followed Samita the warrior through the portal, then helped her friend Demie pull the Pandavas through. The concealed-knowing within recognized that her husbands were waking up, but they were still not as awake as she was.

One by one they came through, and she pushed each toward Samita. But without any clear direction, the brothers tried to gather around her and blocked the passageway. Finally, she had to leave Demie at the opening and moved toward Samita, and then the warrior was able to pull the group down the stairs.

Draupadi felt a tight grip inside her chest and stomach as she started back to the portal, where Demie and Sahadeva struggled to keep the doorway open.

"Let's go through together," Demie urged Sahadeva.

He shook his head, "The opening is now hardly large enough for one. I could not live with my dishonor if I passed through before you."

"Suit yourself," Demie yelled, stepped through and turned. The doorway shimmered as Sahadeva came through, then Draupadi screamed when the opening closed with a snap on her husband's upper torso. Only his right arm, shoulder and head made it through to their side of the doorway.

"No!" Draupadi cried. She grabbed her husband's arm, pulling with all her strength.

"There is no sacrifice I would not gladly make for you," he said. "My only regret, beloved Draupadi, is that I could not do more to protect you." Then, as he squeezed her hand, the portal vanished, along with Sahadeva. Only a featureless gray wall remained.

The princess dropped to her knees, "Sahadeva! He is gone!" All thought, all feeling emptied out of her.

"I know. I'm so sorry," Demie said, as she placed her hand on Draupadi's shoulder.

"Such wrongness. Such wrongness. What am I to do?" She looked up at her friend.

Demie pulled Draupadi to her feet and turned her toward the stairs. "What you do, is we get your husbands the heck out of here. We'll remember him later, but not now."

Draupadi looked down the stairs, as Nakula moved into the courtyard. She felt empty inside, but hurried to join the others in the square outside. Samita gathered the remaining Pandavas together, but Demie was nowhere about. Draupadi again felt tightness inside, then it eased when she saw her friend slowly emerge from the palace entrance. But the tightness returned when she saw that Demie's movement was hindered by a great loss of vital life energy.

"Were you injured by the doorway that took Sahadeva away?" Draupadi asked.

"I don't think so," Demie replied. "I was feeling sick before that."

"Where shall we go?" Draupadi asked, as she applied a healing touch to her companion. The healing did not fail, but Demie's condition did not improve. She didn't know whether she could handle losing her friend too. "Whatever ails you, my good friend, is beyond my ability."

"You'll have to take charge," Demie told her. "It's all I can do just to walk."

"I will do that which I must," Draupadi promised her companion, then directed the remaining Pandava brothers to follow her. They fell in line without a word, and the courtyard guards ignored them as she led the group onto the streets of Hastinpura. After checking that Demie and Samita joined the end of the line, she considered how to exit the city itself.

Reaching into the concealed-knowing which led to the cave of weapons, she was surprised to find a drawing of the city streets. The city inhabitants ignored her troop as she guided them through the streets, and they passed unchallenged out into the countryside. Her injured friend moved even slower than before, so it took some time to return to the clearing where they encountered the horsemen, and then Draupadi turned west once more.

Two day cycles passed before they managed to cross over a range of hills because several times they ran into dead ends, and three times Draupadi sensed great danger lurking ahead, which they had to work their way around. On top of that, more than once Draupadi had to double back to look for Demie, just to find her frozen. Her friend called it sleep when the princess pushed Demie awake.

They started descending into a forest on the other side when Demie froze again, and this time the girl would not awaken. Draupadi felt a great tightness inside, because nothing in her concealed-knowing explained what to do and she didn't know what her friend needed. They couldn't go anywhere, so Draupadi gathered the group around Demie's form and waited.

While Demie remained frozen, Draupadi thought about Sahadeva. She felt a powerful rightness that she had no word for, toward each of the four brothers standing watch with her. Something connected her to each one, like an unseen rope or chain. And though Sahadeva was gone, she also still felt a rightness inside for him.

In fact, the rightness was now stronger than before, but unlike the others, she no longer felt that unseen chain connecting to him. Where Sahadeva's chain had once been, lay an emptiness every bit as deep and strong as the rightness. She didn't know what to do with that emptiness. Or how she would carry it another step.

Demie stirred and asked, "Where are we?"

Draupadi answered, "We have crossed the Kuru mountains, and shall continue west until we come to the Sarasvati, the great river that my people tell of. It brings life to the fields and animals, and there is no other river like it in the world. Then we follow the mighty river downstream until we come to the ancient city of Amaravati."

Demie indicated she was ready to continue, and Draupadi turned to her.

"My friend Demie, you are a wise person, almost a rishi. I am much troubled."

Demie made a strange noise Draupadi had not heard before, then responded, "Okay, if you say so. What is it?"

"It is about Sahadeva. Now that he is gone, there is such wrongness inside me. It makes me want to be gone, just as he is. What is this wrongness?"

Demie paused for a moment before she answered. "It's called grief. I felt that way once, when I lost someone very close to me."

"What can I do about it?"

"There's really nothing you can do. It does get better after a while, but it never completely goes away. My loss was a long time ago, but I still think about her every day."

Draupadi thought for a moment, then replied, "My good friend Demie, you truly are a rishi, for I do not understand your answer. Perhaps, in the fullness of time, I will find the wisdom of your words."

Demie did not respond, but simply stood up and indicated she was ready to continue.

Taking the lead as the Pandavas fell into place behind her, Draupadi wanted to do whatever she could for her friend, as they headed west once more. They descended through the forest, and eventually came across a trail that ran in the right direction. Although they came across other sojourners, they were well out of the land of the Kurus, so Draupadi stayed on the path, and soon her concealed-knowing told her they were near the river.

"We are about to come to the Sarasvati, Demie. It is quite unlike any river you have ever seen."

Then, the trail opened up to a huge expanse. Before them lay a huge, dry riverbed that stretched to their right and left, as far as they could see.

The one thing Chandar hated about online gaming were these mindless cross-country trips. So, after ensuring that Draupadi was leading them somewhere, though God only knew where, he set his character on auto-follow. Then he could just check occasionally to see if anything unexpected happened, or if they finally reached their destination.

While killing time, he decided to surf the internet. He was curious about something that his instructor mentioned about 'ghost limbs' in Philosophy class the previous semester, which might be related to Demie's problem. Sometimes after having a limb amputated, patients still felt sensations even though the limb was gone.

A search on 'ghost limbs' came back with hundreds of thousands of hits. The chaotic mess of responses frustrated him, but after opening a few pages, he figured out the key words needed to refine his search and eliminate junk responses such as rock bands, movie references and artistic references to poetry and paintings. Still a daunting list of results. He then filtered out the medical references that required several years of medical school to understand.

After confirming that the party was still wandering through some jungle, Chandar went back to the search results and read through a number of pages with yoga and Tibetan references. Those looked really interesting, so he bookmarked them and then started reading through blogs by people with personal experiences.

Time and again, they kept referring to a specific doctor doing research on the subject. A doctor in some European country.

Another check on the party, and then Chandar ran a search on that researcher. Much to his delight, among the first hits was a page describing a free, public lecture: "The Reality Of Ghost Limbs." The only problem was that although the lecture was still two months away, it would be in New York City.

And Chandar had no way to get there.

Cassie clenched her teeth as she buried her head deeper in the pillows, trying to shut out the hammer that kept pounding on the back of her head. There it was again, 'Bang, bang, bang.' Then her brain was split by the sound of piercing chimes, and she groaned. Someone ringing the doorbell. Slowly, she pulled herself up, and when the pounding on the front door resumed, she was ready to pound on someone herself.

"Okay, I'm coming. Just hang on a minute," she shouted as she shuffled to the front door, and glanced at her clock. It was only 8:10 in the morning. When she opened the door, one of the two nurses who took turns coming by every morning glared at her, and started making a comment about knocking for five minutes. Without a word, Cassie left the door open and walked back to the kitchen.

It had been years since she'd had a drink, but she was sure she could scrounge something up to deal with a killer hangover. She was just in the process of opening a can of V8 to wash down some ibuprofen, when Nurse Nightingale stormed into the kitchen.

"What the hell is wrong with you! When did you last check on her?"

Cassie simply stared at the unexpected assault, and shook her head. Instant white-hot pain split through her forehead, and Cassie moaned as she closed her eyes.

"You just come with me. I want you to see this."

Barely restraining herself from ripping the nurse's face off, Cassie followed the woman into Demie's room, and the odor of unchanged diaper assaulted her. While the nurse cleaned Demie, she berated Cassie for letting the drip bag go dry overnight, not changing the diaper and not shifting Demie's body. Cassie pretended to listen, since that was the least painful option.

Then, just as the nurse was winding down, the doorbell rang again and Cassie answered the door to find Sherman. She followed him back into the den and the moment the nurse saw him, she proceeded to launch once more into her lecture.

"Do something useful, and get rid of this," the RN said as she handed an overflowing diaper to Cassie.

The sight, in addition to the smell, pushed Cassie over the edge and she cursed as she dropped the bundle on the carpet and raced to the bathroom, then knelt on the tiled floor while her guts heaved. After rinsing her mouth out, and stopping in the kitchen for some more ibuprofen to replace the ones her stomach rejected, Cassie stumbled back to the living room couch, where she stretched out in a barely controlled collapse.

The world finally stopped spinning, and Cassie dozed off. Until Sherman roused her with some nudges on the shoulder.

"So," he said, holding the half-empty bottle. "It's this again? How long has this been going on?"

Cassie weakly waved him away. "Last night was the first time. I was celebrating your good news."

He stared at her, "Don't do this to yourself again. If not for your sake, then for Demie's. Get some help if you need to, but pull yourself together. I'll talk to you later."

Cassie watched him head out of the room, taking the bottle with him, and flipped off his retreating backside. When she heard the front door open and close, she turned over, pulled a pillow over her head and faded back into sleep.

Afternoon light was streaming through the living room window when she woke again. Pulling herself up, Cassie was greatly relieved to find that Nurse Nightingale had left, then went to the kitchen where she retrieved the bottle Sherman missed.

She dumped some ice in a glass, then took cola and the Crown Royal out onto her back porch. Every time the glass was about half empty, she refilled it and by the third or fourth refill, the world felt right again. She still hadn't gotten back to that warm glow she felt the night before, but she had the rest of the afternoon to get there. Cassie closed her eyes, sat back and let the warmth of the sunlight complement the warmth in her stomach.

So she didn't notice Chandar watching from next door.

Demie stood at the edge of a barren riverbed. She wasn't sure whether she was more surprised or disappointed, but the view reminded her of the time Dad took her camping in the desert and explained about flash floods. The biggest flash flood in the world must have happened here.

"I have to admit, Draupadi, you're right. I've never seen a river like this."

Draupadi stepped down into the riverbed, as if to confirm that it was actually dry. "I do not understand. This was not in my knowing."

"So does this mean we're not going to wait for a barge?" commented Demie.

"My friend Demie, what would it serve us to wait? There is no water to carry a barge."

"Never mind." Demie was going to have to work with the princess on developing a sense of humor. "Which way to your city?"

Draupadi moved further out onto the riverbed and turned left. "This way."

"Ah, so we're going downstream?" Demie said, then hastily added, "Yes, I know, there is no stream."

As the group clambered down to join Draupadi in the riverbed, Demie was surprised to get a message from Chandar. She'd almost forgotten he was in the party.

"I found something interesting on the internet. There's a doctor who has done some research on ghost limbs and he..."

"Now hold on," interrupted Demie, feeling heat rise within. "I'm not a ghost!"

"Then what are you? Maybe your body is still alive, but you're not in it, are you?"

"That's really creepy. Maybe I am part ghost, but I don't like that word. Don't use it."

"Okay," Chandar conceded. "So anyway this doctor says that patients can connect with gh..., um, missing limbs through a process he is experimenting with."

"Have you talked to him?"

Chandar paused before responding. "Not yet. I'll have to work on that."

"What about my mom? Have you said anything to her?" This whole process of contacting her mom was taking far too long, and Demie was starting to get worried.

Again, Chandar paused, "She was in your backyard this afternoon, so I thought about going over there to talk with her and, you know, see where it went. But it didn't look like a good time, cause she was kinda drinking and..."

"What!" Demie actually stopped, stunned. "No way, my mom doesn't drink."

Chandar paused again, which was starting to annoy Demie. "Unless she makes iced tea in a booze bottle, she was definitely drinking."

"That doesn't sound right. You've got to talk to her now!"

"I'll see. Look, I'm setting Samita back on auto-follow, so I can do some more searching on the internet. Will check back soon." Then Chandar was gone, leaving Demie alone, with her thoughts racing after her fears.

Even before the lightning incident, her memories of the before-time with Kori were already fading, but Demie was pretty sure Old Mom never had a drinking problem. During the three years that Demie lived in a Kori-less world, she heard vague references that New Mom struggled with drinking at one point, and it may have even contributed to the divorce. But her mother regularly went to AA, and never touched a drink. Heck, Mom never even took cough syrup because of the alcohol.

So if she really had started drinking, something was really bad.

She was so lost in thought she didn't pay attention to how far they traveled down the riverbed, but eventually Demie needed to take another break. Maybe not really sleep, but some sort of rest.

"I have to take a break," Demie sent to Draupadi.

Turning, the princess replied, "This is not an auspicious place for you to freeze."

"Please, just for a little while." Demie pleaded. More often than not, Draupadi made no sense at all. The middle of the riverbed didn't seem very suspicious, nor was it cold. But Demie definitely did need to stop.

While the princess rounded up the troops, Demie sat on a half-buried log and tried to relax. Sensei sometimes had her do something he called meditation, where she took deep breaths and then slowly released them, while letting things fade away. She didn't really breathe in this world, but she could certainly imagine herself breathing.

Demie relaxed and imagined the breathing exercise, just like focusing her chi. She pictured the rabbit at the pet store, where she stopped on the way home from school...the storeowner explaining that bunnies were basically mute, which was when she decided she needed one...petting the soft brown fur...Demie reached a restful state.

Then her mind snapped like a whip back to the riverbed, jarred by a loud bestial roar.

Demie jumped up as she saw a glowing, blue furry alien with four arms and a long tail race into the middle of her group. It roared again, swung a couple of wicked swords, and came straight at her.

Tony got up early on Monday mornings, so he could beat the morning traffic, but that was getting harder to do. It wasn't so much a question of whether it would be bad, but rather bad, worse or really awful. The traffic this morning was just bad, so Tony had plenty of time to upload his updated version of Kali before his team arrived.

Still, he was somewhat surprised when Karen came in unusually early, while he was in the midst of reviewing logs for the Hastinpura module that he re-booted the night before.

"How's it going?" She asked as she settled into her workspace.

"It's going," Tony replied, "It's just not going away."

"It will, sooner or later," Karen responded, as she logged into her systems.

Tony turned back to the Hastinpura logs. The sequence of error codes indicated a continuity problem. The module was supposed to interact with certain NPC game characters, following a set storyline. These characters came into the module as expected, but from a later part of the story line rather than earlier. It was like putting page 100 before page 50 in a book, then trying to make sense of it.

Because the module couldn't make sense of the parameters, something changed the programmed outcome. Then the result exceeded the capacity of the artificial intelligence to adapt the storyline. As Tony examined exactly where the continuity broke, Karen gave a loud whoop.

"Yes! Yes!" she said, as she locked her keyboard and stood up. Obviously she found something important, and he gave her a questioning glance as she gathered her belongings. But she ignored him and left, looking like she had just won the lottery. He'd follow up with her later.

Eventually, Tony came to the conclusion that the logs must've been damaged, because what they claimed simply was not possible. That was when Frank Beck's secretary called him.

The CEO wanted Tony, now.

Demie felt panic rise within her, as she barely grabbed her own sword in time to fend off the first blow. She prepared to parry the creature's next attack, when something dashed in front of her. One of Draupadi's husbands, Bhima.

Wielding that ginormous club, he smacked the alien right in the middle with a mighty blow. Demie expected the monster to fly back and started to run forward. Instead, she yelped and jumped aside, as it came to a dead stop and turned toward Bhima.

Whipping that small tree trunk around faster than should have been possible, Bhima hollered a challenge as he struck again, "Foul creature! I will rip off your limbs and feed them to you one by one."

On the other side of the alien, Arjuna notched an arrow in his bow and loosed a series of bolts, while Draupadi landed some kicks on the creature's back. Then, the fiend dropped his swords and jumped onto Bhima, wrapping him in a bear hug on the ground.

Wondering how long Bhima would last, Demie joined the remaining brothers and Draupadi as they all swarmed over the critter with their weapons, and a flurry of flashing swords swung up and down onto the thing. Until, with a loud cry, it rolled over and started fading.

As it did, Demie felt a rush of energy, similar to but much stronger than the energy drink feeling she got from taking out those rabid rabbits.

Turning to Draupadi, she asked, "What the hell was that?"

"That, my friend Demie, was a rakshasa. An evil spirit that was protecting the river."

"Well, it obviously didn't do a very good job."

Draupadi reached down to where the rakshasa had fallen and picked up a scroll, then said they needed to continue. "We are nearly there. That is why the rakshasa attacked us."

When they reformed their marching order, Demie was still thinking about her mother and feeling lonely as she moved up to the front of the party to join Draupadi. They proceeded in the direction that would have been downstream, and the riverbed began to drop into a gorge, so Draupadi led them to the far bank and up the hillside. Then they continued downstream along the ridge.

"Tell me what you know about this ancient city of yours," Demie asked.

"Amaravati is the capital of my ancestors, and it was a center of great learning for many thousands of years. Countless ships came across the great sea to trade goods, and caravans from far lands traveled thousands of miles to barter with us. The number of people in Amaravati are too many to be counted, like sand upon the beach."

As they walked, Draupadi waxed on about the splendor of the city her people built, and Demie started feeling like she was in a history class. She kept glancing over the side, noting that the gorge continued to deepen until it appeared to be hundreds of feet deep.

"All languages share a common root, and that tap root of humanity leads back to the civilization and city of my people: Amaravati, the greatest city the ancient world has ever known."

They came around a bend, and Draupadi stopped talking. They all stood in silence at the edge of a precipice, where the mesa they stood on dropped sharply down to a plain that stretched into the distance.

Below, the riverbed emerged from the gorge and extended across the plain. On one side of the dry river lay a maze of broken walls, crumbled towers and piles of rubble. Nothing moved among the scattered trees and bushes that had taken over and found a foothold in the shifting sand that half buried the plain.

Demie looked out over the greatest ruins the ancient world ever knew.

CHAPTER FOURTEEN

Cassie finished tucking in the sheet and stepped back, quite pleased with herself. So what if it was a little crooked? She completed the evening checklist and felt good. It didn't really matter that her headache prevented her from changing the bedding. It took some work but she managed to slide a clean sheet on top of the dirty one. That would make laundry easier, because then she could wash them all at the same time.

Before turning off the lights, she checked the drip bag once more and ensured it was full. After the rude way that Gestapo nurse talked to her that morning, she had some suggestions for what the nurse could do with her drip tubes and would be happy to help implement them.

Cassie strolled out to the living room where her drink waited and picked up the cold, smooth glass. She relished the soft clink of ice cubes on glass, as well as the feel and taste of the drink. She was savoring a third sip, when someone knocked on the door.

What the hell? She damn well hadn't invited anyone over. Debating whether or not to leave the drink behind, Cassie decided to take it with her and lurched to her feet, then navigated to the front entrance. Swinging the door open, she found Lauren standing there. Her personal nightmare come to life.

Cassie slammed the door closed on the nightmare and walked away.

Until the doorbell rang again, and Cassie re-opened the door.

Lauren still stood there, looking like she was ready to rip Cassie's head off.

"Oh, I'm sorry." Cassie leaned against the door for stability. She wasn't really sorry, but she was dead tired. "I thought I was just imagining things. Whatcha want?"

Lauren shifted toward the door, as if to make sure it stayed open. "Sherman asked me to come by and check on Demie."

"More like check on me. Right?"

"You don't have to be like this. He's just concerned. We're both concerned."

"How very touching. Sure, go ahead and check. You know where to find her." Cassie reluctantly stepped back and let Lauren in, before closing the front door and following Lauren into the den. Hopefully, the woman would just be quick so Cassie could get the hell off her feet.

While Lauren checked the drip bag and tubing, Cassie noticed the trash bag containing old diapers and bags. She meant to take that out earlier. As Lauren ran through the daily checklist, Cassie used her foot to nudge the bag under the desk, and started to fall over as she lost her balance.

Lauren sighed and turned back to Cassie.

"Satisfied?" Cassie smugly asked.

Lifting up the top sheet, Lauren pointed to the stained sheet underneath. "You're kidding, right?"

"I was in a hurry." Cassie shrugged, "So what? She's clean, and she's on a clean sheet." Cassie headed back toward the kitchen with a dismissive wave of her hand; there was just no pleasing some people.

"In a hurry?" Lauren followed her into the hallway. "To get back to, what is it now? Jack Daniels? Smirnoff?"

Cassie wheeled on her unwelcome visitor. "I'm going Canadian, not that it's any of your business. Crown Royal."

"Cassie, what are you doing? You have responsibilities here."

Cassie pointed at Lauren with her free hand. "I don't need you, of all people, to tell me what my responsibilities are. You, with your happy little world, and your happy little husband to be. That is, if you can keep him."

"I'll keep him. Unlike you, I won't burn my own house down and then wonder why I'm standing out in the cold."

Without thinking, Cassie flung her glass at Lauren; it passed over the woman's shoulder and smashed on the wall at the end of the hall. "You've seen Demie. She's okay. Get out of my house. Now."

The whore didn't even flinch. She just stared at Cassie for a few seconds, then slowly, without a word, walked to the front door and let herself out. Cassie looked at the broken glass at the far end of the hall, then went into the kitchen to get a new one. She'd have to clean things up in the morning.

Seated back in the living room, Cassie thought about where her life had gone. Once she had all the things that were supposed to make someone happy. A husband and family, a home, a good job. Then, bit by bit, a gnawing discontent devoured all those pieces. But even when it was down to just her and Demie, she at least had some core of meaning to hang onto.

But now, even that buttress had become an anchor, wrapped around her, dragging her deep under the water of her despair. This latest development with Sherman and Lauren's marriage cast the hollowness of Cassie's life in stark relief.

That was as much honesty as she could face, and Cassie headed into the kitchen to refill her glass. But when she tipped the bottle, it was as empty as her existence had become.

Draupadi stood looking at the ruins of Amaravati. A growing not-rightness inside confirmed that, although the city was not as she expected it to be, this was the right place. The rishi they searched for was down there somewhere. But that knowing mixed with other knowings, and the chaotic swell confused her.

A knowing that she had absolutely no clue where they were going. A growing awareness that the world around her was changing, it was not right. The sense that she was much more than what even she herself thought she was. She didn't understand where these knowings came from, which caused a desire to just run, somewhere, in any direction. A stirring of what must be the thing called fear.

She longed to talk with the rishi that was down there, somewhere in what remained of the city below her. Draupadi turned to her companions and said, "Come, what we seek is down there."

They continued along the ridge until they found a trail down the hillside, and after some time the stirring she called fear slowly faded. Soon after reaching level ground, they passed the first crumbled walls of the ruins. Up close, the walls were the main sign that humans once lived here, and they ranged from waist-high mounds of rubble to relatively intact stretches of wall reaching above their heads. But everywhere, sand had moved in and taken over, creating a timeless blanket covering everything. This was not what her concealed-knowing led her to expect.

Just within the outer walls, they came across a doorway in one of the partially standing buildings, and Draupadi turned to enter the shell of a roofless dwelling. In one corner were the remains of a table, which had been split apart by force. Next to it lay a mound of rubble, mostly shattered pottery and wood which sand had not quite covered.

The pile of rubble appeared to cover something, and she bent down to examine what looked like human bones. They could've lain there for 100 years or 10,000, and her knowing gave no clue.

"So what is it we're looking for?" asked Demie from the next structure.

"We seek the great rishi, who has wisdom and knowledge like that of the gods."

"Nothing like that in there," Demie said as she joined the group. "What does a rishi look like, anyway?"

"He'll be dressed as am I, only worse."

"Nice," Demie replied.

"No," Draupadi corrected, "Not nice, worse."

"Never mind," Demie said as she exited the building.

Draupadi went back out into the street, and turned deeper into the ruins.

Following what had to be a street, mostly because it was relatively clear of debris, she followed the roadway until it branched. Examining both directions, she noticed tracks in the sand, which could've been made by a bird or lizard. Except these tracks were as wide as her shoulders. Her knowing did not speak of the footprints, and that caused great uneasiness inside.

Saying nothing about the tracks, she turned toward a street that led further into the city, then saw a flash of movement from the other direction. She carefully watched, but nothing moved again, so she decided it was a sign calling her to go that way instead.

Time and again they came to intersections, and each time

Draupadi saw a hint of movement in one direction or the other that led her toward what she sensed was the center of the city. As they pushed deeper, they found strange markings on the walls; swirls and lines that held some kind of meaning, even if they couldn't tell what it was. And the deeper they went into the city, the deeper her uneasiness grew.

Eventually they came to an intersection with a small park in the middle of the junction. The space was enclosed by a low wall, and the strange markings were etched on all sides. An arm and head towered above the debris, the remains of a statue.

As they circled the small park and Draupadi waited for a sign to indicate which road to take, Demie came up to her.

"I don't think we are the only ones looking for this rishi dude."

"Why do you say that?" asked Draupadi.

"I just looked back at the hill we came down, and saw someone running down it."

Whatever guide brought them thus far, now failed to reveal the next branch. Draupadi had to choose, but felt torn both ways. So she led the group down the largest street, which appeared to open onto a large square in the center of the city.

Draupadi halted at the end of the street, where they could see clearly into the square. The open space spanned several hundred feet on each side, and the center held what remained of a huge fountain, filled with rubble and stagnant water. Around the water danced at least a hundred armored creatures twice as tall as a human, with horns, tails, wings and crow-like feet.

The dancers encircled the decayed waterworks, moving in unison as they chanted. They took turns swinging enormous clubs at the remaining stonework of the fountain, breaking it apart and splashing the water. Several creatures used stones to chisel glyphs onto the pedestal of the fountain, identical to the writing throughout the ruins. They were so absorbed in their activity, they didn't notice the small group of humans at the edge of the square.

Except the one walking directly toward them.

Chandar came in the front door, dropped his backpack in the corner and headed for his room, until Maa gave him that disproving look. He tried not to show how tired he was as he shuffled back to retrieve his pack, and then Baba called to him from the living room.

"Son, we need to talk."

Chandar groaned, "Oh, Baba, can we talk later? I had a hard day at school today."

"This is most important. You may rest after we talk."

By the time Chandar got to the living room, Maa was already sitting next to his father, both watching as he sat. He sucked in his breath, because they only sat like that for big announcements. They better not be selling the house and moving to India!

His father started in, "You will be so happy, we have the most wonderful news. We have talked about this many times, and our whole family has long waited for this day. Your Aunt Goshi has probably told everyone in Bangalore by now."

Oh God. Chandar sank deeper into the couch. It was true, they were moving back to that overcrowded country his parents came from. It was bad enough that he had to visit every year, but it was their land, not his. And he really needed to start getting ready for his date with Sierra tonight, after she got off work. He was already running late, even without this talk.

Maa prodded Baba. "Go on, tell the boy. Can't you see how excited he is?"

"Chandar, I know you will always remember this day, because I remember the day it happened for me." Maa prodded Baba again, and he continued. "Sanjali's parents called and said that she has agreed to marry you."

Chandar sat down, mouth dropping, while his parents beamed with joy glowing on their faces. At first, he was just relieved that they weren't moving to India. Then, what his father said gradually sank in. Along with the real meaning of the conversation the night before.

"Wow, Baba." Chandar smiled, there was nothing else he could do. "I don't know what to say." Especially to Sierra.

Baba turned to his wife, smiling. "Do you remember, how speechless I was too?"

She patted his hand. "Not for long, as I recall." Maa turned to Chandar. "Now here's the best part. I know this is very sudden, but they have agreed to have the wedding next month."

Chandar rose halfway off the couch. "What!? Next month, are you kidding me?"

Maa hugged her husband, "See, I told you he would be excited!"

"Yes, it is true." Baba looked at Chandar very seriously. "You'll be starting your new job soon, and although Sanjali still has two more years of school, she has a full scholarship, so that will present no financial hardship. Her family found a hall to rent, the Saturday after your finals. Aunt Goshi's travel service is already booking flights for half of Bangalore."

"But...I don't understand, why so soon? Aren't there some rituals and...you know." Chandar didn't really care about the ceremonies that were so important to his parents, but he needed to slow this down.

Maa leaned forward. "Sanjali's parents agreed that we could follow the traditions later and move forward with the wedding, considering the circumstances..." His mother stopped talking, and then slowly sat back.

Chandar stared at one silent parent and the other. He knew they weren't telling him something, and they didn't want to tell him. Finally, he couldn't stand it anymore and broke the ensuing silence. "Considering what circumstances, Maa? What are you talking about?"

His father looked down as Chandar's mother wrung her hands, then turned and quietly spoke to her husband. "You tell him. I can't." She turned away, looking off into another room, which might've been in another universe.

"Chandar, we are hurrying the marriage, because it is your mother's deepest wish to see you happily married, while she can. You see, we recently learned that she has cancer. The doctor isn't certain how long, but she only has months left."

Demie watched the oncoming creature with grave misgivings as she asked Draupadi, "What are those things?"

"They are daityas, a kind of demon."

"Just how bad is a daitya?"

"Even Bhima could not stand up to one by himself. As for the whole group of them, the gods together would be hard pressed to prevail."

That was exactly what Demie didn't want to hear, as the daitya had clearly seen them and was walking straight toward them, waving an enormous club with spiked nails as big as her arm. Demie couldn't tell whether this was a he- or a she-thing, but she could never tell with rhinos either. Which gave her an idea. Not a good one, but it was all she had.

"Take everyone back to that park, and put people on all corners of the square. When I get there, you'll know what to do." The demon was getting closer, and they could hear a snake-like hissing as it flicked a long, black forked tongue at them. At least so far, it didn't look like any of the others had noticed them yet.

"Go," Demie pushed Draupadi back down the street. "Go, go, GO!"

Draupadi took off down the street, and Demie turned back toward the demon. It was now about twenty feet away and the thing was actually hopping like some sort of bird. A pretty fast hop at that, and that filled Demie with cold fear.

Demie carefully backed down the street a short ways, keeping herself between the daitya and the retreating party. She learned the hard way from messing around with rhinos, that it was best to start this little game well out of the view of the other nasties. When she felt her position was as good as she was going to get, she readied her sword and let it close.

Taking a swing, she connected with a solid hit just as the thing whipped that club around, and its blow sent her flying against the side of the building. She never saw something move that fast, and the attack shook her senses and rattled her more than any hit she had taken in this world. She might not be able to handle even one more of those.

She felt another strike coming, and only her unusual speed enabled her to roll to the side and somehow miraculously dodge it. She was already racing down the street when the club smashed into the wall where she had just been. Time to get the hell out of there.

The thing screeched, sounding like a cross between a dying cat and a rabid eagle, then started hopping after her. Normally she had to slow way down when pulling, but this son of a demon was fast! Rather than trying to stay close, she had to make sure she didn't stumble or run into any obstacles. This thing was hot on her heels.

She reached the end of the long street and shot into the small square. The park lay directly ahead and Demie burst for it as hard as she could, desperately aiming for the partial statue. Hitting the top of the wall with a bound, she sprang for the head, and as she landed, jumped for the upraised limb.

Dangling from the top of the arm, her legs frantically flailed for something to push against as the demon climbed right up the statue after her. Demie was screaming as the Pandavas ran in from the corners and surrounded the daitya on all sides, landing ferocious blows. But not before the thing managed to hit Demie once more.

Her vision faded, but somehow she clung to the statue, until the static in her eyes and ears built up and she slowly began to slide down the arm, into unconsciousness. Demie was hoping the Pandavas were really as good as Draupadi seemed to think, when she felt the princess scramble up and press her hands against Demie. Suddenly, a cool spring of strength flowed into her body, and it felt so good it was like a religious experience.

Renewing her grip, Demie looked down to see the Pandavas holding their own, but not making much progress against the demon. Then, Chandar's character moved into action and advanced toward the daitya.

"Watch out, that's some kind of demon or something," she warned him.

"I know," he responded. "This baby needs a special weapon that will kill the undead spawn of hell. Lucky for you I have one."

The Samita-character reached over her back and whipped out a nasty-looking sword which appeared to be made of glass, with a brilliant green glow. Samita slipped in behind the demon and administered a tremendous blow to its backside. The thing shuddered and turned, but before it could get off more than a couple swings, Chandar finished off the demon.

"I'm glad you finally decided to join us," Demie said as she scrambled back down the rubble pile. She would've kissed him, except...Samita was just a girl avatar, and not really Chandar.

"I've been pretty busy lately. There's a lot going on."

Draupadi followed Demie down, and the princess did more of that hands-on stuff that made her stronger. Demie was going to stay closer to the princess from now on.

"Well, as you see, we've been pretty busy too. Did you talk to my mom yet?"

"Not yet. This really isn't a good time for me."

"Look, just do it. I need to tell her...holy crap." Behind Chandar, Demie saw the one thing that scared her more than one of those daitya things, running up the street.

Entering the park intersection, racing straight toward her, was that Kali thing.

Tony slowly put the phone handset down and stared at his phone as he slumped into his chair. Frank's secretary didn't say what the meeting was about, nor whether he needed to bring anything. Just that he better be in Frank's office in five minutes.

Which left Tony just enough time to call a couple of other project leads to see if they knew what was going on, but no one answered. That in itself was ominous. He couldn't put it off any longer. Standing up and taking a deep breath, he told Joachim and Carolyn he was going into a meeting, and asked that they let Karen know when she got back.

On the way, he made a quick stop in the washroom to splash his face and that helped him gather his thoughts. When he came out, Karen was heading into the ladies room, and she gave him a big smile as she passed through the door. The fact that she was so happy surprised him as much as it worried him.

Tony walked up, and the secretary waved him on in with a neutral look that had pity written all over it. The door to the CEO's office was ajar, and as Tony entered, Frank Beck gestured for him to sit.

For a couple minutes, Frank simply looked at him without a word. Just studying him, it seemed, like some kind of abstract painting. Unable to take it any longer, Tony opened his mouth to say something, when Frank narrowed his eyes and barked a question.

"Do you think it's important to trust your team?"

"Absolutely." Tony wondered what the hell they could have done. "I have complete faith in my team, and I know that we have some of the best contract resources under us."

"I'm glad to hear that. But I'm talking about my team, the people I have to trust to get things done, and to be honest with me. You are one of those people, Tony."

"Of course, I know what you mean."

"The problem is that I don't trust you now." Frank let that sit for a few seconds before continuing. "I understand that you've been covering up some critical mistakes, and hiding the facts."

Tony sat, nodding. He knew he had just gotten run over by something, he just wasn't certain what it was, yet. But he had a pretty good idea who the driver was.

"You are one of the best designers that ever walked these halls, which is the only reason I don't have a security guard standing behind you with a box."

Tony couldn't help glancing over his shoulder. No one standing there.

"I'd rather not make any changes at this point in your team, considering the complexity of your project. But if for one minute I think you are hiding any more programming mistakes from me, you're going to spend the next year running backups on the night shift. Is that clear?"

"Yes sir." At least, the part about running backups was clear.

Frank gestured that he was done, and Tony silently rose and left the room. The secretary looked at him with one raised eyebrow, then turned back at her monitor.

Karen was at her desk when Tony got back to his office, and he went over to see what she was up to. She saw him coming and glanced over her shoulder, and then returned to studying her monitor. Whatever just happened to him, had Karen's name written all over it.

"I logged in to see what Kali was up to. It has acquired another target and it seems to be another Player Character. But all we can do is monitor the program now."

"What do you mean?" Tony asked. "We can't let it keep attacking Player Characters."

Karen swiveled her chair around to face Tony. "You don't understand, we don't have any option. We've lost control of Kali."

CHAPTER FIFTEEN

Demie jammed the cold fear rising from her stomach back down, and readied her sword. Kali raced across the square, a mass of black disheveled hair streaming behind the ebony goddess. Ruby red eyes fixed on Demie, as the ebony giant bore down with a curved samurai-like sword in a left hand, and a massive trident on the right. Demie braced for the attack as Chandar stepped up beside her.

"Maybe I'll join the fun this time," Chandar said. "Can't stay long but I'll do what I can."

Kali made a final leap and the warrior came down in front of Demie, who desperately started to flail with her sword. Then Demie jumped back, startled, when Draupadi flipped over the front line and planted a kick in the middle of Kali's chest. That brought both of them to a complete halt, but it was the only apparent effect on Kali. The female warrior watched Draupadi land a series of ineffectual punches, followed by the same roundhouse kick to the head that finished her off in Krivi.

Demie muttered a curse, this was not the same Kali they faced before.

The goddess swatted the princess aside like a cloth doll, and Demie slipped to one side and landed a blow. Dodging Kali's trident, Demie struck again on her opponent's leg, as Chandar hit with his glass sword.

This wasn't so hard, Demie thought. Then Kali swiveled the

trident like a baton and jabbed her in the side. Fiery pain flashed through her, and she fell back just as the trident dug into the ground in front of her, triggering an explosion that blew Demie back about fifteen feet. It took her a few moments to regain her senses, and she realized that Kali had inflicted a lot of damage. Less than what she took from the daitya, but not much. She had to be careful.

Having beaten back Chandar's Samita-character with an equally devastating sword attack, Kali advanced to re-engage and Demie slowly backed away. But thankfully, before the warrior reached her, Yudhishthira and Arjuna moved in to head off the attack.

Demie was maneuvering around, looking for a weak point, when she felt a healing touch on her backside. She glanced back to see Draupadi's hand gripping her shoulder.

"Thanks, I needed that! What happened when you hit her?" Demie directed a quick question at the princess, as most of her strength surged back.

"I know not how, but Kali is immune to my attack. Now I can do naught but heal." Then Draupadi moved toward Yudhishthira, who bore the brunt of Kali's attacks. Demie was afraid to get too close, but she wasn't sure what else to do, so she moved toward Yudhishthira when something pushed on her backside.

At the same time, Chandar sent a message, "Take this. You aren't skilled with it but it's better than nothing."

Demie accepted the push, and gasped as a bow materialized in her hands, along with a quiver on her back. As she experimented with it, she pulled the bowstring back and an arrow automagically appeared, notched and ready in the bow. So she pointed it at Kali and let loose.

The arrow hit with a small spark of damage, and every time she pulled the string back, another arrow appeared. Over the next few minutes Demie happily went through a couple dozen arrows, about half of which had an effect. But since Kali seemed to have her own source of healing, while they were slowly wearing her down, it would take a very long time.

Demie just wasn't sure how much time they had. She sidestepped over to Draupadi, who was applying healing to Bhima, and asked, "How long can you keep this up?"

"In truth, I am almost at my limit. Perhaps two or three more healings, then I can be of no further help. What shall we do?"

Bhima landed a blow on Kali, and then said to them, "You must flee, now. I will hold this devil until you are safe." Of all the times to start showing independence, Demie thought, with some grudging respect.

Reaching toward Bhima, Draupadi pleaded, "No! We can't run and leave you here."

Nakula, who stood next to Bhima, spoke up. "He's right, Draupadi, there is no time to argue. Bhima, I stand with you."

Demie grabbed Draupadi's arm, "I hate to say it, but I think he's right."

Before Draupadi could argue any further, Yudhishthira broke away from Kali and ran to the two women, followed by Arjuna. "Their greatest dishonor would be to do anything less, to ensure your safety and that of your friend. We go now."

Yudhishthira grabbed Draupadi's other arm and together they ran toward the far side of the square, followed by Arjuna. There Yudhishthira paused for a moment, wavering between turning east or south. Heading toward a plaza full of daityas was not an option.

"We go that way." Draupadi pointed south and took off running. Everyone followed, and Demie glanced back once more as she exited the intersection. She quietly groaned when she saw Nakula fall, but said nothing and kept running. They ran down a long street, and reached an intersection as Kali emerged from the square and turned down the street toward them. Draupadi called out, "This way," and turned left.

Again they ran as fast as they could, but Demie started to get a cold feeling in her middle when Kali closed the gap by a third as they reached the next intersection.

Draupadi turned right, and they started down that street when a shaggy figure jumped out of a doorway. It stood upright on two legs and had arms and a head, but otherwise was barely recognizable as a human. It gestured for them to enter the building, and Draupadi darted inside followed by the others.

When she gingerly stepped past the disgusting man, Demie noticed he was covered with a filthy mat of hair. Whether he wore rags underneath the hair or was naked, she hoped not to find out.

The last of the party entered the building, and the wild man closed the door behind them. For long moments no one spoke or moved as they heard heavy footsteps run toward them, and then continue on past, down the street.

"Whom are we to thank, for saving our lives?" Draupadi asked.

The wild man turned toward them. "I am the Rishi Durvasa. But I may have only postponed the inevitable, for a great darkness is coming upon all of us."

Karen tried several times to time her movements, and she was not giving up until she got it right. For the fourth time that morning, she grabbed her coffee cup and went to the kitchenette stocked with coffee and soda. She lingered as she fixed her cup, partly because she was in no hurry, but mostly so she could watch the conference room door across the hall.

Just after she emptied her cup so she could fix another, the door opened and her reason for waiting walked out. As the CEO entered the hall, Karen released a sigh of relief, tossed her spoon and moved to cut him off.

"Frank, I was about to send you an update." Not really, there was no way Karen would put what she was about to say in writing. Which was why she needed Frank Beck to react just as she hoped, by stepping into the kitchenette and dropping his voice.

"So what's going on?"

"It's Tony. He lost control of the Kali program, and we can't terminate it. The problem is, that's not all he's lost control of."

Frank frowned. "What do you mean?"

Karen paused to purse her lips with worry, and took a deep breath as though reluctant to continue. "I don't know. Since Panchala went online, it's obvious that the whole project is spinning out of control. He's a great designer, but this was a lot more than he was ready for. We may have to take the whole module offline."

Frank scowled, "TerraMythos has never taken a realm down, that's not an option. What are you suggesting?"

"You need someone who knows all the pieces, all the players and exactly what is going on. Someone who can take over without missing a beat. No one cares more about this project than I do."

Frank tightened his eyes as he examined her for a moment. Then let his breath out. "Okay, but what are you going to do about Tony?"

Karen smiled. "I'll find something, completely safe and completely unimportant, for him to do."

Demie stared at an old, feral man clothed only in a filthy mat of rastafarian hair that cascaded to his knees. She came all this way to get answers from some nut who hadn't taken a bath as long as she'd been alive? What could she have been thinking?

On the other hand, Draupadi didn't seem to be fazed. The princess put her palms together, bowed toward the bum, and said, "Namaste, Rishi Durvasa. We can not thank you enough for your aid."

"That is correct. You can not thank me enough, therefore I will not make you try."

Demie made a gagging noise. For someone who looked like a caveman, this guy thought he was pretty special. Whatever. The best way to deal with people like that was ignore them.

Demie briefly acknowledged a message from Chandar that he was signing off, then cautiously moved to the door leading onto the street and listened. There were no windows to peer through, but it sounded like the coast was clear. "Can we go back out now?"

"We shall take another path. Follow me." The rishi-dude went to a corner of the room, reached down, and lifted a trap door that appeared out of nowhere. Without a word he dropped down, and Draupadi led the group after him, with Demie bringing up the rear.

Demie examined the hole, skeptical of anywhere this guy was leading them. Since the alternative was to be left behind, she descended down a ladder into a dimly lit tunnel. It ran as far as she could see in opposite directions, and Durvasa headed down one branch. Faint phosphorescence lit the tunnel and, though they were at least thirty feet ahead, she heard Draupadi and the rishi speak as if they were next to her.

"Great and wise rishi," Draupadi asked, "We thank you for your succor in our time of great need. Therefore I tremble to ask, but would you bestow yet another boon? We have sought for you these many days, to ask questions only one with your great wisdom can answer."

My God, Demie wanted to tell Draupadi, the guy has a big enough ego already. Don't encourage him.

Durvasa didn't even slow his pace. "The foolish student seeks answers he will not understand, while the wise student does not need to ask because he already understands. Nevertheless, ask what you wish, but be not foolish."

She only saw one fool in this tunnel, Demie thought, but kept her silence.

"Rishi, my companion searches for someone that she has lost, and would then know how they may both return to their home."

The party continued moving down the tunnel. Fuming, Demie began to think that the great and wonderful rishi was going to ignore the question, when she heard him respond.

"We all seek to know from whence we came, for we seek to return there. To answer that question is the reason why we are here, and I can give no answer that she does not already know, or can not find."

It was a good thing she was at the back of the party, Demie thought, because she was ready to strangle this guy with his own hair. Or at least gag him.

"Will you not answer her question, then?"

The tunnel came to an end, and they climbed up a ladder inside what appeared to be a dry well. At the top of the forty-foot hole, Demie stepped over a small wall onto the desert surface outside the city walls.

She walked up to the rishi and directly addressed him. "Look, we came all this way because everyone said you were some kind of Einstein or something. I'm not getting it, because I could've gotten dumbass answers like that from my mom."

Draupadi stepped forward and did her bow thing. "Please forgive my friend, for she has traveled far and is weary, and likewise her respect is weary."

Durvasa turned toward Demie and stared deep into her. This was not simply a game character. His eyes were fuzzy and nebulous, just like the eyes which looked into her when the mist took Kori. Could this be the Shadowman? An icy shiver swept over her, through her.

"Knowledge comes only with a price, and the greater the knowledge, the greater the cost. Are you certain, young one, that you are willing to pay the cost for what you seek?"

Demie sensed that more lay behind the rishi's question than she could know. But in the end that didn't alter what she had to do. "Some things are important enough to pay any cost."

Rishi Durvasa looked into her soul for another moment, then seemed satisfied with her answer as he replied, "Go into the desert and find the Kamadhenu, which will set your feet on the path you must take." He turned and walked toward the wall.

"Are you kidding? That's your answer?!" Demie cried out. "I have to find some kama-whatever? What the heck is that?"

"You will know the Kamadhenu when you find it." A whirlwind of sand rose up and swept over the rishi. "When the interval is complete you will see me again."

The whirlwind collapsed and the rishi was gone.

Cassie groaned. That stupid alarm was chirping again. She tried shutting the damned thing off twice but it kept starting up again, so she hurled it against the fireplace. The thing stopped only when it shattered.

The previous night, she made it to the liquor store just before it closed at 10 PM, and started on the rum as soon as she got home. Lauren was right about one thing, she needed to stop drinking Crown Royal. Rum was much healthier since it had a natural color.

A shaft of sunlight slipped between the living room curtains, falling on her face as she lay on the sofa. Why wouldn't that damn light just go away? Groaning, she sat up; there was something she was supposed to do. Something the alarm was trying to tell her.

What idiot would make an alarm that sounded like a bird? She wasn't a bird, what good was that? She needed an alarm that told her exactly why it woke her up, what she was supposed to do. One of those smart alarms. Surely someone made them, and if they didn't, they should.

She would get one, but not right now. Her head was exploding from the inside out, and the room spun like a broken swing, so Cassie turned her back to the window. It wasn't her fault she couldn't remember what that stupid alarm should have told her. She would remember when she woke up, and then she'd get a good talking alarm. But first she needed more sleep.

An hour later, Cassie didn't hear the nurse knock before letting herself in the front door. So she didn't know that the nurse found Demie neglected, soiled and with an empty drip bag. Nor did she stir as the nurse entered the living room, surveyed the scene and checked her notebook.

Cassie started snoring while the nurse called the phone number Sherman gave her.

Draupadi watched the rishi disappear so suddenly that she jumped. The empty space where he had stood reflected the emptiness inside her, as she sought what to do next from her concealed-knowing. She led her friend Demie to Amaravati because of friendship and the debt she owed, but did her obligation go any further? At what cost? So far, she had lost three of her five husbands, and she didn't want to lose Arjuna or Yudhishthira.

"What is this kama-whatsit thing?" Demie asked.

"The Kamadhenu," Draupadi patiently corrected. This, her concealed-knowing could answer. "She is a divine creature, and the mother of all cows. She is said to have the power to grant the wish of those who seek her."

"Oh, like some kind of genie?"

"I know not this genie you speak of. But if it also grants wishes, then yes."

"So where is this desert?" Demie asked.

The rishi must have meant the Thal Desert, and Draupadi knew where that was. But she didn't really want to go there. Yet, something inside Draupadi that she could neither explain nor describe compelled her to accompany Demie. The time they spent together, the experiences they shared and the hardships and losses they endured had forged a bond between them. A strange bond that was now something as deep and important as her own existence.

Perhaps, Draupadi thought, this is friendship.

"I will take you to the Thal Desert, my good friend Demie," Draupadi said. And, she thought, wherever your path may lead from there.

Arjuna and Yudhishthira fell into place behind Draupadi as she set off alongside the city wall, and Demie brought up the rear with the unresponsive Samita in the middle. Draupadi didn't understand why sometimes Samita came to life, then went lifeless again, but Demie seemed to understand. And if Samita was Demie's friend, that was good enough for her.

Crossing into the desert took less than half a day cycle to circle the outskirts of the city and then head into the dry, red desert stretching into the distance.

The nearly featureless land consisted of gently rolling sand dunes, randomly broken by thorn trees which Demie called tumbleweeds on a stick. They wandered for several day cycles and found many bustard birds, which Demie insisted were ostriches, but no sign of the Kamadhenu. A few times they encountered wolves and boars, and once they were attacked by a couple of six-foot monitor lizards. But no Kamadhenus.

Finally, by the end of the third day Demie attacked several bustard birds out of frustration. This caused great uneasiness inside Draupadi, and she stepped to block her companion. "The Kamadhenu is an exceedingly peaceful creature. Violence will only drive her away."

"Then what will bring her?" Demie asked. "Do we need to chant or something?"

Demie's words were like a key unlocking a closed chest, and the answer came into Draupadi's mind.

"We must do a ceremony to summon a dakini. A sort of sky witch."

Chandar signed out of Panchala. His hands were shaking as he started dressing for his date with Sierra. He wanted to chat with one of his online friends about his mom and Sanjali and Sierra, but no one other than Demie was logged on. No way he could talk to her about this.

On his way out the door, he told his parents he was meeting some friends from work. As he drove over to the theatre to pick up Sierra, he wondered if he was doing the right thing, and twice considered turning around and claiming he had car trouble.

She was waiting when he drove up and hopped into the passenger seat. Before he could say anything, she slid over and slipped into his arms. Her hand rested on his shoulder as she leaned into him, along with a light flowery scent. Desire swept away any clouds of doubt, as her hair brushed his cheek. She tilted her face to him with soft, deep eyes that she slowly closed as she brought her mouth up to his. Soft, warm lips brushed his, light as a butterfly at first, then bolder and more insistent, until her mouth hungrily merged with his.

A brash car horn broke the timeless moment, and Chandar hurriedly put the car in gear, consumed with the taste of her mouth, the warmth of her bosom and the scent and feel of her hair as he caressed her. He made several wrong turns in the parking lot before his mind cleared enough to drive to the restaurant. On the way, the scent of her perfume continued to tease him, and Chandar pushed back questions about what he was doing and what he really wanted.

Sierra held his hand in her lap, against her thigh as he drove across the small town to the restaurant, and she talked about how Frankie and Jeff tried to sneak some friends in through the emergency exit, and her dad caught them and called the sheriff, and that their parents boxed their ears when they came to pick them up, and...Chandar barely listened. The more she talked, the more her spell dissipated and he realized just how boring she really was. Sanjali was passionate about the things she discussed. Her dreams, social injustice, being a journalist, doing the right thing.

The right thing. One of the drawbacks of living in a small town occurred to him. What if someone who knew Sanjali saw him with Sierra, holding hands and making out? What had he been thinking...Sanjali's parents would draw straws with his parents to see who got to kill him first. Chandar considered suggesting to Sierra that they make some other plans because it was getting late and the restaurant would be busy. What could they do that would be less public?

But when they got to the Red Robin, the lot was mostly empty. At least that meant less chance of being seen. After they were seated, he kept thinking about what he would say to his parents and to Sanjali if they were seen, when he noticed Sierra looking at him.

"Hello?"

"I'm sorry," he said, "What did you say?"

"I asked, so how is school going? You seem like you're somewhere else. Is everything okay?"

Chandar took a gulp of water and set his glass down. There were so many thoughts bouncing in his mind, where would he start? He certainly couldn't tell her about Demie, and didn't want to discuss his mother's illness; he still didn't understand it himself. That left Sanjali.

"Sierra, you know my family is from India, right? Well, they brought a lot of customs over with them, and some of them are pretty minor, like Namaste, when we greet others by putting our palms together and bow."

"Yeah," Sierra smiled. She had a great smile that melted him inside and it now reminded him of her soft but passionate kiss. He wanted her again, for a brief moment. "I've seen you do that a few times when your family and friends came to the theatre. It's really cute!"

Chandar felt a coldness inside, and forced a brief smile. Cute was not a word he would use. Maybe embarrassing or silly, but cute was nowhere on that list. The fact that she considered it cute felt, well, insulting. Which made his next words much easier to speak.

"Yes, and there are some bigger customs too. One of them is that parents...umm, they kind of look for someone for their children to marry."

"Like an arranged marriage or something?" Sierra snorted derisively, then continued, "Yeah, aren't you glad you live here in America? So what does a stupid custom like that have to do with...wait, you don't mean...?" She trailed off, looking confused and disgusted.

And at that moment, Chandar thought about what a nice smile Sanjali had. What would Sanjali's lips taste like?

"That's right, my parents are kind of old fashioned like that. And they've kind of, sort of...well, they found someone they want me to marry." For a moment he felt defensive, and then realized he didn't need to defend himself.

"So, are you telling me that you're engaged? Have you even met this girl? You know you don't have to marry her if you don't want to, don't you?"

Chandar took a deep breath. What did he really want to say? He knew he didn't have to marry Sanjali, it wasn't his idea after all. "We're not officially engaged yet, but they've pretty much made the arrangements. And yes, I've met her. She's actually quite nice, there's something special about her."

Sierra sat back, and Chandar saw her body stiffen into a 'just friends' mode. And as he described the engagement and marriage customs, he realized that although he was struggling to find the right words to explain why, he now knew what his decision was.

He was going to marry Sanjali.

CHAPTER SIXTEEN

Demie felt like a complete idiot, standing outside a ring of stones as she held a pathetic bongo-like drum. Draupadi went around the circle, which the princess very carefully arranged earlier in the day, tending the squat candle and small bowl of incense sitting on each large stone.

When Draupadi decided to summon a dakini, whatever that was, she provided a list of items they needed to find in the surrounding desert. Animal fat, sinew, bones, a rare flower, boar hide and tree bark. Tree bark was easy, there were thorny trees all over the place. They got the animal fat from those giant lizards, but only every fifth lizard had fat and Draupadi insisted they needed six pieces of fat. So they had to kill a whole mess of them. Apparently even a lizard found it hard to get fat in the desert.

Boar hide came from a boar, of course, and fortunately they only had to kill one, because those suckers were a lot tougher than the ones she hunted down with Lizat! None of the animals they killed yielded bones, which didn't make sense to Demie. But she didn't create the rules. They finally stumbled across a cow skeleton which provided the bones, and they found the rare flower on the bank of what had once been the Sarasvati River. Sinew finally turned up when Demie got bored and killed one of those ostrich birds. Which was lame, because who would think of an ostrich for sinew? Not that Demie had any idea what sinew was.

Once they had all the items, Draupadi wandered around looking for the right spot, though as far as Demie was concerned one patch of sand was as good as any other.

Eventually the princess found a level area with plenty of rocks, then proceeded to re-arrange them into a wide circle. Satisfied with the layout, Draupadi called for the items and put four of the fats together with the sinew and then candles automagically appeared on all the rocks. When she put the remaining fat together with the flower, incense appeared next to the candles. Then she put the boar hide, more sinew and the bark together to produce three drums.

Demie had to admit, she was impressed. She wouldn't have thought of putting those things together like that. Once the night cycle began, Draupadi went around the circle lighting the candles and incense. She stepped inside the ring, sat with her back facing them, and gestured for them to begin beating on the drums.

Which was the point when Demie felt like she was back in elementary school. At least Yudhishthira and Arjuna were banging on drums too, so it wasn't a solo performance.

Thrum, thrum, thrum. The instruments produced a deep, penetrating note which vibrated even the ground and rocks and startled Demie. She hadn't expected these pathetic things to actually produce a meaningful sound.

Inside the circle, Draupadi started a hypnotic, rhythmic chant in sync with their beat as she slowly swayed. Thrum, thrum, thrum. Her chanting increased in intensity, and as her rhythm quickened the drummers increased their tempo to keep up. Then, with a loud cry, Draupadi raised her hand to signal that they should stop drumming. In the darkness beyond the princess, a shape began to form. Demie just hoped it wouldn't be yet another thing they had to fight.

Like a reflection on a glass window, the dakini was mostly transparent, but gradually she solidified into a slim young woman wearing scarlet and yellow garments, with jet-black hair and glowing, light blue skin. Demie expected a sky witch to have wings like an angel, but the dakini maintained a sitting position, suspended in the air before Draupadi.

"Who is this that has summoned me?" The dakini's voice was light and whispery, like a gentle breeze, yet sharp as a shard of crystal. Demie clearly heard every word.

"Namaste, honorable dakini. I am Draupadi, Princess of Panchala. With me is Demie, a Lord of the Overworld."

Demie stifled a laugh; a Lord of the Overworld? Where did she get that from?

The princess continued, “Please excuse our disturbance, for we have need of your assistance.”

The dakini strengthened in appearance and her colors became more intense, as she drifted closer to Draupadi. “I know well why you disturbed me, though you may not. If you wish an answer from me, then you must first give me one. A restless shepherd travels back and forth, dressed the same one direction as the other, and always he passes the same roads yet finds not what he seeks. Who is he?”

Demie set down her drum and stepped to the edge of the circle. The princess shook her head and whispered to Demie, “My concealed-knowing is of no help to me. Does your concealed-knowing give to you an answer for this question?”

“I have no clue what the heck you are talking about,” Demie replied. “So, umm, yeah. No.”

“You do not know of any shepherds?” Draupadi asked.

“There were a few ranchers where I came from, but I don’t think they would’ve been much help, even if I could somehow talk to them. Hey, you said Yudhishthira was almost as wise as a rishi, so maybe he’ll know.” Demie turned to Yudhishthira, and he stepped forward.

“Great and wise dakini,” he began, “One who always passes over the same roads and yet never finds what he seeks could only be the sun.”

With a delicate laugh, the dakini responded, “Well spoken. And who is it that travels day and night, sometimes walks and sometimes runs, never rests and yet at the end of his journey has gone nowhere?”

With a bow toward the sky witch, Yudhishthira replied, “Such a tireless sojourner could only be the river.”

“Indeed, and like the sun and the river, one age ends and another begins; the beginning of the Kali-Yuga.” the dakini said as she faced Draupadi. “Now you may present your riddle.”

Draupadi spoke, “Whatever age we be in, we seek the kamadhenu and the gift it can bestow.”

The dakini started fading, as though to leave, and then firmed up again. “The kamadhenu will appear when it is time. What has led you here, and all that which is to follow, is the coming of the

Kali-Yuga."

The dakini started to fade again, as she continued, "I shall return one night hence, and tell you where to find that which you seek."

Lauren hummed as she re-arranged the suitcase once more, layering the blouses and shorts without wrinkling them. They would only be at the bed and breakfast for five days, but she wanted to make the most of her honeymoon. She finally located a spot for the toiletry bag when the phone rang.

Glancing at the display, Lauren frowned. Sherman said he was meeting with his managers, preparing them to take the reins of the business while he was gone. Why was he calling now? He better not be trying to cancel their honeymoon because of some weekend sale, or a store that needed a facelift.

"Hello, Sherman? What's up?"

"Hey babe. Were you busy?"

"Just packing. Why?" She wasn't sure she really wanted to know, but it better not involve unpacking. Lauren sat on the bed.

"I got a call from one of Demie's day nurses. She just came to the house and found Cassie almost as comatose as Demie. I'm running a management meeting here, so...could you run over and check things out?"

Lauren clenched her fists, wishing they were wrapped around Cassies's throat, and then flopped back onto the bed. She should've seen this coming a mile away. The woman was like an emotion suicide bomber.

"Lauren? Are you still there?"

"Yeah, Sherman. Okay, I'll run over there, but I think we both know what I'll find. I'm worried about Demie. Are we sure this is a good time to leave town?"

"We'll make sure it's a good time." Lauren heard the tightness in Sherman's voice, "We can't let Cassie keep dictating what we do."

Lauren tried to keep the anger out of her voice. "I know. Look, just go back to your meeting, and let me go check things out. We'll talk later."

"Thanks Lauren! Have I told you lately that I love you?"

"Just five times today. Bye." Lauren pressed the off button, and stared at the phone for a moment. She didn't tell Sherman that yes, she would make the ten minute drive to Cassie's house and check out the damage...after she made a phone call.

Slowly, Lauren dialed a phone number she hadn't called in years.

Draupadi felt that the dakini left questions instead of answers, which created an emptiness inside herself. She watched the dakini fade, and the candles and incense went out on their own. Her concealed-knowing told her they would re-light the next night on their own again, when they were to summon the dakini once more.

"So, did we learn anything helpful from this dakini?" Demie asked.

Draupadi turned toward Demie, and solemnly answered, "We learned that we would learn more tomorrow night."

"Yeah, now that's really helpful." Demie turned away and started walking off. "I'm going to go hunt some ostriches. Maybe they'll know something."

Draupadi watched Demie walk off into the darkness, awed by the great wisdom of her friend. The dakini's answers had not been at all helpful to Draupadi, nor did she understand what the bustard birds could possibly know. Perhaps in time she would become as wise as her friend Demie.

When she dwelled in the tower room, Draupadi had not noticed the passage of time between one event and the next. But since Demie freed her from the tower, Draupadi now noticed not only when events took place, but also the times when nothing took place.

This was such a non-event time, now that Demie walked off. Ever since the attack of the rakshasa, Yudhishthira and Arjuna kept watch whenever the group paused or rested. An emptiness surrounded Draupadi; no sounds, no movement, no action. Tension built up within Draupadi which she could not understand, pushing her to move, or do something.

Finally, to break the silent moment she turned to Yudhishthira, the wisest of her husbands. "What can you tell me of the Kali-Yuga?" she asked.

Yudhishthira turned, and she sensed a desire within him to please her.

"A yuga is a time period, such as an era or age. The Kali-Yuga is literally the 'age of vice' which is ruled by Kali, a terrible demon said to govern with dreadful vengeance."

The first time she saw Lord Kali, Draupadi sensed that Kali brought something terrifying, beyond anything she could comprehend. She shuddered, an action she never experienced before, and that also caused a feeling of not-rightness. She didn't like it, yet it was very powerful at the same time.

"What happens during this Kali-Yuga time?" Draupadi asked.

"There will be a tremendous loss of moral values during the Kali-Yuga. Materialism will become dominant, and moral values of honor and respect will be all but forgotten. War will follow war without end, and society will degenerate until men are little more than beasts."

"Dark days, indeed." She pressed Yudhishthira further. "These words, honor and moral values...what do they mean?"

"I know the words, but I know not what they mean." Yudhishthira looked puzzled.

Draupadi stood at the edge of a decision, to seek after answers and wisdom the way her friend Demie did. She realized for the first time that she could reach to become more than what she was now.

"How does one gain understanding?"

Her husband replied, "Understanding comes through meditation; the extended thought, reflection or contemplation of a deep or obscure subject."

Yudhishthira remained on watch as she returned to the circle and sat down. Her concealed-knowing did not explain how to do this thing called meditation, but she would try. As she sat, Draupadi thought about the words Yudhishthira had spoken and turned inward, toward a bubble of confused thoughts and ideas clustered within the center of her being.

How much time passed she could not say, but it was still night when she saw a large, colorful beast walk up to her, which she recognized as the kamadhenu. It had large, soft eyes which looked deep inside Draupadi, and the beast gave birth to another smaller beast. Then another and another until there were many. Then the beast died. The images vanished and Draupadi realized she had seen them with her thoughts. Somehow she knew the images meant that she would be called upon to do something important.

And that brought a great wave of that strange not-rightness she called fear.

Chandar felt more nervous meeting in the living room with Sanjali than he ever did before, now that he realized he wanted to marry her after all.

Part of it was that he feared she might have heard about his dinner with Sierra. Until now, Sanjali had been just one more Hindu girl his parents dragged by. He hadn't really cared what those other girls thought, and sometimes he intentionally made a bad impression with them, but never too obviously. Usually Baba would smack him on the back of the head afterwards, commenting on what a foolish son he had raised.

But since Sanjali accepted the arrangement, Chandar had actually become the foolish kid he pretended to be in the past. And he wasn't even trying!

She poured tea for them both and when he took his cup, he dropped his spoon. Reaching down for the spoon, he knocked the sugar over and as he sat up again quickly, the edge of the tea saucer caught on the table and flung tea across his front. His face felt as hot as the liquid that splashed over him.

"Don't worry," Sanjali said, as she dabbed his tie with her napkin. "Just don't spill at our wedding." Her smile and crinkling eyes laughed along with her voice, and he relaxed.

Chandar slipped the tie off and set it aside. "The date is so soon, just a few weeks. Are you worried about getting everything ready in time?"

Sanjali sat back down, crossed her legs and took up her tea. "Not really. My mother is pretty much making all the arrangements. She rushes in, shows me a bunch of pictures of flowers and asks if I like that one," Sanjali jabbed in the air. "And I just say sure, that's fine Maa. I guess one good thing about this happening so fast, is that I don't have time to get nervous."

"I know what you mean," Chandar emphatically agreed.

"There is one thing, though, that I'm not going to let my mother choose for me."

"Oh," Chandar paused, "What would that be?"

"Our honeymoon. Promise me, you won't laugh."

"Okay, I promise. I would never laugh at you." Chandar crossed his heart.

"Liar!" Sanjali laughed and poked him. "I'm sure I'll give you plenty of reasons to laugh at me. Just don't laugh at this one. Okay, ever since I was a little girl, I never really thought or cared about a fantasy wedding. But I've always fantasized about my dream honeymoon."

Chandar smiled, "That's not silly. Not at all. So what is your dream honeymoon?"

"We are standing on our own private balcony, on a cruise ship looking out over a moonlit ocean, as soft music plays and a warm breeze washes over us. Let me show you the brochure of the one I've picked out."

As Sanjali moved over to sit next to him on the couch, and pulled a pamphlet out of her purse, Chandar thought about that lecture in New York City that he had wanted to go to.

Did any cruises leave from New York?

Demie tried real hard to just keep her mouth shut and not tell her friend how stupid this whole exercise was. She spent the rest of the night cycle and most of the day cycle, since the first encounter with the dakini, hunting ostriches, wolves and anything else that had the misfortune of crossing her path. Wherever this mumbo jumbo was going, it was a complete waste of time.

Still, when the moment came, she quietly watched Draupadi light the incense and candles, then Demie took her silly drum and stood alongside Arjuna and Yudhishthira. Again, they played their drums while the princess did her chant thing and went into a trance. Then the translucent blue woman re-appeared within the circle.

"We thank you," Draupadi greeted the dakini, "For returning once more. You said you would tell us where we may find that which we seek."

The dakini responded with a tinkling laugh, as if she shook a crystal chandelier, then replied, "Answers are like shadows cast upon a wall. The art of getting the answer you seek, is to ask the question which has the right shape."

Demie couldn't take any more of these stupid riddles. Dropping her drum, she crossed into the circle and stepped up to where Draupadi sat. "Look, lady, I'll shape a question for you. I've come a long way to look for someone, so just tell me where she is and how we can get home. Do you have an answer that fits that shape?"

When Demie entered the circle, the witch's image wavered and faded. Then, as Demie spoke, the dakini stood up while dark storm clouds formed around her, and static caused the young woman's hair and clothing to rise. The witch's eyes turned a deep glowing red, and Demie wondered if it was too late to say please.

"What you seek lies buried in a very deep place, one which you can not yet see. Where you need to go does not exist, for it is eclipsed by what does exist. You must search not for the answer but rather for the question, and only then will you find what you are not looking for."

"That's really helpful! Any other shadowy answers?"

"Yes," the dakini replied as she started to fade again. "There will be more than one answer, and they will all be true."

"What answers!?" Demie shouted. "How can they all be true, are you nuts?"

"I can not tell you the answers, but when I return the last time, I will tell you where to look for the question."

Tony logged into yet another TerraMythos server, opened up its management console and frowned. All the servers were running, and there were no significant errors or alarms. But he tapped on the desk in frustration. Something just felt wrong. They were missing something.

Karen took him completely by surprise when she told him they could no longer control the Kali program. Tony spent the rest of the morning trying to track and isolate it. But Kali's processes were embedded like a virus which he couldn't nail down, because the damn processes changed and adapted so quickly every time he thought he found one.

Maybe Kali would be easier to find if he could bog down the processing on one of the servers. He pulled up a handy utility that he used in the past to induce heavy processing loads and waited while it uploaded to the machine he decided to pound. Karen normally managed server operations, so he was reluctant to hammer one of her servers without talking to her. But she had been missing all morning just when he needed her the most, and he was running out of patience.

That seemed to be her pattern, whether at work or outside of work. When they briefly dated, every time things started getting serious she would disappear. Like the time his father died and she was supposed to accompany him to the funeral. Later, she claimed he drove away just as she came to her door and dodged explaining why she wouldn't answer her phone. When he got over grieving for his father, he got over her as well. For the most part, anyway.

What he needed right now was some insight into the program she created and unleashed in Panchala. It was really just a hunch, but he believed Panchala was becoming increasingly unstable. He couldn't say when or how it would happen, but unless they nailed down exactly what was running loose in the online world, Panchala would collapse into chaos.

The utility finished uploading and Tony launched it, but before he could start looking for Kali, the utility finished running. Annoyed, because it was supposed to run until he stopped it, Tony re-started it. Again, it completed almost immediately.

Tony took a deep breath, closed his eyes for a moment to clear his mind and then carefully re-launched his program with new settings. When it spit the results right back, Tony examined the output in disbelief. What he was seeing simply was not possible. He had just authenticated that the data returned by the utility was valid, when the IM popped up.

Terse and to the point, the message simply said, "Frank's office, five minutes."

Stunned, Tony let his breath out and sat back. Frank was the kind of CEO who ran his schedule like clockwork. It was never a good sign when you were summoned to his office. Before he stood up and headed for the hallway, he signaled for the attention of his other core team members, Joachim and Carolyn.

"Frank wants to see me. I don't know what it's about, but keep an eye on Panchala and let me know right away if you see anything odd. Anything at all." Tony started to head out, then he turned back. "And if you see Karen, tell her to come to Frank's office."

He made the walk to the CEO's office in three minutes flat, while replaying the meeting from the day before. Tony didn't hide anything and sent updates with excruciating detail. What could it be now?

Just outside Frank's office, he stopped in his tracks as the answer hit him. There was only one explanation for the output from his utility. It explained the instability. The anomalies they were seeing. Why applications and modules behaved in ways they were never designed to behave. It explained everything.

Except how it was even possible to begin with.

When Tony entered Frank's office, there were two chairs in front of the CEO's desk, and Karen occupied one of them.

ॐ

Once again Demie watched the dakini take form, and determined that this time she was going to kick some witch butt if she didn't get straight answers. But this time Draupadi didn't even have time to greet the dakini before it spoke. The sky witch turned to directly face Demie, who stood outside the circle.

"I will tell you where you must journey for that which you seek, but first I must warn you. What you desire will exact a far greater cost than you can realize."

"What do you mean?" Demie asked, stepping forward, ready to reach down the dakini's throat and pull the answer out if she had to.

"All those here, and many not here, will suffer loss in the days to come. But you, Lord of the Overworld, will pay a grave price indeed. For when the time comes, you and you alone will face a dreadful choice, when you must choose one path and forsake many others."

Demie didn't like the sound of this answer. Stepping into the circle she reached toward the dakini, but her hand passed right through the apparition. "What are you talking about?"

"In the fullness of time you will understand. Until then, mark my words. For now, all of you must go to the city of Dwarka and there you will face your first challenge."

With those words the sky witch stood up, bowed to them and started to fade.

Demie yelled at Draupadi, "Bring her back, I need to know more. Where do I find Kori? And how do we get home?"

Draupadi shook her head and pointed to the dakini, which now turned into a brightly colored, painted cow. What struck Demie most were the eyes, which were as soft and deep as jet black marshmallows.

Just before vanishing, the dakini/kamadhenu spoke a last time. "You will have great need for what you gain in Dwarka. Moreover, the one whom you seek will need what you gain there."

CHAPTER SEVENTEEN

Demie felt bitter disappointment as she stood where the dry riverbed met the shore of an ocean. Here, where the great Sarasvati River once emptied into the sea, she surveyed dry rivulets, scattered boulders and nearly petrified tree trunks.

It felt like the river's graveyard.

What she didn't see was Dwarka. She walked down to the edge of the surf where waves lapped the beach in a way that at first appeared to be natural, but when she looked closer she found a repeating series of patterns. The deep blue water had a glassy sheen, with bone-white foam on the wave crests, and she could walk right up to the edge of the water. But when she tried to walk into the water, she encountered an invisible wall no matter how hard she pushed, kicked or jumped. The freaking thing prevented her from even sticking her toes in the surf.

Demie had been to a real beach twice in her life, and real sand had a grainy feel whereas the tan sand on this beach felt very similar to the dirt or pavement in this world. Where footsteps tended to sink into real sand, this sand impeded movement as well, but did so by being sticky instead. So it felt more like a bog than a beach, which was distinctly unpleasant. At least it didn't stink like a bog.

Demie gazed out to sea and heard the rest of her party walk up behind her.

"So," she asked Yudhishthira, without looking at the one who had guided them here, "You said we would find Dwarka where the river met the sea. There's no city here, unless it's a sand castle."

"In truth, it should be here. I can not say why it is not."

"Would a dakini ever lie?" Demie asked Draupadi.

"She may withhold some of the truth, but she would never speak an untruth. In that respect, she is not unlike a rishi."

"So I've noticed," Demie said. "Which means that since she said we have to go to Dwarka, it must be somewhere. The question is, where?"

"It is there." Yudhishthira pointed out toward the middle of the ocean. "I can not say how far, but Dwarka most surely lies in that direction."

"Oh really, Sherlock?" Demie angrily picked up a stone and hurled it toward the ocean, but it bounced off the invisible wall and fell at Demie's feet. She surveyed the shoreline both ways. Desert met sea as far as she could see to the right. She'd seen quite enough of the flippin desert, especially because there was so flippin little to see. At least the left offered palm trees.

"No point in just standing here, let's see what we can find." Demie turned left and started walking along the seashore.

The rest of the party fell into place behind Demie, as she led them along the beach. Distance was still difficult to judge in this world, but she was getting used to the basic passage of day cycles and night cycles, so that was becoming Demie's yardstick for long distances. Chandar's character brought up the rear, and Demie was getting annoyed because he seemed to be avoiding her. She wanted to know whether he had talked to her mom, and what was going on back home. Mom's drinking was a very bad sign. More than bad.

They trudged along the beach for the better part of a day cycle, and twice they encountered other groups running up the shoreline toward them. In both cases the people, whom Demie now recognized as Player Characters or PC's, ran past them without comment, apparently intent on their destination. And once she saw a sizable group walk down to the beach ahead of them and enter the water, but they were long gone by the time her group reached the spot where they vanished.

Demie was just about ready to turn around and head back to the ruined city, daityas or not...at least they knew where that was. Then they came around a sandy point and discovered a small group of grass thatched huts on the beach laid out in a semi-circle around a large fire pit, and down at the water's edge several men stood next to boats. The vessels looked like huge rowboats, but with high sides and a single mast. Every so often a boat pulled up to the shore and disgorged a fisherman, while one of the waiting men on the shore pushed his boat out into the surf and hopped in.

When they entered the wannabe-village, the occupants ignored the party as if they weren't there. Demie felt totally dissed as she walked up to a weatherworn fisherman dressed in a ragged white shirt and shorts, and he looked right through her as she waved her hand in front of him. She could've been a ghost.

Turning to the wooden boat, she tried to push it out into the water, the way she saw them do it. But the vessel refused to budge, and the owner continued staring out to sea, unconcerned by the attempted hijacking. She then tried to jump into the boat, but encountered the same invisible wall which prevented her from entering the sea. She was getting nowhere, literally. Frustrated didn't count as somewhere.

"Demie," Draupadi said, "It is uncomely to meet strangers and not greet them. Perchance if we introduce ourselves, they may venture to aid us in some fashion."

Demie glared at Draupadi for a minute, but as hard as she tried she couldn't think of an appropriate response. Then she walked around the boat to the fisherman and pushed on him, which was about as comely as Demie was in the mood to be.

Instantly, it was as if the old man 'turned on' and became alert, and she felt a focus of attention from him. For the first time all day, things were starting to look up. This was very much like when she interacted with the shopkeepers, and she could do that.

He turned to face her and responded, "Welcome to the humble fishing village of Sapura. We do not get many visitors in this lonely place." He paused, waiting, so she pushed him again.

"The fishing has been exceptional lately, and in the traditions of our fathers and their fathers before them, we have smoked many baskets of dried fish." Pause, yawn, push.

"But then many months ago..." Boring. Demie pushed.

"Since then..." Push.

"Now we..." Push.

"Do you want..." Push, but this time he kept going. "Do you want to buy some of our baskets of dried fish? YES or NO."

Just another shop vendor selling something; Demie examined

the options, responded with a 'No' and then started to leave.

"Do you want to go on a fishing trip? YES or NO."

Demie almost felt yanked off her feet by this unexpected response. She decided to try a new tact. "We don't actually want to fish. Can you just take us somewhere?"

He repeated, "I can take you on a fishing trip, if you would like. YES or NO."

What the heck? Demie replied, "Yes." The moment she responded, the space around their party twisted, convulsed and spit them into the boat, kind of like a cheap carnival ride. Her head literally spun for a moment, and she would've instinctively run if she could have.

At the same time, the fisherman pushed their boat out into the water and jumped in the back. Standing at the rear of the vessel, he grasped a rudder as large as he was, and asked, "Where do you want to go fishing?"

They sat, motionless except for a bobbing up and down movement, until finally Demie said, "Anywhere but there," and pointed back at the shore. The instant she pointed at the beach, the boat vomited the whole party back onto the sand, and Demie let out a startled yelp.

Then she was annoyed, because of course they had to go through the fisherman's whole spiel again, but soon they were back in the boat and this time Demie pointed straight out to sea. Although the sail was down and the boat lacked any other apparent means of propulsion, as soon as she raised her arm, the vessel darted in the direction she pointed until she put her arm down, at which point it simply stopped moving. Then she pointed left, and the boat turned and moved to the left until Demie put her arm down, and she smiled. That gave her an idea.

"Which way is Dwarka?" she asked Yudhishthira, as she passed the tether to him.

"It lies in that direction," he pointed, and the boat took off.

"Good. Just keep pointing until we get there."

Ever since they started on this trip, Demie found that she needed some rest from time to time, not physically but rather mentally. She sort of napped by closing her vision, but it wasn't quite like closing her eyes, because with real eyes she would've seen spots or shapes or something. This was more like turning off a monitor.

She hadn't 'rested' for a full day cycle, so while Yudhishthira guided the boat, Demie turned off her vision and drifted in her mind, until eventually the boat came to a stop and Yudhishthira said, "We have arrived at Dwarka."

Demie opened her eyes, looked around in shock and said, "You've gotta be kidding!"

They were surrounded by completely empty ocean in every direction, as far as they could see.

Except for a spire which rose out of the water in front of them.

Chandar checked on Samita occasionally but remained inactive. That was the best way to keep Demie from pestering him about her mom. Not that he had much else to do, after quitting his job at the theatre. He still saw Sierra at the college but it was easy to avoid her there.

It was awkward enough to see Sierra while trying not to remember the taste of her lips. But more than that, it was her unblinking ice-cold stare as if she were trying to dismember him with her gaze. He wanted to say that he never meant to hurt her, that he did care about her but just not in that way. In the end, he only said goodbye when he resigned and he wasn't certain she'd heard that. He simply told his parents that he quit because the popcorn smell was making him start to throw up.

After checkng on Demie's party, Chandar scanned through the 'ghost limbs' search results he bookmarked a week or two before. He wanted to confirm a hunch that nagged him. One search turned up numerous reports from some New Age institute in California, which specialized in teaching a modified form of yoga to amputees. Many of their students reported actually seeing or feeling limbs that they had lost. The thing was, these weren't just reports of pain or phantom sensations. These were actual experiences with missing limbs.

The other search identified a European doctor who did research on ghost limbs, also with amputees. This was the physician who was speaking in New York soon, about using patients' experiences with ghost limbs to animate artificial limbs. What made his research so intriguing was that in some cases, the patients experienced sensations of touch and temperature through these artificial limbs, even though the prosthetics had no such sensors.

Chandar confirmed that the California institute and the European doctor had never crossed paths. Not only that, apparently no one had connected the dots between them. If he was the first to see the correlation, it opened up all sorts of interesting possibilities.

After bookmarking his finds, Chandar closed the searches and logged into Panchala, but failed to make his own association. The one between his research and the thought that lurked unseen in the back of his mind.

That his mother was dying.

Cassie warily walked into the coffee shop and saw Sherman sitting at a table in the corner by the fireplace. She wasn't sure exactly what he wanted to talk about, but at least he picked a private spot. He pushed out a chair with his foot as she approached.

"I figured you could use a latte, so I took the liberty of ordering you one. You still take it the same way, I trust?"

She skeptically stared at the drink on the table as she sat, then picked it up without a word and slowly sipped. Another time she would have enjoyed it, but right now her head felt like she had an ax buried in it. He was right, though, she did need it, and she gave an appreciative sigh.

"Okay, Sherman. I'm here. What do you need to talk about?"

Sherman forced a smile before replying, "Still cutting right to the chase, eh?"

"Socializing was never your style. You're a businessman who never calls a meeting unless there's a reason. We're here, it's your meeting. So let's start."

"Well, this isn't business, but we both know what this is about."

Cassie was waiting for this and slammed her cup down. Her anger blocked out the pain from the hot liquid that sloshed through the top. "Yes, we both know. Me and my drinking. There, it's out on the table. What do you want to say about it?"

"Why are you drinking again, Cassie? After what happened, I thought you put that behind you for good. Why, after staying dry the past ten years?"

"Really? You called me here to ask that? My life has fallen apart, my only child is basically brain dead, and you wonder what pushed me over the edge?"

"No, that's not why I asked you here. But I did want to know."

Sherman paused for a minute, looking out the window, before turning his attention back to Cassie. "Your drinking is part of it, but only indirectly. Really, it's Demie and whether you can handle her."

Cassie's headache was growing, and the pulsing pain expanded into her neck as if Sherman's words were physically choking her.

"Okay. I know I've messed up a few times, but this is a really hard time. I just need to get through this. Then I'll be alright."

Sherman leaned forward, "It's not just that you messed something up with Demie. It's why you messed up, because of your drinking. If you can't handle that, there's no way you can handle anything else. You need to pull yourself together."

"You're not telling me anything I don't know. What's your point?"

"My point is that Lauren and I are going on a honeymoon after we get married. How can I trust that you'll take care of Demie while we're gone?"

Cassie's headache now blurred the vision in her eyes. She couldn't take any more pain, and she sure couldn't take any more of his words. "I guess you'll just have to figure that one out. But I'm not worried, because you're good at coming up with reasons to avoid responsibility." Taking her coffee, she stood up.

Resisting the urge to smash the coffee over Sherman's head, she simply said, "Thanks for the coffee, by the way." Then she turned and strode out to her SUV.

Cassie carefully backed up and then drove off. No one was going to take Demie from her, except over her cold dead body. She wanted to rip Sherman's head off but, at the moment, anyone's head would do.

Chandar was surprised when he re-connected with his character, Samita, to find that they were in a boat somewhere out in the middle of an ocean. Curious as to where the heck they were going, he pulled up the game world map and saw that they were heading north toward an island.

"I'm back," Chandar announced to the party.

"Nice of you to drop in," Demie shot back.

"I did not notice you left, Samita," Draupadi responded. "Where have you returned from?"

"What are we doing now?" Chandar ignored Draupadi, directing his question to Demie.

"Well, we found Dwarka, about 100 feet under water. Then I told the boatman to take us to the nearest land, so we're on our way there now."

"I'm not sure where this is taking us," Chandar replied, "But we really should have brought a high level magic user on a major quest like this. I have a pretty good collection of magical items, but that's really not the same thing."

"I'll be sure to give you an itinerary next time," Demie replied. "By the way, have you talked to my mom yet?"

"No, not yet. I've been really busy, and I don't know what to say."

Demie's response came back immediately. "Just tell her the truth. We don't know how it happened, but I'm here and I need help to get out. Listen, if she doesn't believe you, tell her that she used to call me 'watermelon' because I had more hugs in me than a watermelon had seeds."

Chandar sat back in his chair, thinking. He was reluctant to talk to Demie's mother because, face it, no matter how he tried to explain it, he was going to sound like an idiot. But then he thought about his own mom, and how much it hurt to even think about the idea that she would be gone. At that moment, he understood how Demie felt.

"Alright, I'll give it a try. But I can't promise anything."

"I know. The best time to catch her is when she's coming home and getting out of her car. She's always distracted, thinking about what she wants to do."

The sound of tires pulling into the driveway next door came through the bedroom window, and Chandar replied, "It sounds like she's coming home right now, in fact. I still think this is a really bad idea."

"Please, just try. I promise, this is a good time, so go right now."

Chandar stood up and looked through his window, and saw Cassie getting out of her car. Maybe Demie was right, that it was a good time. He would have to hurry.

Demie cautiously examined the path that led from the island beach where the boatman deposited them. On the way in, they observed that the island was not particularly large, maybe a mile or two long. A small volcano peak rose on one end, sloping down to flatland on the other end. Jungle covered the whole isle, including the peak, and the beach where the boatman landed them was on the flat end.

Draupadi came up behind, and spoke. “My friend Demie, to be sure I can not tell you where it comes from, but the concealed-knowing within tells me that what we require lies at the end of this path.”

Demie replied, “But you don’t know what it is? I guess that’s why it’s a concealed knowing.” She shrugged and set out up the trail. Nothing was ever direct in this world, but so far everything had worked out one way or another.

The path wound up a slight incline, through a deep green jungle similar to the one outside Kampilya, except the trees here were palm trees and the vegetation sported a variety of brilliant red, yellow and orange flowers. After a brief trek, Demie gasped as they emerged into a broad clearing containing the last thing she expected to see. A small village alongside a tiny lake.

Numerous brown natives, bare-footed but dressed in bright red sarongs with yellow shirts, darted back and forth between grass covered huts, ignoring the strangers in their midst. It wasn’t clear exactly what their activities focused on, but the faint murmuring of conversation hung in the air, mixed with the clanging of an anvil in the distance and the sound of wood chopping somewhere. Demie waited for a villager to pass nearby, then pushed on the woman.

The native turned, bowed and addressed her. “Namaste, most honored guests, you are welcome in our time of need. You will wish to speak to Chief Munda.” Then she continued on her way. What annoyed Demie the most was that the villager didn’t even wait for a response.

Demie stopped several other natives, but the idiots all said the same thing and resumed their activities before she could ask where they hid the chief. Finally, at the far end of the village, they came to a large space that centered on a large fire pit where a man stood wearing a robe in addition to the sarong. Going up to him, Demie hoped for the best as she pushed.

He turned to face them, threw his arms wide open in greeting and said, “Thank the Gods for sending us mighty heroes. A terrible curse has come upon our village, and we would reward you well to help us in our time of need.” Like the boatman, Demie had to push on the chief throughout their conversation.

The chief continued, "An evil graha has preyed upon my village for many months. We know not where this foul creature came from, but every fortnight he has taken one of the children from our village. Only last night, he captured my own daughter."

"What is a graha?" Demie asked the princess. She was learning that if she didn't know what something was, then it probably meant trouble.

"A graha is a malevolent ogre-like demon from another dimension, brought here by some great wickedness."

"Oh great, Lauren followed me all the way here," Demie replied, then prompted the chief to continue.

"My daughter Ashlani is fair to behold and beloved by all in the village. The evil graha intends to devour the maiden this very night." Push. "Our strongest and bravest warriors have ascended to the lair of this terrible demon to do battle, but none have returned." Push. "Our village is powerless against this great evil, but if you can rescue my daughter Ashlani and rid the village of this scourge, I shall reward you with a rare and wondrous gift. Dare you face the foul creature? YES. NO."

Demie didn't feel particularly moved by the chief's plight, but she was intrigued by the fact that the graha came from another dimension. Wherever Demie came from, it definitely wasn't this dimension. She replied, "Yes."

The chief responded, "You will find the evil graha in the cave at the top of the mountain. Please hurry, before Ashlani is consumed." Then the chief turned away to face the fire pit once more.

Demie faced her small band, determined to bag a graha. Chandar was still away, hopefully talking to Mom, so she warned Yudhishthira and Arjuna to keep their weapons ready and advised Draupadi to be prepared with her special healing magic. Demie made sure to select, as her weapon of choice, the special glass-like sword designed for killing the undead and demons. Samita/Chandar gave it to her after the daitya incident, with the admonishment to use it only when needed. She was pretty sure that was now.

They were as ready as Demie thought they could be, so she turned to the path beyond the chief's fire pit and headed for the other end of the island. It was convenient for the graha that it had a path right down into the village, but that could work both ways.

The trail crossed the small isle and then ascended the volcano in a winding series of switchbacks until it ended on a ledge the size of Mom's driveway. A dark opening, about as wide as a garage and two stories high, led deep inside the mountain. At least, it looked like an opening, but as she approached the threshold to the cave, she sensed that this was a doorway into a new 'area' just like entering a shop. Maybe this wasn't such a good idea after all.

Chandar was still offline, for who knew how long. But everyone else was prepared, so ready or not, she pushed on the entrance and like an elevator door opening, they were inside.

The interior was dark, like one of the night cycles, but they could see clearly. The cavern was large, perhaps a hundred feet across, and on the far side stood what had to be the demon, with a young girl behind it. The tall creature had the body of a lion from the waist down, and a man-like body above its waist. Except for the fact that like Kali, it sprouted four arms instead of two.

The moment they entered, the improbable beast saw them, roared and charged. Demie screamed, scrambled to find the way back out but whatever opening let them in seemed to be a one-way door. After fumbling blindly for a few moments, Demie turned back to face the graha.

The freaking thing was so fast that Arjuna only managed to get off three ineffectual shots before it reached them. Since Yudhishthira had the best armor, Demie let him take the brunt of the attack, while she moved to the demon's side and cut loose with her sword. Arjuna's arrows and Yudhisthira's sword did nothing except distract the graha, which was fine with Demie. But Chandar's demon-killing sword flashed with glowing green sparks every time she struck the demon, and her adversary was starting to slow down considerably, when she felt a deep, burning stab in her side. A quick glance confirmed that Arjuna had actually shot her.

"What are you doing!?" Demie indignantly asked, as two more arrows struck.

Draupadi raced over and answered for Arjuna as her healing countered the arrow damage. "Arjuna's will is now under the control of the graha. Possession is one of the special powers of this type of demon."

Demie hit the demon again as she replied, "That's kind of an important detail, don't you think? You should've told me sooner. What do we do about Arjuna?"

"Arjuna may only be released from the demon by death, either his own or the demon's. There is no other way."

"Then just keep healing me."

Demie desperately redoubled her attacks on the graha, hoping to slay it before Draupadi ran out of healing power. The moment the demon keeled over, Arjuna lowered his bow and acted like nothing had happened. Demie decided there was no point in saying anything and turned toward the chief's daughter to check whether she had been harmed.

Ashlani wore a torn red sarong, like the other villagers, and appeared to be no more than ten or twelve years old. The child had wide brown eyes, with a moon-shaped face and bangs across her forehead that reminded Demie of her little sister. Demie unsuccessfully tried to pick up the girl and then gently pushed on the child.

The young girl responded with a small, trembling voice. "I can not thank you enough for sparing me from this horrible fate. You have slain the terrible creature that terrorized our poor village for so long. We will tell of your mighty deeds to our children and their children." Then she fell silent and started back to the village.

As the cute little girl walked by, Demie instinctively reached out and grabbed the child's hand. When she did, the girl froze and Demie felt an electric charge surge through her arm into Ashlani's body, along with a faint blue glow. At the same time, Draupadi came over to the frozen figure and placed her hands on the girl. The same faint blue glow formed around the princess's body, gathered into her hands and then spread into the child's body.

Ashlani blinked several times, looked up at Demie, and giggled. Demie was shocked by the transformation at first, but then pleased when the girl grasped Demie's hand and led them back down the trail to her village.

When they entered the small community, the girl walked up to Chief Munda and took his hand. Demie had to jump back out of the way when faint blue flashes darted from the child to the Chief, like sparks jumping across a gap. Then the flashes multiplied into over a dozen streams throughout the tribe, like a small electrical storm that eventually died out.

As if nothing happened, the chief smiled at Demie, reached into a bag slung behind his robe and held out a number of conch shells that were creamy and tan outside, with a vibrant pink glow on the inside.

"These shells were given to us by the great sea goddess, and now we give them to you in gratitude for your invaluable service." This time, the chief responded naturally, the way Draupadi and her husbands did, without needing a push. "Breathing through these shells, you may enter the realm of the sea goddess at will and go where you will. They are yours to keep."

Surprised but grateful, Demie took the shells and Chief Munda added, all on his own, "You have set us free and awakened us from our deep slumber. We are deeply in your debt."

"You have given us much as well, Chief," Demie replied, and as she looked at Ashlani, she genuinely meant it.

"Nothing we have to offer may compare with what you have given us. Namaste, Demie." The chief turned to lead his daughter away to his hut and Demie led her group back toward the beach.

On their way out of the village, each native stopped and greeted the party with a bow and "Namaste" as they passed, rather than ignoring them like before. A train of laughing children followed them to the end of the village, and as Demie's group reached the edge of the clearing and passed into the trees, the group of children all bowed in unison and wished them farewell with a chorus of "Namaste". Demie hugged each child and wished she could've stayed longer.

As soon as they stepped out onto the beach, Demie cursed. That worthless boatman was gone, leaving them to swim all the way back to that spire. No tip for him. She passed out the conch shells and led the group down to the surf. This time, the ocean offered no resistance as they walked forward and then sank below the waves.

Demie smiled inside her shell as she submerged, and failed to notice Kali climb out of the waves at the far end of the beach.

Tony was stunned as he followed Karen back to their office. He was just as confused about what she had done as he was about why, but there was no confusion about the outcome. Frank made it clear that Tony's future was in Karen's hands, for better or for worse. Probably worse.

She didn't say anything as they walked and Tony was not inclined to break the silence. Just outside their office, Karen firmly pulled him over to the side and she fixed her gaze on him for several long seconds. Her eyes narrowed and brows wrinkled as her intensity reached a peak. He looked unflinchingly back into Karen's emerald green eyes, which didn't have the allure for him they once held.

"I need to get a handle on what's going on with Panchala," she hissed. "The only thing I want you to do is keep tabs on Kali and see what it does. That shouldn't be too hard. Think you can handle it?"

"Whatever you want, Miss de Havilland," Tony quietly replied. "You're the boss now." Tony shrugged and walked on to his cubicle, refraining from throwing his chair across the office only because that would have pleased her. While Karen went to her desk and proceeded to make some hushed phone calls, Tony logged back into the Panchala servers to see where Kali was and what it was up to. Whatever he found might be just as useful for him as for Karen.

Tony frowned, and almost blurted out his surprise. For whatever reason, Kali was on an obscure island in the western ocean of Panchala, part of an insignificant upper-level side quest. Although they no longer controlled Kali, his tracking utility still monitored the status of the Kali program, which apparently lost track of whatever anomaly it had been hunting. When that happened, Kali should have switched into search mode, or gone inactive. That was not what it was doing now.

Inserting a virtual character, Tony watched Kali enter a small village and start attacking villagers with mighty swings of its weapons. The chief greeted the Kali avatar, only to be annihilated with one blow, and then Kali chased down the fishermen, women and child NPCs. He couldn't believe that they actually tried to run, but they were all trapped in the village area. Why would they run? Even more bizarre, the last NPC was a young girl who actually appeared to drop on her knees and plead with Kali, before it obliterated her as well.

That done, Kali turned to the huts and began demolishing them as well, striking all of them until they were eliminated, and then it turned to the remaining infrastructure. The program did not stop until every well, fire pit and other created item was destroyed. When Kali finished, not a trace remained; only bare ground existed where Chief Munda's village and its inhabitants once stood.

Tony snagged a snapshot of the module for this area, and when he opened the code he found that the programming for this area had not just been shut down, it had been completely erased. It would have to be reloaded, but now he suspected it wouldn't be quite that simple.

He turned his attention back to Kali, and he was surprised to see that the rogue program had acquired a new anomaly as a target. It left the barren wasteland it had created and ran toward the shore. When it reached the water, it didn't hesitate as it plunged into the surf and continued on a beeline, swimming out to sea. Tony sat back, wondering where the heck it was going now. When Karen finished her call, he updated her on what he had observed.

She crossed her arms and replied with a smug grin, "Well, it sounds like we've only got one option left, then. When all else fails..."

Tony simply shrugged without a comment and turned back to his workstation. If he was right, she would be in for quite a surprise.

But she would find that out for herself soon enough.

CHAPTER EIGHTEEN

Chandar dashed down the hall, wondering if he was insane. He barely paused to slip his shoes on and swung the front door open just as Maa asked where he was going. "Outside," Chandar hollered, just before he pulled the door shut.

Trying not to run, he saw Demie's mom heading around the front of her car and met her as she walked to the front door. When Chandar came trotting up, she turned to face him, and the narrow tightness around her eyes opened a cold hole in his gut. His steps faltered and he almost turned around.

"Yes?!" she said, putting down a bag she was carrying.

Chandar considered muttering, 'never mind.' But then he realized Demie would never stop pestering him. He needed to just get this over with.

"I'm really sorry about Demie, Miss Morris."

She looked hard at him for a few moments, released a sigh and held out her hand. "I'm sorry, I don't remember your name."

"Chandar," he replied, awkwardly taking her hand, and then releasing it after completing the formality with a brief, light touch.

"Did...do you know Demie? I mean, she never mentioned you."

"Well, not really. Until recently that is. We knew each other from school and all."

A puzzled look flashed over Miss Morris' face.

"How's Demie, you know, doing? Physically, I mean." Chandar didn't want her thinking too much about the school part. Or asking what grade he was in.

"She's still in a deep coma, and we really don't know when she'll wake up. But her body is healthy, so when she does come back..." Demie's mom trailed off, leaving an uncomfortable silence.

"Yeah, right." Chandar caught himself digging a hole in the lawn next to the sidewalk with his shoe. He wished he could climb down inside it.

"You're the one who called 911, right?" Chandar nodded, and the woman continued, "Thank you. Even a minute or two later and she would've been...gone."

"Yeah, that was me. You know, the thing is, she's not really gone."

"I know what you're trying to say. She may not really be here, right now, but at least she's not in heaven yet."

Chandar decided it was now or never. If he didn't make the leap now, he would never find the courage to try again.

"Well, this may sound crazy, but wherever she is, I think I've been talking with her. Online, through the computer."

Cassandra Morris stood, motionless and expressionless, as if Chandar had turned her into a statue. He had no idea whether that was good or bad, and decided to just keep going.

"Somehow, I don't know how, she contacted me online through my computer. I didn't believe it at first either, I thought it was just a prank, but then she kept telling me things that other people wouldn't know."

"Like what?" Miss Morris barely whispered loud enough for him to hear.

"Personal things." Chandar wasn't about to explain going into Demie's room to retrieve her diary. "She keeps pushing me to tell you about her, and that she's okay. And she told me to tell you, that you used to call her watermelon, because she was full of hugs."

Demie's mom continued to stare, silent and still. Chandar decided he'd said enough for now. In fact, probably far more than enough, and he better go before he dug himself any deeper.

"Anyway, she just wanted me to tell you that she's alright."

Chandar turned and walked off, thinking that hadn't gone too bad after all.

Demie was having fun for the first time in quite a while. When she went under the surface, she started swimming and automatically breathing through the conch shells, which molded to fit over her face like some weird Halloween mask.

She also had perfect buoyancy, neither rising nor falling except through her movement, although she bobbed to the surface a few times before she got the hang of maneuvering in three dimensions. One nice surprise was that although they wore those odd shells over their faces, everyone in her little group had no problem speaking.

"So where is Dwarka?" she asked Yudhishthira once she got acclimated to the undersea environment. When he pointed off in the distance, she told him to lead them on.

The difference between day and night cycles was less pronounced than on the surface, so Demie couldn't really gauge how long they swam. But just like running in this world, they could swim all day and not feel tired. Which she would miss if she got home. When she got home. Since that time on the barge she tried not to think about home, it was just too painful.

As they swam, Yudhishthira kept them about thirty feet above the sea floor, and they passed numerous critters, most of which moved considerably faster than her people could swim. The sea life probably followed the same kind of rules of engagement as the land animals, but she wasn't anxious to test it out by pulling any of them for the party to kill. Especially those big sharks with wicked teeth—just looking at them gave her the heebie-jeebies.

After what Demie estimated might have been a full day cycle, they began to glide over what looked like submerged farms and houses. Demie swam down closer to examine them, half expecting to see mermaids come out. She was disappointed when nothing emerged aside from an occasional octopus or fish. A short while later, Yudhishthira led them over a large wall and then they passed above the city proper.

At one time, this metropolis must've been every bit as large as the lost desert city. So Draupadi hadn't been exaggerating, after all, about a lost great civilization. Maybe this was even Atlantis, except wasn't Atlantis supposed to be in the Atlantic Ocean?

Demie tried to recall her geography lessons, wondering what the heck ocean they were supposed to be in anyway. She had eliminated the Arctic and Antarctic oceans when Yudhishthira led them directly toward a tall, white marble column which rose from the seabed. It went as high as they could see, right up to the surface. This must be the spire.

Yudhishthira stopped in the water about thirty feet away from the structure, and turned toward Demie. "We have now come to the center of Dwarka."

Demie looked at him doubtfully, then swam around the column and examined the ruins spread out below them. Off in the distance in every direction, nearly at the edge of their vision, a massive stone wall encircled the area below, and a dozen broad avenues ran from the protective walls toward the spire, like spokes on a wheel. The roadways converged on an enormous square larger than any Demie had seen before in this world, and the tower occupied the center of the open area. If the whole city were a wheel, then the spire would've been the axle.

Amid the ruins, all Demie could see were sea fronds, kelp and fish. And not a clue as to what the heck they were supposed to look for. She turned toward Draupadi, "Now that we're here, do you have any idea what the dakini wanted us to do?"

"She merely said we are to face a challenge. She did not say how to find the challenge."

"Where would you hide, if you were a challenge?"

Draupadi paused for a moment before responding, "I will have to think deeply on that question, my friend, for I am not a challenge."

"You might be surprised. Never mind, just follow me." Demie turned down, and swam toward the base of the spire. And sure enough, there at the base was a large opening, big enough for a couple of monster trucks to fit through. After making sure her party was following, Demie swam through the opening and into the darkness of a large tunnel.

The fifty foot wide tunnel sloped downward, and though it was dark, at least the passage was clear of the aquatic vegetation that covered everything on the sea floor. They passed several small branches that led off to the side, but none which seemed to contain a challenge. They continued swimming down the tunnel for about a hundred yards until it opened into a huge cavern.

Demie paused, as much surprised as overwhelmed. The square well-lit chamber appeared to be unoccupied, and as wide as a football field on each side. Piles of gold, jewels, chests and various weapons and armor covered the entire floor. If they hadn't found the challenge, they'd certainly found the reward.

As they swam into the vast chamber, Demie turned around to face Draupadi and froze. Pointing with her sword, she asked, "What in God's name is that?"

Draupadi turned to look. "Demie, that would be Makara, a beast whom the gods ride as a mount. Perhaps this is our challenge."

Slowly moving toward them, filling most of the tunnel they just exited, was what looked like a crocodile in the front half and a dolphin in the back half. Except that it was the size of a blue whale.

Lauren slowly twirled her brush and lightly swayed back and forth, as she contemplated the canvas and Rimsky-Korsakov played in the background. The violins in Scheherazade moved the deepest part of her soul. Light pencil marks outlined an alpine scene waiting to emerge, but she struggled to tease out of the canvas what background color it wanted to be. She began to hum with the music as she mixed a color that felt right, and it clicked when she tweaked the hue.

She was applying the first strokes when Sherman came in. "Back already?" she asked over her shoulder, without looking.

"Be glad you weren't there."

"That good, huh?" Yes, the color was just right. It would do. "So I'm guessing she didn't tear her clothes, dab herself with ashes and repent." Turning to face Sherman, Lauren mocked, "Ah have seen mah wicked ways, and may the Lawd strike me down if anuther drop passes mah lips."

"It's not funny. Right now, I'd settle for her just admitting that she has a problem."

Lauren felt a pang of guilt and set down her palate and brush, then sat on her stool. "You're right, it's not something to joke about. I'm sorry."

Sherman sat on the other stool which Lauren kept around, for him to sit on when he visited her in the studio. "It's partly about Demie, of course. We don't know what's going to happen to her in the long run, and she needs to be cared for until something happens for better or for worse. But it's also hard to see someone you know, someone you were once very close to, self-destructing before your eyes. And know there isn't a damn thing you can do about it."

Lauren came over and laced her arms around his neck. "Yes, I can understand that," she whispered. "Believe it or not, even though she makes it hard, there are times when I see the person she once was, and could someday be again. But you can't do anything for her, when she won't do anything for herself. None of us can."

"Well, the bottom line is that we can't trust her to take proper care of Demie while we go on our honeymoon, so there's only one thing we can do."

Lauren settled her head on Sherman's shoulder. "I know, hon. There will be other romantic getaways when the time is right."

"Don't be silly! We're still going, I'll just hire round-the-clock care."

Lauren released her fiancé and stepped back. "What!? You are going to abandon your helpless daughter? We can't just run off."

"Why not?"

Lauren couldn't believe what she was hearing. "Demie needs us. Now more than ever."

Sherman laughed, "She doesn't need us, she needs a nurse. Or rather a team of nurses."

Lauren jabbed her finger at Sherman. "You think it's funny? To just leave her in the hands of strangers? You emotionally abandoned that girl all her life, and now that she's bed-ridden you're abandoning her physically as well. I have loved that child more from a distance than you ever have up close."

"Great!" Sherman yelled. "Then you stay here and wipe her butt, and I'll send you postcards." He slammed the door as he stormed out of the studio.

Her hand shaking with anger, Lauren dabbed paint on the canvas and wept.

Tony sat at his desk, arms crossed and monitored Kali's progress on his computer. He couldn't have cared less about the furtive glances and hushed whispering between the other two members of his core team, on the other side of the small office.

After Tony updated Karen on what happened with the Munda Village quest area, she had hurried out to consult with upper management on her intended next steps. But before she left, she gave him very explicit instructions: Watch Kali and do not touch anything, change anything or do anything.

It was bad enough the way she talked to him on the way back

from Frank's office. But then not only did she talk down to him as though he were an intern or child, she did it in front of the other team members and didn't even try to lower her voice. After she snatched up her purse and stalked out, Joachim and Carolyn avoided all eye contact and didn't say a word to him. They could tell he was a corporate leper at the moment.

So he did exactly what she instructed. He merely observed Kali swim across the sea to the mainland and set a course down the beach. After a time, the rogue program reached a small fishing village on the coast and proceeded to wipe it out, eliminating every trace of the NPCs as well as the whole area they operated in, just as completely as it had with Munda's Village. The damned thing even waited for the remaining boatmen to come back to shore and erased them as well.

Then, having apparently acquired a new target, Kali turned inland and made a beeline for the interior. Along the way it encountered a couple of small adventure areas with a few NPCs, and paused to wipe them out as well. When it paused at the second spot, Tony made a note of the coordinates and then pulled out a large printed map they had made of the Panchala realm.

He didn't want to make any marks, so fingering the locations of the fishing village and the two adventure areas, Tony used a ruler to extend Kali's path. Then, he quietly whistled to himself when he saw where it was going.

After rolling the map up, Tony laughed as he shredded the notes he had made and logged out of his computer. Karen simply told him to watch Kali; she hadn't said anything about actually documenting what it did.

Tony probably didn't have much time, but he knew what he had to do. He swept a few particularly valuable Star Wars keepsakes into his backpack and told Joachim he had to run an errand. Heading into the hallway, he turned toward the HR department to make a brief stop before he got the heck out of here.

He knew what Karen was planning, and this was the last place he wanted to be.

Demie had a really bad feeling about this 'challenge.'

If that Makara thing got out of the tunnel and into the chamber, where it could move freely, she didn't think they would have a chance. Calling to her companions, she swam forward to head the leviathan off at the entrance.

Fortunately, when they confronted Makara at the opening it started snapping at them with its jaws, apparently not realizing it could've powered right past them. Demie was willing to maintain that illusion as long as possible.

Because the beast halted its progress just inside the tunnel, Demie, Yudhishthira and Arjuna were able to position themselves in front of the thing, while Draupadi took up a position right behind them where she could provide healing. Samita just drifted off to the side since Chandar was offline, predictably enough at the worst possible moment.

This Makara thing moved fairly slowly, so most of the time Demie and her partners were able to dodge many of the attacks, but now and then a blow did land and the effect was serious enough that they couldn't take a second hit without some healing. So, although they were holding their own, they were pretty much at a stalemate until Makara started getting lucky. Demie didn't want to wait for that, so she was looking for an escape route when Samita finally stirred.

"What's up?" asked Chandar.

"You pick the best times to just drop in," Demie angrily replied. She quickly explained their situation while dodging a couple more attacks, narrowly avoiding the last one.

Samita/Chandar swam up, and pulled out a small stick. "Darn it, I told you before we shouldn't be doing this without a high level mage. Alright, when I tell you to, everyone swim out of the tunnel as fast as you can."

Demie looked at the stick, which was about as big as a sapling. A small one at that. "You can't be serious. Are you going to fight it with that, or floss its teeth?"

"Just trust me. Now!"

Demie and her companions frantically paddled out of the tunnel, and Makara surged forward while the water in the tunnel started to froth and boil. Then, just as the snout poked through, the froth turned into a mass of stone. The snout jerked back and rock filled the gap.

Swimming over to Samita, Demie asked, "What did you do?"

"Just a wand that I happened to have. Creates walls of various types. In this case, a stone wall."

"It certainly came in handy. Does it remove walls too?"

Chandar paused before answering, "Um, no."

"Well, that's a great exit plan. We're going to have to get out of here somehow, so see what else you have that might be handy. I'm going to look around."

Demie swam along the floor of the cavern, glancing over the riches for something that would be useful. Somehow, she didn't think all the gold in the world was going to buy their way out of this place.

At the far end of the chamber, she found a throne which appeared to be carved out of the rock that made up the rest of the building. The throne was simple, without any jewels or precious metals, so Demie had a hunch about it. Sometimes the plain things were the most valuable. Drifting down to it, she examined the throne and found, on the front of the backrest, a curious diagram with some writing that she couldn't read.

The large diagram portrayed a man in the center, surrounded by symbols in a circle all around him. Those symbols included a mountain above the man, pictures of jungle and desert on each side, a boat upon an ocean below the man, and between the landscape symbols were various animals including an elephant, tiger, boar and lion.

Calling Draupadi over, Demie asked her translate the writing. Draupadi first pointed to the writing that ran around the circle of the diagram.

> "The World holds many challenges for a man,
> "From the highest peaks to the depths of the ocean,
> "Yet one of these presents the greatest challenge of all,
> "Which only the truly strongest can conquer."

Then, pointing to a line underneath the diagram she translated, "The wise man who recognizes this foe can realize his greatest desire."

Demie looked closer at the diagram, and ran her hand over the symbols around the man, determined to crack this puzzle. She felt a tingle very similar to when she was going to open a door and recognized that she could press the symbols. So, this was some kind of riddle, and she needed to figure out which of these challenges the man in the middle would find the greatest.

They had passed through a lot of lands and encountered many of these animals. The elephants certainly were tough, but nothing like the demons they had faced. If one of the symbols were a demon, the choice would be a no-brainer. Then of course there were the areas or regions. The desert hadn't been particularly hard, and she hadn't been in the mountains but she figured that probably wouldn't be very different.

After swimming through the sea and seeing some of the critters down here, especially that makara, if she had to pick one of the symbols it would probably have to be the sea. She touched that symbol and prepared to press, but something just didn't feel right.

Something that Sensei used to say nagged at her; 'If you can defeat yourself, you can defeat anyone else.' She wasn't sure what the heck he really meant, but he always said that when he was telling them to challenge themselves. Maybe whoever created this was some sort of sensei.

That was it! She pressed the symbol of the man, in the middle of the diagram, and felt what she could only describe as an electric shock pulse through her body. A deep rumble shook the cavern as the water to the right of the throne churned and a large stone door swung open. Then, a figure walked out, one of the oddest that Demie had seen yet in this world.

From the shoulders down, this figure was human. But on the shoulders sat an elephant head; trunk, tusks and all.

Immediately, Draupadi and the others swam over and Draupadi greeted the figure with a full bow, placing her hands together above her head. "Namaste, Lord Ganesha. We are honored by your visit."

The elephant-man, who Demie presumed was Lord Ganesha, acknowledged the princess by returning the bow, but then it was to Demie that he turned.

"Who are you?" Demie asked, giving her own bow.

"I am called Lord Ganesha, but to explain who I truly am would take both more time and more knowledge than you have." His voice was deep and rumbled so much, she wondered if the walls would hold. "You will face many challenges, young one. And you are wise indeed to recognize that conquering yourself is the greatest challenge any of us face. Because you have chosen wisely, what is your greatest desire?"

Demie waited for Lord Ganesha to present some kind of list, like most of the merchants seemed to offer up, but he simply waited for her response. She hadn't expected to come up with her own answer. Chandar might suggest asking for some kind of weapon or something, but that wasn't what she had in mind.

"I wish to conquer myself," Demie replied.

"A wise desire, to be sure. And yet, only you can bring that to pass. Even I cannot fulfill such a request. What can I give you which you can not give yourself?"

Demie didn't have to think about that one, she knew what she wanted and maybe she'd finally get it. "I want to find my sister Kori and bring her home, back to where I came from."

"I can give you the key to fulfill your wish." Lord Ganesha bowed toward her, and continued, "But it will be up to you to find the lock and turn the key. You have much further to go and less time than you realize. Mark my words, what you ask for may not be what you think it is. Take heed and waste not any time."

Lord Ganesha reached into a pouch on his waist, and held out something in his hand. "Listen closely, young one, and stray not. You must take this token of great power to the forgotten city of Musi, deep in the Dandaka forest. There an old friend of mine, whom I have not seen in an exceedingly long time, will explain what you must do with it. Now follow the passage I opened and make haste."

Demie took what Lord Ganesha held out and stared at it dubiously; a small black egg. As she held it, though, it squirmed and she almost released it. Examining it, she found that it was pitch black, with brilliant sparkles within it. The fact that it seemed alive creeped her out in a way nothing else ever had, and she stuffed it in her pack immediately so she wouldn't have to look at it.

The Lord bowed toward Demie and the others, then continued. "I am required elsewhere, and can stay no longer. I have given you all that you need."

And then he vanished.

Cassie wasn't sure how long she stood there, completely oblivious to anything around her, but eventually she picked up her bag of groceries and went inside.

Whether it was because of Sherman's comments, or what the boy next door had said, Cassie went into the kitchen and opened the two remaining liquor bottles. She did not hesitate as she turned them upside down and poured them down the drain.

Then she went into the den and checked on Demie. Although the drip bag was not empty and it was not yet time to change Demie and clean her up, Cassie worked her way through the list of tasks. She took her time, and was especially diligent with the cleaning, tending to some things that the nurses often overlooked. And all the while, she kept thinking about what Chandar had claimed.

The whole idea was preposterous, of course. The kid probably got it from some movie he watched, and thought she would be desperate enough to fall for it. But why would he try to con her? He hadn't asked for money, at least not yet.

On the other hand, he appeared to actually believe what he was saying. Cassie didn't know much about her neighbors, but she never got the impression that their son had mental problems, or was as some people like to put it these days, 'intellectually challenged'. As she knew all too well, reality was enough challenge in itself.

She gently wiped Demie's face, arms and hands with a washcloth, and then Cassie stroked her daughter's face and lightly kissed the child on the forehead. Although she tried to hold them back, sobs forced their way up, as Cassie began to let her pain out in gasps.

Then, as she hugged Demie's still body, her cries grew into animal-like wails of pain and anguish. After a time, the anguish drained out of her until Cassie found herself sitting on the floor next to Demie's bed, head in her hands, moaning "No."

Chandar's words came back to her, and a cold fury stirred within her like a bitter winter wind. Pulling herself to her feet, she barely paused to wipe her eyes and nose and stalked outside to the house next door.

When Chandar answered the doorbell, Cassie snarled at him, and hissed, "You are sick and disgusting. I don't know what kind of game you're up to, but you are a pathetic excuse for a human being."

Then, before she left, she grabbed the door from him and slammed it shut.

CHAPTER NINETEEN

Chandar returned to his computer just in time to see Ganesha vanish.

Luckily, his parents were on the phone with family back in India when Demie's mom rang the doorbell. She rang it two or three times before Baba asked him to get the door, but then he had to run for the door when she started punching the buzzer like a jackhammer.

The moment he opened the door, Chandar feared that the red-eyed, snot driveling disheveled woman was going to attack him. The hatred in her eyes drilled into him as she hissed her words, and the walls actually shook when she slammed the front door.

Chandar stared at the closed door, wondering what had just happened, then jumped when his mother spoke right behind him. "Was that Miss Morris from next door?"

"Yes, Maa. She's a little crazy."

"What did she want?" Apparently his mother only caught the tail end, thank God.

"I think she's looking for her daughter."

"But...the child is in a coma, is she not?"

"Yeah, I know. That's what I'm trying to say."

His mother muttered something about wandering spirits and left for the living room to pray at the family shrine. The irony was that Maa probably wasn't too far off about Demie. Of course, then he had to explain everything to his father as well, so it took him a while to get back online in Panchala.

His nerves were starting to settle down as he found Demie herding the group into a long winding passage, which she managed to discover behind the throne. Chandar let her know he was back and she filled him in on what Ganesha told them. He had to admit a grudging respect for her.

"By the way, did you talk to my mom?" she asked.

"Yeah, let's just say that it didn't go very well."

"You mean she didn't believe you?"

"That's one way of putting it," Chandar replied.

"So? What happened?"

"I don't want to talk about it. Just don't ever ask me to tell her again. Ever."

"Okay."

"Really, I mean it. Don't ask."

"Look, I get it, okay?"

Chandar had done enough talking, and wasn't in the mood to chat. Setting his character to auto-follow, he pulled up the game world global map. It listed all the major features in Panchala, but not what he was looking for. Then he went through all the area maps which were much more detailed, but required a lot of time to scroll through. Again, his objective was not on any of them.

The group was still trudging through what looked like a very long tunnel, so Chandar switched out of the game and browsed through some walk-through sites, where people posted detailed steps on how to complete quests. Because Panchala was so new, there were only a few walk-through posts and none had what he was looking for either. Finally, he scanned a number of chat boards before he came to the surprising but inevitable conclusion.

There was no Dandaka Forest in the Panchala world.

Karen strolled into the office, whistling to herself. The CEO approved her plan and now she would make Tony actually pull the trigger. That would be almost as good as one of her Saturday morning aerobics classes; she just happened to despise soccer moms more.

The first thing she noticed when she strolled into the office was that Tony's prized C3PO was gone. When she saw that his monitor was off and Carolyn said that he had left, she assumed he was blowing off some steam. That was fine, she would let him run out the line for a bit before she reeled him in. It was when she checked her email that her bubble burst a little, as she read the memo from HR that Tony would be taking some personal leave. Oh hell.

Turning to Joachim and Carolyn, she said she had an announcement to make.

"This morning, I took over the Panchala project. As of now, the two of you and Tony will report directly to me. We have some anomalies we're dealing with and now this rogue program, Kali, is running loose and wiping out customer characters and accounts. All thanks to our friend Tony."

"Well, if I remember correctly, it was actually..." Joachim started to respond and then stopped, halted by Karen's cold stare. "...something I don't remember at all."

"As I was saying before I was interrupted, I'm cleaning up Tony's mess. We need to contain the damage which this rogue program is spreading. But because we can't find the processes running in the sub-system, there's only one option left.

"This evening we shut Panchala down. Every single server."

Demie finally saw light at the end of the tunnel, literally. There was no day or night in the tunnel, just the same phosphorescent glow that lit the tunnel in Amaravati, so she had no idea how long they walked down that endless tube. It was a long time until the passage eventually sloped upward. When she saw the faint spot of light ahead, she was so relieved she started running.

They burst into bright sunlight and green foliage, in a small glen surrounded by jungle. The moment the last of her group emerged from the ten foot opening in the rock outcropping, the tunnel entrance shimmered and vanished from the rock face with a snap. Hopefully, they hadn't forgotten anything.

"So, Yudhishthira, which way to Dandaka Forest?" Demie asked.

The Pandava brother paused, turned in a circle and then responded, "In truth, I can offer no guidance as to our course. The place you ask of remains unknown to me."

"I'm not surprised," Chandar/Samita chimed in. "I searched everywhere I can think of, but there is no reference to Dandaka Forest anywhere in Panchala."

It seemed like up to this point, she always had someone to guide her, whether it was Lizat, Draupadi or Yudhishthira. There was always someone else she could get directions from, but now they were looking to her and Demie felt suddenly inadequate, unprepared.

Demie examined the surrounding terrain, looking for a clue to follow. The vegetation was similar to the jungle outside Kampilya, but deeper green and the trees had some kind of moss hanging from them. They might be further to the south but that didn't help much.

She reluctantly opened her purse and took out that black egg, hoping it might provide some clue. The slimy cold thing creeped her out as it squirmed in her hand like an egg-shaped frog and she resisted the urge to fling it away. There was something familiar about it and she didn't want to examine it, although she decided that she had to.

The thing was as black and featureless as before, aside from brilliant specks of light deep inside, and it revealed no pattern or map as to which direction they should go. However, as she lifted it to look closer, she jumped when she felt a tug in her hand toward the two o'clock direction. It was much like the pull that led her to Draupadi's tower.

No trails led from this small clearing, which meant she had to forge her way through the vegetation. She sighed as she tucked the orb back into her purse and told everyone to follow her, just hoping for the best. They spent the better part of a day cycle working their way through the fairly thick undergrowth, with frequent stops as Demie consulted the egg-compass. The day cycle was ending when the orb led them up to an impassable wall of thickets.

"Do you know where we are?" She asked Chandar. She certainly had no idea.

"According to the global map, we are at the edge of the Panchala world. There isn't anything further, so I don't know what to suggest."

Demie moved to the right along the thicket wall, but the barrier remained as impassable as ever. The further she moved the more the egg pulled leftward. Returning to her starting point, Demie tried the other direction with similar results pulling her back to the first spot where she encountered the wall.

Back where she started, she pushed, kicked and struck the mass of thickets but it remained impervious. Finally, in frustration, she threw the egg against the wall, and it sank into the barrier. The thickets melted away, and an opening developed similar to the portal in Hastinpura that swallowed Sahadeva. This portal had the appearance of a very blurry piece of glass with the egg suspended in the midst, but when she pressed on it, her arm passed through.

"I don't know how long this will stay open, so come on through," Demie called out to Draupadi, while keeping the black object in place on the wall and stepping though herself. Moments later, Draupadi, Yudhishthira and Arjuna came through but there was no sign of Samita. Demie waited a couple minutes, but either Chandar was asleep at the keyboard or didn't want to come through. The portal vanished when Demie pulled the egg away and then she looked around to see where they were.

In most respects, the jungle was similar to the one on the other side of the barrier, but the colors were different and something felt very different. Then it hit Demie...she was sweating and breathing, for real.

She jumped and went higher than expected before gravity pulled her down to smack on the ground. Warm sticky air clung to her skin and a musty earthy odor filled her nose. The plants had a definite texture, and the sound of birds and insects echoed through the trees. Demie inhaled deeply, laughed and spun around, feeling truly alive.

Draupadi and her husbands were touching themselves, each other and the plants around them in wonderment, looking around as if they were in the ultimate candy store. Demie still held the egg in her hand. It no longer had that slimy, squirmy feel, though it did continue to pull her forward, toward a path that lay ahead of them.

"What magic have you wrought?" Draupadi asked, as she slowly turned, gazing with wide eyes. "What is this strange land which you have transported us to?"

"I can't explain right now," Demie replied, which was the ultimate understatement. Feeling a bit like she was in Disneyland, she grasped the princess's hand. "We have to keep going, so come with me."

The path wound through a dense, dark jungle for maybe a quarter mile and then ran alongside a small stream, where Demie paused for a moment to run her fingers through the cool, refreshing water. She never thought anything could feel so spectacular. After splashing her companions, they continued until the trail turned uphill, away from the flowing water. Even under the tree canopy everything was well lit, but Demie saw no source of light in the sky. That was another way that this world was both like, yet unlike the one she came from.

The trail climbed back and forth up a fairly steep incline, and they ascended a couple hundred feet. They were actually panting, which the Panchalans complained about, when the trail leveled out at a small lake which was several hundred feet across. A cliff towered high above them on the other side of the expanse and a tall thin waterfall fed the lake, while the stream they earlier followed emptied out of the other side of the lake.

Once she caught her breath, Draupadi turned to Demie, "I have a very unpleasant feeling where my body touches the ground!"

"Yeah, well, you're giving me an unpleasant feeling where my body sits on the ground," Demie replied, then continued following the trail around the water until it came to an abrupt end at the cliff, near the waterfall. She pulled out the egg, but was disappointed that it no longer pulled. It seemed there was no forgotten city of Musi. Maybe it was called forgotten because someone forgot to build it.

Disgusted, Demie was about to toss the useless egg into the lake when she saw a figure step out from the edge of the waterfall. The rastafarian shroud of the rishi Durvasa was unmistakable, and Demie shivered. This had to be Kori's Shadowman and she felt torn between trust and fear. She needed his help, but he was the reason she needed help to begin with.

While the rishi approached, Draupadi and her husbands immediately greeted him with their Namaste bows, and Demie warily followed suit. When Durvasa came up to them, he returned the greeting and then turned to Demie.

"As foretold," he said, "You found the path that led you here. Events that have long been set in motion are nearly complete, so it is time to finish what has begun."

"You're not just a rishi, are you?" Demie asked, her arms crossed. "I don't care why or what you are doing, I just want to get home."

The rishi gestured for them to follow and walked back to the edge of the waterfall, then vanished. Following him, they passed through a thin veil of water and found an enormous cavity on the other side, hollowed out of the cliff wall. Above them, level after level of houses and buildings were carved out of the rock, linked by a bewildering spider web of stairs.

The entire city had a worn look to it, the sharp edges of steps and walls worn smooth by time and use. Aside from the hewn rock, the space was barren, but images flashed through Demie's mind of a time when crowds thronged through streets vibrant with life. Merchants and students, lovers and politicians, young and old occupied with things important and trivial.

But now, the only sound Demie heard was the constant roar of the waterfall next to them. Before she could ask the rishi where all the population went, he gestured for them to continue following as he led them to a large open space, centering on a dais which supported a simple table or altar made of what appeared to be obsidian. Durvasa led them up to the altar and gestured at a round black basin half filled with water.

"You ask how you may return to the world you came from. Place the egg you brought in this basin of water and I will show you. Then you will choose your path."

Demie retrieved the egg, and placed it in the basin without hesitation. She was more than ready to go home, and get this dream-nightmare over with.

The black egg rapidly expanded into a pitch black sphere about four feet across, full of countless fuzzy bright dots. She felt a searing cold coming from the sphere, as if it sucked the heat from all around them.

"The purpose for which you were brought here is complete, so you may return now," the rishi said. "Simply step into the portal and you will return to what was before you came here."

"Are you kidding me, step into that thing?" Demie asked.

Demie reached out to touch the surface of the sphere. It had a spring to it, similar to the other portals she had encountered. But she shivered when she looked at the fuzzy dots of light within and they reminded her of what she saw when Kori was taken.

Without taking her eyes off the sphere, she addressed Durvasa, "When you say everything will be the same, does that mean without my sister?"

"You are correct. To recover that entity you must first find it, for only if you use the egg together will you return together. Understand this. If you return now, the path is clear and the waters smooth. Turn away, and I can not see where that new path leads."

Demie turned away from the dark sphere to face the rishi and emphatically stated, "Your purpose for bringing me may be complete, but my purpose is not. I left her behind once before, this time I will never return without her."

Durvasa turned and walked away from the altar. Demie followed, yearning to rip his head off and frustrated because she knew there was no way she could. He stood facing out at the waterfall, and without looking at her, continued, "This is your choice. But if you do not return now new paths will open, while others will close to you forever."

Demie flatly replied, without hesitation, "Just tell me what I have to do, okay?"

The rishi turned back to the altar, gesturing for Demie to come with him. He guided her hands to touch the sphere on its sides, and the thing collapsed again, until it was just a strange egg again. Except that the water was now gone. "You will find the one you seek when you look at the beginning. After you find her, activate the egg again and cross the threshold together."

Demie returned the egg to her backpack. "Can I ask one more question?" Durvasa nodded, and Demie's voice hardened as she continued, "Why did this happen to me? I deserve to know at least that much."

As he led them back to the glistening sheet of water, the rishi replied, "I could answer your question now. But if I did, you would not yet understand the answer."

With that, he pointed the way through the water and Demie emerged on the other side, standing outside with only her friends and more questions than answers.

Chandar helplessly watched online as the others in the party entered the portal. He was dumbfounded when he tried to follow, because Samita was blocked from entering. Nothing should have prevented his character from following wherever the others went, especially since they were in a party. Samita's experience level and items were on par with the others, so it just didn't make sense.

In any case, the portal vanished, so wherever they went was either a secret game area or they had entered a new realm. He just had to wait for them to return.

Chandar glanced at the cruise brochure Sanjali left. She circled two cruises which she equally preferred, and asked him to pick one.

He turned to the first, a one-week trip through the Caribbean, leaving out of Miami. The other was an eight-day tour of the Mexican Riviera, leaving out of San Diego. Unfortunately, neither left from New York City.

Frankly, spending a week stuck on a ship wasn't his idea of fun. He was susceptible to motion sickness, so he really didn't care whether he was puking into the Pacific or the Caribbean. But Sanjali gave him the booklet with such a deep smile and blissful eyes, he would have gone to the Antarctic if she had wanted. Still, the itinerary of the San Diego cruise gave him an idea.

"Yes!" He pumped his fist when an online search confirmed that the yoga center specializing in amputee yoga was located in Los Angeles. It shouldn't be hard to talk Sanjali into visiting a famous yogi. Then he thought of something else.

Yes, there it was, on the TerraMythos home page. Their headquarters was located in Long Beach, not far from the yoga center. He wouldn't say anything, not until they were out there. But how much could there be to do at a yoga center?

Chandar wasn't sure what he would accomplish, but if he explained to them what happened to Demie maybe they would understand how she got there. And more importantly, how to get her back. The key was to figure out whom he needed to talk to. It took a while, but after poking around on the website and teasing the code for the credits, he eventually discovered that the development team for Panchala was headed by Tony and Karen McClure.

Chandar picked up the phone to call Sanjali and tell her they were going to California.

Exhaustion hit Cassie like a bus out of nowhere. Night crept up before she knew it and when she saw that it was 9:00, her stomach growled to life with a vengeance. Along with an urge to smoke.

She gathered the spray bottles of all-purpose cleaner and glass cleaner, along with rags, paper towels and furniture polish and tucked them away in the upstairs linen closet. Then she went back into Demie's room and carefully placed all the clutter on the dresser and side table exactly as she found it. Her own room and the upstairs bathroom hadn't taken long to clean; it was Demie's room that had taken most of her time.

Her spirits felt high, and she hummed as she skipped down the stairs to the kitchen. Keeping busy all evening not only got things done which she had neglected, it also kept her from thinking about drinking. Demie's evening care still needed to be done, so Cassie only had time to warm up a frozen dinner. She pulled out a lasagna meal and got it going in the microwave.

As she watched her meal rotate in the oven, she thought back to what that creepy boy next door said. It was unnerving that he somehow knew her pet name for Demie. In fact, she couldn't remember the last time she called Demie that, but it was long enough that she completely forgot about it. So there was no way that he could have over-heard them in the backyard. Just the thought that maybe there was something to what the kid said gave Cassie goose bumps, but she dismissed the notion as the microwave signaled that her meal was ready.

After eating and cleaning up the kitchen, Cassie went into the den and she was on top of things as she ran through the evening checklist. The basics taken care of and Demie settled for the evening, Cassie hummed to herself as she spread skin moisturizer on some dry areas she found while rotating Demie's body. She finished one arm and was gently massaging lotion on her daughter's right hand, when she felt an electric hum on her palm and fingertips.

Startled, Cassie jerked her hand away, then cautiously placed her hand back. Again, she felt an almost magnetic, tingling connection as she grasped Demie's hand and she couldn't explain it, but she felt that her daughter was in grave danger.

Her heart pounding, Cassie checked the IV, Demie's pulse and temperature, and even ran the automatic blood pressure machine. Everything was normal, but she couldn't shake the haunting premonition. Maybe Demie really was trying to contact her through that boy after all, and passed along the watermelon comment so she would understand.

If that was true, maybe she could talk to Demie too.

Karen spent the rest of the afternoon re-arranging the office to suit her. First, she had to clear off Tony's desk and pack his silly trinkets and toys in a couple of boxes which she picked up from the facilities manager. Really, that was something Tony should've done, but she wasn't going to wait. She wanted the view now.

Swapping computers didn't take long, and she positioned the keyboard and monitors to her liking, then started everything up. The books and files she could move later. Better yet, she would have Tony move them. She was going to be too busy running things. As she signed onto her primary computer, she glanced out the window and saw Tony out in the parking lot.

He was walking out to his car, with two security guards escorting him. Apparently, his visit to HR didn't go as well as he expected. Karen grinned, sat back with crossed arms and watched with delight as he walked to the back of his car. Then one of the guards unslung a set of golf clubs from his back and slid them into Tony's trunk, while the other deposited a box he carried on Tony's front seat. Then they both shook Tony's hand.

An emphatic "Uhh!" forced its way through her clenched teeth as Karen flung her pen at the window. In the reflection of the glass, she saw both of her underlings look up as it bounced off, but they were smart enough to just glance at each other and say nothing.

Okay, so Tony was chummy with the guards. That had always been one of his problems, associating too much with riff-raff, and not with people who really mattered. Like the CEO.

Karen swung her chair around to face Joachim, who had been on the phone with the server farm for the past half hour. "Alright, it's time. Turn the lights off."

Joachim spoke into the phone, and every Panchala server shut down.

PART THREE – THE NASCENCE

CHAPTER TWENTY

Cassie rolled over in bed, unable to get comfortable. The pillow over her head didn't shut out the midnight thoughts haunting her—that Demie was in trouble and trying to contact her. Each time she drifted toward slumber, memories of the eerie connection she experienced earlier that evening with Demie jumbled with that strange boy's words and rushed out onto the field of her mind. Finally, in the dwindling hours of the night she surrendered to the conclusion her thoughts led her to, and fell into a dreamless slumber. Until sunlight oozed between the blinds and poked her eyes.

Groaning, she sat up. At least this headache was from lack of sleep instead of a hangover.

After slipping on a robe, she went into the kitchen and set up the coffee pot. Somehow or other, the kid knew Demie's pet name. He had to be in touch with Demie, because there was no other logical explanation for what he knew. For the first time since that awful EMT call, Cassie felt a glimmer of hope.

While the coffee brewed, Cassie checked on Demie. Her daughter was unchanged from last night, and Cassie quickly tended to the drip bag and other early morning cleaning chores. Finished, she paused to examine Demie's face.

"I haven't taken very good care of you, have I?" She stroked her daughter's brow. "I'm so sorry. Mom started down a path she should've stayed away from. But I'm not going there again, sweetie. I promise, pinkie swear!"

Cassie walked around the bed, gently moving and rotating Demie's body to prevent bedsores. "I'll bet that feels better. When you wake up, we'll do that camping trip we keep talking about, you'll see."

After fluffing the pillows and carefully replacing them, Cassie checked the blanket and sheets, then started applying lotion to Demie's limbs.

"Do you know, that foolish boy next door claimed that he's been talking with you on the computer! Must be a sign of the times, because when I was a kid we tried to contact the dead using Ouija Boards and séances and stuff like that. I guess it makes sense; if everyone else is going high tech with email and instant messaging, why not the dead too?"

"What?" Cassie gasped. "Oh, honey, don't get me wrong! I'm not saying you're one of the dead. You know what I mean, the dead and the sleeping share the same world. I just wish we could communicate somehow. Even by computer."

At that moment, just as the coffee pot chirped its readiness from the other room, Cassie swore she felt Demie's hand squeeze hers. It was very slight, and she almost missed it. But she knew it was a squeeze, praise the Lord. Demie was telling her something!

Cassie waited for a few more minutes, encouraging Demie to try again, but apparently she just had one squeeze in her that morning. But that would do for now.

She went back to the kitchen, and as she sat down at the table with her coffee, she knew she had to contact Demie. Her daughter needed her, and wanted to tell her something important; something that required more than hand squeezes.

That boy, Chandar, had been in contact with Demie. Cassie was going to find out how.

Demie stood next to the waterfall, ready to cry with disappointment and frustration. What was the whole point of this trip? The cool mist of the waterfall raised goose bumps on her arms, so she started moving away from it when Rishi Durvasa emerged from the sheet of water. He walked the path around the lake, and a barely perceptible wave of his hand conveyed that they should follow.

"I will accompany you to the trees," he said. "Now that you have chosen not to return to what is, you must make haste if you wish to preserve what will be."

Demie pondered whether to bother asking the rishi what he meant by that, but figured a riddle upon a riddle would only add confusion. The bottom line was that he was telling her not to waste time, she got that.

"So what is this place and who are you, exactly?" She asked, trying a different approach.

Durvasa answered without looking at her, "This is a paradigm that conforms to what you can recognize. When you understand why you were chosen, you will understand who I am."

That was helpful, Demie thought. Was it too much to ask for a straight answer? "And when will that be?" she asked as they reached the far side of the lake, where the trail turned to go downhill toward the stream and eventually the spot where they created the portal.

"That will be up to you," the rishi replied. Then the ground began shaking.

The quake was not so much ground shaking, as it was a rippling of the whole world. Nothing was thrown around, but it felt as if the gods were shaking the universe the way one shakes out a rug. The whole incident lasted only a few seconds, but Draupadi grabbed onto Demie's arm and clung to her as they both screamed, even after the ripples stopped.

"What was that?" the princess asked, still trembling.

"It was the opening of an egg," answered Durvasa, "and it was the reason you were brought to this place."

"Don't even try to explain that one to me," Demie answered. "Just tell me the best way to get out of here." And hopefully the fastest.

The rishi pointed to the trail leading downhill. "Stay on this path and you will find your way back. Remember what I said, that evil is loose in the world and if you do not make haste, it may destroy that which you seek. If you are not wary, it may destroy you as well."

"What do we need to be wary of?" asked Demie.

"That which hunts you, and which you must hunt in turn. Therefore, you would do well to find you some hunters."

Demie should've known better than to expect a useful answer and led her group down the path they came in on. Once they reached level ground, she got them to jog until they made it back to the thicket barrier.

The Panchalans were all gasping heavily, and Draupadi collapsed on the ground as she cried out, "Demie, my friend, what is happening to us? I fear we are about to die."

Demie shook her head, "Just take deep breaths." Then she turned to face the thorny wall.

It appeared as impassable from this side as it had from the other, but once again when she struck it with her black egg, it sank in and dissolved an opening big enough for them to traverse. After the Panchalans went across, Demie slipped through and when she pulled the orb from the wall, the opening vanished. How the heck did Durvasa manage to enter this place? He probably had some secret path that only the most enlightened could walk on. Whatever.

Back in the Panchalan jungle, they found Chandar's character Samita standing, patiently waiting. And Chandar-less, of course, so he was still offline. Demie paused to consider where to go next. That dumb rishi could've told them something useful, but no, he had to talk nonsense about breaking eggs.

When Mom was looking for something she lost, she always said start at the beginning and retrace your steps. And the rishi said look at the beginning. So she needed to return to the field where she first woke up, and start looking for Kori from there.

"What was the name of that city again, where I found you?" she asked Draupadi.

"It was in Kampilya that you freed me from my bondage," Draupadi replied, and then bowed to her.

"Which way to Kampilya?" Demie asked Yudhishthira, wishing for the first time they had some way to fly. He pointed toward what had to be the densest part of the jungle.

"I should've guessed," Demie said, and after pushing Samita to make sure she followed, dashed off in that direction. So she didn't notice the surrounding vegetation taking on deeper colors, the ground becoming more textured or the flowers giving off scents they never had before.

After they left, the growing circle of change continued to spread and trailed after them like a boat wake.

Karen sat back in her chair, arms crossed as she glared at the monitor and watched Kali's movement across the Panchala countryside. It moved in a straight line, over hills and across streams in a steady pace. Occasionally, it encountered an unfortunate small party of Player Characters and paused just long enough to annihilate all trace of them. The hapless parties never offered enough resistance to cause any measurable damage to the avatar.

She turned to Joachim.

"I told you to shut it down."

"They just did."

"Oh really? Then why am I still logged in?" she pointed at her screen. "Tell them to check again."

Joachim spoke for a few minutes and then looked up. "They checked twice, every server is off. And yes, the backup servers as well."

Karen flung herself out of her chair. "Do I have to do everything myself? The idiots you're talking to obviously couldn't find a server if it fell on them! Okay, let me draw a picture for you: one of the virtual servers must have moved somewhere, so just do something any kiddie hacker could do and find the damn thing. Preferably by the time I get back."

She stormed out into the hall to get some coffee. It was obviously going to be a long night, and she needed to give herself some space before she ripped Joachim's incompetent head off. Now that Tony was out of the driver's seat, there would be some staffing changes. But not tonight.

After pacing down to the cafeteria and ruling out all of the worthless vending machine selections, Karen figured they should've had plenty of time to find one lousy server. She swung by the coffee station in the kitchen, and headed back to the office.

Joachim was getting off the phone as Karen came in. She sat at her desk and spun around to face him, "So? Is Panchala shut down?"

Joachim shook his head.

"Then where is it running? I see you're not on the phone with the Ops Center."

Again Joachim shook his head. "They checked and double checked, and I double checked them. Every trace we attempt goes off-net and fails to return. They go to IP addresses that aren't registered, and every time we check DNS the assigned addresses change."

"So what are you telling me?"

"Panchala is indeed still up and running, though I don't understand how. Wherever the servers are, they're not anywhere we can find."

Chandar and Sanjali sat side-by-side on the living-room couch, reviewing the cruise brochure while their mothers wrangled over wedding plans in the kitchen. The look on Sanjali's face told Chandar that he chose wrong when he said he wanted to do the Mexico cruise.

He still didn't get it. Why do girls give you a choice, when you really don't have one? Either you make the wrong choice, or you weren't really supposed to choose and you got into trouble because you did. How do you pass a test that you don't know you're taking?

Still, Sanjali's excitement about the trip was infectious. As they planned the details of the trip, things they could do onboard and what they would do when they returned, all the little pieces of building a life with Sanjali started to fit together naturally, in a way he never expected, like a comfortable tailor-made coat. But Chandar really did want to go on the Mexican trip. And it wasn't just the yoga center. He found some really fun activities on the Riviera while doing some online research. Which gave him an idea.

After taking Sanjali to the kitchen so they could tell their parents where they would be, he led her back to his room where he could show her some of the web pages he found.

"Oh, wow." This was the first time she had seen his room.

Chandar cringed inside. He hadn't planned to bring her back here, so clutter lay over the room like a fresh snowfall. While she watched, he scurried to gather up clothes and school books, and at least made neat piles he could deal with later. When he turned back to her, the hint of a smile vanished from her face as she tried to look stern.

He sat her down at his computer, and eagerly scrambled to get another chair from the dining room. Then he pulled up the websites he bookmarked. The bedroom door was open, of course; their parents might forgo some traditions but certain standards were not negotiable.

Sanjali warmed up quickly to the Riviera, and they were actually deciding which stateroom they should book on the Mexican cruise, when Chandar heard a knock at the bedroom door. Miss Morris stood in the doorway, as his father walked away.

"Hello?" Demie's mom said, "Oh, I'm so sorry, I didn't know you had company."

Chandar was so shocked to see her, after their last encounter, he had no idea what to say. Instead, he just stood up and mumbled.

"I'll be quick." Cassie took a step forward. "I can come back another time, but I just wanted to say that I'm really sorry about what I said the other day. It was very rude, and I was under a lot of stress. Anyway, I do believe what you..." Cassie's words trailed off as she stared past Chandar, at something on his desk. Taking several quick steps to the desk, her hand darted to the shelf and picked up Demie's diary.

"So, that's how you know private, intimate details about my daughter! How dare you play with me like that. How dare you!" Sanjali sat riveted in her chair as Cassie stepped up to Chandar and grabbed him by the shirt, pulling his face to within inches of hers. Cold sweat broke out on his neck and back.

"But she wanted me..." Chandar started to protest.

"She wanted you? I'll bet she wanted you. Don't even try to explain why her diary is in your room. I'm going to read through it myself, and when I find out all the nasty things you've been doing to her, I'm calling the police." Cassie shoved Chandar halfway across the room, and as she exited with the diary, she turned to face Chandar one last time.

"For God's sake, she just turned sixteen, you sick pervert!" Then she swept from the room.

Stunned, Chandar turned to face Sanjali, who stared at Chandar in shock. Then, as she started crying, she stood up and slapped Chandar. "You disgust me," she cried, then fled the room.

By the time Chandar got out to the hallway, Sanjali had already gathered her bewildered mother and they were heading for the front door. Sanjali's last words, as she went out the door, were, "I don't want to see you again. Ever."

"What did you do to her?" his mother hissed at him. "What if she calls the wedding off?"

"I didn't do anything, Maa. And I really don't care." But he turned to hide the tears as he looked out the door, the handprint on the left side of his face glowing red.

Demie led the way through the jungle. She didn't notice the structural change in the environment that trailed behind her, spreading out on both sides. As they went the terrain became less hilly and the vegetation thinned out, so they maintained a fairly decent pace. She could easily leave the others behind, so she regularly checked behind to make sure they kept up.

She was anxious to get back to Kampilya, so it was frustrating that the few trails they came across went off to one side or another. But they encountered few animals and no people as they went cross-country, and eventually found a path that ran mostly in the direction they wanted to go.

Soon, a couple of PCs came down the trail toward them. Now that Demie knew these were avatars for real-world players she paid them little mind, because unless she ran across Lizat she wasn't adding anyone to her group. So she was caught off guard when the avatars both turned and attacked her in a frenzy.

Since they had not engaged in any combat since Makara's den, she was unprepared and didn't even have a weapon ready. The two characters savagely hacked at her, but they were pretty low level and she still had the Rakshasa armor on, so the few blows they landed were absorbed. The Pandava brothers took them down before Draupadi could even join the melee.

Demie examined the vanquished avatars before they disappeared. The weird thing was, they were in the same state as Samita, which meant 'disconnected' from their real-world players. So how the heck could they have acted with some kind of purpose or intent? And why choose to attack Demie?

There wasn't any point in asking Draupadi, so Demie continued up the path and came to a dead stop at the edge of a small town. Or what had once been a small town, before every individual, building and structure was reduced to dirt. If this world had machines, Demie would have sworn the place had been leveled by a bulldozer.

From the other side of the clearing, something missed by the demolition came running out of the jungle. A shorthaired brown dog, wearing a collar that came from a now-erased master, ran up to Demie whining and wagging its tail like a small propeller.

Demie smiled as she leaned down to pet the critter and found that it had an invisible leash, similar to the tether she used when pulling animals for Lizat. She quickly passed the 'leash' to Yudhishthira, so she didn't notice the dog breath it suddenly developed.

What she did notice was a broad path on one side, cleared by the bulldozer. And on the other side a slightly wider trail extended into the distance, flattened by a somewhat larger bulldozer. She felt chills ripple through her body as she saw where it led.

The larger path headed the exact same direction they were going.

Karen slammed down the phone and glared at the screen again, tracking Kali's progress across the Panchala landscape. Night settled outside the expansive window of her new office space, and she had sent the rest of the team home half an hour before. Mostly because she didn't want them to hear her make some phone calls.

"Arrrrrgh," she vented as she threw herself in frustration back into her chair. She tried every number she collected over the years, some of his favorite hangouts, and even mutual friends. Tony was nowhere to be found. It was as if he had fallen off the face of the earth.

She got up and started pacing. This was too convenient. She takes over his miserable project, he heads out the door and all of a sudden they've not only lost control of Panchala--they've somehow lost Panchala altogether.

For the first time since taking Tony down, she was scared. She had seriously under-estimated him. Whatever he did, however he did it, somehow Tony pulled off the ultimate poison pill. He didn't merely crash the company's system, he took the whole damn thing with him.

And now she couldn't find him to save her life. Or her job.

CHAPTER TWENTY-ONE

Demie was grateful for one thing. At least that bulldozer created a path not only clear of obstacles but also straight as an arrow, so they could run at full speed and not even waste time on curves. The trail extended over rolling hills like an interstate highway at home, and the sheer power of whatever did this frightened her.

While pausing for a moment to let her companions to catch up, Demie got a message from Chandar. Although his Samita character was still inactive, it continued following behind the Pandavas and Chandar could still communicate.

“Something’s really wrong with Panchala. I can log in but can’t do anything with my character or even see what’s happening. What are you doing over there?”

“Why do you think I might be doing something?” Demie shot back. She didn’t even want to be here, let alone be blamed for the world’s problems.

“The last time Panchala froze up like this, you were taking over my character.”

“Well, there haven’t been any lightning strikes on my end, but if I see a thunderstorm that’s not a bad idea. Maybe I’ll get back the same way I came.”

“Don’t count on it, they’re just graphics on your side. Not real.”

Draupadi and her husbands came trotting up, with Samita not too far behind, so Demie turned and resumed running, while replying to Chandar. “By the way, have you talked with my mom anymore?"

Chandar immediately replied, "I told you, don't ask. But I do have a question, did you write anything about me in your diary?"

"I don't know, just that I thought you were a geek. Why? You're not reading the diary, are you? You promised not to read it."

When the Shadowman dropped her back into a Kori-less life, Demie not only refused to speak, she spurned any friendships in a world she didn't belong to. But her bedroom window looked out over their backyards and over the years, she watched Chandar and fantasized about the exotic boy next door. So yeah, maybe she wrote a few fantasies down. Well, more than a few, and Demie felt a queasy embarrassment just recalling some of them. There was a phase when she thought he was uber hot, but as long as he kept his promise to stay out of her diary, what difference did it make?

"I assure you, I'm not reading it. I was just curious is all. Anyway, I can't do anything here, so I'm going to log off. I'll try again later."

"Before you go," Demie asked, "Can you check your map and see what direction we are going?" Not that she didn't trust Yudhishthira, but he had led them to the edge of an ocean.

"It looks like you are heading straight for Kampilya." Then he was gone.

Demie stopped as she came over the next hill. Below and ahead of them, the cleared highway came up to a small town and ended there. What the heck? She stepped into the cover of some nearby trees.

A small crowd was gathered in the center of the town, in what appeared to be some sort of riot. Then one of the buildings suddenly vanished, with a brief flash. Demie went deeper into the forest and cautiously weaved her way downhill toward the small town so she could get a closer view. They reached the edge of a drop-off, where they could look down onto the settlement below.

That Kali devil marched throughout the village, using her weapons to vaporize every person she came across, even the dogs and cows and chickens. Except every so often, she would grab someone and stare at the person for a moment until her victim shriveled and turned as black as the darkest night, then set the person down behind her.

Then Demie gasped. Those charred figures joined a growing retinue of jet-black individuals that trailed behind Kali, also attacking anything that moved. Together, they cleared out all of the inhabitants in the town. Once every person had been eliminated or converted to the dark side, Kali's force proceeded to flatten all the buildings. And when the buildings were gone she wiped out any remaining traces of the town, even the streets themselves.

Then Kali resumed the direction she was heading when she came across the unfortunate town, spearheading the small corps that fanned out behind her, scorching the earth as they went. As they went over the next hill, Demie thought they looked like a swarm of army ants.

Once she was certain all of Kali's troops were gone, Demie led the group down to where the town once stood, and felt a deep cold fear when she looked around. Nothing remained but bare ground. Kali's motives were as mysterious as any rishi, but Demie didn't need a rishi to point out the obvious.

Somehow, Kali had to be stopped. Based on what she had just seen, nothing in Panchala would do more than slow her down. It was up to Demie to do what she could, because if Kali reached Kampilya, it would be the equivalent of flattening the entire city and everyone in it with an atomic bomb.

Along with Kori, wherever she was.

Cassie sat on her couch, flipping back and forth through Demie's diary. She didn't believe it at first, but after skimming through it from cover to cover, the only places where her daughter mentioned Chandar were about clearly unfulfilled fantasies. Demie had never done anything with him, which both surprised and relieved Cassie at the same time.

On the other hand, Demie hardly mentioned her mom, though she made a lot of references to an imaginary sister she called Kori. That worried Cassie, because while a lot of kids had imaginary friends, Demie should have grown out of hers long ago. But mostly the entries were concerned with the girls on the team, who liked or hated whom, and how that carried over into school. All in all, the diary was surprisingly boring.

Not finding anything incriminating about the boy, Cassie spent some time reading those few parts where Demie wrote about her, usually after some sort of argument. Cassie turned to the last couple pages, which Demie wrote the night before the incident with the lightning.

Mom really blew it this time. She promised that if I kept my grades up she would let me have a pet. The report card came in the mail today and not only did I keep them up, they are the best grades I've had in high school. So I said I want a rabbit, but she said no because I couldn't even take care of a backpack let alone a rabbit. I can have a fish, or a hamster, or anything else that lives in a closed home, but no rabbit. Really? Why would I want a stupid fish? You can't pet a fish, and everyone knows hamsters bite. Only a rabbit would understand me, because they're mute too. So I'm going...

Cassie lowered the book as a car pulled into the driveway, and moments later the doorbell rang. Wondering who could possibly be visiting, she reluctantly set the journal down on the coffee table and went to the front door. Sherman stood there, while Lauren sat in the idling car.

"We're on our way out of town and I wanted to give you our contact information. Just in case anything comes up with Demie." He held out a folded piece of paper.

"Thanks. I'll let you know if it does." Cassie took the paper without opening it. "So this is the big trip, huh? Finally tying the knot and all?"

"Yeah, it's time. First a quick stop at the courthouse to see Judge Wheeler, and then we're off to a bed & breakfast overlooking a California beach. One of my business contacts gave me his reservation, and claims it has the best view on the West Coast. We'll see."

"Believe it or not, I'm glad for you. Best of luck." Cassie reached out to shake Sherman's hand.

"Thanks."

"Well, you better go, you know how the Judge hates to be kept waiting."

Cassie sighed with relief as he walked back to the car, and then she closed the front door once they backed out of the driveway. Before heading back to the sofa, she went into the kitchen and fixed a cup of chamomile tea. Sweetening it with a touch of honey, Cassie returned to the living room, sat on the couch with tucked legs and read the rest of Demie's diatribe.

The playoff game is tomorrow, and I know we're going to win, so I'll have to wait until after the state championship. Then I'll run away to live with Dad. I can't stand Lauren, but I bet they'll let me have a rabbit and not lie about things like that.

She almost dropped the book as she read the last page. The tea forgotten, she shut the book with shaking hands and closed her eyes. So her daughter had been planning from the very beginning to leave home and run away. Eventually, Cassie silently got up and went into the den where Demie lay. It wasn't time yet for another check, so Cassie pulled the chair over by the bed and sat, holding Demie's hand.

"Oh Honey, Mommy didn't know getting a rabbit was so important to you. We can work these things out. Really, I promise, just come on back home. Okay?" She paused, and put her ear near Demie's lips, desperately trying to catch the response when she saw Demie's lips twitch.

"You're right, trying to run away like this won't solve anything. And that Chandar boy. I still don't trust him, so I want you to tell me everything that's been going on." Again, she paused with her ear poised to listen.

"Yes, I know it's hard for you to talk right now. Don't worry, I'll come up with something that will help. You just be a good girl, and I'll be back before you know it."

Cassie rose, and after tucking the sheets in, gathered up her purse and headed out of the house. She knew a shop that specialized in the kinds of things she needed and would be able to help her. Plus, she had another errand to run as well.

Just as she entered her SUV, she glanced down the street and saw an unfamiliar car parked there. In the other direction were two other suspicious cars, all of them with men in them. They were scrunched down in their seats so most people wouldn't see them, but Cassie knew they were there. And one of them looked at her with binoculars. She wouldn't let them see fear.

Her hands shook as she backed out of the driveway and drove down the street. She kept glancing in the rearview mirror to see if any of them followed her, but they didn't. Which meant they had colleagues positioned ahead to pick up her tail and follow.

Yes, they were clever. But she was on to them now.

Chandar watched on the map as Demie's party ran across mile after mile of countryside, but with his avatar unresponsive, he couldn't even see what was happening let alone help if they ran into problems. Fortunately, Samita was already set to auto-follow the party so he logged out of Panchala and briefly logged into a couple of the other TerraMythos realms. Which was really strange, because his other avatars worked normally. Whatever technical problem TerraMythos had was isolated to Panchala.

It was near dinnertime but he hadn't heard anything from his folks. His mother was usually nagging him to wash his hands by now. Chandar signed off and went out to the kitchen, where he found his father sitting at the small kitchen table, comforting his sobbing mother.

When Chandar saw them, he started to turn and leave, until Baba saw him and called out over his mother's shoulder, "Sanjali's parents just called. They've canceled the wedding." Chandar felt like spears were piercing him when Maa let out a wail and continued sobbing.

Vegetables lay unchopped on the counter and the rice hadn't even been started, so dinner was obviously going to be delayed. Feeling useless, Chandar went out to the front room, and sat looking at the shrine which dominated their living room, the way televisions dominated most American living rooms. Chandar's parents had a TV in here as well, but it was off to the side, and he was not in the mood to watch anything anyway.

The news was hardly a surprise, though for some reason he hadn't expected it so quickly. Having heard that Sanjali canceled the wedding, an unexpected reality hit him. This was an event that Chandar hadn't originally wanted, one that he told his mother he didn't care about, so he should be happy. Yet, sitting silent on the sofa, he felt as if someone had replaced the real Chandar with an empty mold of a Chandar.

It wasn't just because Maa was upset. At first, he went along with the whole thing because he was taken by surprise, and then because he knew how important it was to Maa before she...before that happened. The truth was, Maa would get over it. But as he thought about the way Sanjali hid her smile when he was cleaning up his room, her quick wit and her hand on his arm, he realized he didn't want to get over her. Sanjali had come to mean something to him.

Chandar looked at the shrine, sitting in the center of the far wall where fireplaces or televisions would sit in most American homes. And he saw it in a way he had never looked at it before, the way he sometimes saw his mother look at it. He'd watched his parents offer prayers to the shrine, and when he was a kid he had gone through the motions. But it had never really meant anything, at least until now. Maybe because he never really had something he needed to pray about before.

He quickly rose and stepped toward the kitchen, just enough to confirm that his parents were still occupied in the kitchen, then came back and sat down on the big couch. No one was here to watch, but he still felt awkward and embarrassed as he turned to the shrine and began to offer the ritual prayers he'd heard so many countless times. This was not the first time he had uttered them. But it was the first time he meant them.

At first, he just felt silly and almost stopped a couple times. Then he began to feel a connection to something deeper, bigger and more powerful than himself. Something he had no words to describe. The words and thoughts of his prayers became deeper, more real and impassioned. And, whether it was God, some higher dimension or the Collective Unconscious his teacher talked about in Psychology a few weeks ago, Chandar felt a sense of peace come over him. And with it a realization of what he had to do.

What he didn't realize was that his parents were watching from the hallway.

Draupadi found her friend Demie as inscrutable as a rishi. She knew Demie was greatly troubled because, for some reason, her friend wished to pursue Kali the Destroyer of Worlds.

They continued following the path of destruction across the countryside until the Destroyer came upon another hapless village. When the ravaging host stopped to swarm over the small town, Demie again led them off to the side like before, but this time didn't bring them to a vantage point where they could witness the destruction. Instead, she led them too far ahead and then back into the path Kali would take when the goddess resumed her course. Draupadi felt great not-understanding inside when her friend brought the group to a halt on a grassy plain, and turned to face the direction of the town that lay just over a nearby ridge.

First of all, they could not see the village from here. Moreover, her friend did not realize where they had stopped, so Draupadi approached Demie. "My good friend, I must tell you that this may not be an auspicious place for us to remain."

Demie turned, "What kind of place?"

"A fortunate or favorable place."

"That's okay, you're not going to remain here. I want you to take your husbands back to Kampilya as fast as you can and look there for any kind of help you can find."

Draupadi felt a great not-rightness inside, as if she did not know which direction was up or down, or north from south, but most especially, what she was to do or how she was to help Demie. "I can not possibly leave you, my friend. I owe you everything."

"Why would you owe me anything?" Demie replied, as a noise resumed in the distance.

"Because," Draupadi said, dropping to her knees, "You have awakened life within me. I was sleeping and in darkness, and you have brought me to life. Let me tell you all the ways that you have touched me, starting with..."

Demie pulled her up, "We don't have time for this. Kali will be here soon. I can stay ahead of the bitch, but not if you're with me. This is something I must do by myself."

"Then do that which you must do, and I shall do what you ask. When I find what help there may be, how then will we come to your aid?"

"I have no idea, but I'll let you know." Demie pushed on Draupadi. "They're coming, so just get going. No matter what happens to me, keep going straight to Kampilya and don't stop for anything."

A terrible sound approached, as if a great swarm of monstrous locusts were chewing and crunching everything before them. They were still over the ridge but closing quickly. "Namaste, Demie. I will not fail you."

Demie continued to face the source of the grinding and crunching and didn't even turn to look at Draupadi. The not-understanding inside threatened to overwhelm her as Draupadi turned and grabbed Yudhishthira and Arjuna, then raced to the north across the small plain. The dog they found in the first ruined village, which Yudhishthira named Darm, followed close behind.

When she reached the edge of the trees, she looked back and saw the trees and vegetation at the top of the ridge fall, as the dark mass of figures came over the crest and began to swarm down the hillside. She went perhaps a hundred yards into the forest before she heard the crunching stop behind them.

Draupadi paused and glanced behind, feeling great emptiness within. She had lost Sahadeva, she had left Bhima and Nakula behind in Amaravati; now she was leaving her best and only friend. Only her promise to Demie kept her from turning back.

The silence caused great not-rightness within her, as Draupadi thought of her companion. Then she heard a tremendous thrashing and crashing for a moment, before the grinding and crunching resumed, but now headed away, in a westerly direction.

Draupadi turned north again and resumed running as fast as possible. She did not know if Demie was now gone, to join Sahadeva. But she felt rightness inside of herself for Demie, a rightness greater than anything she had ever felt. Demie was more than a friend to Draupadi, she was a sister. Whatever she could do for Demie, she would.

Even if it meant the end of her own existence.

Karen groaned and stretched, then turned over. The sleeping pad tucked underneath Tony's desk was better than sleeping on the carpet. Better, the way getting hit with an eight pound bowling ball was better than getting hit with a sixteen pound ball. Either way, you were still in for a world of hurt.

Sunlight poured in through the office windows she had coveted for so long, driving away any chance of going back to sleep. Karen shuffled down the hallway to start a fresh pot of coffee brewing, and then went into the bathroom to clean up as well as one could with water, dispenser soap and paper towels. God, that was the one thing she regretted about being put in charge. Working around the clock to solve an intractable problem was a part of Tony's job she hadn't thought about. Or prepared for.

Once she obtained her caffeine fix, she felt at least vaguely human. Back at her desk she found no messages from Tony and no phone calls. No surprise there. Panchala was still running despite having been shut down, Kali was wreaking havoc and wiping out everything in its path, and all she could do was watch. Again, no surprises.

Out of curiosity, Karen decided to check on how many characters Kali managed to whack so far. That was when she did get a surprise; one that woke her up more than a whole pot of coffee. When she compared the database of player characters in the archive with those that had been eliminated in the area module, the number Kali eliminated was higher than the number in the archive. In fact, some of those were player characters that never existed in Panchala.

How could Kali destroy characters that weren't there? Characters that she herself saw being eliminated.

As Karen pondered this question, her cell phone rang. It was Frank, the CEO.

CHAPTER TWENTY-TWO

Demie wasn't sure just how many day/night cycles had passed, but she knew they were more than she could've counted on one hand. The fatigue weighing her down was more than anything she felt since waking up in the field outside Kampilya. She longed to stop even for one minute and do a chi exercise, but she couldn't. A quick glance back confirmed that Kali still followed after her like a faithful puppy dog. She had wanted a pet, but this wasn't quite what she'd had in mind.

The scariest part of this plan had been the initial encounter, because she had to let Kali get close enough for Demie to physically hit her. The moron was so focused on getting to Kampilya, she actually ran right past Demie. That caught Demie by surprise, so she had to do a couple of quick flips over Kali's front line, but landed on her feet and ran up behind the huge black demon.

A solid blow to Kali's backside with that glassy sword got her attention, all right, but the arrogant fool couldn't believe that someone would dare attack from behind. Kali stopped in her tracks and just stood looking about for whomever had the audacity to strike her. Demie gave the demon another whack in the leg, and then it was mostly a matter of running like hell.

By the time Kali whipped around, Demie was already fleeing and managed to dodge the goddess's first blows. What scared the crap out of her, though, was that she almost got bogged down in the crowd of Kali's followers. Perhaps that was their main purpose, to pin people down. In any case, she finally broke free and took off in any direction but north.

Since Demie made her play on Kali in the late-afternoon, she simply headed toward the setting sun and followed her nose for a couple of day and night cycles. When she came to the banks of the dried up Sarasvati, Demie turned south and retraced her earlier path. Kali pursued Demie along the side of the riverbed until they came to the end of the mesa, and then dropped down toward the ruined city of Amaravati.

As she slogged around the outskirts of the city, Demie toyed with the idea of seeing if she could lead Kali inside and get her adversary tied up with the daityas. But Demie would likely be the one that got nailed by the birdlike demons. And even if she didn't, with her luck Kali would just turn the daityas into allies, which wouldn't be helpful to say the least.

So Demie made an arc out into the desert instead, and sure enough, Kali stayed on her tail the whole way. The great thing about the desert was that there were very few obstacles to get in her way. Until she literally ran out of desert. The one thing Demie couldn't risk was running into one of those edge-of-the-world walls, so she turned north.

After a while, a very tall mountain range started to rise up ahead of her, spreading both to the east and west. She couldn't estimate how far away they were, because she had never developed a good sense of distance in this world. Unfortunately, Chandar and his map were offline and those peaks were getting too close for her comfort. Demie decided it was time to turn east, since that was the direction she sent Draupadi to get help.

The problem was, she still didn't have a plan for how to use any help the princess managed to dredge up. When she started this wild-Demie-chase, her plan had been very simple: Get Kali's attention, lead the bitch away from Kampilya, and while running come up with Plan B. Many cycles later, she was still looking for Plan B, but so far all she'd found was Plan F.

Demie surveyed the terrain ahead. She was entering gently rolling foothills, but they were starting to turn into forests and that worried her. She didn't want to get into an area where vegetation would slow her down. More importantly, the last thing she could afford was to run into an area that only had one way in, or out. Or it might indeed be the last thing she did.

Which was why that mountain range really worried her. When she saw it the first time it seemed to run straight east and west, but as she ran, in fact it curved inward. Toward her.

Demie was literally running out of foothills. And time.

Dusk was falling when Cassie pulled up into her driveway. Now she wished she had gotten that garage door opener the year before. Those strange cars were gone, but they would be back. She whisked herself out of the SUV and grabbed her bags, then couldn't help letting out a startled yelp when she saw the man walking up the street on the far side. He had a pretty good cover of walking a dog on a leash, but she knew better.

Scrambling to get her front door unlocked and safely inside before the man could run up, Cassie suddenly remembered what she left in the back of her SUV. Carefully scanning the street through the blinds before fully opening the door, she dashed out to her vehicle, popped open the back, and then lugged a large cage into the house and set it in the den, opposite Demie's bed.

After checking the house and making sure everything was secure, Cassie tended to Demie's needs, then ate a snack as she eagerly unpacked the contents of the bags she brought in.

Sharon, the owner of The Mystic Pyramid New Age Shop, explained to Cassie what she needed to do in order to communicate with another energy plane. The owner said Demie was a regular customer and Sharon would do anything she could. They were constantly interrupted by students from the small community college, but Sharon wrote out all the instructions and drew a diagram for her. Only while driving home did Cassie wonder what Demie had been purchasing.

Cassie carefully removed and unwrapped twelve tissue-wrapped crystals, then set out seven candles, each with a distinctive color and scent. The drawing Sharon provided displayed the exact placement of each crystal and candle, and Cassie kept slowing herself down so she could meticulously follow the diagram. One candle at each compass direction, and three candles in a triangle around Demie. Then the crystals formed a circle around the room, three crystals evenly spaced between each candle.

Once she had the candles lit and the lights in the room turned off, Cassie went over to the cage and removed the restless inhabitant. She brought the grey lop-eared rabbit over to Demie's bed and held it in front of her. Now, her daughter would stop running away and come home.

"Look, Baby, here's your bunny. It's a girl, so what do you want to name her?" Cassie leaned over to listen but didn't catch the response. "Would you like to pet her?"

Cassie held the rabbit with one arm and guided Demie's hand over the soft pelt for several strokes.

"That's it for now, Hon. You can pet her some more tomorrow. She needs to get used to her new home." Cassie placed the rabbit back in its cage and then went upstairs. She eagerly raced back and forth as she brought Demie's computer system downstairs, and set it up on the desk in the corner. Once the monitor, keyboard and mouse were hooked up, she turned to Demie.

"Now, you have to concentrate Sweetie, and focus real hard. The energy from the candles is being channeled by the crystals, so all you have to do is tune into the right vibration and we can chat on the computer."

It took several tries, and then Cassie pumped her fist when she got some responses from Demie. They were very faint and Cassie had to look hard to catch them, but Demie would get better with practice. Her daughter said she was doing well, she was having a good time, and she wanted chocolate milk. Also, the bunny should be named Ashley, because it was the color of ash.

Cassie stood up and stretched. "I'll get the chocolate milk next time I'm out, okay? Good night, Sweetie." Then, she gave her daughter a kiss on the forehead after blowing out the candles. They needed to make those candles last, so they could keep communicating.

She didn't notice as she left the room that her foot kicked the computer's power cord, which she forgot to plug into the wall.

Draupadi and her husbands ran across the field outside the gates of Kampilya and passed into the city.

She wasn't sure what to expect, but it certainly wasn't what she found. The streets were full of people running around, many just dashing back and forth without any purpose. Though she tried to ask some of them to help her friend, they all ignored her. Perhaps that disrespect was why Lord Kali the Destroyer was coming to eliminate the city.

Uncertain exactly what to do, she began to wander around and soon noticed the same people more than once. At first she thought she was mistaken, but then she saw two of the same person actually run into each other. Whatever help Draupadi was sent to find, this definitely was not it. Even if she somehow guided these helpless fools wherever Demie needed them, at best they might get in Lord Kali's way. More likely, they would get in Demie's way.

Draupadi turned to Yudhishthira and Arjuna to ask if they knew where to find help, but remembered that they were less 'awake' than she was. This was her responsibility, and she would either succeed or fail of her own accord. At this point, it looked like that would be failure because she had found nothing useful. When Demie needed her the most, she had let her friend down.

Whatever else Demie did, she had sparked an awareness in Draupadi that she didn't understand. Was this spark a new thing, or had Demie awakened something which was there all along? Draupadi suddenly realized that before she met Demie, even before she was in the castle, there had been a 'before' time. Whatever it was, this spark inside Draupadi was the reason she now did things that she couldn't do before. Like exit the castle that had held her captive. Or, perhaps, enter it.

Draupadi felt good-things-will-happen stirrings inside, as she hastened down to the lower level and the tower where she had once been captive. The entrance to the small castle remained closed and locked. Boldly walking up to the door, Draupadi gave the door a firm push.

The door opened, and Draupadi entered.

Chandar heard the phone ring on the far end and held his breath, waiting to see who would answer. It took him all morning to get the courage up to call, and he was just getting ready to hang up after the seventh ring, when he heard a voice on the far end.

"Hello?" Fortunately it was Sanjali. Her parents probably wouldn't have let her talk to him.

"Sanjali? It's me, Chandar."

"Why are you calling? I'm sure your parents told you the wedding is off."

Chandar took a deep breath, wondering how he was going to

handle this. "Yes, they did, but I wanted to find out why, from you."

Sanjali gave a tart laugh, "We were both there, you know why. Do you want to explain to me why you had a sixteen-year-old girl's diary in your room? Exactly what is your relationship with her?"

Chandar hesitated. "It's kind of hard to explain."

"Yeah, I'll bet it is. Well, spare yourself the effort, you don't need to explain anything to me."

"It's not what you think, Sanjali."

"Let me tell you what I think. Anyone who is involved with a young girl is a pedophile. End of conversation." The phone clicked on the far end and Chandar hung up.

Tossing the phone on the bed out of frustration, Chandar headed into his backyard to get some fresh air and think. How could he tell Sanjali about encountering Demie in TerraMythos? She would think he was not only a pedophile, but certifiably insane as well.

As he paced the backyard Chandar saw some movement in the yard next door and, looking through the fence, he saw Cassie standing on her porch with her eyes closed while she chanted inside a strange shape drawn with chalk.

Karen sat in front of the CEO as he stared at her in disbelief. They were the longest seconds of her life, before he stood up and exploded, "What do you mean, you've lost Panchala? How in the hell do you lose an entire world?"

"When we shut the servers down, it just went somewhere. And we haven't been able to track it down."

"It just went...where the bloody hell did it just go?" Karen had never seen someone's face get truly beet red, but Frank's was as close as she was ever likely to see.

"Well, if we knew that, it wouldn't be lost, now would it?"

For a long moment she thought Frank was having an actual heart attack. But then he sat down, let out a long sigh, and stared at the ceiling for a minute or two.

"Okay," he asked, "I presume you tried to restart the servers?"

"Of course, and it had no effect. We were able to connect to them on our network, but Panchala wasn't running. Or rather, I should say it wasn't the Panchala that the rest of the world is seeing."

"So what do you think happened?"

Karen licked her lips; if she wasn't careful she would just set herself up to take the fall. "Someone moved the virtual servers. It has to be an inside job, and there's only one person who both could have done it, and had reason to. Tony."

Frank sat back and regarded her, before responding. "I agree. So what are you going to do about it?"

"What do you mean?"

Frank leaned forward, "Karen, you asked for this project, and I gave it to you. I don't know what your problem is with Tony, and I honestly don't care. This project, the people on it, and everything that goes with it is your problem and I expect you to deal with it."

"So what am I supposed to do now?"

"I don't know, but if you need to find Tony that's your problem. Or do I need to make it someone else's problem?"

Karen didn't reply as she stepped out of Frank's office. She was sweating by the time she stopped at her desk just long enough to grab her purse. There was only one place Tony could've gone, and she was finally desperate enough to go there.

A place where she had sworn to herself that she would never go again.

ॐ

Demie was screwed, plain and simple. Another day cycle was nearing an end when she realized her luck had run out. What at first looked like a very long rise of hills turned into valleys, then began to narrow. And as she ran out of valley, the hills converged ahead, with mountains rising up all around her. She was in a trap.

Now that she was less concerned about keeping Kali in sight, Demie ran ahead as fast as she could. The path followed a stream, and Demie came around a bend to find that the stream originated from what amounted to a small lake in the center of a cul-de-sac. The water was surrounded on all sides by steep un-climbable hills, and she screamed out her dismay.

Demie drew her sword and faced the bend, where the passage through the canyon walls was most narrow. She intuitively knew this would be the best place to make her last stand. What would it feel like to become dirt? Would she end up back home, or would she just end?

Demie looked at the water, the sky, the hills and trees and they appeared more beautiful and real to her than before. She ran her hand through the water and it felt as cool and refreshing as the water in Dandaka Forest.

Did those about to die always appreciate their final moments so deeply?

She heard the familiar crunching before she saw them, then Kali and her forces came into view. When Kali saw her, the demon actually slowed down and let her forces gather around. Then, slowly, she resumed a walking advance toward Demie.

Demie looked around one more time to make sure she had not overlooked some kind of escape route, perhaps a cave or even a hidden path. But there just wasn't that much to miss.

Desperately, Demie searched the hillside for an escape route, and saw that not only were Kali's forces slowly advancing up the valley toward her, but the surrounding ridges were crowded with additional forces of soldiers.

She would learn soon enough whether they were there to watch or participate.

CHAPTER TWENTY-THREE

Desperately, Demie turned to face her nemesis, determined not to go down easy. Kali halted at the entrance into the cul-de-sac and sent her dark forces marching forward. The tramping of countless feet echoed as they spread out, filling the floor of the canyon while Demie slowly backed up toward the small lake. And if that wasn't enough to worry about, she was concerned that some misfortune had overtaken Draupadi.

During the past day cycle she repeatedly tried contacting the princess the same way she talked with Chandar and Lizat. But apparently Draupadi had not fared well in her search for heroes, because Demie was only rewarded with silence. Now she stood utterly alone.

If nothing else, maybe she could buy enough time for Draupadi to escape. Then she saw a familiar figure step into view on the ridge above her, surrounded by two others. Demie started to yell, "Yes! Yes!" and did a passable end zone dance when she saw the princess and the Pandavas.

"Namaste, Demie," Draupadi called down. "It is well met to see you again, though I would that it were under more favorable circumstances. As promised I have brought aid, such as there was to be found."

"Why didn't you tell me you were coming?" Demie sent back.

"All is not right with the world, my good friend," Draupadi replied. "I could not sense your location, let alone share speech with you. However, the presence of Lord Kali the Destroyer shines as brightly as the sun. So I thought by coming to face her, we would find you as well. Did I do well?"

"You did very well," Demie laughed, eyeing Kali and her advancing minions. Then, more seriously, she continued, "Wait until I tell you, and then have everyone jump down."

Demie stood her ground until the leading edge of the cohort that Kali sent forth was about fifty feet away, then she resumed retreating to the end of the valley, maintaining the distance. Like an unending swarm of insects, they poured through the gap Demie abandoned and spread out on both sides of the lake until they filled the valley.

Fighting back feelings of dread, Demie reached the far end of the valley. When both prongs of the advancing forces converged and no further retreat was possible, Demie sent the message to Draupadi, "Now! Time to start this party."

Like a golden cloudburst, a mass of soldiers wearing scarlet plumes and gold-plated armor rained across the valley, and Demie cheered while battle erupted across the entire expanse. Draupadi and her husbands landed nearby, and the two women put their backs together to face the oncoming waves of attackers from both directions, while Arjuna and Yudhishthira likewise stood back to back next to them.

"Where did you find these guys?" Demie asked, eagerly slashing the first fighters to reach her. Fortunately they seemed very weak, probably previous farmers or fishermen. She could practically hit them with her eyes closed and they were gone with one solid blow. These were just pawns that Kali wanted to be rid of. Stronger ones were certainly not far behind.

"You empowered me, my esteemed friend, to go with boldness and strength where once I was held captive. The tower from which you liberated me held those forces belonging to the king of Panchala. I simply commanded my father's troops to follow me."

Demie knew better than to ask Draupadi why she hadn't commanded them to release her from the tower to begin with. Plus, now that the first round of wimpy fighters were defeated, she had to start paying more attention. This next wave of opponents were somewhat tougher and required several hits to vanquish, but her side continued to hold.

Although Kali's forces outnumbered the small army that

Draupadi brought with her by almost four to one, the king's troops took out almost half of their opponents by surprise when they literally dropped in. Now the remainder were being forced back through the gap by the disciplined soldiers. Surging forward, Demie and her companions took the point, and pushed the battle around the bend. The enemy, with Kali in the back, retreated down the valley.

The front line of ebony fighters began collapsing like a crushed milk carton, and those which didn't fall, turned and fled. When they ran into Kali's irregular troops behind them, those forces started to flee as well, and the flood pushed Kali back by sheer force of their mass.

With a shout, Demie urged her own forces to press forward as hard as they could.

Chandar entered the living room and quietly sat down next to Maa, empty of both words and feeling. She looked thinner than he remembered, and the lack of color in her skin made the bags under her eyes almost seem to pop out. Guilt swelled within him because the events of the past twenty-four hours left her deflated and drying up, like a plant that lost its source of water.

As he sat on the sofa, she dabbed her eyes with a tissue. Taking her free hand, he said, "It's going to be okay, Maa."

She patted his hand. "I know, but I just don't understand what happened. I had such hopes for the two of you."

"I'm sorry it didn't work out. I know how important it was for you..." Chandar trailed off. Aside from that first statement from his father, his parents said nothing further about his mother's illness, nor had Chandar inquired. And really, he didn't want to know; but not knowing didn't make the reality go away. It was a reality she now unmistakably wore, and he could no longer avoid seeing.

"Don't worry, Chanja." That was her pet name for him. "Her parents say that Sanjali will give no reason, but absolutely insists on calling it off. What happened between you two?"

Chandar sighed. "I can't explain it. Just a misunderstanding, but one that was important to her."

"My son, I wanted someone good for you, and she seemed like just the right girl. But if something is not meant to be, you can't fight karma."

In a flash, Chandar realized this was the hook he was seeking, and he felt a surge of hope. "Maa, speaking of karma, this is a bad way to end things. If it has to be like this, I think it's important to end everything properly. Please call her parents and tell them it's because of karma or something, but I want to formally apologize to them. Including Sanjali."

Maa wrinkled her brow and studied Chandar for a moment, then responded, "Are you certain? This is very unusual, and I'm not sure they would be willing to do that."

"Absolutely. We do not want to carry this karma forward into another lifetime, so I need to set things right."

Setting things right meant he would have one last chance to fix the hole Sanjali left in his heart.

The next morning Cassie woke up in her bed, smiled and enjoyed some glorious stretches underneath her comforter. She felt more refreshed than she had in a long time. No headaches, no hangover and a sense of peace. After dumping all of her liquor again, she slept through the night without waking up once, something she had not experienced since Demie's accident. It was also the first night she actually spent in her bed rather than on the couch.

Heading downstairs, she checked to make sure Demie was fine, and confirmed that Ashley had water and food. The little rabbit wrinkled its nose as Cassie stroked it, and chomped down the baby carrots she fed it. Cassie hurried through a yogurt and granola breakfast, eager to be on her way, then let Demie pet Ashley for a few minutes before she put the bunny back in its cage.

"I have to run a quick errand, Hun." She knew Demie was listening now, and gave her daughter a lingering kiss on the cheek. "Don't worry, I'll be back soon."

Cassie walked out to the SUV and discreetly checked out the neighbors, trying not to let them know she was onto the fact that they were watching. Sure enough, she caught that woman across the street peeking through the blinds, probably taking pictures. It made sense now. Cassie always thought the former teacher was too young to be retired. The woman must have ten years worth of pictures.

While she drove to the market, Cassie was careful to obey traffic rules so the cops would not have a reason to pull her over. All they needed was an excuse, and no one would ever see her again. In the parking lot, and as she strolled through the store, she carefully kept her face averted from the hidden cameras and the two-way mirrors. No point in making it easier for them.

When she got to the checkout stand with the fresh carrots and the quart of chocolate milk, she ran her card through. The clerk pulled out a pen from under the counter and handed it to Cassie to sign the receipt. She started to hand the pen back, and then stopped and put the pen in her purse.

"Lady, that's our pen."

Cassie smiled and wagged her finger at him. "Nice try, I almost fell for it! But not this time." They wouldn't get her fingerprints that easily. The clerk shook his head and waved her on.

She drove back home as carefully as on the way out, and when she got out of the car, she deliberately arranged the seatbelt to drape in a specific spot and placed a hair on the steering wheel. If they went through her vehicle, she wanted to know about it.

Inside, the first thing she noticed was that the rabbit cage was out in the hallway. Inside the den, the nurse sat in a chair, finishing up her morning routine and writing in the log. Cassie would check that log later.

Picking up the cage, she hauled it back into the room, and the nurse looked up.

"Demie wants Ashley in here," Cassie scowled.

"Demie wants a clean room so she won't get sick. The rabbit goes."

Cassie set the cage back in its spot, set her feet in front of the pen and crossed her arms as she glared at the caretaker. "I decide what goes and what stays."

The woman shook her head and turned back to her paperwork. Cassie went over to the bed, to double-check the nurse's work. She examined the monitors hooked up to Demie and lifted one of the wires.

"Why did you change this?"

The nurse glanced up with a puzzled look. "What are you talking about? I didn't touch any of the monitors."

"Oh, no, that's not true. This was a different color, I know." Cassie went and got her digital camera and pulled up a picture she took the previous evening. The cable was the same color, which meant this woman was really sharp to catch that detail and change the image. Someone that astute must be a government agent. Looking around, Cassie noticed that the candles and crystals were all neatly stored in the corner.

"You took apart the sacred sphere! What are you trying to do?"

"The candles are a fire hazard. And smoke is not good for her."

"You just don't want us talking to each other!" Cassie accused her, "You think I might find out what you're doing."

The nurse rose, now obviously irritated. "And just what do you think that is?"

"You can't fool me. You're trying to kill her."

"Kill her?! If there's anyone in this house trying to kill her, it's you!"

Grabbing the woman's purse, Cassie swung it at her and gestured toward the hallway. "How dare you! Get out of my house, now. And you better not come back."

Snatching the purse, the nurse headed out and replied without looking back, "Don't worry, they don't pay me enough to put up with this kind of crap."

When Cassie heard the front door slam, she checked to make sure the door was locked and then went back into the den. Just as she thought. The drip bag had a slight discoloration, from the poison the nurse put in it. Disconnecting the bag, she took it into the kitchen and poured the contents out, then thoroughly rinsed the poison out.

Reconnecting the bag to Demie's drip line, Cassie carefully poured the chocolate milk into the bag, and watched the brown liquid snake through the tube and into Demie's body.

Demie yelled encouragement to her troops as they surged forward like a tidal wave and swept over their opponents. The bulk of Kali's forces were crushed and annihilated, reduced to a small circle of core fighters that surrounded Kali. Demie gave a victory cry as she raised her sword to lead the final assault, when a sudden wave of dizziness all but knocked her over.

She felt stunned. No opponent had hit her, and as far as she could tell neither Kali nor anyone else had waved any of those magical sticks or hands against her. Yet, her strength continued to drain, and as she weakened, her vision and hearing began fading as well.

With the sickness melting the core of her being, and fear sweeping away her resolve, Demie stumbled back, and the surging force of allies faltered. Then they began to pull back, like a wave on the beach which had reached as far as it could before sliding back into the ocean.

Draupadi fell back with Demie, staying at her friend's side while Arjuna and Yudhishthira covered Demie's retreat. The princess placed her hands on Demie, administering one of her healing touches. The curative effort had no effect, and Demie could tell that the affliction lay outside of the game world. This was not something Draupadi could heal. Where was Chandar when she needed him the most?

"What ails you, my friend?"

Demie forced a reply, "I wish I knew." Struggling to stay on her feet, she staggered back around the bend into the small valley, then halted when they reached the edge of the small lake. Friendly troops streamed in around them as their dark enemy pushed forward, turning the rout to their favor.

"Gather everyone at the gap there. It's narrow, so if our strongest soldiers can hold them, we may have a chance." Demie remembered something in history class about a small band of Greeks holding off a whole army. She took little comfort in remembering that while they held off an overwhelming force for days, things didn't work out too well for them in the end.

Draupadi directed Arjuna and Yudhishthira to flank her sides, and they stepped forward to stem the flood pouring through the gap. Just in time, it turned out, as the first of Kali's fighters came into view.

Her vision faded in and out, as Demie watched Draupadi and her band firm up the remaining soldiers from the king's army and hold the passage. After a brief surge back and forth, the skirmish reached a stalemate and the fighting began to subside. Then Demie noticed the enemy force begin to part.

Demie started to pass out as Kali moved forward to the center of the front line and for the first time, the enormous black goddess prepared to directly engage the battle.

And Draupadi.

Tony was enjoying a brand new day. It had been far too long since he took the time to drive up the coast to his cabin, nestled in a stand of trees that looked out over the Pacific Ocean, atop a 400-foot cliff.

He made the winding drive up through the trees the night before in pitch-black darkness; there was no residual light in the sky this far from any major cities. When he awoke that morning, the bright sunlight, fresh clean air and solitude of the forest helped Tony shrug off the events of the past days, which now felt a hundred miles away, literally. And he was quite ready to leave them there permanently. Maybe it was time to retire, perhaps do some public service.

The few provisions he'd brought with him would only last another day or so, but then he'd be ready for the twenty-mile drive to the nearest food mart. Until then, he was content to just lie in the sun and listen to the surf far below. The warmth of the sun had lulled him into that blissful state between dreaming and waking, when the hiss of tires coming up the gravel road brought him back. A car door closed with a thud, and he glanced at the sky to gauge the time and then closed his eyes again. She was right on time.

The steady crunch of footsteps approached, and then stopped. Tony ignored them, enjoying the last moments of peace. He didn't have to look to know who it was.

"I know you have cell phone coverage up here," Karen said.

"Not if I have the damned thing turned off," Tony responded with a smile, keeping his eyes closed. "What took you so long, sweetheart?"

"This isn't exactly my favorite place."

Tony sat up and turned to look at her. "It used to be."

Ignoring his last comment, Karen turned and slowly walked into the cabin. Tony sighed as he gathered his t-shirt and book, and trudged to the cabin as well. It was nice while it lasted.

Karen had the fridge door open, and held up the last two beers. Tony said, "Sure, I'll have one too," and sat at the small kitchen table.

Without hesitation, Karen retrieved the opener from a drawer and picked out a couple of cozies from a cabinet to slip over the cold bottles. She popped the tops and joined Tony.

"Everything right where it used to be," she said as she sat.

He took a swig of the beer she handed him, and then examined her for a moment before responding. "Let me guess. You shut down the servers, and Panchala didn't go down."

"I don't know how you pulled it off, Tony, but you got us good. I have to say, I'm really quite impressed."

Tony laughed, "You give me too much credit. I didn't do it, I just saw it coming."

Karen frowned. "What are you talking about? If you didn't do this, who did? Are you working for someone else?"

Tony laughed again, "You still don't get it, do you? I don't understand it all yet, but this is something much bigger than you. Or me. Or Panchala and TerraMythos."

Karen slowly set her beer down. "Just tell me this, do you think you can get us back online? Can you re-connect us back into Panchala?"

"I honestly don't know. But why would I want to even try?"

Karen reached across the table and took his hand. "Because I need you."

Tony understood what she meant; she needed his expertise, his ability to see connections where other people missed them. She didn't need him the way he wanted her to. The way he never stopped wanting her to need him, and knew she never would.

But it was enough; he would drive back with her.

CHAPTER TWENTY-FOUR

Demie struggled to retain consciousness. Dropping to her knees, she fought against the fog in her mind. Something was occurring back in the real world; nothing here caused this fainting attack. Which scared Demie, far more than Kali. There was no defense against what was happening to her, only resistance.

Through blurry eyes, Demie watched Kali push her own minions aside and move toward Draupadi. In response, the princess dropped back slightly to fortify her position, and sent a message to Demie. "Should I fall here, my good friend, I ask only that you remember me well. For you have become as a sister to me, and none other is more dear to me than thou."

Demie desperately wanted to help but could only implore, "Then don't fall."

Kali launched a fierce assault on Draupadi, and the princess desperately deflected the dual-weapon attack with the help of Yudhishthira and Arjuna. She slowly fell back toward Demie while the line between the opposing forces slowly pivoted with them. The dark goddess continued to press the attack and forced Draupadi back step by step, ever closer to Demie, until the combatants reached the girl's helpless body. The princess could retreat no further.

As if sensing victory at hand, Kali paused to fortify her line, then launched a renewed attack on Draupadi to bring down the princess. Stepping forward to take the brunt of the assault, the Pandava brothers parried Kali's blows, but their weapons had little discernible effect. Weak and barely hanging on, Demie watched the brothers wane under the relentless onslaught until they both collapsed. With the Pandavas down, Kali turned to face Draupadi, the last remaining obstacle between Kali and Demie.

Demie desperately fought back waves of dizziness with her chi exercises, and her condition began stabilizing. Not improving, but at least she wasn't worsening. Unlike the situation before her. Remembering Lord Ganesha's words about conquering oneself, Demie focused her reserves into one last burst of energy and opened her eyes in time to see Draupadi fend off another punishing series of attacks which left the princess on her knees.

"No!" Demie cried, rage pushing her to her feet as Kali swung both weapons in order to finish off the now defenseless Draupadi. Just before the weapons struck, Demie seized the princess and yanked her backward.

Kali turned her aim on Demie, who dodged the demon's trident while using her own sword and armor to parry her adversary's sword. The two pressed back and forth, and Demie didn't know how she managed it, but they reached a balance where neither could overpower the other.

Rather than weakening, the ongoing combat sharpened Demie's focus. She was stronger and more capable than the last time she fought Kali. Something else was different as well, as she wiped sweat from her eyes. The water here felt as real as in Dandaka Forest, and it was not just an illusion. The sounds, the smells, the very feel of this world was becoming real.

She had seen changes in many of the inhabitants of this world. The odd awakening of the village and fisherman, and more so with Arjuna and Yudhishthira. But the strongest transformation was within Draupadi. The rishi said look at the beginning, and this whole adventure started when the glowing yellow ball led Demie to the princess. Draupadi didn't realize that when said that she was like a sister to Demie, she was speaking the truth.

What was awakening in Draupadi, was Kori.

Chandar stood in his living room, in front of Sanjali and her parents, fumbling with his tie and adjusting his sport jacket while he searched for the right words. After his mother spent an hour on the phone pleading and wheedling with her parents, they finally agreed to come back once more to hear Chandar's apology. His own parents sat on one side of the room while Sanjali sat with her mouth drawn, face hard as marble and eyes hating a hole right through him. Chandar nervously licked his lips and coughed, uncertain how to start.

"The only reason I'm here," Sanjali spat, "Is because I don't want to take even the smallest chance that I might have to meet you again in another incarnation to work out any unresolved karma. So please, let's just get this over with."

Sanjali's mother touched her daughter's arm and whispered something, but the girl's narrowed, unblinking eyes never wavered from Chandar. Chandar took a deep breath and launched into it.

"Sanjali, Mr. and Mrs. Kumari. You have my deepest apologies for the great unhappiness that has come upon both of our families. I never meant for this to happen, and you may not believe me, but it really is all a terrible misunderstanding. Some things happened which are hard to explain. I'm not sure I really understand it all myself, and if I tried to explain it, I'm sure it wouldn't make sense. The important thing is that I'm truly sorry for how this has looked to you."

Sanjali glared at Chandar and started to rise and leave, but her mother pulled her back down, and Chandar heard her whisper something in Sanjali's ear about being rude.

Chandar desperately forged ahead, sweat starting to bead up on the nape of his neck. "Sanjali, you told me what you think, and I don't expect you to change how you feel. However it's important that you at least know the truth. Because if you want to call the wedding off for some reason, that's fine, and I respect that. But things are not what you think they are, nor what they look like."

"So tell me what I should believe, after what that woman said about her daughter?"

"What woman?" Sanjali's father turned in confusion to his wife.

"What daughter?" Chadar's mother almost rose out of her seat.

Ignoring them, Chandar knelt before Sanjali. "She jumped to conclusions, and so are you if you believe her. You never gave me a chance to explain."

"Why would...?" Sanjali blustered, and then faltered, her certainty cracking for the first time. "Okay, then just tell me why she would say those things?"

"I honestly don't know." Chandar stood up again, and as if on cue, he heard loud chanting through the window he left open, facing the backyard. He was about to take the biggest gamble of his life, and he could only hope his earlier prayers were more than mere words.

"But if you come with me, maybe I can show you." And Chandar led Sanjali toward the backyard.

Draupadi searched deep inside herself for the strength to hold off Kali the Destroyer as long as she could, in order to give her sister/friend Demie time to recover. Even though her own attacks were ineffective, it was a goodness that at least Lord Kali was not attacking Demie.

But Draupadi was worn down, and she readied herself for Kali's final attack. This one would finish her off and end her existence. She never thought before about what would happen to her after she ended. Maybe she would see Sahadeva, or just stop being. She felt a deep not-rightness.

Then, Demie stepped forward and pushed Draupadi backward out of danger. For a moment, her mind swirled with not-knowing. She had to do something, anything.

Draupadi applied some healing to herself and regained what strength she could, and watched Demie hold off Kali. Demie's skills had grown greatly, yet for all that, the best Demie could do was match Kali. She would not overcome the terrible Lord.

The concealed-knowing spoke to the princess, that somehow Demie had the key she needed, if she could but see it for herself. Puzzled but renewed, Draupadi moved to aid Demie, who managed to parry most of Kali's attacks but still suffered serious injuries.

"You are more than you realize," Draupadi said, as she healed her friend. "You must see yourself for what you are, while you still can."

Since Cassie had to rebuild the sacred sphere, she reassembled it on the back patio. Which was necessary anyway, after Demie explained in whispers what they needed to do. At first Cassie resisted, but Demie was right.

Setting up the candles and crystals was easy. The hard part was pushing Demie's medical bed through the house and out onto the back porch. Especially getting it over the porch threshold. But everything was in place, and she had Demie's bed meticulously aligned to face north.

Cassie went into the bathroom and found the electric shears she purchased years ago and only used three times. Once to give Sherman a disastrous haircut, and twice on Demie, before Demie made her promise to never try any more hair styling.

Ten minutes later, Cassie's hair lay on the bathroom floor and she examined her own bare scalp. She probably ought to use a razor, but this would be good enough for them. Using an extension cord for the shears, she went out to the patio and shaved Demie's hair, carefully catching the locks on a sheet under the girl's head. After giving Demie a few final touches with the shears, she cleaned up the hair.

Taking up the medicine drum, afraid and excited at the same time, Cassie maintained a slow steady beat on the bongo-like drum as she chanted.

> "Hear the angels, their lovely song.
> "Closer they come, on the wind.
> "Angels coming, we welcome you,
> "Coming to bear us home."

After repeating the chant at each point of the compass, Cassie gently spread a white sheet over Demie and lit the candles around the sacred sphere. While she fumbled with one of the candles, she failed to notice the man hidden in the bushes behind the fence.

She finally got the candle lit as he pulled out his cell phone and placed a phone call.

Demie didn't know how she managed it, or how long she could keep it up, but she continued to match Kali, blow for blow and parry for parry. But she couldn't shake the sense that she faced another danger. She couldn't see or combat this other peril, but it threatened her as much if not more. The danger had to be back in the real world, which meant she might not have much time. She and Kori needed to return soon.

What had Draupadi/Kori meant, that Demie was more than what she thought she was? The answer had to be connected to the changes she now sensed in the fabric of world around her, changes in the inhabitants of this world, especially Draupadi. The princess was awakening from a sleep, which meant Kori was awakening. But what caused this awakening...an awakening from what?

Whatever, the bottom line was that she found her sister. Demie didn't understand the rishi's riddles, but he had been clear about one thing. When Demie found what she was looking for, she should use that creepy egg portal thing.

"Draupadi, you are also more than you realize," Demie said, "You also have to see yourself for what you really are." Reaching with one hand into her backpack, Demie grabbed the black egg, and cast it into the nearest water, which happened to be the lake. And immediately an enormous black sphere sprang into existence behind her.

Was Draupadi/Kori ready to go back? And what would they go back to?

Tony sat back in Karen's chair, and anxiously waited for the first servers to come up. Not that he thought it would really do any good, but his moment of truth was at hand.

Karen followed him during the two-hour drive back into town, probably worrying the whole time that he might change his mind. Which he very well might have, had he known that his belongings were in boxes under her old desk. When they walked in, she paused nervously and then gestured toward her 'new' cubicle. "It's going to take a while to set your workspace back up, so why don't you just use my computer."

"Very kind of you," Tony dryly responded, biting back on his anger. The other two team members quickly vanished, remembering urgent meetings they needed to attend. Which was just as well, because he didn't want anyone around to see what they were doing.

While he waited, Tony logged into the public Panchala. Just as Karen reported, he was able to observe but could not interact with anything in the game world.

When the servers came up, Tony verified that they synced with each other, and that all the Panchala modules were loaded. But as he expected, the TerraMythos Panchala servers were not connected to the public version. TerraMythos essentially had the world's biggest computer lab. Tony bounced them once more, and then finally sat back and let out a sigh.

Karen nervously broke the silence, "At the cabin, you said you didn't do this, but you saw it coming. What exactly did you see?"

Tony rubbed his eyes, before responding, "Okay, this is going to sound crazy. I ran some processes that started and completed without any actual processing time. Some of them were processes that even a bank of supercomputers would've chewed on for at least a few hours.

"I believe what you see here," Tony gestured toward the screen displaying the live version of Panchala, "is a massive quantum computer."

CHAPTER TWENTY-FIVE

Demie felt her strength grow as the pieces fell into place in her mind. It was a strength which had always been there but which she hadn't known or tapped into. Or believed that she had. Now she finally understood her own existence in this world.

The Kali she faced was a powerful and capable fighter but, in truth, little more than just another character of this world. Giving a gun to a toddler made him an extremely dangerous toddler, but he was still a toddler.

On the other hand, while the fabric of this world was woven into Demie's being, she also retained the essence of the world she came from. So Demie was not just part of this world, she was part of what created this world. She still didn't completely grasp what that meant, but she knew she had far more capabilities within herself than she understood even now. Certainly more than Kali had.

"Now you face the true Destroyer of Worlds," Demie told the faux Kali and confidently pressed forward. Not once had Kali actually spoken. An example of the difference between the real thing and a poor imitation, she thought.

Demie now effortlessly moved forward and forced Kali to back up, then began working the demon around in a circle until she backed it up against the canyon wall. Another difference between them, she gleefully thought. The not-living don't recognize danger.

With a final push, Demie overpowered her opponent and crushed Kali like an empty soda can. She whooped with excitement and spun around in a brief victory dance, before looking for her next opponent. Around them, the direction and focus of Kali's forces collapsed along with Kali. Although they kept fighting, the enemy fighters moved and attacked at random.

Draupadi directed her palace guard to hold the gap leading into the valley, and they watched the wandering fighters gradually cut each other down, until only a handful of stragglers left the valley. Meanwhile, the guards tossed the bodies of the enemy into the lake, which apparently had an infinite capacity to absorb Panchalan bodies.

While the guards mopped up, Demie turned to face the large black sphere. She knew Kori was awakening within the princess, but Kori hadn't yet seen it for herself. Until she did, there was no way that Demie was going to risk taking Draupadi/Kori back home. They would probably only get one chance.

Demie found Draupadi standing over the motionless forms of her two husbands.

"What foul deed has Kali done?!" Draupadi wept.

"Can't you heal them?" Demie asked, surprised as she realized the dead didn't vanish now.

"I have tried for naught to apply my healing touch. Their shapes remain, but they are no longer there."

Demie examined the forms of Arjuna and Yudhishthira. Neither contained the traces she normally detected in Panchalan characters. In that sense, they were indistinguishable from a rock or tree.

"Why didn't they disappear?" Demie asked. "Won't they re-form, like everything else in this world?" Then she thought of the bodies of Kali's fighters, filling up the lake.

"I do not feel their presence elsewhere. Indeed, since you made Kali go away, the world has changed. None of those defeated have been removed. You have the touch of Life, Lord Demie, and if you please, your touch can restore them." Draupadi fell to her knees, and bowed with her palms together over her head, which just felt wrong to Demie, coming from her sister.

"Really, you don't need to do that," Demie pulled Draupadi up, and then knelt down next to Yudhishthira. When she placed her hands on his form, she did not feel any spark within him, but then the dog that followed Yudhishthira, Darm, came up and licked the man's face. Placing her hands on the animal, Demie found that it harbored a spark of Yudhishthira that had not yet left. Closing her eyes, Demie willed for the ember to be re-kindled. She felt for it, cradled it and carefully fanned the flame until it burned once more and she could transfer it back to his body. She felt Yudhishthira stir, and moved back as he sat up and Draupadi rushed to his side.

But when she turned to Arjuna, she found no spark in him. She wished for him to resurrect, with all the willpower she could muster, but she might as well have been trying to animate a rock. Arjuna was dead, in a way Panchala had never known before. She had grown fond of Arjuna, and Demie stood to embrace the princess with her own sorrow.

Though she couldn't revive him, Demie and Draupadi were able to move Arjuna's body to the far end of the valley, near the head of the small lake. Demie, Draupadi and Yudhishthira gathered rocks, and created the first monument in Panchala.

As Demie put her arm around Draupadi, she pondered how she would fully awaken Kori.

Tony tried very hard to ignore Karen's perfume. Just like her to put on the scent he bought her a lifetime ago.

"A quantum computer?" Karen stared at him. "How do you know?"

"A few nights ago, I wanted to slow the processing down so I ran a utility program that tries to crack the strongest computer security key known. If you linked all of the most powerful secret intelligence-service computers together to do the same thing, it would take them years to crack the key." Tony paused.

"So how long did it take?" Karen asked.

"About two seconds. And I think that was mostly due to the physical limitations of the speed of light; it took longer to transmit the answer back to me than it took to find it."

Karen slowly responded, "That's just not possible. That kind of quantum computer doesn't exist."

"I don't know how, but at least one does."

"So what do we do?"

"When you shut our servers down, you dropped our connection to...whatever this is. So we have to try to find a way to re-connect to it." Tony crossed his arms as he sat back and looked at Karen. "But first, there's something you're going to do."

Karen sighed, "Yes, I understand. I was actually expecting this."

He watched as she pulled out her cell phone and dialed a programmed number. She spoke for a couple minutes, and then handed the phone over.

"Hello Tony." It was Frank, the CEO, and he was obviously at some kind of party. "I can't say I'm surprised to be talking to you. Karen tells me she was wrong about the Panchala project, and that you had almost solved the problem when she pulled you from the project."

"You could say that." His voice wavered with anger as he replied, but Tony wasn't about to try explaining the impossible right now, over a cell phone.

"We'll work out the new team structure in the morning. Just get Panchala sorted out." Frank hung up, as direct and curt as ever, and Tony handed Karen's cell phone back to her.

"Tony, I'm not very good at this, but...I'm sorry. I wasn't always like this, you know."

"I know." And she hadn't, but that was then and there would be more things to figure out in the morning than just the team structure. "Look, I'm not sure how all this happened with Panchala. I'm not even sure where it happened. But I'm pretty sure when it happened, and that may help us get re-connected, whatever it is that we're re-connecting to."

Karen pulled her chair over and watched while Tony logged into the Panchala servers and started searching through the logs. It was going to be a long day, because there were quite a few servers, and each one had numerous logs. So he was searching for a needle in a field full of needles.

But while he wasn't sure exactly what this needle looked like, he knew he'd recognize it when he saw it.

Lauren was practically chewing her nails as Sherman drove up to Cassie's house, and the car was still moving when she jumped out. They were still at the airport in California when she got the first phone call, and they jumped on the next flight back home. And she didn't say a word as Sherman broke every speed limit in the county getting here.

The private investigator she had hired met them by the car, and Lauren rushed through the introductions, anxious to just see what the hell was going on. She would have some explaining to do later, but that was the least of her worries now. While they walked toward the fence, the PI filled them in on what he had observed over the past couple days, and the brief conversation he'd had with the nurse as she left. Then they glanced through the fence and Lauren's legs went weak.

She didn't see Cassie anywhere, but Demie lay in her bed on the back porch, completely covered with a white sheet except for her shaven head. And what were all those candles about?

"What the hell is she doing?" Lauren whispered to Collin, the PI. Whether that was his first name or last name, it was the only one he ever used.

"Who knows? I wasn't going to ask her, but as soon as she came out and started cutting the kid's hair, I figured that wasn't a good sign and called the sheriff."

"Where is he?" Sherman asked.

"Who knows, probably had to finish his donut." Then Collin nodded toward the backyard as Cassie emerged from the house. The bald woman walked up to Demie's prostrate body, started chanting toward the sky and raised a large kitchen knife.

For a moment, Lauren's reflexes were to climb the fence. Then she spun about but the two men were both already dashing around the garage. They had half a dozen steps on her, but she caught up as they opened the gate, and they all burst into the backyard together.

Cassie turned her head to look at them but kept the knife raised above Demie. For a few moments she gaped in confusion, and then recognition showed on her face.

"You!? What are you doing here? You're not the ones who are supposed to come," Cassie asked, in a strangely wavering voice.

"That doesn't matter. What are you doing, Cassie?" Sherman responded.

"You don't belong here, none of you. Demie and I are going to be together, just the two of us. You...you can't come with us."

"Just put the knife down, and let's talk about this." Sherman took a step toward them. Cassie jerked the knife down toward Demie and he stopped, while Lauren screamed.

"Oh God, Cassie, please!" Lauren stepped toward Cassie and dropped to her knees. "Don't do this. Take me, I'm the bad one. Just, please...don't hurt her." Lauren closed her eyes and held her arms back, leaving her chest undefended, and Cassie took a step toward her.

"Maybe that would...no. No, that wouldn't work." Cassie shook her head, then looked at her ex-husband. "We don't need to talk, Sherman. This is what they told me to do."

Arms shaking as she held them out in supplication, Lauren pleaded again, "Cassie, this isn't what Demie wants."

"How do you know what Demie wants?" Cassie hissed. "She told me last night that she was ready for this. This was her idea."

"What else did she tell you?" Sherman asked as he edged another step toward Cassie. He was still about fifteen feet from Cassie, too far to stop her even if he jumped.

"Just what in tarnation is going on here!?" They all involuntarily looked toward the gate as the sheriff walked through.

Then Sherman cried out, "No!" and Lauren looked back just in time to see him lunge toward Cassie and Demie.

But not before she plunged the knife into Demie.

Demie had never seen a real eulogy. She tried to recall bits and pieces she had seen on TV and in movies, but none of them seemed to really fit. Nothing that seemed very royal.

After Draupadi/Kori gathered a small group around Arjuna'a monument, the princess turned and looked expectantly. The spotlight was on Demie, so she decided to keep it simple.

"This is a very sad day for Panchala, because we lost someone special. I can truthfully say that he was the bravest and most virtuous warrior I ever fought with. Arjuna gave everything for Panchala, and his spirit will soar with the gods."

Demie turned to Yudhishthira and nodded, while Darm howled mournfully. Those words sounded like the kind of talk he and Draupadi liked. Yudhishthira seemed satisfied because he nodded back and then turned to face the group, to add words of his own.

But as Yudhishthira spoke, a shaft of pain struck Demie like an enormous spear piercing her from head to toe, and an avalanche of heat crashed upon her as she cried out. A maelstrom of static filled her vision and hearing, like when she first arrived in this world, but in reverse. She felt herself falling away, drifting apart.

"Kori, help me!" Demie desperately cried out to the princess, reaching for her sister. "I don't know what's happening, but I don't want to lose you again!" Panchala faded, as Demie called on her chi exercises. Whatever this was, the exercises were ineffective.

She floated, and something tugged on her, almost as if she was being pulled through water. A distant, garbled voice came through, one that was strangely familiar. It was Kori.

"You must try harder Dee-Dee. I can't hold you much longer!"

Demie felt herself holding numerous threads, one of which was dragging her into darkness. Either she released that one, or she would lose them all. It would be so easy, she just had to relax and let it take her away...and she felt so tired. Holding onto the other threads was hard...but that was what the voice wanted her to do...it called to her again and it wouldn't leave her alone. Maybe if she let go of the one thread pulling her away, then the voice would just leave her alone.

Demie responded, and it became a little easier as the static started to dissipate again. Panchala came back into focus for her, and a warm peace filled her as Demie realized she was lying in Kori's arms.

Demie had almost left, again, without her sister. She started crying as she thought about the cliff she had just been pulled back from.

Chandar and Sanjali watched in horror as Sherman tried to stop Cassie. When Demie's mother stabbed the girl, Sanjali grabbed onto Chandar and started screaming and sobbing. The sheriff yelled over the fence for Chandar to get her out of there, and Chandar slowly led Sanjali back into the house.

Both sets of parents rushed outside and met them near the back door, and Sanjali's parents took over comforting her while Chandar explained what they had witnessed. His mother, of course, raced into the living room to offer up prayers for the poor girl and Baba stayed with Sanjali and her parents, guiding them into the kitchen to make some tea and calm them down.

Once he determined that Sanjali was settled, Chandar went back outside to see what had happened. The paramedics had arrived and already taken Demie away, so he couldn't tell what happened to her. But one paramedic was working with the sheriff to control Miss Morris, and after he gave her some sort of injection, within a few minutes the woman fell silent. The sheriff helped bundle her into a straitjacket and they wheeled her limp body away.

When Chandar went back into the house, he found a subdued Sanjali sipping tea in the kitchen. As soon as she saw him, she set down her tea and walked up to him, eyes downcast.

"She really was the crazy one. I was wrong to judge you, and I promise to never doubt you again. For the rest of my life." Then she put her arms around his neck, rested her head on his shoulder and held him close.

CHAPTER TWENTY-SIX

Demie looked around. Nothing had changed in the valley or the world around her, but for a few moments she had felt torn between two sources of light, until she finally went with the one that had Kori/Draupadi's voice. Demie still felt disoriented, like when she had fainted on the softball field, and Coach got mad at her for not drinking enough water.

She had faced death, and it was not what she expected. She couldn't explain why, but now she knew she could face whatever came up. She had been to the abyss and back, and while she didn't want to make that trip again anytime soon, she didn't fear it now.

Standing up, Demie gave Draupadi/Kori a hug. "Do you remember now, who you are?"

"Yes, I'm Kori...I think. Where are we? What happened?" Kori asked, returning the hug and not letting go.

"I wouldn't know where to even start. What do you remember?"

Kori/Draupadi replied, "I remember the forest, and some kind of tornado, and then...this strange dream where I was the Princess of Panchala. But it wasn't a dream, was it?"

"I don't really understand it, and I don't know why it happened to us. Not yet." As she said that, she felt a foreboding and shivered. "But no, it wasn't a dream."

Surprisingly, Demie was going to miss this place. But she was ready to go home, whatever that might be, as long as it was with Kori. Which Mom would they go back to? Would Dad be there, or would he still be with Lauren?

How was she going to explain Lauren to Kori?

Tony glanced over at Karen, still dozing under her desk, and recalled when they were dating and she fell asleep while they watched a movie. He returned yesterday because of his feelings for her, but he could not allow the past to continue haunting him. Or blinding him. His feelings for her might never change, but he wouldn't let his guard down again.

Walking over, he gently nudged her with his toe, though a part of him still wanted to lie down with her. It always would. "Time to wake up, the rest of the gang will be here soon."

She stirred, peered up and nodded as she sat up. Tony returned to his computer and his search, while Karen left to freshen up and get coffee for them. When she came back a while later, she pulled a chair over and handed him a cup.

"So what are you looking for?" she asked.

"Whatever we are dealing with, it started the day we launched Panchala. The rest of you left to celebrate, but Panchala locked up for about half an hour. That was when it happened."

"When what happened? You said we're dealing with a quantum computer, but how can that be? That's way beyond anything we could do. It's beyond what anyone can do."

Tony swiveled in his chair to face her as he took a long sip of coffee. "I honestly don't know, at least not yet. But my best guess is that some freak coincidence bridged a number of parallel universes together. Or more specifically, the TerraMythos servers in a number of parallel universes. I'm not sure how many other timelines are involved, but I have a hunch there must be at least half a dozen other universes very similar to ours, linked together on a quantum, sub-atomic level. It could be more, maybe not, but it would be some finite number."

"So," Karen slowly interjected, "That's why Panchala stayed up even though we shut our servers down?"

"The other timelines must have kept their servers up, and Panchala along with them. That's also why, even though we bring our servers back up, they aren't connecting with the real Panchala."

"So how do we re-connect to this...quantum Panchala...then?"

"That's why I'm searching the logs from the day we launched.

Something is keeping our timeline connected, even though our servers are offline. I'm hoping it left a trace in the logs, something we can also find in Panchala. And then use that as the set point to re-sync with."

Karen started to respond, as Joachim and Carolyn walked in. They both stood, gaping at Tony and Karen, and then Carolyn looked at Joachim with a raised eyebrow before they silently took their seats.

Tony turned to Karen, and pointed at the screen of his computer. There it was, exactly as he remembered it that day Panchala first opened its gates and he almost re-started the servers. Whatever this was, it was the point of origin for what they were dealing with. Switching over to the account that was logged into the live Panchala, he searched for the trace of that particular process, and pulled up a world map of Panchala.

"That's it. Right there, next to the lake in this valley. Now, I have no idea if this is going to work. Hell, I don't even know why it would work, but if I just..."

Tony started the re-sync on the TerraMythos servers, and just like before, the world of Panchala froze while it synced. He knew he would be living here over the coming weeks and months as he tried to decipher exactly what they created. But after spending so many years on this project that had become like his child, he felt relief wash over him.

Panchala came back online. What he didn't know was that it also reloaded the Kali program.

Lauren let herself fall backward onto the bed and wanted to pass out from exhaustion. She had completely expected to die, certain Cassie would plunge that knife deep into her heart. The trip to the hospital was a fog of hysteria while they followed the ambulance to the hospital, and then they spent over twelve eternal hours sitting in the waiting room. She went on an emotional teacup ride every time a doctor or nurse came out to update them on blood transfusions, near organ failures and surgeries. But in the end, although things were precarious for Demie a couple of times, she pulled through and was stable.

It took Sherman eight more hours to pry Lauren from Demie's bed, but eventually he convinced her to come home for a break, with a firm promise from the on-duty nurse to call if there was any change. At least they were only fifteen minutes away if they had to rush back.

"Not much of a honeymoon, Mrs. Anderson," Sherman commented as he began unpacking his suitcase.

Lauren groaned. "This wasn't exactly the way I dreamed it would be. Did you call the bed and breakfast?"

"Yes, and the good news is that we'll just lose the first night's deposit."

"That's good news? What's the bad news?"

Sherman came over and sat on the bed. "They're booked solid for almost twelve months out. No vacancies until next year. So we'll have to come up with a plan B."

Lauren rolled over and propped her head up on an elbow. "Let's go on a cruise. Just think how romantic it would be, watching the sun set, and dancing all night long."

"But I get seasick," Sherman protested, "And I don't want to just be cooped up on some ship for a week."

"There are some really good medications now for that, and they have cruises out of California that go down the Mexican coast so we can stop at several ports. You'll have plenty of time on shore. Please!!!" Lauren gave him her best puppy-eyes pleading look, and he finally started laughing.

"Alright, when should we go?"

"Once Demie is recovered and home with us, and we've arranged for full-time nursing while we're gone. Two months should be plenty of time."

Sherman got up. "Okay then, I'll call the travel agency, and book us on the best cruise they have available two months from now."

As her husband went downstairs to make the phone call, Lauren lay back with her eyes closed and smiled to herself. Between Demie, their aborted honeymoon and what happened with Cassie, their marriage had gotten off to an unexpectedly rough start.

But everything was going to be okay now.

Chandar and Sanjali left both of their sets of parents in the living room, wrangling over the finer details of planning a wedding. Taking her by the hand, he led her back to his room, and this time the room was in order.

As they entered, Sanjali let go of his hand and, after silencing him with a finger to her lips, closed the door. Then she came up to him and slipped into his embrace with a sigh, resting her head on his shoulder for a few minutes. At first Chandar held her awkwardly, until she seemed to melt into him and then it felt so natural he couldn't imagine it otherwise.

Then, she ended the moment with a long, lingering kiss and murmured, "This isn't just an arrangement for me anymore."

"It isn't for me either," Chandar whispered back.

Sanjali looked into his eyes for a long minute, and whispered, "I'm glad." Then she slipped away to re-open the door. "Did you bookmark that cruise we were looking at?"

"No, but it should be in the history file." Chandar sat at his computer, and within a few minutes pulled up the reservation they had been looking at. He also saw the link for TerraMythos and twinged. Although he heard Demie was recovering at the hospital, he had tried to contact the girl online numerous times in the past day and she hadn't responded. Opening the cruise website, they found that even though the cruise was only eight weeks away, the stateroom they wanted was still available.

Chandar was about to click on the 'Complete Transaction' button, and then paused. "This wasn't your first choice. Are you sure you don't mind doing the Mexican Riviera?"

"Not at all," Sanjali said, and reaching over, clicked the button for him.

Cassie had no sense of what time or even what day it was. Or how long she had spent in this room, talking with this guy. He claimed to be the court appointed psychiatrist, assigned to evaluate her, but he couldn't fool her.

"And you say that Demie told you to do those things?"

"Of course she did, why else would I do them?"

"Well, I have to admit that I'm just curious to know how she did that, given that she was in a coma from the day of the accident up until the moment you killed her."

Cassie shifted in her straitjacket, and leaned forward. "Yeah, I'll bet you do! That's what this is all about, but I'm not giving my secrets up."

"Miss Morris, we've gone over that. I'm not from the CIA or any other intelligence service. I can assure you, they really have no interest whatsoever in you."

Cassie jerked her head to face away from him and stared at the wall.

"Alright then, let's talk about the reason you're wearing the jacket again. Why were you digging into your arm with a fork?"

"You know why, doctor. Your people put the implant in there, and they stopped me before I could get it out. So you can listen to my thoughts if I'm not careful, but that's why you're here, right? Because I'm blocking my thoughts and you can't get them."

The so-called doctor, whoever he was, sighed and closed his notebook, and then knocked on the door. When an orderly let him out, she could just make out a few words: "She's still...increase the dosage...don't let her...just in case..."

The door opened and the doctor stepped halfway in. "I'm booked up the next couple days, Miss Morris, so we'll take a break for a while. I'll see you again at the end of the week, and maybe we'll have a better talk then."

The orderly came in and after unhooking Cassie from the restraining clip, helped her to her feet and escorted her down the hallway back to the wing she now called home. As they passed the courtyard, she asked if she could stop there for a couple minutes of fresh air and he shrugged, then opened the door.

Cassie sat on a bench in the sunlit corner, and felt a cool breeze blow over her face. And for a moment, as though pushing back some cobwebs, she felt some clarity take hold in her mind. She was in this place because she stabbed and killed her daughter. It would be a long road back from wherever she was.

The orderly made a noise behind her, and Cassie jumped. As she flinched, like a swimmer clinging to a rock in the middle of a raging river, her grip gave way and she slipped back into a world of fear and shadows.

"You're trying to hear my thoughts!" she snarled at the orderly.

"I'll tell you what my thoughts are, Cassie. I think it's time for your meds and some happy quiet time."

Grasping her jacket, the orderly firmly guided her back into the building and down the hall. She went with him quietly because, if she was good, maybe in time they would give her access to a computer.

Then she would contact Demie like that boy had; she knew

Demie was still out there.

Demie was getting impatient. She had come a long way since running up the driveway at home, and there was nothing left for them to do here in Panchala. Whatever changes were happening, they would continue without Demie and Kori. In fact, Demie felt a growing unease about remaining here, almost like some subsonic vibration grating on her nerves.

"Draupadi and I must leave, now." Demie said to Yudhishthira. She wasn't even going to try explaining that Draupadi was really Kori. Or was Kori really part Draupadi now too?

"Surely you can remain long enough to help us celebrate this remarkable victory, and the birth of a new age?" Yudhishthira protested. When Demie shook her head, he bowed toward her and continued, "Nevertheless, I have with great sadness forseen that you both must leave. The form which holds Draupadi has become greater than what this world can contain."

"What will you do here in Panchala after we leave?" Demie asked him.

"I also have forseen that Yudhishthira will be a great king," Draupadi/Kori answered as she turned to Yudhishthira and bowed to him. "This is what you were made for, my good lord."

"Well spoken. Alas, I shall lack for nothing but my queen by my side." Yudhishthira bowed back to Draupadi. "Your throne will always be here for you, Draupadi, if you take form in this world again. I would have none other than you sit on it as long as I am king." The man then leaned down to pet Darm and scratch behind the dog's ears. "Until your return, I will have my faithful companion and no man could ask for more." The dog barked several times and eagerly wagged his tail.

It was time to go home. Demie stood next to the sphere, and began a turn toward Kori, when she saw a large black body rise behind Yudhishthira.

Kali the Destroyer stood, looked at Demie and swung with both sword and trident as she pounced. Demie readied herself to receive the charge, when a figure jumped from the side and tackled Kali. Draupadi/Kori wrapped her arms around the demon's waist, and they both pitched off balance to the side—directly into the black sphere that was to take the sisters back home.

As they fell in, a flash of light enveloped their shapes when they crossed the surface of the sphere. Then they were gone. All Demie could see of Kori was a vague shape within a tunnel for a moment, then the tunnel darkened to a pitch black. Kori was no longer there. The sphere started to collapse and Demie didn't even think. She leapt into the darkness of the black orb.

She and Kori had dealt with Kali more than once, and they'd do so again. But boy, were Mom and Dad in for a big surprise.

ACKNOWLEDGEMENTS

It would be fair to say that it takes a village to raise an author, at least in my experience. So many people have played a part in my journey as a writer, it's impossible to mention everyone. Whatever is good in my writing, I have the following people to thank for it. The flaws are on me.

An important part of my early journey was the Downtown Tacoma Critique Group, including Allen Cox, Gretchen Wing, Leslie Birnbaum, Marcy Rodenborn and Matt Rizzo. We could not have forseen at the time how a whimsical offhand exercise would turn into this amazing story. I miss you guys.

Another important writing proving ground has been the Southsound Algonquins, including Caroline Street, Chris Dahl, Dolly Cehaar, Kate Diamond, Laura Petersen, Liz Shine, Manek Mistry, Mark Henry, Megan Pottorff, Monica Britte, Nancy Grace Campbell, Ned Hayes, Shelly Shellabarger, Thom Marrion and others I just can't recall at this moment. All of you deserve medals for enduring countless iterations of a specific passage that refused to surrender. You know which one I mean.

Another group which has been central in my development as a writer is the Cascade Writers. Writers, instructors and friends from that group that have touched my life in ways both large and small include Alaina Ewing, Amanda Clark, Beth Meacham, Brian Hunt, C. Sän Inman, Danielle Myers Gembala, David Levine, Elizabeth Coleman, Geoff Hulten, Heather Roulo, Jay Lake, Karen Junker, Katie Cord, Ken Scholes, Pandem Aelion, Patrick Swenson, Randy Henderson, Rebecca Birch, Shannon Page, Spencer Ellsworth, Stephanie Bissette-Roark, Stephen Sottong and so many others. I hope I have given back to you at least a fraction of what you all have given me.

There are also those who contributed directly to this project either through feedback and input on the manuscript, or work they did on the Kickstarter project. These (in no particular order) include Mark J Ferrari, Darren VanderVort, Rob Carlos, Barbara Kenyon, Amanda Wright, John Waugh, KC Stegbauer and Lynn Perry. Thank you for your contributions, and sorry the project didn't get off the ground. It would've been awesome.

Other people that contributed to my journey include Dr. John McCann (for teaching me where to find passionate digression), Bill Johnson (who first showed me how to give voice to characters), Paul Racey (my creative backstop), Belinda Wright and Bridget Kenyon (readers par excellence), Cat Rambo (teacher par excellence) and Monique-Cherie Snyman (you never forget your first).

Finally, I want to give a specific shout out to Mark Henry, who may not realize it, but he has been like an unofficial mentor to me. That Saturday road trip down to Portland changed everything.

ABOUT THE AUTHOR

Tom D Wright lives in the Puget Sound area with his wife, cat and a small pack of dogs. When he's not writing, he works in IT.

Tom graduated from Bowie State University with an M.A. in Psychology, so when people call him with an IT problem, he can tell them "I understand, and how does that make you feel?"

A collection of short stories and a novella will be available in November 2014, titled "The Baylah Run, and Other Quantum Leaps of Imagination" and a novel, "The Archivist" will be released in April 2015, by Evil Girlfriend Media.

Check his author website for details at www.TomDWright.com

The following is an excerpt from:

The Archivist

By Tom D Wright

Available from Evil Girlfriend Media
April 2015

Chapter One

Even before the heavy oak door shuts behind me with a dull thud, I sense a setup hanging heavy in the smoky air of The Broken Mast. I cannot say precisely what the game is, but I have been on too many retrievals to miss the signs and usually I am right. Not that I ever let being right stop me.

At least the tavern is warmer than the brisk autumn evening outside.

I am merely cautious as I stand at the entrance and take my time, loosening my dark brown oilskin duster while I survey the room. Dim, primitive, handmade electric bulbs dangle over the bar and harsh yellow light from the incandescent bulbs randomly flickers which means this town actually has a generator somewhere. The unsteady light means they only have a crude rebuilt, and I recall seeing a watermill when the ship that brought me into town sailed into the small port. The mill is probably multitasking as a generator and nowadays taverns tend to be social centers, which explains why it warrants the luxury of electric lighting.

The lights are such a luxury they only hang over the bar. The rest of the place is lit with candles on wooden chandeliers that illuminate lively sailors and weather-beaten fishermen, gathered in sturdy if rustic chairs around a dozen roughly hewn tables in the center of the tavern. A handful of jovial farmers sit in a group off to one side. There is a comfortable camaraderie in the air and I see why Wally chose this place for a clandestine rendezvous.

This port town sits on what was called the Pacific Canadian coast a few decades ago. This is my first time here and I am placing it at a late 1800's tech level. In the thirty years since the Demon Days, following the collapse of the Intelligent Internet, I have seen a lot of towns far worse off than Port Sadelow, so they have not done too badly here. No one takes particular notice of my entrance except the two goons at the table in the shadows by the door.

I struggle not to laugh as a short pudgy man and his taller stick-thin companion make an obvious show of not looking at me while they fiddle with their cups and nervously glance at each other. These amateurs, dressed in sewn-leather rather than the cloth-spun garments worn by the rest of the patrons, are my clue that something is afoot. I survey the rest of the candlelit room and, sure enough, I see him sitting at the bar bracketed by empty stools. A Disciple wearing the long black cape and a black hat with a wide, flat brim reminiscent of the Amish style typical of the brethren. He blends in about as well as a raven in a flock of pigeons.

The Disciples of the Earth would be what you got if the Amish and the Taliban mated. For all I know they did; I was preoccupied with helping to establish the Archives when the first Disciples appeared about thirty years ago right after the Crash. Throughout my travels there are few things in this broken world that I have found to be as utterly devoid of redeeming value as this bunch. Not that I have anything against nature-loving activists, but these guys are filled with far more hate than love. I have not seen this particular acolyte before and I have seen more than my fair share, but he is fairly young so this might be his first assignment. He avoids glancing my direction but I know why he is here. Few things short of an Archivist would induce a Disciple to enter a tavern with electric lights.

My contact, Walecki, is nowhere to be seen, so I decide to play along and head over to the counter that runs the length of the room. I snag an empty stool at the opposite end from the Disciple. After a long sea journey I could use something to take off the edge—but not too much edge, not yet. The spot I settle into faces toward the entrance so I can keep an eye on my nemesis and at the same time watch the privy behind me reflected in a mirror on the wall behind the bar. Who knows, maybe Wally had to take a piss. The seat is near a corner where I lean my heavy walking stick and shrug off my pack so I can set it down and hang my duster on the knobby handle of the stick.

The barmaid comes over, an uncommonly winsome wench. Not just because I spent two months on three vessels in close quarters with unwashed sailors. Her thick fire-red locks cascade over her shoulders, covered by a loose cotton shift which flashes hints of ample womanhood while still concealing more than it reveals. Her skin is fair and light freckles cover her face like a faint mask, complementing her green eyes. She looks to be in her twenties, old enough to know herself while still retaining youthful playfulness. As she approaches, I notice her waist is bound with a thin leather belt that sports a small leather medallion.

She pulls a rag from under the counter and sweeps the area in front of me clean in one swift movement and opens up a broad, warm smile. Not a turn-up-the corners-of-your-mouth smile, but a mouth-and-eyes-and-every-muscle-in-your-face smile in which her whole being greets me. I am as human as any other man, and due to the nature of my work lonelier than most. The genuine warmth of human sociability can be hard to find anywhere these distrustful days, so I hope Wally takes his time getting here.

"I'll bet ya just floated in on some cargo ship." Her voice is deep yet not husky, and utterly feminine.

"What gave me away?" I am sure I was not followed here from the Bridget's Secret.

"This is a small port town. Half of my customers are here every night, and the other half are sailors or traders that drop in when they come to buy wool and sheep." She sets an empty ceramic mug in front of me, then pauses to look at me with narrowed eyes. "You're obviously a traveler but you don't look like a butcher or weaver."

"What do I look like, then?"

She winks and flashes me a wistful smile. "Someone waiting for a friend to show up." The sureness of her voice conveys that she knows more than she is revealing, but I am more curious than concerned. She has an authenticity that makes it hard to be wary. Behind me a patron calls out for Danae, and the woman's glance dances back and forth before it settles on me once again. "So what'll you have?"

"A draw of your house favorite, Danae, and whatever food you sell the most of." In the course of executing countless retrievals, I have learned that the safest fare is whatever the locals find popular. Except in Reyeston, where the only safe option is to bring your own food.

She fills the mug from a tap before she turns away to serve some other patrons. I quench my thirst with a pint of thick brown ale that looks like the muddy river we came up, but the cool brew has a nicely rich and smooth taste. Danae brings me a refill along with something that smells heavily of garlic and rosemary, and looks like a thick bratwurst skewered on a stick with some roasted vegetables. I do not ask what it is, I have found it is better that way.

Instead I turn around to survey the room as I eat. At the other end of the bar the Disciple is getting antsy. I struggle to contain my mirth as small rivulets of sweat bead and then roll off his shaven head into his splayed whiskers, but the rigid believer refuses to remove his robe or look my way. Time and again, like a child that cannot keep his eyes off a sweet, he glances at the pair of hoods seated in the shadows near the door. I am not worried; he will not do anything before Wally comes because he is not nearly as interested in me as he is in what I am here to collect. Unlike me, he wants to destroy it.

The distant toll of a town bell marks that another hour has passed. Partly to pass the time, partly to blend in, but mostly to annoy my watchers, I head over by the privy and join in a game of wall-bully. The dart game uses three targets which resemble traditional dartboards, except that one of them swings like a clockwork pendulum. The object of the game is to score the same number of points on both fixed boards without exceeding the score on the moving board, which is called the bully.

The four farmers are wrapping up a round when I approach and they eagerly let me go first as they start a new game. First I toss three darts at the bully and set the mark at a total of twenty-three points. I want to start out easy on these guys. Then a gangly farmhand gives me a roguish smirk while he gives the bully a shove and the pendulum swings back and forth. He would not be smiling if he knew that I introduced wall-bully to this region seventeen years ago. It was invented by an engineer friend of mine back at the Mars colony, but I rarely play because it reminds me of a home that

I have not seen in more than three decades.

My first two darts on the left wall target add up to nineteen and I let the bully hit the third dart as it flies. Then my third dart on the right target takes my second total to twenty-eight and I am busted for this round. The evening wears on as the game stakes build up, but Wally does not show. By the time I clean the unwitting farmers out of their share of the local currency, the candles have burned low and half the pub has cleared out. The losing players take their losses in good stride and begin to disperse, so I let the poorest of the farmers win my gains. I do not plan on hanging around this town long enough to spend it.

The Disciple closes his tab and retrieves his staff. The thick wood is almost a post, and is topped with a snarling wolf head forged out of pewter. Over the past few years an increasing number of the brethren have started using these ornamental staves as walking sticks and I suspect the metal decoration can pack a nasty punch. He must have come to the conclusion I arrived at an hour ago, my contact is not showing up. I pause in the middle of a dart throw to observe Danae, who stands behind the counter.

The Disciple waves her over and the woman deliberately serves a table across the room before she slowly walks behind the bar, and places her rag on the counter between them like a symbolic shield. He leans forward to make a hushed comment and then takes his deepening scowl outside trailed by the hired thugs. As he passes through the door the woman's shoulders visibly drop as if the man pulls the tension out of her when he exits the tavern. She is clearly glad to see him leave and anyone who is not a friend of a Disciple could be a friend of mine.

I head back to the bar for a refill, and as she takes my mug Danae murmurs to me, "You know what they say, K'Mar. Whenever you see a Disciple, an Archivist is not far away."

The smile on my face barely twitches, while a shiver dances on the nape of my neck and then wriggles down my spine. I never mentioned my name to the barmaid. "Yes," I reply, "But would you know one if you saw him?"

Danae lifts an eyebrow as she whispers back, "Well, I heard about an Archivist that was about a hand's breadth taller than me, in his mid-thirties, with short black hair and a nasty scar over his left eye. Oh yeah, and I was told that his hat was so ugly some towns considered it a deadly weapon. Based on that description, I'd say I'm looking at one right now."

The reference to my headwear persuades me that she has some connection to my contact. Wally has never appreciated a genuine akubra and every time we meet, the first thing he says is how obnoxious my hat is. Okay, she knows who I am, so I toss a challenge back to her. "Then I suppose you can tell me where Walecki is?"

"The one who called himself Wally is dead." The words hit me like a freight train, something Danae has certainly never seen; nor have I for several decades. I sit back on my stool and turn away for a minute. I will not shed any tears for Wally; this harsh new world wrung those out of me years ago, but this is as close as I have been in a long, long time. It takes about a dozen slow, deliberate breaths to wrestle my emotions back down until eventually I turn back.

Her voice is somber, "I'm sorry, I can tell you knew him well. But if you have what he promised to provide, you can still find what you came for."

"And just what do you think that might be?"

She chuckles, "Something Intellinet left behind, of course."

"Really?" I blurt out. I am not sure which surprises me more, that she knows exactly why I am here or her reference to the Intellinet. Aside from Disciples and Archivists, few know or even care anymore that the machines left anything behind other than collapse and chaos. It is definitely not something the average barmaid chats about. "Maybe we do have something to discuss, but first I need to know what happened to Wally."

"You can ask my associate when you meet him, after I close up."

"If Wally's dead, just how much can you trust this associate?"

"With my life," she replies, banging down my refilled mug. "He's my father."